Where it all began...

"Mr. Longyear, where do you get your ideas?"

I refused to cry.... I turned back to the interviewer.

"Members of the Science Fiction Writers of America are supposed to answer that question with a post office box number in Schenectady. You send in two dollars and a self-addressed stamped envelope, and you will be sent back an idea."

The interviewer stared at me. "Schenectady?"

"Schenectady."

—from "Forepiece"

*　　　*　　　*

IT CAME FROM SCHENECTADY

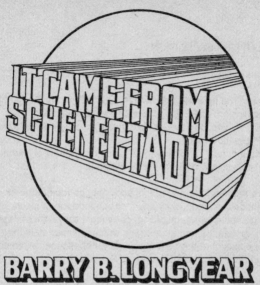

IT CAME FROM SCHENECTADY

BARRY B. LONGYEAR

POPULAR LIBRARY

An Imprint of Warner Books, Inc.

A Warner Communications Company

To
Mary Ann Drach
and
To Terry and Kathy Lynch
Without whom not only this book
but a whole bunch of other things
would not exist.

Contents

Forepiece

I have seen it happen so many times. At an autograph party or at a science fiction convention a science fiction writer will be innocently trying his or her best to answer an inexperienced interviewer's questions. Most times the interviewer has never read any science fiction. It is guaranteed, however, that this investigative bulwark of the *Milltown Daily Thunderclap* has never read anything at all by the author being interviewed. Armed with this ignorance and an assumption that "sci-fi writers"—as the pencil-wielding trolls insist on calling us—all do the same thing the same way, the interviewer attempts to elicit from the interviewee some items of information that might possibly be worked into a couple of relevant column inches for the readers of the *Thunderclap*.

The author sits in giddy anticipation, the interviewer confidently opens its mouth, and then ensues a moment of mutual wide-eyed silence as the interviewer suddenly realizes that it doesn't know what questions to ask. From the stunned look on the interviewer's face, the author numbly realizes that it's going to be one of *those* experiences and shifts into creeper gear. The author knows what's coming next. With the inevitability of Earth's eventual incineration by Sol's declining gas attack, that creature is going to ask—

"Where do you get your ideas?"

I have seen grown men weep at being asked this question. Early on I resolved not to be one of them.

My first opportunity to exercise my resolve came at Chattacon, a science fiction convention in Chattanooga, Tennessee. I was innocently minding my own business when one of the convention's staff people asked me if I would mind being interviewed on television.

I said I thought a chair would be more comfortable.

Taking this observation at face value, the committee person deposited me on a couch and cued the electronic ambush. The next thing I knew, a 650-watt klieg light was microwaving my retinas while some woman was trying to stuff a gray golf ball on a stick down my throat. Perhaps you have heard of delayed stress. There I was, my vision filled with blinding light, being threatened with a blunt instrument while a slinky female voice interrogated me.

"Mr. Longyear, just what is this convention all about?"

The lights! All I could think about was the lights! "Name, rank and serial number is all you're getting out of me, buddy!"

"Excuse me?"

"Ho Chi Minh's mother is a 20-piaster Saigon hooker!"

The lights went out, and a woman wearing a confused look was staring at me. The golf ball on a stick turned out to be a microphone. "I'm sorry," I said. "Could you repeat the question?"

She nodded at another person, and the lights went back on. Before the light hit, I deftly inserted my genuine Harlan Ellison shades between my eyes and the oncoming photons. Don't ever let anyone tell you that faster-than-light travel is impossible.

In any event, the interview continued. She smiled sweetly at me obviously trying to put me at ease. "Mr. Longyear . . . You *are* Mr. Longyear?"

Her new strategy appeared to be to start me off with simpler questions. Something that I could handle more easily.

I thought carefully, then answered. "Yes. I am."

She seemed somewhat relieved. Then she moved on to the tougher questions. "Are you a sci-fi writer?"

"I have never written a sci-fi in my life."

She looked confused. "Isn't this a sci-fi convention?"

"I didn't know sci-fies had conventions."

A dark figure in the swim of images beyond the lights

leaned over and whispered something into the interviewer's ear. As the dark figure moved back and blended again into the background, the interviewer faced me and began again. Her face, if anything, looked even more confused. "You dislike the word 'sci-fi'?"

I thought about it some, then shrugged. "I don't much care one way or the other. I don't have anything against 'sci-fi.' Interface."

"What?"

"'Interface.' Now that's a word I really hate. 'Interface' and 'viable.' And 'parameters'! Now that's a word that really puts the blood in my eye! Damn 'parameters'!"

While the interviewer conferred with another dark figure behind the lights, perfumed hair brushed my cheek and soft lips came next to my ear as a low sexy voice whispered: "If you don't stop screwing around, fathead, you can sleep someplace else tonight." I looked around and it was my wife, Jean.

She marched off into a cloud of science fiction fans, and since sleeping in the hall during a convention is a contradiction in terms, I resolved to treat this particular interview with the seriousness that it deserved. The interviewer concluded her talk with the shadow, and then she smiled at me and asked . . . *it*!

"Mr. Longyear, where do you get your ideas?"

I refused to cry. I looked around to make certain that Jean was not within audio range, then I turned back to the interviewer. "Members of the Science Fiction Writers of America are supposed to answer that question with a post office box number in Schenectady. You send in two dollars and a self-addressed-stamped envelope, and you will be sent back an idea."

The interviewer stared at me. "Schenectady?"

"Schenectady."

The interviewer smiled. "I see."

"Roger Zelazny says that every evening he leaves a glass of milk and a dish of cookies on his back porch. In the morning the milk and cookies are gone and on the dish is a slip of paper containing an idea."

The interviewer began looking grim. "That's cute. Who is Roger Zelazny?"

I swallowed my pipe. "You don't know who Roger Zelazny is?"

She shook her head. "No."

I pulled out another pipe, filled it, and thought as I set its contents aflame: this person is from another planet. "Roger Zelazny," I said, "rides sci-fies in the sci-fi rodeo."

"I think I'm confused," she remarked.

I nodded. "But all these people," I swept my arm about indicating all intelligent life within the known universe, "I know where they *really* get their ideas. They get them from the same place that I do."

"And where is that?"

"TV commercials."

The interviewer frowned. "You are saying that science fiction writers get their ideas from TV commercials?"

"Not just science fiction writers. Fantasy, horror, and occult writers use TV commercials for source material. Every occult writer can recite every single Prudential Insurance Company commercial from memory."

"Prudential?"

"Certainly. Just think about it. You fade in to see some poor wretch who has either run over a fire hydrant, been in a three-car pile-up, destroyed his neighbor's house by accident, incurred the wrath of an entire motorcycle gang by wrecking their vehicles, or had his own house fall on his head because of a wind storm. The very next thing you see him do is pick up the telephone and say 'Prudential?'"

The interviewer shook her head. "What does that have to do with the occult?"

"It's obvious: Who is the insurance carrier for all of these disaster prone souls? Prudential: the insurance company for cursed people.

"And think about the fantasy ideas. You know, the temperance bull that busts up parties and saloons every time someone opens a can of Schlitz Malt Liquor and then goes off and sells stocks and securities for Merrill Lynch?"

The interviewer coughed. "Mr. Longyear—"

"Even the porno writers. Just think about that one Preparation H commercial. The guy says to the druggist: 'Say, Ben. I got this itch, and I don't know what to do about it.'

Now get this. The druggist tells the guy that Preparation H will offer relief, *and* it comes *both* in suppository form *and* this handy squeeze applicator.

"And what does the guy say? 'Hey, Ben. Why, I think I'll take *both*!' Think about it. Where's he gonna stick the other one?

"What about all those sado-masochists in the aftershave commercials slapping themselves, 'Thanks, I needed that.' Yeah, I'll just *bet* they needed that.

"Talk about your weird sexual fantasies. Imagine standing in the center of a crowded pedestrian thoroughfare shouting at all the women: 'Show us your Underalls!'

"Then there's the Whipple Syndrome: an unnatural desire to squeeze rolls of bumwad. My God, this year Whipple is *hugging* the damned stuff! Can you believe that?"

The interviewer twitched a bit.

I continued. "Those fantasy writers have the real deal. A TV commercial revealed the true God to us all. The Eleventh Commandment: 'To make drains go, better use Drāno!'

"Just try to imagine it: a universe in which the all-knowing, all-powerful supreme being makes ends meet by selling Drāno. Kinda makes you wonder how baptism originated, doesn't it?"

The interviewer just sat there with an expression on her face that had me convinced that she had been smacked on the back of her head with a splitting maul. After a minute her eyes became a bit less glazed. "Mr. Longyear, what ... what does any of this have to do with science fiction?"

I laughed. "You don't think some science fiction writer hasn't stolen a few ideas from the Budweiser universe? Just think about sapient tastebuds for a minute. I mean thousands of intelligent beings, living on your tongue, knowing what your breath smells like—"

The interveiwer dropped the microphone and rushed to the ladies room. The camera kept rolling, so I picked up the mike and proceeded to elaborate upon my theme.

"Just try and think of the socio-evolutionary mechanisms that result in a culture where disputes are settled by duelling with bottles of Mello-Yello. Remember last Christmas when TV had the Devil on selling Milton-Bradley games? And what did God say? 'I wanna play.' Think on that a minute: God is a wargamer! That would explain a lot of things, wouldn't it?"

Well, by then the cameraman had animated himself enough to stop the camera. When the interviewer returned, she grimly set about the task of continuing the session. The camera started rolling, she took the mike from my hand, and asked: "Mr. Longyear, could you please give us a specific example of an idea you got from a television commercial that you subsequently turned into a story."

"Certainly."

"What was the commercial?"

"I believe it was for the Playtex Living Bra." The interviewer just sat there with her mouth hanging open, so I trucked on. "I pondered the concept of a living bra for quite some time, trying to think of what kind of environment could evolve such a lifeform. That's when I came up with the planet Bilumpus."

"Bilumpus?"

"Yes. You see the ruling lifeform on Bilumpus, the Bilumpians, were shaped like double grapefruits. They came in six sizes: A, B, C, D, Super, and Training.

"This is not particularly unusual in itself, but the Bilumpians were attacked by a voracious parasite. The parasite was so effective because it adapted itself to the shape of the Bilumpians, and there was no defense. The parasites only had a lifespan of eighteen hours, but in that time they would reproduce, leaving the host lifeform limp and withered.

"Well, by and by the Bilumpians discovered that the parasites could be destroyed by fire. A movement was begun, and soon great assemblages of Bilumpians were tearing the parasites from their bodies, casting them into the flames. The Bilumpians were finally free. Liberated.

"But a few of the parasites managed to escape. They fled Bilumpus, went dormant, and for thousands of years they drifted through the galaxy, awaiting only the presence of a suitable environment to once again bounce to life. Eventually they reached the blue planet called Earth—a land of nourishing detergents, bleaches, softeners, and suitable hosts. They spread over the face of the globe, stalking the country roads and city streets in search of human—"

The interviewer interrupted at this point. "Mr. Longyear, do you expect me to believe that this was an actual story that you wrote?"

"It was," I answered.

She looked at me steadily. "And it was published?"

"Yes."

"I don't seem to recall ever hearing of anything quite that bizarre."

I shrugged. "Well, I don't suppose you can read everything."

"What is the story's title?"

"The original title was 'The Big Bust.' The movie came out under another name."

"This was made into a motion picture?"

"Yes."

"What was its title?"

"Certainly you have heard of *The Invasion of the Booby Snatchers*."

Well, that was the end of the interview.

Now, don't get me wrong. I *like* being interviewed. Center stage is my favorite location, and publicity helps peddle the product. In addition, I happen to think that from where a *particular* idea came from is a fascinating subject. So when an interviewer who has done some homework asks me a question like "Where did you get the idea for your alien in 'Enemy Mine'?" I'm as happy as a piranha in a crowded swimming pool.

Thus the excuse for this colleciton, *It Came From Schenectady*. Contained herein are several stories of which I am particularly fond along with discussions about the various places from which their ideas came (there is no central repository). Among these stories is my all-time favorite, a Hugo nominee, an experiment, a joke, and one story that I wrote because I had become fed up with dinosaurs.

Except for a seat in Congress, I can't think of another occupation besides that of science fiction writer where one risks becoming fed up with dinosaurs—and gets paid for it.

The first selection, "Collector's Item," is my personal favorite. The original idea began a few years ago when a friend of mine asked me to talk to her sixth-grade English class about writing. Ever since, I have done stints with her classes, and have read and critiqued what seems to be a million or more themes and stories. One thing that came out of this is seeing how many children use writing assignments as an opportunity to think over problems, unburden themselves, escape, and reach out. Many of these writings were virtually "dear diary' letters to their teacher.

After a few times doing this, without knowing the individuals by sight, I got to know some of the kids through their writing—their attitudes, situations, hopes, goals, fantasies, fears. I could see them change, and the direction in which they were changing. I became intrigued by these attempts at communication—the mechanism. Whatever it was that intrigued me was tucked away in the back of my head until Stanley Schmidt, editor of Analog, bought my wife and me dinner and leaned on me for a story. During the meal we got on the subject of education (Stanley has flogged a student or two in his time), and he suggested I might want to do a story related to education.

At the time the suggestion sounded about as interesting as an evening watching a granite fence post erode. And then several blasts from the past hammered their way into my *awareness through television specials, the news, and some folks that I knew. The remains of my generation's exercise in international affairs were filling up the rehabs, the jails, the unemployment lines, and forming self-help groups to try and place Vietnam into some sort of perspective that would allow sanity to exist. And when I sat down at the old word processor to tickle the keys, my experiences with those kids and their writings leaped on the screen with a vengeance.*

Incidentally, "Collector's Item" is one of two stories in this collection that I could not have written without a word processor (the other one is "The House of If"). If you write on a word processor you probably know why, and if you don't I can't explain it any more than I can convey what color is to a person who has been blind since birth. Nevertheless, a word processor adds a dimension to the writing process that I needed to do this story.

Collector's Item

As per the instructions in his will, I was going through my father's things, and it was a pitiful small lot indeed to represent the entire life of a man. Although he had been an English teacher, he hadn't accumulated very many books. He loved books, which is why he rented the dark little room over the candy store. It's right across the street from the library. The few books he did have were piled atop a dusty mirror-mounted dresser. Among them: Coleman's *Relativity For The Layman,* Einstein and Infeld's *The Evolution of Physics,* and one of those Barnes & Noble college outline things, Bennett's *College Physics.*

They were all paperbacks and all half-read. I smiled wondering what bee in my father's bonnet had driven him to take on physics—especially physics. My father did not belong in the Twentieth Century. He would have been more than happy believing the sun orbited the Earth and that things twice as heavy fell twice as fast. He had his English in which to glory. That was all the world he ever needed, or had, or wanted. The books being half-read seemed to indicate that he had either found his answer, or had satisfied himself that if he did find it, he wouldn't understand it.

The walls were hung with a few dark photos and a drawing or two. His closet had two threadbare suits and several equally

threadbare shirts and pairs of casual slacks in it. As a dev-
ilishly hard rain rattled the two windows in the room, I closed
the closet door and went to my father's desk.

Thunder rumbled away, and I turned on the desk's goose-
neck lamp. It was still early afternoon, but dark. I sat in the
chair and looked at the desk calendar—one of those sheet-
per-day things. It read: Wednesday, 2 July 1980. That was
the day he had died across the street in the library. The
remainder of the ruled sheet was empty. I absentmindedly
flipped through the sheets until I came to July 30th, 1980,
the day his son had finally arrived upon some lawyer's instructions to gather up the effects of the late Nathan B. Hall.
That sheet, too, was blank.

There was a telephone on the desk, and I lifted the receiver
to see if it had been cut off. A dial tone. The man is dead,
but credit lives on. I dialed the lawyer's number and waited.
"Wayne and Bowman, attorneys at law, may I help you?"

"Yes. This is Jay Hall. I'd like to speak to Mr. Bowman."

"He's out right now. May I take a message, Mr. Hall?"

"Look, I'm supposed to gather up my father's things. You
know, because of the will. But there's nothing here to gather
up." I fingered a framed coin that stood on the desk. It was
a beat-up 1978 Washington quarter. A real collector's item.
"The furniture is rented and everything else is junk—and not
much of that."

"One moment, Mr. Hall." I heard the eternal movement
of papers in the background. "It's just a formality, Mr. Hall.
Your father's will was specific in that you examine his effects.
Just check to see if there is anything of value. Perhaps something of sentimental value."

I shrugged. "Thanks."

"Would you like me to have Mr. Bowman call you back?"

"No. Thank you." I hung up the receiver and sat staring
at the quarter in its cheap dime-store frame. The frame had
to have cost more than the quarter was worth.

I rubbed my eyes, feeling slightly regretful that my father
was a mystery to me. All the old clichés applied: you don't
miss them until they're gone; etc. He wasn't a mysterious
character. I just never bothered to get to know him. He was
a dusty, dull little man teaching a dusty, dull little subject.

He was absorbed in teaching sixth-grade English. I couldn't stand the subject in that or any other grade. Geology interested me, and when I tried to interest my father in the subject by explaining how the mountains around our Pennsylvania home had been thrust from the sea and then eroded away, he simply shook his head and said "Jay, I'd rather not hear about it." It bothered him to think that there was once a time when those mountains were under water, and that a time was coming when those mountains would be gone. My father's Earth was a solid, unchanging entity, and that's the way he wanted it to remain.

I had laughed at him. My father was the image of the pioneer driving in a property marker and by so doing declaring "This part of the Universe is mine—forever." And I had tried to explain to him what plate tectonics was doing to his "forever." He didn't want to hear about it.

But as I looked at that quarter at the age of thirty-eight, I understood a little more about my father's uneasiness at geological change. Continuous social alterations washed across the world, Mt. St. Helens continued to pound the hell out of southern Washington State, while the Soviets continued to pound the hell out of Afghanistan. Tens of thousands of Cuban refugees were finally getting sorted out, except that racial unrest now had snipers hunting police 1960's style in Miami and Chattanooga. The Cambodians, the most current recession, the insanity of political party conventions.... The Shah had died the day before, the *Imam* still held America hostage. I was still playing roulette smoking with my heart attack not yet a year old. Nobody knows anything for certain from one day to the next. I understood that much about my father, now; I could use the security of a little permanence myself.

I looked from the desk to see the three paperbacks on top of the dresser. I had done well in physics. He could have asked me his question—if he had thought that I would have listened—if he thought his son gave half a damn.

I suddenly felt a great urge to know and understand this character—to share something of what he thought, knew, liked, hoped for. But what can you learn from a bunch of worn-out clothes, a few half-read books, and a beat-up 1978 Washington quarter in a cheap frame?

I opened the center drawer of the desk and found a clutter of odds and ends. Paper clips, rubber bands, a half-full box of chalk. I smiled at the chalk. He had been retired for nine years; yet he kept the chalk. Pipe cleaners. He hadn't smoked since being diagnosed as having lung cancer six years ago; yet he kept the pipe cleaners. The drawer still had flakes of tobacco in it. I shut the drawer.

The upper left-hand drawer contained blank envelopes, blank stationery. Some of both had been used, which at least meant the old man had been in contact with someone. I opened the lower left-hand drawer. It was crammed with files. I pulled one out and read its identification: Anderson, Mary—1954–1955. I shook my head. Was anybody ever named Mary Anderson? Sounded like Andy Hardy's first date.

Inside the file were childish scribblings on three-ringed wide-lined paper. "What I Did Last Summer" by Mary Anderson, Grade 6, Room 4b, Mr. Hall. And what did Mary do in the summer of 1954?

"What I did last summer was too go too my father's cabun in the Catskill Mountain. We hunted and we fished and cooked fish and marshmellows on a wood fire, though I did not care too much for the bugs. Then we went home. It was good too be home again because my friends are their. The woods are all right if you like them. . . ."

I shook my head as I closed the file. "What are you now, Mary? Probably some wigged-out environmental freak." I flipped through the rest of the file. "My Favorite Dream," "How I See The Future," "What I Wish," "My Secret Friend," "Things I Think About." The topics my father had assigned were about as imaginative as the grind I had been put through in the sixth grade. I put the file down on the desk top and picked out another.

I looked at the label. "Well, Randy Deever, year of 1954–1955, what do you have to say for yourself?" Not much. Last summer he didn't do much. Got up in the morning, ate, played, ate, played some more, ate, watched tv, then went to bed. I leafed through the file and found a short newspaper clipping. First Lieutenant Randolph Deever, 1st Air Cavalry, U.S.A., reported missing in action near Buon-bu-n'jang, Vietnam.

I went back and leafed through Mary Anderson's file more carefully. There were several clippings from bookjackets and newspapers about a writer named Joy Frank. And Mary Anderson is Joy Frank, novelist.

Another file. Stienmetz, Willy, 1954–1955. In the summer of '54 he buried his mother. In the summer of '69 he was killed in an anti-war protest demonstration. At the time he had his doctorate in romance languages.

I opened the file drawer all the way. In it there were, perhaps, fifteen files. The records of a few students out of his forty years of teaching from eighty to a hundred students per year. I sat back and thought. My father had touched the lives of between three and four thousand persons. Forty years of classes, yet he had kept the assignments of just a few. I looked through the files and separated out his bank statements, greeting cards, correspondence, his manuscripts and diplomas. Remaining were the files on five students. Mary Anderson, Randy Deever, Willy Stienmetz, Tommy-Sue Robertson, and Paul Nolan. All sixth grade, year of 1954–1955.

A quick look told me that Tommy-Sue had ditched her "Beach Blanket Bingo" name, became Susan Robertson, and had achieved doctorates in both mathematics and physics. A note scribbled in my father's almost unreadable hand mentioned that Paul Nolan had been accepted at Brown University. From Paul Nolan's file I pulled out his single-page theme "My Favorite Dream."

> I don't have a favorit dream. I don't really dream much at all. But when I do it is scarie. It is about a man. he is covered in mud and blood and black stuff like he was burned real bad. He talks to me and he is not nice the way he talks to me. He uses bad words, and he shouts at me. Sometimes he cries. Even when I wake up I smell smoke. The dream is very smokey. Then if I go to sleep again the man will be there and he will sit and talk. He talks a lot then he yells like he's real mad and he walks off into the smoke. I don't understand what he says because in my dream I can't

here him good. I think that is what makes the man mad.

Tommy-Sue Robertson's "Dream":

It is not a nice dream, like the one I have about my girl friends and the pyjama party or when I dream about my boy friends. Sometimes I start dreaming about those and then this man changes the dream. He is horrible and dirty. His face is all red, and he yells at me and makes me cry. He calls me awful names. Once he called me silly little b---h. I know I shouldn't write that, Mr. Hall, but that's what he called me. Sometimes, when he isn't yelling, he trys to talk to me but I'm so scared I can't hear him. He gets mad again and he walks off in the smoke. The smoke is there for a long time and I can smell it when I wake up.

I thought for a moment. A remarkable coincidence? Or a remarkably inept piece of cheating? Yes, Virginia, there were students that cheated even way back in 1954. Back in 1954, we were the wild, unruly generation while our parents were the sainted ones. I opened Willy's file and took a look at his favorite dream.

I only have one dream and it is not a dream but is a nightmaer. He is a solger that is standing in a lot of smoke. He is hurt real bad and his face looks real mad. He shakes his fists at me. I can see his mouth yelling at me but I can't here him. I can tell he is a solger by his uniforum even though it is dirty and ripped all up. Once he got down on his knees and was talking right to me but I still can't here what he said. I wish I could here him. He wants me to real bad.

I looked at Randy Deever's "Dream":

This man he comes to me in my dream. There is smoke all around. He just stands there and looks at me. I ask him who are you and he just shakes his

head and walks away in smoke. That's all. It's the
only dream I ever have.

And Mary Anderson's "Dream":

My favorite dream is always about the angel who
brings me to Oz to see the Wizard, Dorothy, Glinda,
the Munchkins, and all the other neat people there. I
go to the Emerald City and look through all the streets
and stores. But two nights ago I met the Wizard for
the first time. Above the gate to the city was the word
TURKU. I asked the tin woodsman what it meant and
he said it is the name of the city. The Wizard's court
room was full of smoke and he towered over me. His
face was red and angry. The cowardly lion ran away
and the scarecrow burned up. The Wizard opened his
mouth and yelled at me but I couldn't hear him. I
asked the tin woodsman what the Wizard was saying,
but the tin woodsman couldn't hear him either. Then
everything disappeared except the smoke and I could
see the shadow of a man walking away from me. And
there was a burnt sign on the ground. It said TURKU.
The next day I looked it up in the library. Turku is a
city in a country called Finland.

I thought for a moment, then sorted all of the themes from
all of the files and collated them by title in the order they
were written. "My Favorite Dream" was due Monday, No-
vember 1st, 1954. The next date in order was Wednesday the
10th. Due: "How I See The Future."

Paul Nolan's "Future":

I will be a professional football player in the future.
There is nothing else I want more. I am on the second
string at school now, but Mr. Yates says I will be on
the first string next year. There was a man who talked
to me after the game last Sunday and he said there is
more to the future than football. Not for me.

Tommy-Sue Robertson's "Future":

I see the future as a time when everything is good.

There will be no poverty or hunger or diseases or wars or crime. That is the future I see. My new friend says that if that's what I want, it will only be because I make it so. He says it just won't happen by itself. He is a very sad person, but nice.

Willy Stienmetz's "Future":

The futur will be a horrible place. The man I talked to last Monday says so. He even has pitchurs. It's true. I even saw the dates on the backs of the pitchurs. Everything is burnt and crumbled. Sick and dead people are all over the place. The hungry people have no food. He said that the futur doesn't need to be like that. I don't see how nobody can change it though. He's even got pitchurs. He wanted me to keep the pitchurs, but I ran away because they made me sick to look at.

Randy Deever's "Future":

I don't see any future. But I want one. I want to plan for one. I am very good at art. Mrs. Bule says my drawings and paintings are very good. I like it a lot (I like English, too). My friend says painting is important. But there are other important things too. My friend is a soldier. He is a major, and that's what I call him. I don't think I want to be a soldier though.

Mary Anderson's "Future":

No one can see the future. I like to think it will be wonderful. I don't want any wars. My father was in Korea in the infantry and he says bad things about wars that I shouldn't write. My Uncle Rich was too young to be in the war, and he always is saying that he wishes he could have been in it. My father tells Uncle Rich that he is a bad word. Mother says that I should never use that word. My new friend calls my Uncle Rich the same bad word. Major says that the future will be what we make it. It can be very good or very bad. I hope it will be good.

The next theme, due Monday December 20th, 1954, was titled "What I Wish." I frowned. The titles my father had assigned appeared to be playing off these five students. When I was in the sixth grade, we all did "The Things I Wish" theme right before Christmas. We all turned in either shopping lists of toys or syrupy "peace on Earth" pieces. These five had done something a little different.

Paul Nolan's "Wishes":

I used to think I wished to be nothing more than a profeshional athalete. I'm good at sports and I have fun. But there is more in the world than that. There are things I would like for Xmas, but I don't think about them much. This man I met back during football sees me now and then and he took me to the library here in town. He showed me lots of things that happened to hole civilizashuns and then showed me how those people could have changed things if they knew what was going to happen to them. I think about it a lot. I always hated history. But now I think about it a lot.

Tommy-Sue Robertson's "Wishes":

I wish it could always be Christmas. I don't mean presents, although I like giving and getting presents. I mean how nice people are. I like the music being played all the time and how everyone is nice to everybody else. My sad friend says that many people need an excuse—he calls it an official authorization—to be nice. And to be smart. And to be sane. I don't know what he means by that, but I think I feel what he means. I wish I could invite him home for Christmas dinner, but he can't come.

Willy Stienmetz's "Wishes":

I wish my mommy was alive. This will be my first Christmas without her. We never had any presents. I mean real presents, like you go and buy in a store. But mommy would make things. For my sister mommy would make these little dolls out of apples that were all dryd up. They looked like little old ladys. They had dresses and hair and little shawls. Onct mommy made me a quilt for Christmas and I still have it. I wish mommy was alive for Christmas. My friend says that people die and we should remember the good things and not feel to bad that theyre gone. He says that more people will die in the future. He says that we should make sure that why they die will leave nothing but good things for people to remember. He won't come to Christmas dinner, which is probly just as good since we can't afford an extra place at the table daddy says.

Randy Deever's "Wishes":

I want to paint pictures of happy people and happy places. I hope I get the paint set I asked for. Mom said things to Dad about paints being messy, but I know about how to take care of paints. Besides, whats a couple of spots on a rug if you get a beautiful painting for it? The major says that to paint happy people and happy places, there must be happyness. First there has to be happyness, then you can paint it. The major says that there are things that you must do if there is to be happyness. You can't paint it if it isn't there. I don't know about him. He is always pushing at me to do something else. But what I want to do is paint. And that's what I wish. I wish I can spend the rest of my life painting pictures.

Mary Anderson's "Wishes":

I often think of the fairy tale where the genie grants a person three wishes. If I had three wishes I would first wish for everything in the world to be perfect. Second I would wish for the Major to be happy. He is so sad. I think if got my first wish, the second one would take care of itself. I'll save the third wish in case something goes wrong with the first two.

Due on January 4th, 1955 was "My Secret Friend." My father appeared to be looking for the enigmatic companion of these five kids. They complied.

Paul Nolan's "Secret Friend":

My secret friend is a great man. He knows more than anyone else in the world. Sometimes he helps me with my homework. I talk to him and he talks back, but when Mom or Dad looks in my room to see who I'm talking to, they can't see him. I asked Dad about this once, and he said not to worry about it. He said he had a secret friend when he was a boy that he could see and that no one else could. They would play and have a lot of fun. But my secret friend doesn't play with me. He is always after me to work, learn, and study. He says the future is a ball of clay and that the ones who shape it will either be artists or idiots. He says that there are many kinds of artists. He is tall, blond, and very sad.

Tommy-Sue Robertson's "Secret Friend":

No one can see my secret friend. He knows all about numbers and why things work the way they do. He shows me these things, and it's not like math or science in school. He shows me how these numbers and laws affect people and future events. I told my father about my secret friend, and he got very upset and sent me to a doctor. The doctor talked to me, then told my father I would outgrow it. I told my friend about it and he laughed. His name is Major. He said he would be with me forever.

Willy Stienmetz's "Secret Friend":

My secret friend is named Major. It's a strange name, and he is kind of strange. I am not comfortable with him. He tells me terrible stories about things to come. I talked to my father about Major. He told me to go and do my homework. Major talks a lot about the right and wrong of things. I think he wants me to do something, but he wants me to figure it out myself.

He is tall, blond, and very sad looking. Denise Jordan told me she had a secret friend called Annette. Annette is her age and plays games with her. Major is an old man.

Randy Deever's "Secret Friend":

I don't know if I can call Major a friend. He is always there, and he helps me with my homework. But he is not fun like a friend should be. Major keeps pushing me to look at history, politics, wars and all sorts of things that don't have anything to do with painting. He says that happiness has to be there to be painted. But I can imagine dragons when there aren't any dragons. Why should happiness be any different? If I paint pictures of happiness where there is no happiness, is that any different than painting dragons where there are no dragons?

Mary Anderson's "Secret Friend":

My secret friend is the Major. He is tall, blond, handsome, and very sad. He shows me how to write. No one can see him but me, and my father says everyone has a secret friend as a child. Still the Major is very real to me. I have touched him, laughed with him, have seen him cry. I want my parents to see the Major, but they never can, even when he is standing next to me. The Major says I should not worry about it. The future is before me and there is enough there to worry about. The present is just an instant. The future is eternity, he says.

Due January 27th, 1955 was "Things I Think About." My father on another fishing expedition.

Paul Nolan:

I think about a lot of things. Things are very nice in 1955, but what will they be like years from now? None of my friends ever thinks about ten or twenty or thirty years from now. Major says that I should think about these things. He said it wouldn't hurt if you did too. I don't mean anything by that, Mr. Hall. The Major said it.

Tommy-Sue Robertson:

I think about the difference between being good and being happy and if there are any differences. And if there are any differences, should there be? Since the Major came into my life, I think about a lot of things I never thought of before. I think I want to be a scientist and learn how to make things work. The Major reads my themes and helps me sometimes mostly with spelling. He can spell very good. That's the way I say it. The Major says I should say that he can spell very well. I don't care myself. He also said I should tell you the title of this theme should be Things About Which I Think instead of Things I Think About.

Willy Stienmentz:

I think about the Major. I don't know much about him, but he knows everything about me. When he helps me with my homework, it looks so important to him, when I don't really think it's all that important. But he makes me learn things. They are awful things. He took me on a trip to see a movie yesterday. It was in a town I never been to before. The movie has a funny name, and the Major isn't here so I can't spell it right, so please don't give me a bad grade for not getting it right. It is Appocolips Now. The movie scared me a lot. I don't understand what the story was, but I think about it a lot.

Just what, I wondered to myself, is being pulled here? The motion picture mentioned hadn't been released until 1980. I shook my head and continued:

Randy Deever:

I think about the secret friend I used to have. I don't see him anymore. Every time he saw me before, he cried. He said I should always remember him and that I should do the things he wanted. He wants me to be a soldier. He says I can paint too, but that I have to be a soldier. He said I will know why when it's the right time. He said he will see me again when I am older. This is his picture.

I glanced at the picture, and it was quite a good drawing for a sixth grader. I turned to the things Mary Anderson thinks about.

Mary Anderson:

I think about the things I would like to write. There are so many stories, and there are so many things you can try to do with stories. I think the things Major tells me about are things I would want to put into my stories. He loves his father very much, but never told him that. He talks about being in a terrible war that doesn't have to happen. Major says there are lessons people have to learn to avoid the war. He says stories can help people understand things like that.

I tossed the themes upon the desk and shook my head. Whatever the major had accomplished, he hadn't avoided the war. I laughed to think about it. I wasn't in a combat unit in Vietnam, but Vietnam had happened. After decades of fighting off Japanese, French, and Americans, Vietnam took a deep breath during its brief moment of peace, then performed as its first act of foreign policy the invasion of Cambodia. Then China invaded Vietnam, got its nose bent, then hustled out. The Russians were up to their samovars in Afghan rebels, Iran . . .

I looked at the small pile of themes. What in the everloving hell did they mean? I leafed through them again. Mary Anderson's dream had the major talking from a holocaust from some place in Finland. Turku. Well, at least we weren't fighting in Finland.

I reached into my father's file drawer again and pulled out his correspondence file. There was a letter of his, dated February 16th, 1955, to a coin company in Illinois. The company's answer was scribbled on my father's letter.

... When I collected the lunch money from the
students, I found this coin among them. Can you tell
me anything about it?
Yours,

*Mr. Hall, this appears to be an excellent forgery,
although I can think of no reason to forge a 1978
Washington quarter. Such date alterations are possible. For example, with a 1950 quarter, the 50 can
be silver soldered, carved, and polished into a 78.
Such attempts are usually obvious, although I could
swear this one is die stamped. However, the many
scratches and other circulation marks might obscure
the telling signs. It is a curiosity, but not much of a
collector's item.*

I looked at the Washington quarter in its frame. I reached
for it and pulled the cardboard from the back. I tilted the
frame and dropped the quarter into the palm of my hand. A
1978 Washington quarter. I looked through the remaining few
letters in my father's files. There was a letter from the FBI
wanting to know why my father was trying to get in touch
with Susan Robertson. Another from the State Department
not admitting that any Paul Nolan worked for them, but also
asking why my father wanted to know. A letter from Willy
Stienmetz's father conveying the sad news of Willy's death
in a street demonstration. Another letter from the FBI wanting
to know what connection, if any, my father had with Willy
Stienmetz. A letter from Mary Anderson:

Dear Mr. Hall,
Thank you very much for the very kind things you said
about my new book. I hope it will be as important as you
think it is.
Yes, I seem to remember Willy Stienmetz telling me that
he had gotten some money from the one we used to call the
Major. He was very poor, you know. He told me when we
were in high school about the Major. I'm sorry to hear that
Willy is dead.
I guess the Major is still with me, in a way. It's as though

he is an idea in the back of my head. I still hear the idea, but I can't remember what he looked like. . . .

A letter from Randy Deever:

Dear Mr. Hall,

Sorry it took me so long to answer, but the mail is all screwed up over here. This nightmare is becoming almost monotonous in its regularity, but it's nothing compared to the one we're avoiding. Yes, the Major is still with me. He is at my side on S&D missions, and he's saved my hide more than once. If I told anyone else about the Major, they'd think I was crazy, which might not be a bad thing. At least I'd get sent home. But the Major says we have at least one more mission to do. We'll do it alone, together.

Here is the picture you asked for. Major Hall hasn't changed much at all—

I sat straight up. *Major Hall!* I looked through the rest of the correspondence file, then through the other papers. There was no picture. I looked around the room and saw the pictures hanging on the walls. I stood, went to the door, and turned on the overhead light. The photos were of my mother, my two sisters, five blowups of yearbook pictures. They had no names, but it wasn't hard to guess who they were. And then there was the drawing. Randy Deever had become quite an artist before heading out on that last mission. I took the picture down from the wall, walked to the dresser, and looked into its dusty mirror. I held the picture next to my face. There was no mistaking the likeness. I saw writing on the bottom of the drawing, and I turned and read it.

Dear Dad, If they can learn from this, it is the price; If they cannot learn from this, it is only the beginning. I love you, Jay.

I can't prove any of it. The papers can all be explained away as forgeries. That Finland hasn't been involved in a devastating war by now, in 1980, is no proof. Neither has

South Dakota. The Major carried a 1978 quarter, but people in 1980 carry 1978 quarters, as will the people in 1990, if there are people in 1990. But I think the Major might have accomplished what he set out to do. Something has changed. I don't know its significance, but the 1978 quarter I carry with me is not one of your cupronickle and copper sandwiches. The 1978 quarter I have is made out of silver.

I suppose the idea for "Dreams" came from an inability to keep my mouth shut in combination with a case of indigestion, an unfavorable review, and a spare Alex Schomburg illustration.

I was in Philadelphia visiting the then editor of Isaac Asimov's Science Fiction Magazine, George H. Scithers. After gabbing for a while, I was looking around his office and happened to see a color illustration on a table. It looked like a refugee from a 1930's Snorting SF Adventure Tales magazine cover. There was an old-fashioned planet Mars complete with flying saucers backgrounded by a couple of moons and a glowing pink nebula. Standing in front of the planet was a silver robot fitted out with antennae, flashing lights, pipes, hoses, a belt full of strange tools, and glowing red eyes. The robot held its left arm extended like a cop halting a stream of traffic.

The illustration tickled my funnybone, and I said out loud to no one in particular, "There's a story in that."

George's voice came from the other side of the room. "Write it."

I may not believe I can make just any old thing into a story, but some people do. And those were the days when it was very important for me to live up to the unrealistic expectations of others—particularly paying editors.

The illustration was an extra color sketch for a James

27

Gunn piece for Asimov's, *"On the Road to Science Fiction."
I took a copy of the illustration home with me to Maine, stuck
it up on my wall, and the robot and I spent the next several
weeks staring at each other. There just wasn't a story in that
thing. I did manage to crank out a two-thousand-word thing,
but it wasn't long enough to rate a cover. That piece eventually went to an anthology, but I was still left with that
damned robot staring at me.*

*Along about then I read a copy of the first review of my
first book. As I read it I could hear the bombs dropping all
over North America. I didn't know whether to throw myself
beneath the wheels of the nearest truck or hire a hit man. I
have since learned that this particular reviewer hobnails all
over anything even resembling science fiction. But when I
first read the review I didn't know that. It upset me.*

*What upset me even more was getting from George one
of those little form letters they send out requesting an author
to come up with one of the thumbnail bios* Asimov's *heads
stories with to update an author to the readership. I hated
writing those things. I still do.*

*That night, my stomach groaning with chili, I had one hell
of a nightmare. I couldn't get back to sleep, so I went to my
office and tried to get my nightmare down on paper. Sometimes I use writing as a therapeutic tool to cut down the size
of my inventory of devils. One thing led to another and what
I began writing appeared as the story "Dreams" in the August
1979 issue of* Isaac Asimov's Science Fiction Magazine, *that
damned robot all over the cover. Keep in mind where this
story first appeared. It's important.*

Dreams

Some think I am insane. Would that my problems were that easily explained. Some people I know believe I am insane, although they point out that I am making quite a good living from being crazy.

They don't understand. The things I write are not for money, although money allows me to keep on going. No, the writing is how I let it out; how I try to piece together the events; how I try to sustain that one lousy, remaining thread I have to reality.

And now I sit here, staring at this damned form letter—this flip, semi-literate request for details of my personal and professional life, to introduce me to the reader. But I do not write for fun. That even less than for money, and certainly not to satisfy the curiosity of any person with a dollar and a quarter to waste and a few minutes of time to kill. But—I look at this bio request again and again. I can't hide from it, and I can't throw it away. What about me, it asks, and the things I feel well up inside me, clawing to be set free—given that peculiar life of ink on paper.

I thumb through a back copy to look at the authors' bios, and laugh. Twenty thirty-word lists of dry events attempting to be amusing through lame humor. I already have over two hundred, and I've hardly begun.

But, if it's a rule—this thirty-word limit—I might as well break it. I've broken just about every other rule of writing.

I don't read much—I never have. I don't plan anything, I don't revise, and I don't give a damn. I'll break another right now by telling you the ending of this tale first—two rules, in fact, since the ending is one that is *verboten*. "It was all a dream" is considered a cheap ending in fiction. Lewis Carroll can pull Alice's cookies out of Wonderland that way, but the rest of us are supposed to gimmick, slug, slash, or reason our way out. *Reason*? What a laugh. What a thigh-thumping, tear-rending *laugh*.

Let me sprinkle the pieces of my broken rule before you. They are dreams I have, yet . . . they are something else. They are where I have been, they are the experience I draw upon to write, they are nightmares to the nth power that let me meet the horrors all of you laugh off with the morning sun and try to describe to bored listeners at the breakfast table.

They are dreams, I am sure; that they are *nothing but* dreams, I cannot tell. No one can.

Let me tell you about when they started. It was three years ago. (My god, I almost said it was a dark and stormy night! Well, it was.) I had stumbled into bed about three in the morning, my sinuses packed from too much smoking, my stomach writhing from the bowl of chili I'd eaten at midnight, and my head slightly soggy from the several beers I'd used in an attempt to extinguish the chili. It had been one last attempt at saving a forty-thousand-word start on a novel that had kept me up. Soon after the novel expired, I did as well.

Helen had the covers wrapped around her head and was well through her second cord of wood. Snoring usually drives me to distraction, but that night I was asleep before I hit the pillow, and I mean *asleep*.

Usually sleeping for me is a fitful state of semi-doze as I mentally thumb through bits of plot or dialog, discouraging events of the day, or particularly humiliating episodes of my youth. Many times, while I am "sleeping" in this manner, I will come wide awake with a story idea. Then it's another all-nighter while I try to get it on paper before I forget it. When I stretched out that night, however, I was blank.

Then it started.

* * *

Whoever directs my dreams was trained by Orson Welles. Dramatic angles, startling contrasts, and deep shadows.

I was in a roundish room with one continuous wall. There were doors in the wall spaced only a few inches apart, with swirling, black mists serving as curtains. In the center of the room, one of the black mists shaped itself into an irregular column, then opened its eyes. Eyes covered the column from top to bottom. Horrid, red-irised things. "Which door?" the column asked.

In my dreams I can usually tell that I'm dreaming. Lots of times, if I enjoy the premise, I'll go along just for the fun of it. If I don't want to play along, I can force myself to wake up.

"All right. Wake up!"

A number of the eyes crowded together on my side of the black column. "We are awake. Which door?"

Without moving my legs, I was beginning to whirl around the wall, passing the doors in a blur. "Wake up! Wake up!"

"We are awake, for we never sleep. Which door?" Twice more I whirled around the room, heard the column say something about "random dimension"; and then I was walking at night on the boardwalk at Coney Island. There were no lights anywhere, and the place was a shambles. Windows were boarded over, and scraps of paper skittered across deserted walkways. I don't remember the ocean being there, but I heard music—some of that incoherent jazz that I don't understand at all. I walked a little further, the wet night air making my face sticky; and I saw a light ahead.

I held my hand to my face, felt the moisture on it, then stopped. This was too real for one of my dreams. When I dream, the pictures I form, the things I experience, are remarkably devoid of detail. Feeling the moisture in the air and on my skin is the kind of detail my dreams never have. I stooped down and felt the boards under my feet. They were worn, and grains of sand rolled under my fingers. I picked up a splinter, then jerked up my hand and sucked on my finger.

As I squatted on the boardwalk, trying to catch the end of the splinter with my teeth, I kept asking myself, "Why

Coney Island?" I hadn't been there since I was kid—twenty-five or more years ago. The bad-news novel I had been fighting with had nothing to do with Coney Island, and my chili dreams usually involve bug-eyed characters riding on snakes forming up a posse to come and get me. I looked at that light again, then stood and began walking toward it while that bleep-honk jazz got louder.

I stopped in front of an open doorway, a single naked bulb illuminating the entrance to what looked like a ride of some kind. Behind a counter stood a fat man in rough clothes chewing on the stub of a cigar. He looked at me. "Care to take a chance?"

I backed away from the door a little, then began wondering about the plot change. My dreams usually find me being driven through circumstances with no volition of my own. I want to get out—get free—but off I go into flame, disaster, off tall buildings or whatever. But in front of that cigar-chewing fat man, I knew I had a choice. If I wanted, I could turn around and go away. That puzzled me, because I never reflect in my dreams—I just experience. I looked at the fat man again, then stepped through the entrance. He smiled around his cigar, then pulled a ticket from a huge wheel. "That'll be fifty dollars."

"Fifty dollars? You're out of your mind." Something compelled me to reach for my pockets just to see how much money I had. Money is something else I never have in my dreams. I reached to my right side pocket and closed my fingers around a handful of paper. I pulled it out and counted the bills. "I only have thirty-seven dollars."

"Too bad."

"Whaa—" The floor dropped out from underneath me, plunging me first into darkness; then as I hit a huge wooden sliding board, I was in a corkscrewed shaft lit with red, yellow, and green lights. I started falling over to one side, stuck out my hand to right myself, then withdrew it as friction burned my palm. I went over on my shoulder and decided the time was right. I began screaming. That was my sure-fire way to wake up from a dream, because if my own noise didn't wake me up, it would wake Helen. In turn, she would shake me until it was over.

The screams followed me down the giant corkscrew until the slide leveled out and deposited me in a huge wooden bowl. I came to a stop, took a few breaths, then looked around. There were seven others sitting in the bowl. One of them stood and walked over to me. "You're the eighth. I guess it begins now."

"Eighth what, and what begins?" I sat up, then pushed myself to my feet.

The one standing, a man dressed in a gray business suit, shrugged. "The game. I don't know anything more about it than that."

I took a chance. "Did you see that black thing, the one with all the red eyes?"

The man raised an eyebrow at me, then shook his head. "I wouldn't worry about it. You do know this is a dream, don't you?"

"Yeah, sure." I nodded, then smiled. "Yeah. It's good to hear someone say it, though."

"BEGIN!" At the boom of the signal, all of us were on our feet. The man I had been talking to looked up at the colored lights.

"Begin what?"

Swords, maces, and axes appeared in our hands. The ax in mine startled me so much I dropped it. I looked up at the lights. "What in the hell is this?"

"BEGIN!"

From above the lights began a rumbling, then soon all of us could see a shape descending, the outside of a bowl. A woman holding a sword stared at the shape, then looked down at me with wild eyes. "They're going to crush us! They're going to crush us, unless we fight it out!"

She brought the sword back over her head with both hands, then rushed at me. She brought the blade down, but I stepped to one side. The weight of the heavy blade pulled her off of her feet, and she fell on it. Then she was still. "SEVEN!"

I looked up at the bowl shape. It had slowed a little. When I looked down again two couples were swinging it out on the side away from mine and two men were coming at me—one with an ax, the other with a mace. "Wake up, you two! This is only a dream!"

The one on the left brought up his ax. "Then it doesn't matter what we do."

I held up my ax. "Like hell, it doesn't!"

"SIX!"

I saw a body drop on the far side of the bowl. A woman dropped her sword and screamed as a man ran at her with an ax. I turned to face my two opponents, wondering why they were ganging up on me. Sooner or later they'd have to slug it out between themselves.

"FIVE!"

The one with the mace swung at me with a vertical stroke, and I stepped aside and gave him a horizontal whack in the kidneys. His scream almost drowned out the signal caller.

"FOUR!"

The guy with the ax came at me, but I'll be damned if I didn't recognize him. Roman something—Roman Janeway. Yes! Roman Janeway. The slimy, ignorant, two-faced . . . the others! I recognized them all. Martin, Wertzle, Simmons— all book critics. I looked at Janeway. "Janeway, don't you recognize me? It's me!"

Janeway hefted his ax. "Of course I recognize you. Why do you think I have this?"

I threw my ax at his face. "THREE!"

I bumped my head on something and fell to the floor of the bowl. When I looked up, I could see that the matching shape was only a few feet from crushing us—those that remained.

"TWO!"

I saw a body drop—Van Zandt from the *Times*, I think— then a second body, still on its feet, came at me. He was crouched down to avoid bumping his head on the shape. I grimaced and picked up Janeway's ax. The one coming for me was Bettnor from the *News*, and I knew from experience that there was no reasoning with Bettnor—not after his review of my first novel, there wasn't! At a crouch I moved toward him, but then slipped in a pool of blood. "Hah!" He rushed at me, swinging his ax. I rolled over as Bettnor sunk his blade into the wooden floor. I swung my ax at Bettnor's head.

"THE WINNAH!"

Again, I was in that circular room looking at that black column of red eyeballs. "Which door?"

"Home! I want to go home!"

"... home!"

"Wake up! Come on, wake up!"

I opened my eyes and saw Helen staring down at me. She was on her knees shaking my arm. "Helen ... Helen."

"No more chili for you, buster." She pointed at herself with her thumb. "I can't lie around here all day like you do. I have to punch a time-clock. Now, go to sleep and for God's sake quit eating before you go to bed!"

She stretched out, rolled over, and in a minute was again sawing wood. My pyjamas were drenched with sweat and I got up to put on a dry pair. After getting the fresh pair from the dresser, I went into the bathroom and turned on the light. Except for a wild look, the image in the mirror looked the same. I shucked my old pyjamas, then pulled on the bottoms of the fresh pair. As I thrust my arm through the right sleeve of the tops, I felt something jab my finger. I remembered the splinter from the boardwalk. I swallowed and looked at my right palm. The heel of the hand had a friction burn. I spent the rest of the night drinking coffee.

Have you ever tried to tell a dream to someone? You wake up, realizing that you've just gone through an experience of incredible importance, then you try to convey the impact of the experience on someone. "That's something, but you should have seen the dream I had." And everything piddles away into unimportance. Helen was even less sympathetic.

"See these bags under my eyes? That's what I think of your damned dream!" She pointed at the wastebasket. "All of the cans of chili are in there."

"What if I just take them out?"

"I opened them first. Enjoy."

I pushed a piece of bacon around on my plate. "Helen, what if I saw a shrink?"

"You just want someone to humor you. Look, everybody knows you're crazy. If you want someone to humor you at fifty dollars an hour, pay me. I'll humor you."

* * *

Helen had gone to work and, as usual, had taken the car. "All you do is write. What do you need a car for?"

"What if . . . what if I wanted to see someone?"

"Like a shrink."

"Yeah, like a shrink."

She leaned over and kissed me on my nose. "I can tell you everything a shrink would, and for free. You are totally off your bezonko. Now, get in your office and write another best-seller, poopsie. Mommy can't keep this show on the road all by herself."

I was beginning to get the impression that I wasn't being taken very seriously. I shuffled into my office, flopped down in my chair, and picked up the paper. For some reason when I unfolded my paper the headline caught my eye: SEVEN CRITICS BRUTALLY MURDERED.

Was it Descartes that didn't know whether he was awake or dreaming? I remember something like that from my one year of bonehead philosophy. I had assumed I was dreaming. But that was before finding out that all those critics had awakened from their dreams to find themselves dead. I couldn't get it out of my head. What if I had been responsible for the deaths of Bettnor, Janeway, the other one? But I didn't kill them all. Terrific. What a defense. You see, your honor, I only killed Janeway, Bettnor, and the other one. Somebody else killed the rest.

I had to talk to someone. The trouble with writing at home in La Suburbia is the lack of willing listeners within walking distance. Even the housewives were thinning out as they discovered that there was more to life than manufacturing babies and unplugging toilets. Gary Wertzle, my dentist, had a home office two blocks away; but he cost more than the shrink. Besides, he'd probably be up to his elbows in somebody's gold mine. The sole remaining member of the endangered housewife species, Claudia Fenner, was a block away; but I couldn't bring myself to endure another recitation of "My son the lawyer." As far as I'm concerned, her son the lawyer ought to be her son the convict.

David Ross wouldn't be out of school until three-thirty. In those rare moments when David wasn't mining his lode of blackheads, he studied to become a SF writer, and he had picked me as his mentor. This great honor was bestowed upon me because I was within walking distance of his house, "and none of those other guys ever answered my letters." Our relationship matured—I might even say flowered—when I found out that David was a whiz at doing research (something I hate) and was a walking reference shelf of current science fiction. I never read the stuff myself. His value to me? I told him once that I needed a Faster-Than-Light drive for one of my stories. In a week he had compiled, in terms that I could understand, all of the currently fashionable reasons why FTL is impossible, in addition to a breakdown of every FTL drive ever cooked up by every writer since the 1940's. I was thinking of adopting him.

It was while I was mulling over the paucity of my choices that the doorbell rang. I figured it was the mailman, and I sat at my desk and waited for the creep to leave. The Christmas before, his gaily decorated blackmail note suggested that the amount of mail I get left me in his debt. I told him what he could do with his note; and ever since my manuscripts and other mail shows up ripped, soaking wet, or covered with suspicious, footprint-sized marks. The bell rang twice more, and I got up and looked out of the window beside the door.

It wore an ankle-length overcoat and had a brown stocking cap pulled down over its ears, leaving scraps of black hair sticking out between the hat and coat collar. Under its left arm was a suspicious wad of papers. "Will you look at my story and tell me what's wrong with it? It'll probably bore you, but I'd really appreciate it."

"Why, young tyro, would I want to be bored?"

"I'm sure you don't. But can you tell me why it's boring?"

"Probably because you can't write..."

I have these little flashes of conversation I wish I'd had. They help pass the time. The bell rang again, and I moved to the door and opened it. "What?"

"I'm Tilly Winters."

"Chilly Winters? What is this, a joke?"

"Tilly. Tilly Winters. You said you wanted to see the manuscript I'd written based on the multi-dimensional idea I told you about."

"I did?" I frowned and looked down at the bundle of papers. My great aunt Fanny, it would take me all day to wade through it. "Kinda long, isn't it?"

It smiled. "Oh, these are all the drafts, in case you wanted to see how I developed the idea. I did twelve drafts."

The load on my heart eased, then a germ of memory began to announce itself. "Tilly . . . you're the one . . . the psych major I met at the con in . . . in . . ."

"Washington."

I nodded. Suddenly "it" became a qualified listener—or at least as qualified as anything else I could get. "Come in, come in."

Tilly Winters came through the door, pulling off cap and coat, transforming an it into a she. I took her cap and coat, put them over the back of a chair, then motioned for her to follow me into my office. She stopped in the doorway to my office, bugged her eyes and hung open her mouth. "Oh, this is just the way I had imagined it!"

I sat down at my desk. "Imagined what?"

"This office." She looked at me. "I've been a fan of yours for ever so long." She pointed at a chair. "May I sit down?"

I nodded, then held out my hand for the manuscript.

"Just the final draft."

She pulled out a few sheets and handed them to me. Its title was "Dimensanaut." Bells went off and recollection stampeded its way into my awareness. I had been working on the idea of a traveler between dimensions when I had met Tilly at a con and she told me about her story idea. That forty-thousand-word fizzle had been my result, and now here was Tilly's try. She had told me . . . about a dream she had. Black mists and red eyes. Yes! It had seemed vaguely familiar then, but that was before my trip to play chop-chop with the critics. I had three words of the opening sentence read when she leaned on my desk. "What do you think?"

I looked up. "Tilly, do you jog?"

She frowned. "Yes, I do."

"Then take a few laps around the block. I can't read this

with you hovering over me like a mother hen."

She smiled. "I'm sorry." She stood and left the room. I leaned back in my chair, put my feet on my desk, and began reading. When I put down the manuscript, I was soaked with sweat.

Tilly's experience was a trip through flowers, with golden boys and silver girls prancing to the strains of "Tiptoe Through the Tulips." In fact, her trip had no story possibilities whatsoever. The sweats came when her trip ended and she found herself in the round room with the black gas peeking at her with those red eyes. She came puffing and wheezing into my office, then flopped down in a chair. She actually *had* gone and lapped the block a few times.

"Well . . . what do you think?"

I tapped the manuscript with my finger. "Did you take this from a dream?"

"Most of it. That business at the end, with the director sending people to different dimensions, was mostly made up. I remembered something like that, but it was pretty vague. Why?"

I shrugged. "Nothing . . . in your dream, did you see the director at the beginning of your trip?"

She shook her head. "It started in the flowers. But what about the story? Is it any good?"

I shrugged, then held out the papers. "You need conflict. Sally whatshername shows up in happyland, frolics around, then finds out that it was a trip to another dimension. She hasn't had to struggle to achieve anything. You need a guy in a black hat—something like that."

She stood up, snatched the papers from my hand, then stomped toward the door. "Good-bye!"

I jumped up and ran around my desk. "Hey, wait! I was only—" The door slammed and Tilly Winters was gone. Back at my desk I cracked out my forty-thousand-word flop. I leafed through the pages, then closed the thing and thought. The premise was that what everyone thought was dreaming was actually experiences in another dimension. Most people go to sleep, but then have a long blank period until they wake up in another dimension. My hero had figured out the gag and had found out that by remaining in a state of half-sleep, he got to visit with the thing that ran the show.

My director was an oversized ant at the head of a magic tunnel—both complete fabrications. But Tilly had seen the real director; and now, so had I. It couldn't be mere coincidence.

I nodded. I had been working hard on the manuscript before I went and hit the sack. I looked at my finger, then squeezed at the splinter. It popped out along with a little gob of pus. I nodded again, then began studying the portion of the novel concerned with meeting the director. The next time I was going to choose my door, and maybe ask Old Redeyes a question or two.

The black column opened its eyes. "Which door?"

I licked my lips. "I'll pick one. First, I want something."

"What?"

"Look, I can't get anyone to believe me about this. They think I'm dreaming."

"Everyone calls it dreaming."

"Look, I picked up a splinter the last time. I know where I got it, but Helen says I got it when I fixed the kitchen cabinet. But that means I can bring back things."

"We must hurry. You are backing up the travelers. What do you want?"

"Give me something—anything—that I can take back with me to prove where I've been."

The black column snaked out a tendril that shot at my face and touched my left cheek. "Ouch!" I opened my eyes and Helen was sitting up, looking at me.

"Again? Are we going to have another night with you jumping around?"

I touched my cheek with my fingertips and could feel a lumpy area. Helen had rolled over and I shook her shoulder as I turned on the bed lamp. "Look. Look at this."

She half-turned, squinting against the light. "What did you do to your cheek?"

"I asked the director—the guy in my dream—to give me something to bring back. Well? Believe me now?"

Helen shook her head, then pulled the covers over her

shoulder and turned away. "You are sick. Burn yourself like that just to make a point. You are a real sicko. Now, good night and shut up!" She reached out a hand and turned off the light.

I got up, went to the bathroom, turned on the light, and looked in the mirror. My cheek was bright red with a dime-sized welt in its center. I turned off the light and went back to bed. As I lay there, thinking, I decided that I'd have to bring back something that couldn't be explained away. I half-dozed, concentrating on again meeting the director.

Moments passed, then it opened its eyes. "Which door?"

"Mars. I want to go to Mars."

"You two better get down to the *Eagle VII*."

I turned from the port, with its view of the red planet, then nodded at the orbiter pilot. "Right, Skip." I looked over at my copilot for the *Eagle*. "Let's go, Hap."

I turned to my buckles and began releasing myself from the couch. In this dimension I was an astronaut; and I knew my two companions, as well as what I was doing. None of that panicky groping around in fogs with fanged things hot on my heels; none of that embarrassing silence where everyone waited for me to do whatever it was that they knew I should do, but that I did not. I slapped the armrest of the couch. Damned good, solid reality-dream this time.

I pushed up from the couch, made my way to the rear hatch, and pulled my way into the *Eagle*. As I turned at the deck, Hap came in, closing both hatches behind him. As I began strapping myself into the swivel couch, Hap pulled himself down and began on his buckles. By the time he was finished I was three-quarters of the way through the separation check.

Hap completed his part, then we both leaned back as the countdown began. He looked over at me, looking a bit nervous. "Like a dream, isn't it?"

I nodded and smiled. "Sure is."

"I mean, like a *dream*."

I frowned. "Are you trying to tell me something, Hap?"

Hap shrugged, then rubbed his eyes. "I don't know. It's too late to scrub the mission now, so I'm going to get right to the point." He looked at me. "Are you in dimension right now?"

This had to be a trick; another little game of Old Redeyes. "I'm not sure I get your meaning."

Hap studied my face until I turned away. "You get my meaning, all right! How did you get here?"

I twiddled my thumbs, then darted a glance at Hap. "I asked to go to Mars." That was safe. If worse came to worse, I could say that what I meant was that I had volunteered for the Mars mission.

Hap nodded. "Sure you did. What are you in your own dimension?"

He was really closing in. Was he another dimensanaut trying to make sense out of all the bizarro things that were going on? I took a chance. "I'm a writer. What about you?"

"I have a little souvenir shop in Miami Beach. You know, coral, shells, things like that."

"You sell sea shells by the seashore?"

Hap glared at me. "This is no time for lame jokes, buddy."

"Sorry." I looked at the elapsed-time indicator. "You all settled in? We'll be going down soon."

He stretched out a hand. "Do you have any idea what we're getting ourselves into?"

"I don't know. But what I do know is that I'm going to walk all over Mars and bring back some of it."

"But what's down there? This reality is made up out of our minds."

"What are you talking about? Mars is Mars." I shook my head. "Don't you think you're getting a little excited about nothing, Hap?"

"From dimension to dimension there are differences. The traffic cop . . . what do you call the thing with all the eyes?"

"The director."

Hap nodded. "Yeah. Well there are billions—trillions of doors. More. Perhaps an infinite number. Each one an imaginable reality. That's how we get these dreams or dimensions. Something in us *wants* them."

"Hap, I can only think offhand of perhaps a thousand dreams that I'd rather not have had."

"Only part of you. Part of you wanted to explore a certain

dimension—a dimension dictated by your own mind." Hap studied the instruments, then turned back to me. "I do a little backyard astronomy. Mars has always interested me, but as an astronomer. You said you were a writer. Where does your interest in Mars come in? What kind of writer?"

I shrugged. "I write a little science fic—"

"Science fiction? Pop-eyed monsters and that sort of stuff?" Hap shook his head. "Damn." He pressed a button on his hand console. "Skip, do you read science fiction?"

Long silence. "Yeah." Another long silence. "What about you two?"

Hap closed his eyes and nodded at me. I pressed my button to open a channel to the command module. "Hap reads the stuff; I write it."

Another very long silence. "I'll take a chance." Skip seemed to weigh his words. "Are you two . . . talking about traveling between dimensions?"

"Yes. There's some common desire that put all three of us into this dimension. That's what Hap thinks. That we all wanted the same dimension. What do we know about Mars?"

Hap shook his head, then broke in. "It's not what we know; it's what we want—what we want Mars to be." Hap looked at me. "What about you? What do you . . . wish Mars to be?"

I shook my head. "I don't know. I told the director, 'I want to go to Mars.' That's all." I bit my lower lip and looked at Hap. "But deep down, what was the Mars I asked for?"

Hap pressed his button. "Skip, is there any way to abort this mission?"

I began unbuckling while Hap waited for Skip's response. When I was loose, I pushed off for the hatch and tried to open it. "Nothing. It's jammed tight!"

I heard Skip's voice through the *Eagle*'s system. "No good! It's under computer control and I can't stop it! Separation in twenty seconds!"

I pushed back to my couch and buckled up. Hap was shaking his head. "My God, what are we getting into?"

I reached out and punched him in the arm. "Look! We're in control just as long as we don't panic."

"God, when I think about some of the monsters I've read about . . ."

"Knock it—" I was cut short as the *Eagle* lurched, then began its entry burn. I switched to the radio. "Skip? Are you reading me? Skip?" I looked through my view port but couldn't get a look. By the time I'd adjusted the *Eagle*'s attitude, we were a long way from the command module. "Skip, do you read?" Three white streaks came from the direction of the planet, passed by the command module; then the sky filled with a bright flash. "Skip!"

Hap was blubbering. "Skip's dead. Poor Skip. Dear Jesus. What's happening?"

I craned my neck to peer after the streaks, sweat dribbling into my eyes. "If I were you, Hap, I'd start thinking about those streaks coming after us."

If my comment was meant to calm my companion down a bit, it had a slightly opposite effect. Hap began flailing his arms and screaming as we approached the Martian atmosphere. Then he grabbed onto his half of the dual landing controls and froze. Through the view port I could see Syrtis Major rushing up at us. I reached out a hand and shook Hap's arm. If I didn't get him loose of the controls before the computer program expired and turned the flight over to us, it would be splat time. "Hap? Hap, you want to let go? Hap?" He kept staring straight ahead, arms frozen. I leaned over and punched him in the side of his head.

"Ow!" He released the controls and held his hand to his head. "What'd you do that for?"

"You were frozen on the controls, idiot. We're landing."

The readout on the computer indicated thirty seconds to landing, but the transponder showed us to be two and a half minutes from the surface at the rate we were going. I grabbed the controls and the computer let go. So do I believe my eyeballs or the transponder? I went with the instrument and plunged toward Syrtis Major.

"We're going to crash! Decrease the rate of descent!"

"Look at the transponder. We're still twenty kilometers up."

"You never heard of an instrument going haywire? Slow this thing down!"

"If I use up our fuel to land us ten kilometers short of the surface, we get to fall the rest of the way. A ten kilometer drop, even at this gravity, won't be pretty."

"But... what if the transponder is wrong? You'll smear us all over the place!"

"Why would I wish a bad transponder on us? Hell, I didn't even know what a transponder was until this dimension. You have a secret thing against transponders?"

Hap began blubbering again. "What has this got to do with anything?"

"This is a dream, Hap. Ride with it and see what happens."

"Jesus. Jesus, Jesus, Jesus..."

I turned back to the job and held my breath as the surface rushed up to meet us. We passed through it and Hap passed out.

The ground below was green, the waters blue. We were descending through a blue sky with chubby tufts of white clouds sprinkled about. The distance to ground peeled away and I headed for a plowed field to keep out of the trees. *Trees?* I threw the coal to the *Eagle VII* as we approached the surface, slowed to a hover about five meters above the ground, then the fuel ran out. We dropped like a stone and slammed into the field.

I cleared my head, looked out of my view port, and could swear that I was in a Virginia rural scene. I reached over and shook Hap's shoulder. "Hap. Hap! Wake up!"

"Waaa—" He looked out of his view port, then back at me. "I don't get it."

I thought a moment. "Hap, you were right—about those secret wishes. I remember when the Viking lander reports came in—how disappointed I was about the lack of life upon Mars. This dimension is Mars with life!" I began unbuckling. "Come on, let's go outside."

Hap undid his buckles. "What about our pressure suits?"

"Trees, grass, plowed fields... oh, go ahead and take readings of the atmosphere, if it'll make you feel better."

"It would." Hap performed the checks, then nodded. "We have air; enough and the right kind." Hap frowned. "Why haven't we been in touch with mission control?"

I shrugged. "The orbiter had the rig, maybe? Anyway, no

mission control is necessary for this dimension. It's you and me on a Mars with life." I reached to the hatch and opened it. The smell of freshly turned earth—uh, Mars—filled the *Eagle*. I climbed out, went down the access ladder, then stood on the field as Hap's head poked through the hatch. I waved him on. "Get down from there and let's look around."

Hap climbed down, then stood beside me. "When we were landing, did you see any structures? Habitations?"

"I didn't notice." I pointed toward a gap in the trees at the edge of the field. "Look. I think there's a road over there. Let's head for it."

We made our way over the furrows, and as we reached the trees at the edge of the field, something roared overhead and both of us went into the underbrush. "Look!"

Hap was pointing his finger into the air. I glanced in the indicated direction to see three saucer-shaped crafts banking toward the *Eagle*. As they made a pass above the field, the *Eagle* disappeared in a bright flash. They roared overhead, then from behind they banked around and came over the field again. Two of them continued on while the third settled to the ground. The side of the craft split and a long ramp extended from the opening. Ten metallic creatures emerged from the opening and clanked down the ramp. Hap looked at me and went for my throat. "What kind of a sicko mind do you have? What are those?" I punched him in the head again. "Ow!"

"Now knock it off! Let's see what they want."

"After killing Skip and blasting the *Eagle*, I'd think it's pretty damned obvious what they want!"

"Shut up!"

The creatures fanned out and began a search of the tree line. They were robots, no doubt, with almost a cartoon, Buck-Rogers quality about them. I frowned and searched my mind for a clue. I don't know how many stories I'd written that I didn't know the ending myself until I had gotten it on the paper. If those walking garbage cans were creatures of my own mind, what ending had my sicko mind already thought up for hapless Hap and myself? I turned away from the field and looked through the windbreak to a field on the other side.

Beyond it was a farmhouse. I tapped Hap on the shoulder. "Let's go."

Hap and I worked our way through the brush until we reached the field, then we ran toward the house. The thing had a gabled roof, clapboard siding and needed a fresh coat of paint. "What kind of . . . habitation is . . . that for a Martian?"

I puffed and shook my head. "Don't know." I looked over my shoulder to check on the walking junkyard. They were still poking around in the other field. I tripped on something and went sprawling into the dirt.

Hap grabbed my arm and pulled me to my feet. "Come on! Before they trace us!"

We began running again, and I winced every time my right foot hit the ground. I had twisted my ankle. We reached the house and went running around its corner to be out of view from the field. Hap leaned against the wall while I went to a screened-in back door. I knocked, and in moments a yellow, narrow-headed thing with suckers on the ends of its fingers came to the door. It wore denim coveralls and was sucking on a piece of straw. "Yep? What kin I do fer ya, young fella?"

I felt my upper lip curl as my eyebrows went down. "Knock off the Walter Brennan impression, will you? You've got to hide us. There's an army of robots after us!"

The creature put its thumbs under the straps of its coveralls and nodded. "Yep. I don't mind sayin' we pay a lot of good tax money for them robots, sonny."

Hap pushed himself away from the wall and stood beside me. He looked at the creature, then shook his head. "What are the robots for?"

It sucked on its straw a bit more, then rocked back and forth on its toes. "Well, we seen whatcha done to your planet, sonny. We sort of like things the way they are. Them robots, along with the ships and projection system, make sure that you folks don't see nothin' but a dead planet. Too bad you fellas made it down here, 'cause now them robots'll have to kill ya."

Hap grabbed my arm. "Run! We've gotta run!"

I took a few steps after him, but I had a question that

needed answering. I turned back. "What about the Viking probes? How come they sent back pictures of—"

It turned its back and walked from the door. "Don't know nothin' 'bout no Vikin's, sonny."

I heard clanking, rushed to the corner of the house, and saw the squad of robots approaching the house. I turned and headed off into the woods after Hap. I couldn't find him or his trail. "Hap! Hap!"

I rushed through the trees, sharp branches swatting my face, I called and called again. Then I heard whirring and crashing behind me. A meter to my left, a swath of forest disappeared. I turned abruptly to my right and ran clang-smack into one of those robots. I looked up from the ground, my head spinning, and saw two coal-red eyes peering from under a helmet of silver. It raised a hand toward me as I blacked out.

"Which door?" It was Old Redeyes again.
"Did Hap come through here?"
"Which door?"
I sighed, then hung my head. "Home."

I opened my eyes in the dark room and could hear Helen snoring. I sat up and turned on the bed lamp. My hands were all scratched, and I could feel a lump on my head. The palms of my hands were crusted with still-wet dirt. The snoring stopped, Helen rolled over and opened her eyes. "My God, sicko, what have you been up to now?"

I looked at her. "You wouldn't believe me if I told you. But this time," I looked at the dirt on my palms. "this time I can prove it!"

The next afternoon I sat at my desk looking with disgust at my envelope of dirt scrapings. The stuff crawled with organics, said the soil chemist. About the one place he could guarantee that it didn't come from was Mars. I threw the envelope into my wastebasket, then leaned forward to finish the breakfast Helen had prepared for me. That was a new twist, since Helen never prepared breakfast. I looked over my mail—bills, a fan letter, a fat envelope from a publisher.

I opened the fat one and pulled out a set of galleys for a story of mine. Whatthehell, life must go on. Livings still must be made. I picked up my red pencil and began proof-reading the sheets. Then I saw something that I *never* do: the word "said" as well as all of the other half-million inane alternatives do not appear in my stories unless they cannot be avoided. If I find where I have to use something of the sort to clue the reader in who is speaking, I'll rewrite the story before I start with: he said, she replied, he suggested, she wailed, he murmured, she denied, he speculated, she confirmed—or anything like it.

I reached for my telephone, had the editor's number half-dialed, then I hung back the receiver. I stared at my filing cabinet for a solid minute, then got up, went over and pulled the manuscript for the galleys I had been checking.

There it was in glowing black-and-white: he said, she promised . . . he pleaded, she coaxed. . . . The bloody thing crawled with them! I moved to my chair and sat down.

All right. Perhaps there are no immutable laws—especially when we're talking about multi-dimensional travel, dreaming, or whatever. But *that* is something I *never* do. *Never*. I don't care what kind or style of dimension anyone wants to cook up. I just don't do that!

The doorbell rang and I jumped up from my chair. After a few deep breaths I went to the door and opened it. A man wearing an overcoat and a wild look pushed his way in. It was Hap! "Hap," I exclaimed.

"I thought I'd never find you," he replied.

"Then I'm not going crazy," I blurted.

"No," he confirmed. "Can we go somewhere and talk?" he suggested.

"My office," I nudged. "What happened to you?" I inquired.

We moved into my office, and Hap dropped into a chair. I walked around my desk and sat down. "I ran," he bemoaned. "I ran until I could no longer move. Then I fell down. I guess I fell asleep," he concluded.

"I was worried," I confessed. "But then you saw Redeyes," I stated.

"Yes," Hap agreed. "I was in such a state, I hated to think

what dimension my mind would pick for 'home.' So I told the director to send me where you went," he admitted.

"Hmmm," I muttered. "But what now?" I tempted.

"I'm going to kill the director," he ranted. "The very next time I get in that little round room, I'm going after that pile of eyeballs," he sputtered.

"Why tell me?" I coaxed.

He looked at me. "I owe you that much. I wanted to give you a chance to get to a dimension that you prefer before I put an end to this business once and for all," he declared.

I nodded. "Considering the way I write in this dimension, I think I'll try another," I explained. "But won't killing the director leave you suspended between dimensions?" I hinted.

"I don't care," he roared. "When I got home this time I found my wife in the arms of another man," he wailed.

"But that's this dimension; she'll be faithful in another," I offered.

"It doesn't matter," he babbled. "I could never bear to look at her after this," he cried. "Remember," he cautioned, "be certain you get into the dimension you want first thing tonight. I'll wait until eleven before I go to sleep."

I spent the rest of the day making up a shopping list of the things I wanted in my dimension. Then I spent the evening memorizing it. This time when I said "home" I wanted to know what I meant. I felt almost sorry for Redeyes. After all, he was just doing his job. But that's how it goes. I'm here now. This Helen doesn't snore; and if I decide to stay up all night working, she stays up too and makes me coffee and brings me great bowls of chili. I'm not very well-known right now, but on my shopping list I ordained a happy future for my writing. Someday I shall be numbered among such present science fiction greats as Robert O. Heinlein, Frederik Pole, and the namesake of this inestimably superior publication, Isaac Karamazov.

I have always had a horror of prisons. The absolute loss of freedom, the regimentation, the brutality of prison was frightening, but there was something more than that. Ever since I can remember, books and movies about prisons and prisoners have always drawn me like a magnet. I have never known why. I never wanted to know why, suspecting that my fascination bordered on the ghoulish. I managed to lay this particular ghost to rest through writing "The House of If."

This story, all sixteen thousand words of it, was written in one twenty-hour sitting. I began after reading a letter from a reader. The letter was from an inmate in a Federal prison and he was being very complimentary about one of my stories.

I correspond with countless readers, a number of them currently in the joint. This particular reader's letter, however, got me to thinking again about what I considered my sick fascination with the subject of prisons.

I immediately wrote a very short story (I can no longer remember the title) where the gimmick was an instrument that forced one into a state of dreaming, locked in the dream's premise (you are in prison), and regulated the time distortion experienced by the dreamer. In this story a petty thief is the first person ever to have his sentence carried out by this gadget.

What it amounted to, for next to nothing in the way of cost, the thief begins serving a sentence of years (which *because of the time distortion will only take minutes). And there is no escape, no appeal. The horror of this to me seemed sufficient to make a story, but George Scithers sent it back saying "What you have here is a gadget. What are you going to do with it?"*

Obviously the horror I felt hadn't been conveyed to George. It was a personal thing of my own. Why did I feel the way I did? I kept asking myself that question and began tickling my word processor. Twenty hours later I sent "The House of If" off to George.

As I mentioned in the introduction to "Collector's Item," this is the remaining story in this collection that the added dimension of a word processor made possible. With a typewriter I can only work on one part of a story at any one time. To write "The House of If" I had to be able to write and see all of the parts of the story at the same time.

The House of If

. . . A vague swim of colorless walls. The shadow of bars; but no door, no window, no bars—just the shadow. The sound of footsteps, but no floor, no boots, no feet—still the sound. I tried to push my hands forward into my vision. I reached, stretched, strained; but no wrists, no fingers, no hands— only the reaching. I opened my mouth to scream and heard silence—

I *awakened with a start*, my eyes still shut. I was lying on my back; a hard, cold surface under me; my heart still pounding from the nightmare. The nightmare; part of me, or part of Krenmyer's lockup? I felt the surface beneath me with my fingertips. It was smooth. My eyes opened and in the dim, sourceless light I could see four gray, featureless walls. The walls were only as far apart as it took for me to stretch out full-length on the floor. The ceiling extended to infinity. I laughed.

"Krenmyer! Krenmyer, can you hear me? I hope you can, because you blew it again. I hope the audience can hear me, too. This is no prison. I recognize it. It's my secret nook— my childhood hideout. Do you hear me, Krenmyer?"

I listened. Silence. I sat up, then pushed myself to my feet. "Krenmyer, can you hear me?" I listened again. Nothing. I chuckled, moved to the closest wall, and felt its surface. Smooth. Not a bump; not a crack. This was it, all right. My prison. My imaginary prison; the tool shed in back of the house. In a few minutes Aunt Pam would call me to lunch and I would curse her for popping my bubble of fantasy.

I stood back from the wall as icy breath touched me. The tool shed walls were rough sawn planks. These smooth, impenetrable walls were creatures of my childhood imagination. I walked around the walls, touching, examining all four. I looked up at the endless height of them and closed my eyes. Little Marty Colter sneaking into the tool shed; jeans and jersey transformed into prison grays; the shed into the impossible lockup; the boy into a tragic figure condemned for eternity. I hung my head, felt the tears on my cheeks, and whispered:

"Damn you, Krenmyer. No one should be allowed to know that much about another human."

I placed my back against the wall and slid down until I was seated on the floor. I rubbed my eyes, then looked at the walls again. So even then—ten years old—this was my abstraction for the word "prison." I started to laugh, but stopped short. Not just prison; little Marty Colter used to serve time in an *escape-proof* prison. No doors, no windows, no guards to bribe, no way out. Nothing to do but endure.

"I still have to eat, Krenmyer! How is the food going to get in?" I folded my arms, stretched out my legs and crossed them as I began whistling *La Marseillaise*. The food had to get to me somehow; a guard entering; machinery; an opening of *some* kind. That was the key to my escape from Carcel Ultima in Coahuila: if food can get in, word can get out; dreams, temptations, visions, of wealth to underpaid guards, bribes. Then Martin Colter was on the other side of the walls while *mucho* jobs went down *El Toileto*.

I looked up. Perhaps the food would be dropped or lowered to me. I stopped whistling and began the process: strategy planning. It would be a poor excuse for an escape artist that couldn't outwit the imagination of a ten-year-old child. Perhaps they would wait until I slept to bring in the food. I leaned my head back against the wall and closed my eyes, my ears alert for the slightest sound.

After several minutes, my eyes opened as a thought slammed the back of my head. Little Marty Colter—through ignorance—had accomplished what Krenmyer and all the world's lock-watchers couldn't. He had designed an escape-proof prison. There would be no food. Food for little Marty came when Aunt Pam called and the fantasy ended. His prison had no provisions for feeding the inmate; there was no need.

I shut my eyes and nodded. There was no need to feed me either. After all, I would be in for only five minutes. *Five minutes. Twenty-five years.*

Sick terror.

"Krenmyer! Krenmyer, you sadistic bastard! *Krenmyer!*" I stood, ran at the opposite wall, and pounded on it with my fists.

"Krenmyer! Turn it off! Let me out of here!"

I flailed at the wall until my breath grew short, my arms heavy. I sank to the floor, weeping. I fought off the sleep as I sensed the outlines of the dream that awaited me. Irresistible tiredness engulfed me.

Logic sets do not a prison make, nor circuitry a cage. Omegon Maximum—was that only last night? I had busted Krenmyer's latest "escape-proof" facility in record time. Krenmyer's singular brilliance included some astounding blind spots, but the flaw in the Omegon system was laughable. In fact I was laughing so hard I almost foiled my own escape from Omegon Maximum Prison.

It *was* funny. The gates opened, the robotic guard with which I had exchanged psychotronic images sped out, then the psychotronic might of the Bureau of Corrections, North American Union, followed in a stampede of honks, whistles, and flashing lights. I almost dissolved on my way to the staff compound after that hapless pile of machinery bellowed out to its pursuers: "Youuuuu, youuuu dirty rat! You'll nevah take me alive, coppah!" Then followed a beautiful fireworks display as eighty million credits worth of psychotronics blew the hell out of itself. The little speech I had planted in the robot's audio system was just a bit of fun; my sense of humor; me rubbing it in.

After borrowing the warden's flyer, I easily made my way through the constabulary's hastily improvised vector blocks, went into the city and registered at the Baltogrand Inn. I toured the shops, then with new clothes and a sumptuous repast, I attended a performance of the stage musical production *Thousandth Night*—all charged to my hotel chit, and that charged to the Bureau of Corrections.

Theater critics, especially those who had branded the 2009 edition of *Thousandth Night* "fluff" and "an evening's escape for the mindless," would have been confused had they observed me studying the wily Shahrazad with written history's first known serialization. My rapt attention was not due to the company's below average performance; I was absorbing the technique—the strategy. I was living the theme. As King Shahryar abandoned his plans to execute Shahrazad and the curtain opaqued, my lusty "Bravo! Bravo!" was conspicuous against the indifferent applause of the rest of the audience. *No matter. The other patrons watched a bad musical; I witnessed an escape.*

I *awakened*, on my back. I pushed myself up and leaned my back against the wall. A deep breath, then my eyes opened. Nothing had changed. The impossible prison. The wall. I looked behind myself and examined the wall against which I was leaning. How could I distinguish one wall from the others? They were identical. The dim light illuminated them equally. I reached for my pockets—must find something to make a mark with. My hands went down the smooth coverings over my legs, then patted where my shirt pockets should have been. No pockets in little Marty's prison. "Jesus." I shook my head, then sprang to my feet.

"This is a simple problem, Krenmyer; with a simple solution."

I placed the pad of my right index finger between my teeth, bit, then tore the flesh. I looked at the blood, laughed, then went to the first wall and marked it with a single red dot. The next wall to the right: two dots. The next wall, three. The remaining wall, four. One, two, three, four. Orientation.

"And, now, Krenmyer." Time. How long had I been there? How to keep track of time? Mental time. Seconds, "One thousand, two thousand, three thousand, four . . ." My pulse! I reached for my wrist and felt for my pulse. The gentle, regular pressure against my finger. Heartbeat changes with activity, emotional state, health. but if I remain calm . . . no. My wrist—*my* wrist—was not in my *mind*. Neither was my finger. I looked at my right index finger and found my self-inflicted wound healed. No trace. I looked at the walls and the blood marks were gone.

I sat cross-legged in the center of the floor, placed my elbows on my knees and rested my face in my open palms.

"You are a hard warden, little Marty Colter." Why? Why, as a child, did I play at this? So long ago . . .

"Dish it out! I can take anything!"

The voice was high, strange, tinny. I opened my eyes . . . seated in the corner, a child. A boy dressed in prison grays. He was looking up at the nonexistent ceiling. Was that Krenmyer's machinery sticking things into my head? "You. You, boy."

The child looked at me. His eyes were narrow with controlled pain. "What?"

I licked my lips. "Who are you?"

The boy closed his eyes and rested his head against the wall. "I don't want to talk."

I studied him: unkempt black hair, muscular, a face bordering on ugliness . . . I crawled over, reached out a hand and grabbed his left arm. "You're . . . *Marty Colter!*"

The boy pulled his arm free. "What if I am?"

I squatted on my haunches and studied him. My pulse and finger might not have been in my mind, but little Marty was. "I'm Martin Colter."

"I know." The boy looked up again.

"Why are you playing this game? Tell me."

The boy looked at me, his eyes wide with surprise. "Game? This is not a game. You *know* this is not a game."

I pointed a finger at him. "You *know* it's a game! I remember all of this. This is the tool shed—"

The boy laughed. "Game? Ask Doctor Krenmyer if this is a game. Ask Krenmyer, Mister Martin Colter. He'll tell you."

I frowned. "You don't know anything about . . . Krenmyer. The game . . . it was different—fun."

The boy's eyes looked at me steadily. "I know about him because you know about him. And I know all about *you*."

"I *don't* know about you. Why the game? What are you playing at? Why are you playing at it?"

The boy hung his head, then shrugged. "I can't say the words." He looked at me. "I never say them. But you're grown up; you can say them."

I moved to the opposite corner, sat down, and stared at the boy. He looked up and shouted, "I can take anything you can dish out! I can take it!"

"I can take it," I repeated as I looked at the boy. I looked up at infinity

and saw through the boy's eyes—*my* eyes. I let myself flow into the image: sight, thoughts, feelings, time. *Defiance.* Defiance flung at unseen tormentors. Locked up and hid away; safe. Shout your defiance in the tool shed, Marty. No one will hear you except your fictional guards. But make them *real*, and make the prison real. Otherwise you're just being silly. But don't shout too loudly. Your *real* tormentors might hear you. Aunt Pam, Uncle Bill, their hulking cruel son Sean. For them . . . for them there is no defiance. You suffer abuse—humiliation, do this do that, you are such a dumb boy, why can't you be more like Sean; fat, cruel, stupid Sean. You don't shout defiance—put everything on the line—for small things; unimportant things. If I'm to suffer, let it be important; for important reasons. Let the reasons be black-and-white. Let the occasion be something to rise to; *then* hear my challenge. I screamed at the nothingness above. "Pigs! I can . . . take it . . ."

I looked down and saw Martin Colter the adult—the so-called adult. His face was confused. What fiction had he constructed to make himself so confused. Marty Colter knew the truth. "That was the one thing you couldn't do, Martin Colter: you couldn't take it." I held out my arms toward the walls. "But here is your black-and-white context; here you are the oppressed and they are the oppressors. Here the issue is clear and there are no sneaking doubts. Here you *must* shout. You will suffer, but tragic heroes always suffer, don't they? And, here where it's important—here in this fiction— you can be brave. The game was never fun, Martin Colter; it was *important*. It stood between you and knowledge of your cowardice."

The man stood before me, weaving. He pointed a trembling finger at me. "You should *see* the things I have done. *Real* things
                    in *real* prisons!" I caught my breath. I was back—looking at the boy. The things he had said—*I* had said...
"You don't... you *don't* know what you are talking about! You don't *know*!"

The boy laughed at me. "I know. I know. I know..."

I sank to the floor, felt myself blacking out. The image of the boy faded. It went black, and I sensed coming at me ... another dream within the nightmare.

After breaking out of Omegon... the next morning. The Bureau of Corrections building. I was immediately ushered into the Secretary of Correction's Office. The glass-walled, gaily decorated room was an ironic setting for the person whose task it was to keep almost three million humans entombed in living deaths. This was the office of the Secretary of Locks; the Chief of Despair; the Minister of Pain and Waste.

As I took my place at the conference table and surveyed the three faces surrounding it, I was reminded of my old friend Mark Twain's observation that man is the only animal that blushes. Or needs to.

The hottest blush was hanging on the thin face of balding Doctor Krenmyer, the Bureau's Chief of Psychotronic Research. The Omegon experiment was his third attempt to adapt psychotronics to the ignoble task of removing humans from the society of their own kind. Omegon was, as well, Krenmyer's third failure at the hands of Martin Colter: professional thorn-in-the-side. If the good doctor's looks could kill, the reports of *my* death would not have been greatly exaggerated.

As I crossed my legs and settled back in my chair, Krenmyer looked down toward his folded arms and concentrated upon the secretary's genuine walnut tabletop. It always does me good to find a fellow who appreciates fine woods.

Secretary Epps—trim, tacky, and transplanted hair—cleared his throat and nodded toward me. "I suppose, Mister Colter, you are to be congratulated on your escape."

I smiled and shrugged. "It was nothing."

Omegon's pig-fat warden glared at me, then joined Doctor Krenmyer in appreciating the tabletop. The warden's voice sounded as though the Hog Street Strangler was working on his neck. "That 'nothing,' Colter, will cost the taxpayers almost a hundred million credits."

I drew down the corners of my mouth and shook my head. "Eighty million—tops." Smiling at that point would have been rubbing it in; hence, I smiled. "However, it might cost a few jobs." Again I shrugged. "When the Bureau hired me as a consultant on the Omegon project three years ago, I said the system wouldn't work. Now, of course, you know why." I faced Krenmyer. "I am disappointed, Doctor. You promised me quite a test." I rubbed my chin and looked thoughtfully at the overhead light panels. "Let's see . . . it took me—"

"Thirty-seven hours, nineteen minutes and eight seconds," Krenmyer completed.

"Yes. Thank you, Doctor." I looked at the secretary and raised my brows. "If that is all, gentlemen, I shall be on my way." I stood. Krenmyer was struggling with something. He started to speak, then clenched his jaws. I pointed at him. "I told you how I would do it three years ago, Krenmyer. Any fixed system of rules, electronic or otherwise, can be cir-cumvented. Find out what the rules are, then invent a plan that the rules don't gather within their comprehension."

Krenmyer's neck veins stood out. "Colter, there *were* no fixed rules! It was foolproof. The system at Omegon was governed by random program."

I shook my head. "Doctor, doctor. Foolproof means proof against fools. Convicts may not be moral giants, but neither are they fools. There is no such thing as a random program. The things called random programs *are* patterns. The patterns are unknown to their inventors; but they are still patterns."

Krenmyer went even redder; his eyes held murder. I was playing with him, and he knew it. "The program evaulation showed that no discernible pattern presents itself within six quadrillion digits. At six minutes per operational program, before you could have seen enough to detect a pattern, this universe would have turned to dust!"

"That was just one of the fixed rules, Krenmyer: a program

change every six minutes. There was no necessity to detect any more of a pattern than that. The physical plant, the structure of the prison itself, was another fixed rule. My own neural pattern—" I nodded my head toward the father of psychotronics. "—psychotronic matrix if you prefer—is how the system identified me; just as similar patterns identified other prisoners and robotic units to the system. Another fixed rule. Need I go on?"

Secretary Epps leaned back in his chair. "Mister Colter, I think you owe us that much, in light of our investment in you."

I chuckled. "As unintentional as that investment might have been." I nodded. "Very well. The fourth fixed rule—the key—was the half-second time delay between program changes. Since neither you nor your machine ever knew what program was coming up, and since each new program might be faced with any manner of prisoner situation, you implanted a half-second delay to enable the system to evaluate and double check current conditions before implementing each new set of operations."

Krenmyer pointed at me. "That was in the interests of both plant security and inmate safety."

I raised my brows. "Very touching. But what that amounted to, Krenmyer, was that the system was virtually shut down for half a second every six minutes. I developed a context that had my section's guard unit within arm's reach during each program change, then went to work switching psychotronic matrices with the guard. Do you require technical details?"

Krenmyer faced Epps. "Colter pulled the identity grid from the guard unit then jumped the unit's detector to its backup identity grid imposing his own matrix on the backup grid."

"Quite right, doctor. In a manner of speaking, I put on a guard's uniform and walked through the front gate." I produced my most credible stage sigh. "I *had* hoped for something less hackneyed to show you, but I *was* in a rush. I have to do a talk show tonight to promote my new book." I put my hands into my coat pockets and rocked back and forth on my feet. "What I don't understand is why the guard units weren't armored. A ten-year-old child could reduce one of those robots to its component parts, given enough time and a bobby pin."

Krenmyer snorted, then fired a brief glare at Secretary Epps. Epps coughed and proceeded to admire his own table-top. The secretary shrugged and glanced at me. "Since they are—or were—robots, it was not considered necessary to go to such extremes to protect them. It wouldn't have been cost effective."

Krenmyer snorted again. "Cost effective! I wonder how cost effective the corrections committee will think eighty million credits worth of rubble is."

I chuckled. "I apologize if I am prodding an old sore, doctor. But you needn't concern yourself. Armoring the guard units would have slowed me somewhat, but it would have made no difference in the end."

Krenmyer slapped his open palm upon the table top. "Damn you, Colter!" With the same hand he made a fist, then pointed a finger. "You have destroyed the work of . . . *twenty years*! Do you have any conception of what this will do to psychotronics as a science? This was just the first step. The contributions it could have made in other areas—"

My smile evaporated. "Doctor, *I* did not make caging humans the first application of your scientific child; *you* did."

Krenmyer stood abruptly. "The Bureau of Corrections provided my funding!"

"Doctor, perhaps you should have been a bit more discriminating about what you used the money for. As they say, the difference between a whore and a homemaker isn't from whom you get the money; it's what you do in exchange for it."

The look on Krenmyer's face as the scientist lowered himself into his chair was, by itself, worth the price of the trip. The warden turned to Epps. "Mister Secretary, can't Colter be held responsible for *any* of the damages? He's rich, and he's going to make plenty more because of this. When the Corrections Committee convenes—"

The secretary held up his hand. "When the committee meets, Bruddick, we are in for a roasting. The contract we have with Mister Colter relieves us of any responsibility in case of his injury or death attempting to escape; but it also relieves him of any responsibility in case of damage to government property, as well as in the event of injury or death to government personnel. It was a test of the system, and Colter lived up to his part of the contract."

Bruddick glanced at me, half-smiled, then addressed Epps. "Mister Secretary, under the Public Information and Security Act we *can* detain him for an indefinite period—"

I snorted out a harsh laugh. My involuntary outburst stopped the warden short. "In what, Bruddick? Detain me in *what*?" I looked at Epps. "Are you certain the bureau can weather two such embarrassments in a row?" Krenmyer again looked as though he were about to speak, but he remained silent, still looking at me. His stare gave me an odd feeling, but I dismissed it. Unvarnished hate is bound to give anyone an odd feeling.

The secretary glared at Warden Bruddick, drummed his fingertips upon the table, then folded his arms. "I suppose, Mister Colter, that you will announce this tonight on the Armand Starks Show."

I smirked. "Of course. We must all wend our ways along this economic coil."

Warden Bruddick hunched his shoulders. "Placing us in the most unfavorable light possible, of course."

"My dear Warden Bruddick, there is no need. *You* have already done that. All *I* will do is tell the story."

Bruddick looked at the secretary, then back at me. "What about my flyer? That's personal property, not government."

"It's as good as new and resting comfortably in the Baltogrand parking tower—along with the hotel bill. Good day, gentlemen."

I bowed, left the room, and closed the door behind me. With my hand still on the doorlatch, I stood silently in the receptionist's office. It had been good; but not good enough. It was never good enough.

"May I help you, sir?"

I glanced to my left and saw the bland face of the young man who served as Secretary Epp's receptionist. *I snorted and marched from the office as I felt my face darkening with rage.*

* * *

I *awakened on my back* looking up at the infinite ceiling. I let the feeling of the dream remain with me. "Of course it was never good enough." A common enough problem. I must have treated a thousand children and young adults whose erratic, self-destructive behavior was a simple manifestation of unexpressed pain; repressed frustration. They aim their hates at fictions, never admitting the truth—never admitting the real hate. All those children—all those frustrating hours trying to dig through the apparent to get at the true. But there were others.

I sat up. Stealie Boy Yokosuji, my cellmate before I escaped from Taiyaku Jima, was a classic case. I looked up and the wall in front of me was the cracked whiteness of my Taiyaku Jima cell. Looking back at me was Stealie Boy's handsome face; a single lock of his thick black hair dangling in front of his forehead.

"After I open the door—very quiet—I begin to move chairs, tables. See, to clear path to door if I must run. If *papasan* wake up, Stealie Boy must run."

Another machine-fiction, I thought. Then the image faded. "No!" I closed my eyes and *believed*. Taiyaku Jima . . . Stealie Boy. I am in Taiyaku Jima, I thought. If I can . . . control these images—if they are *mine* to control . . . but, Taiyaku Jima: I can *escape* from there! I heard the sharp click of stone against wood. "You move, Colter."

I opened my eyes and Stealie Boy grinned at me. He pointed at the *go* board dotted with black and white marble playing pieces. He was, as always, winning. I waved my hand at the board. "I'm tired of this."

Stealie Boy tossed back his head and laughed. "Colter, you *always* tired when you losing."

"I'll get out of here."

Stealie Boy shrugged. "Maybe." He stretched out on his pallet, lit a cigarette, and blew a cloud of smoke toward the wire-sheathed cell light. The ceiling was four meters above my head—*this is Taiyaku Jima*.

I stood and went to the wall of bars that served as the cell's door. "I've gotten out of tougher places than this." I looked back at Stealie Boy. "You know something?"

"What?"

"You are stupid as hell."

He glanced at me, then laughed. "Colter, you put *self* in prison, and *I* am stupid?" He laughed again.

I pointed at him. "The homes you rob. You never make a big killing, and you always do it at night when the family is home. Always in the same district. Is that how you get your kicks? Risking it all for nothing? Why don't you at least knock over houses when the families are away at work or on vacation?"

Stealie Boy shrugged and blew more smoke at the ceiling. His black eyes studied the ceiling for a moment, then

I smiled and looked at the funny round-eyed Colter. "No fun."

Colter squatted next to my pallet. "Stealie Boy, you're a bright kid—smart."

"You just tell me I stupid." I waved my hand at him and turned to the wall.

Colter sighed. "You're ruining your life, that's why."

I turned back and sneered at him. "Become monk and tell to Buddah."

Colter pursed his lips. "Look, you could be doing better— even as a criminal."

I sat up, pointed a finger at the round-eyes. "I folk hero. Me." I stabbed a finger at my chest. "Me they write stories about. On street they greet me with respect. Even who I rob. It kind of honor to have Stealie Boy rob you."

Colter shook his head. "Somewhere there is a reason why you do what you do. If you can find—"

"You, Colter. You do same thing. You do same thing . . ."

I . . . I was back looking at Stealie Boy. "You do same thing and cry at me to do different." He waved a hand in disgust as he stretched out again. "You sick, Colter."

I shrugged and moved to the cell door. It was Stealie Boy's life; let him screw it up any way that amused him. In a few moments the block trustee will bring the food—and the bar spreader. In a few moments I would be out—another story to tell—another prison embarrassed—another round of applause . . . for Martin Colter . . . folk hero. I felt the tiredness coming over me, but fought to stay awake. I *used* the bar spreader. That's part of how I busted out of Taiyaku Jima. I was awake for that. I have to be awake...

Stealie Boy's voice as I drifted off... "You do same thing, Colter. What your reason?"

...evening in my dressing room at the UBC's Baton Rouge studio; a makeup person assaulting my complexion with creams and powders while my agent, Jane Towzawi, bent my ear. "Cool it tonight, Marty, okay? Take all of the bows you want for beating Omegon, but lay off the needles. We're here to promote your book; not to grind your personal ax."

The makeup person's hand removed itself from blocking my vision, and I pointed a freshly outlined eye at Jane. She was entirely too pretty to be a walking anxiety attack. "Jane, we've been through this a thousand times. When I find a fool, I call him a fool. That's why people buy my books." The makeup person completed its chores, removed the napkin from around my neck, and exited. I looked at my image in the mirror. A gorilla anointed with a fresh layer of cosmetic jaundice. I looked back at Jane. "I'm certainly not selling books on my looks."

"*Or* your personality." Jane pursed her lips and looked at the television monitor. The screen was blank. "Just cool it, Marty. Three different jurisdictions have prior restraint actions on your book waiting in the wings."

I shrugged. "Waiting for what?"

Jane glanced at me, then turned back to the screen. "For you to smart off again. You have every constitutional right to be as nasty as you want, Marty; but every time you open your mouth, you make another judge somewhere more sympathetic to some government's argument."

I reached to my dressing table and picked up my bourbon and branch. I studied Jane for a second, took a sip of my drink, then lowered the glass to my lap. "You are acting very strange. Noricon Publishing beat down the prior restraint order here in North America. Why do you think the lawdogs will be successful elsewhere?" I studied her some more. "That isn't it at all. What's really chewing at you?"

Jane tapped her long nails against her chair's armrest. "You are, Marty."

"*I* am?"

Network test images appeared on the monitor and Jane swung her gaze in my direction. "Marty, I remember when you came to me after getting released from Helgavea Prison—"

I laughed and nodded. "That was some time ago—"

"You were different, Marty. A different person."

I shrugged. "We all were. Are you complaining about all of the money I've made for us?"

She shook her head. "You're different. Back then you were a hurt, angry man striking out to get the justice you deserved. Now . . ."

I waited, but when it appeared that she was not going to finish, I prompted her. "Now, what?"

She looked back at the monitor. A silent promo for the Armand Starks Show was running. The polished, wavy-haired Starks was depicted laughing without sound at an unheard joke. Jane stood, punched off the monitor, then faced me. "Now you are way beyond justice—or even revenge. You are . . . *obsessed*."

I downed the rest of my drink and placed the glass on the makeup table. "Am I?"

"Yes. And your obsession is feeding an ego about five times the size of this planet—"

"That's enough!" I took a deep breath, then smiled. "Jane, I am making both of us a lot of money by busting out of this world's lockups; *and* by needling the bureaucrats who build all of those stone monuments to stupidity. Yes I have a case against prisons—against the *concept* of prisons." I held out my hands. "How much money do you think you'd make off of me if I went back to being a psychotherapist?"

"Probably nothing, Marty. And that's not because there's not a market for work in that field; it's because you *can't* go back now. You're too crippled—"

"Now, just a damned second—" The ringing of the dressing room phone cut me short. Jane picked up the handset.

"Yes? Mr. Colter's dressing room . . . Yes, Mina—" Jane

covered the mouthpiece and looked at me. "Mina Jeffer, the producer." She uncovered the mouthpiece. "Yes . . . I see . . . It seems unlikely, but I'll ask him. Hold on."

"What is it?"

"The producer wants to know if you'd object to going on with a representative from the Omegon Prison project."

I chuckled. "Who is the masochist?"

Jane asked, then looked back at me. "Erid Krenmyer. Doctor Erid Krenmyer."

That odd feeling washed over me again. I frowned, rubbed my chin, then pointed at Jane. "What for? Is he showing up for talk, or what?"

Jane spoke into the mouthpiece. "What's the drill on Krenmyer's appearance." I watched my agent's face as she listened. Her expression didn't change, but her skin became pale. She covered the mouthpiece. "Marty, don't do it. Krenmyer is up to something. He has equipment with him; a prison—he says—from which you cannot escape. He wants to demonstrate it on the show."

I laughed, but couldn't shake that odd feeling. I may have made Krenmyer look like a fool, but a fool was something he wasn't. But what kind of portable prison could he have devised that could be demonstrated during the twenty-odd minutes I would be in front of the cameras? He had presented himself at the door, equipment in hand. He must have been fairly certain that I would consent to the demonstration. That odd feeling grew stronger; it was the suspicion that Krenmyer knew something about me that I would prefer he not know. I shook my head, then nodded at Jane. "If he has an escape-proof prison, I wonder why it's only now making its appearance? Okay, Jane. If Krenmyer wants to make himself look silly in front of sixty million viewers, I'll help out."

"It's dangerous, Marty. What if he makes a fool out of you?"

I looked at my hands. They were white-knuckled into two fists. I relaxed them and looked up at my agent. "That *is* the test, isn't it?"

"You don't have to do this."

"Go ahead. Tell them I would be happy to share the spotlight with the good doctor."

"Marty—"

"Go ahead." As Jane talked to the show's producer, I geared myself with my own brand of hate—*a mantle of icy loathing that brought all of my faculties to bear. To escape; to win; to squash like an insect Krenmyer and all that he represented.*

I *awakened, back against the floor*, eyes looking up at that endless ceiling. I sat up, pulled myself to one of the featureless gray walls, and leaned against it. I had escaped from Taiyaku Jima before. Why didn't I this time? Because it's not Taiyaku Jima? Because it's all in my head?

"Obsessed, am I?" I closed my eyes and rested the back of my head against the wall. Jane Towzawi. I could hardly remember my first meeting with her. I had blood in my eyes— anger. I was out to settle Helgavea's hash. Jane was a means toward serving that end.

I opened my eyes and looked again at the gray walls. Time. "How long a time lies in one little word." The Bard, Richard the Deuce. The prison library's copy at Helgavea had that line marked. It had struck a chord in some long dead or forgotten con, and he had taken a pencil, making the line with a bold stroke.

Time. Five minutes; twenty-five years. Krenmyer had sentenced me to twenty-five years; in front of everyone.

I thought back to the library at Helgavea—my sanctuary. My door; my fantasy escapes. I knew I could open my eyes and see that room. I could see Martin Colter, new fish, bending over a book. What did Jane say? I was different then. Different how?

I opened my eyes. I looked up from the book in my hands and saw the library. The only other person was the librarian— a lifer named Stack. Mass murderer. Stack stopped next to my table. "You, fish. I gotta close in ten minutes. You can check out the book if you want." Stack frightened me; all the cons frightened me. Brutes. Yet you cannot survive being anything less.

I closed the book and looked at the cover. *Huckleberry Finn*. My old friend Mark Twain. I thought for a moment. Mark Twain *had* become real to me—had become my friend at Helgavea. Twain, Dumas, Hugo . . . they wrote about lock-ups; fictional characters playing my game—my game that had suddenly become my reality.

That was the terror of Helgavea: my fiction had become my reality. A combination of clerical errors, a computer malfunction, a misidentification, the slow grind of bureaucratic gears, and Martin Colter found himself in prison. Unjustly. All conditions met, except one: the issues weren't black-and-white. I endured, passive, waiting for justice to free me. And endured. For three years.

Stack bent over the table and tapped the book. "You wanna check it out, or not?"

"Yes." I stood and followed Stack to the small desk near the library entrance. He entered my number into the terminal, then took the book from me and passed it over a sensor coding plate. He handed the volume back to me.

"Damage that book, fish, and I come for you personal and rip out your guts." A sour taste came into the back of my mouth. I took the book, made my way through the gleaming white corridors, the rumble slam of security control gates, up into the galleries.

Back in my tiny cell I looked at the part of the story the book had been open to in the library. That constant hard knot of fear left my guts. On the north side of the hut near the ash-hopper Huck Finn and

I . . . Tom Sawyer . . . arguing about the method we should use for liberating Jim—the slave.

Huck looks at the window-hole, one board nailed across it, then he looks at me and says: "Here's the ticket. This hole's big enough for Jim to get through if we wrench off the board."

I felt disgusted at my friend's lack of imagination—his poverty of romance. I say to him: "It's as simple as tit-tat-toe, three-in-a-row, and as easy as playing hooky. I should *hope* we can find a way that's a little more complicated than *that*, Huck Finn."

Huck scratched at his head. "Well, then, how'll it do to saw him out, the way I done before I was murdered that time?"

I nodded. "That's more *like*! It's real mysterious, and troublesome, and good." I thought some. "But I bet we can find a way that's twice as long—"

Stealie Boy looked up from his pallet and laughed. "You call me stupid! Colter, you are crazy!"

"Huck . . . what did you say?"

"I didn't say nothin'." His eyebrows went up. "Tom, is it the witches Nat said about? Voices?"

"What . . ."

Little Marty Colter sat in the corner of the tool shed. He stopped crying long enough to create his escape-proof cell.

"Tom, I don't see no need gettin' all balled up with tunnels, saw blades, mournful inscriptions, and such. Let's just wrench off the board!"

"Hesh up, Huck Finn! You got no more . . . romance'n a fence post."

"It's plain dumb, Tom."

"Just shut the hell up, okay? *I'm* running this show!"

"You are an idiot, Colter."

"God damn you, you simple-minded—"

—It swam. All of it distorted, swam, became dark, Stealie Boy laughed and laughed. "You are crazy!"

As I walked on stage and shook hands with Armand Starks and his previous guest, comic Tabby Glennys, the studio audience gave me a standing ovation. The applause and cheers literally rocked the building. I bowed and nodded toward the audience, then took my seat in one of the empty chairs in the half-circle indicated by my host. The applause lasted for a full minute after I sat down. After concluding the opening banalities, Starks looked over the studio audience, then faced me. "Well, Martin—I may call you Martin?"

I nodded. "It's my name."

Starks waited for the audience's polite chuckle to end. "First, congratulations on your most recent escape—" More applause. "It seems that to a lot of people you are something of a folk hero."

"I think it's more a case of most people understanding that prisons are expensive antiquities. Factories for misfits and institutionalized cruelty."

Starks smiled and raised his brows. "I think your remark

sounds familiar. It wouldn't be from your new book, *Chainbreaker*, would it?"

I nodded. "It would."

Tabby Glennys placed her hand upon Starks's arm as she faced me. "Excuse me, Armand, but I've been simply dying to ask Mister Colter a question ever since I read his first book." Starks held out a hand toward me, and I looked at the comic. Her frizzed-up hair and outlandish makeup disguised what I sensed to be a very sharp mind. "Mister Colter—"

"Marty."

She smiled, but a strangeness was in her eyes. "Marty, then. Marty, if prisons are what you say they are, what are we supposed to do about criminals?"

"As with any disease, it makes more sense to prevent it rather than wait for it to happen and then try to cure it. This is one of the things I am trying to demonstrate through my little escapades."

"I see. According to your first book, you were imprisoned unjustly for three years in England."

"Yes, Helgavea. I was imprisoned awaiting trial on charges of subversion. The trial never took place, and I was eventually cleared of the charges."

She leaned forward, elbows on her knees. "And then you had yourself *put back* in Helgavea?"

I nodded. "I wanted to prove that I could have escaped from there had I wanted to." I pointed a finger at her. "Three years had been snatched from me, my career was ruined, and all I got in return was an apology and two hundred credits."

Starks held up his hand, then dropped it to his lap. "Marty, if you were cleared of the charges, why couldn't you continue your career? You were a psychotherapist, weren't you?"

"Yes. I worked with disturbed children. However, parents are reluctant to have an ex-con treat their offspring. Because of my record I couldn't even get a job as a therapist with the prison system."

Tabby Glennys cocked her head to one side. "And so you had a score to settle."

"That's right."

She nodded. Somehow she didn't seem very funny. "In

the six years since the publication of your escape from Helgavea, there have been no appropriations for new prison facilities in that system. The eleven bond issues that were attempted all failed."

I raised my brows in surprise. She seemed remarkably well informed. "That is correct. I consider that one of my biggest victories."

She leaned back in her chair. "Mister Colter, my mother was assaulted in that same district two years ago. Four months ago she died from the beating she took. I wonder how much of the responsibility for her death is yours."

Armand Starks's face was bright red. His professional veneer leaped upon his face through sheer will, and he laughed. "I understand *now* why Tabby wanted to appear on the show with you tonight."

Tabby Glennys shook her frizzy head and mugged at the audience. "I've been found out!" When the laughter died, her mask was firmly in place. Mine came off.

"The responsibility lies with the fellow who did the crime, as well as with the bone-headed officials in that district who failed to take the necessary steps to prevent the crime. It is true they have stopped building new lockups, but they simply use that as an excuse for budget cutting. They refuse to put that money where it would do some good in *preventing* crime: police protection, mental research, economic rehabilitation—"

The comic held out her hands. "Well, excu-u-u-u-u-se me!" More laughter. I leaned back in my chair and made an insincere attempt to laugh with the audience.

Armand Starks faced the cameras and audience and held up his hands. "A truce you two. Right now, folks, we have a surprise guest. While Marty was busy last night opening doors at Omegon Prison, our next guest was one of the boys trying to shut them. The chief of Psychotronic Research at the Bureau of Corrections, Doctor Erid Krenmyer. Let's give him a big hand."

A brief roll of lukewarm clapping passed as Krenmyer made his entrance and shook hands with the host. As I shook hands with him, I noticed with amusement that Krenmyer was wearing a new suit. We all sat down and Starks continued.

"Now, doctor, Marty's escape from Omegon would seem to put you and the gang at Omegon in something of a bad light."

Krenmyer glanced at me, then looked at Starks. "It would appear so." He looked uncomfortable under the bright lights, and even more uncomfortable as Tabby Glennys mugged again at the audience. But there was something . . . about his eyes. Krenmyer had an obsession of his own. I felt that—in some manner—the scientist had thrown caution to the winds to be in that chair . . . to get at me. "Unfortunately . . ." The laughter died out. "Unfortunately psychotronics will be tarred with the same brush."

Starks nodded. "As I understand it, doctor, you feel that the Omegon experiment was an unfair test of psychotronic's capabilities."

Krenmyer cleared his throat and nodded. "Yes. There were many restrictions imposed on the use of psychotronics at Omegon. There were cost considerations, and . . . some constitutional problems."

Starks rubbed his chin, then waved a limp hand in the air. "Is psychotronics a form of mind control? I don't want to be simplistic or to brand it with a label. But aren't the mind control aspects of your discipline why there are constitutional questions?"

The doctor clasped his hands over his belly. "Yes. With the appropriate hardware, we have the ability to detect and identify neural matrices—human thoughts. We also have the ability to alter and implant matrices."

"You can put . . . thoughts *into* someone's mind?"

Krenmyer nodded, then shrugged. "That is where the constitutional problems arise. The Corrections Committee felt that the active use of psychotronics would be an invasion of privacy. That is why the Omegon project was limited to the use of passive techniques. Psychotronics was used solely as a means to identify and locate individual prisoners. The rest of the system consisted of robotics."

Starks nodded. "I see. And you contend that the use of active psychotronic techniques would be more effective."

"Yes. Less expensive, as well." Krenmyer looked at me. "I agree with you, Colter, that those stone monuments as you call them are obsolete; but prisons are not. There will always be those who need the lesson of time—"

"Guilty or not," I interrupted.

Krenmyer glared at me. "Colter, with the use of active techniques as a perception detector, your innocence could have been established beyond a question of a doubt. If we could use active techniques, you never would have had to have spent a day in Helgavea." He turned back to Starks. "But that, too, is an invasion of privacy, as well as an infringement on one's guarantees against self-incrimination. The technique can establish guilt as well as innocence."

I smirked and looked at Krenmyer. "It sounds like what you have is nothing but a glorified polygraph. What if the subject did the crime, but believes he didn't?"

Krenmyer smiled. "Memory can be suppressed, Colter; it cannot be erased." He turned to Starks. "Psychotronics is advanced to the point where we can identify psychic fact from fantasy. With the proper psychotronic analysis I could know more about you than you do." He looked at me. "For example, just through the passive technique used at Omegon to set up Colter's identity grid, I learned enough about him to know that he couldn't refuse to accept my challenge tonight. I claim to have a prison from which he cannot escape. He doesn't believe that—cannot believe that—and remain sane. Martin Colter is a very sick man."

I forced myself to join the audience's laughter. When the studio quieted down, I looked at Krenmyer. "If you have such a prison, why don't you use it?"

"It employs active psychotronics, Colter. I am forbidden to use it. However, there is no law that says I can't demonstrate it—as long as the subject of the demonstration freely consents."

Starks rubbed his hands together. "And you have your equipment set up behind the curtain, doctor?" He faced me. "And you agree to test it, here, on stage?"

I thought for a moment. Dark, dangerous shapes seemed to be hovering behind me. By putting on the demonstration—probably without the permission of the Bureau of Corrections—he was ruining his own career. Krenmyer would look the fool if I refused right after his declaration to the world that I *could not* refuse. The question that had me licking my suddenly dry lips was: could I refuse? I studied Krenmyer's face. In the past I had seen him frustrated, embarrassed, and helpless with rage. This was the first time I had ever seen him look ... smug. The studio was uncomfortably quiet. I looked at the faces in the audience. Of course they wanted me to accept. But accept what? A try at escaping from a ten-minute prison sentence? I shrugged. "Very well. I accept."

As the cheers and applause began to wane, Armand Starks introduced a commercial, then stood and faced us as the show's theme music began and a shadow behind the lights waved. "This is terrific! What a show!" He pointed toward a curtain. "If you gentlemen will move over there we can get set up before the break ends."

Tabby Glennys waved a hand at me. "Dearie?"

"Yes?"

"Break a leg."

I smiled. "Thanks."

"No, Dearie. I meant *break a leg*."

I stared at her for a moment, then shook my head and followed Starks and Krenmyer to the now open curtain. On stage were three chairs, a simple table, and on the table a silver metal suitcase. Starks glanced at his watch and ran off to say a quick word to one of the shadows behind the lights. Krenmyer smiled at me. "You couldn't refuse, you know."

I laughed. "I could have refused, Krenmyer. But I'll make a bigger fool out of you this way." I put on my best sneer. "You know you're casting yourself as the mad scientist, don't you?"

Krenmyer looked at me steadily. "Angry, Colter. Not mad; angry."

Starks returned and motioned me into one chair, Krenmyer into another, while he sat in the third and faced the cameras. The show's theme music faded and another shadow waved. Starks smiled. "We're back, and tonight we have with us escape artist Martin Colter and the Bureau of Correction's Chief of Psychotronic Research, Doctor Eric Krenmyer. We are about to do a little experiment." He faced Krenmyer.

"Doctor, perhaps you could explain to our viewers a little about what we will be seeing."

Krenmyer crossed his legs and chuckled. Life in front of an audience appeared to be growing on him. He reached out his left hand and touched the metal suitcase. "Unfortunately, all that we will see is Mister Colter taking a little nap. To *him*, however, that nap will be at least twenty-five years in prison."

The audience gasped, then became very quiet. Starks frowned. "I'm not certain I understand, doctor."

Krenmyer stood and talked as he placed the suitcase on its side and opened it. "It's simple, really. The things we call dreams are time distorted. A dream that lasts only a second can seem to the dreamer as if it lasts weeks or even a lifetime. This is because the only time reference framework the mind has is itself." He patted the suitcase. "This provides the mind with a time reference; one minute equals five years. We will see Colter nap for five minutes; he will see himself, in prison, for twenty-five years." Krenmyer faced me. "And you will live and suffer through each and every day of that sentence, Colter. And there will be no escape because this prison is your *mind*. This equipment regulates your time reference, and it also locks in your dream premise. You will be in whatever your mind calls 'prison.'"

Starks looked uncharacteristically troubled. "Doctor... what kind of prison will he see?"

Krenmyer shrugged as he adjusted a few dials inside the case, then inserted a magnetic card into a slot. "Right now I have no way of knowing; to learn that would take rather extensive analysis. But it will be a prison, I assure you. He can tell us about it after he is released." He smiled at me. "Twenty-five years from now."

I looked at the panel of dials in the suitcase, then up at Krenmyer. "What constitutes escape as far as you are concerned?"

The scientist pointed at a simple toggle switch. "All you have to do, Colter, is get up and turn off that switch." He looked at the audience. "Martin Colter has told me several times that any fixed set of rules can be circumvented. All one has to do is find out what the rules are, then devise a plan that the rules do not gather within their comprehension." Krenmyer faced me. "Here are the only rules in this system, Colter: a minute is five years; prison is whatever your mind calls prison; to escape you have to turn off this switch."

Starks leaned forward. "Marty, are you sure you want to go through with this? It was a last minute thing—"

Krenmyer waved a hand. "He is sure, Mister Starks. Colter *can't* pass up a challenge like this." Again Krenmyer faced the audience. "While we are watching Martin Colter serve his sentence, here are a few things about which to think. This piece of equipment cost under three thousand credits to produce in prototype. The per unit cost would be much lower with mass production. And it will take only five minutes to execute a sentence of twenty-five years. This requires a minimum of government facilities, and only a few moments of the prisoner's time. Including overhead, it would cost the government only twelve to fifteen credits to administer a twenty-five year prison sentence instead of the several hundred thousand credits it now takes. The prisoner is out only a few minutes of real time; hence, he goes back into society— lesson learned—and resumes his economic life. Next to nothing cost, and the convict never becomes a burden upon the rest of us. And it is escape-proof. The ideal solution."

I felt a moment of nausea—of panic—then anger flooded my mind. "That always assumes, Krenmyer, that I can't escape from it."

He smiled, his hand hovering above the switch. "We'll see."

Starks glanced at one of the shadows, then looked at me. "If you are certain—"

"I'm certain. Let's get on with it."

Starks looked at the suitcase. "Doctor, don't you have to attach something to Marty? Wires or something?"

Krenmyer shook his head. "No. To program the equipment a psychotronic grid would have to be prepared for each individual prisoner—a matter of a few minutes—but I already have Mister Colter's grid from the Omegon experiment. All I need to do is energize the equipment. It will do the rest."

Krenmyer grinned at me. "Then all you have to do is escape."
He turned back to Starks. "I'm ready."

Starks looked at me. "Marty?"

I looked at my white-knuckled fists resting upon my lap.
Many times in Helgavea cons told me about the voice. A
voice that told them they were about to commit an act that
would end their lives, crush them, change them forever. A
voice that, had they listened, would have saved them. But
none of them ever listened because none of them could. Pain
and death had shown their hands, but the cons swatted them
aside and killed, maimed, or stole regardless of the consequences. Because . . . because it was something that *had* to
be done. *I looked up at Starks, then looked at Krenmyer.
"I'm ready."*

Krenmyer smiled, nodded, then threw the switch.

I *awakened on my back*, those gray walls, that endless,
beginningless ceiling.

I sat up and forced the panic to drain from me. "Rules,
Krenmyer. It's always done with rules."

One minute is five years.

Prison is whatever my mind calls prison.

To escape I must turn off the switch.

"You held a kicker, Krenmyer; there is a *fourth* rule." I
stood up and looked at the walls. How much dream time had
I served? Only a few hours, yet I had fainted once and slept
three times. Five times, including the first awakening, I had
opened my eyes to find myself flat on my back, in the same
position, in the same room. "You have me on some kind of
closed loop, Krenmyer. That's it. Every so often you move
me back to square one. Square one: that's the fourth rule."

Prison. Was there a flaw in rule number two? Prison is
whatever my mind calls prison? Huck Finn and I were *outside*
of Jim's hut. Jim was in the lockup; not me. Prison. What
were my prisons?

I backed up against a wall and slid down it until I was
squatting, still leaning against the wall. The books I read in
Helgavea were my *escapes*—not my *prisons*.

"There are many kinds of prison, my dear child." The

voice first, then the scrufty white-haired Abbé Faria was studying me. Abbé Faria; Edmund Dantes's teacher in the *Count of Monte Cristo*. I let Dantes's stone-walled cell at the Chateau d'If surround us. Faria held out his hands. "You *chose* this cell. Your mind escaped through a story from Helgavea to the Chateau d'If.

I rested the back of my head against the stone wall and examined the old man as he shook his head in amusement. "Faria."

"Yes, my child?" The abbé sat upon the bed, his hands in his lap.

"Did I choose the Chateau d'If, or did I choose you for a cellmate?"

The old man cackled. "Poor, poor child! Can you not speak to your own mind with truth? Can you hide from yourself here in your own head?"

I rubbed my eyes. When I opened them Faria was still before me, smiling. I pointed at him. "You . . . you are part of this—part of me. And Huck Finn, too. Both of you . . . laughing at me." I wiped my hand across my mouth. If this were true—

"We do not laugh at you, child; *you* are doing all the laughing. We are not real. You are the one who is real. Do you not find yourself amusing? What was your prison before Helgavea?"

"Faria, do you mean my childhood fantasy?"

"No. Don't you remember all of those children? All of those unhappy children?"

Those unhappy children. Yes. I saw them. All of them surrounding me; their walls of pain, anger, frustration between me and their freedom—their happiness. As part of the therapy we would play . . . the House of If.

Faria cackled. "That was why you read *Count of Monte Cristo*, my poor child. In your ignorance, you thought Chateau d'If meant House of If.

I looked at the stone-faced girl seated in the chair in front of me. I spoke. "Your mind is a house, Connie. Everything in it can be rearranged, rebuilt. The tool you use is the word 'if.'"

Connie closed her eyes and shrugged. Her eyes opened again. "That's silly."

"Connie, what if you opened up that hard knot of pain you carry around inside of you? What if you opened it up and looked at it; found out what it is; what's causing it? Try it. Say 'what if.'"

The little girl sighed, then closed her eyes. "What if." Her voice sounded very bored.

"Good. What if Connie can see that pain. Say it."

"What if . . . what if I can see . . ." She shook her head, then looked at me with hate in her eyes. "But I *can't* see! *Won't*!"

"Try it again, Connie."

She made two fists, tears in her eyes,

my . . . mouth in a pout. I looked at Doctor Colter. Stupid, hulking, Doctor Colter. I don't want to do this. I don't want to, but he forces me. I hate him. I hate him so much. "Don't you *care* that I *hate* you? I *hate* you for doing this!"

"I'm not trying to get you to love me, Connie. I'm trying to get you to see the things you have to see so that you can love yourself. Try it again."

"I hate you." I wiped my eyes with the backs of my hands, then stared at the floor. "What if I could . . . see? What of it? See what?" I wanted to run.

"What do you want to see?"

I half cried, half laughed. "What I *don't* want to see is Mom . . . Mommy. B-but . . ."

"Go on."

"What if I could see my mommy . . . I can. I can see her."

"What is

she doing?" I sat back, startled at seeing Connie before me—knowing what she thought—knowing . . . what I thought.

Tears dribbled down Connie's cheeks. "She isn't . . . she isn't doing *anything*! She . . . Bobby she hugs and kisses. You should see *his* grades! Just passing. He's so dumb." Connie shook her head violently. "All A's. Mine are *all A's*! I handed her my card'n she didn't even look at me. Just held Bobby. All she says . . . says to me is 'That's nice dear.'"

"Connie, what if you could tell her how you feel?"

The child's chest heaved with sobs. "I can't *mean* it! I *can't*!"

"Mean what, Connie? Say it."

The girl shook her head, sobbed, and looked in my direction, but her eyes filled with wet pain. "Mommy... Mommy..."

"Yes, Connie?"

"I... I *hate* you!" The girl ran at me and beat on my chest with her fists. "Hate you! Hate you! Hate you!" She screamed, then collapsed against me, crying. I put my arms around her.

"It's all right, Connie. It's all right..."

Faria cackled at me. Back against the wall; back in the Chateau d'If. "Oh, you foolish child. What a prison that was for you. The ones you could not help frustrated you; walls that you could not breach. The ones you *did* help you *resented*. Their walls were coming down, while yours..."

"Be silent, old man!" I closed my eyes and forced my way across the space that separated us.

    my eyes opened and they looked at prisoner Martin Colter seated against the opposite wall. I looked down at my hands: thin, scarred from digging, wrinkled with age. I felt the laughter coming out of my mouth as I looked again at Martin Colter. I spoke. "Now, child, you see the fool, do you not? Ah the romance of the dungeon. But even the Chateau d'If was unsatisfactory."

Martin Colter narrowed his eyes. "What do you mean, Faria? Prison is a horror—any prison."

I held up a finger. "And that is its romance, Martin. This is a fine prison for you: a victim of unjust persecution, tunneling through walls, moments with a great teacher, *the escape*! We must remember the escape; *so* dramatic. Chateau d'If would have been your paradise had the guards inflicted white-hot pokers on your skin. Perhaps the rack?" I laughed at the foolish man. "So tragic; so pitiful; such a hero—"

Colter leaped at my throat, his strong fingers crushing the life from me. Such a foolish man. Even as my eyes went dark, my body racked with airless laughs

    Faria's lifeless body dropped from my hands. Before

the old man fell to the floor, he disappeared. I looked up to see the gray featureless walls . . .

On the floor, on my back. The closed loop. Square one. Prisons. This . . . this was my first prison—no! The lockup created in the tool shed was my *prison of choice*. There was another . . . an earlier prison. In this prison I was innocent; in the other, I was vaguely, somehow, someway guilty

The walls became hung with gaudy wallpaper. My fat hands were red and wrinkled from the steaming dishwater. I pushed a straggle of hair from my face, looked out of the open window above the sink, then shook my head as that little brat Marty came from the tool shed. I shouted through the window. "Marty! Marty Colter! You come in here this instant!"

The brat glanced at me, then looked down as he hung his shoulders and heaved a big sigh. "I'm coming, Aunt Pam

I rejected it as something sacrilegious. I was . . . looking through Aunt Pam's eyes! It . . .

I looked again at the boy and shook my head. Mercy, my back ached. I shook my head in exasperation. "I do not understand why Bill took that child in. I really don't!" I dried my hands and placed them on my monstrous hips as I faced the door. "And don't slam the door!" The boy came in the kitchen and began closing the screen door. He held the handle with his right hand and had his left palm against the frame. He was closing it very, *very* slowly. I stormed over, grabbed him by the shoulder and pulled him away from the door with a slam. I faced Marty and he stood there, a hurt look on his face, rubbing his shoulder. "I didn't hurt you, so you stop pretending this instant!" His hand dropped to his side. "Well?"

He looked up at me, his face confused. "I . . ."

I pointed toward the door. "What are you doing out there all of the time! You haven't been getting into your Uncle Bill's tools, have you?"

He shook his head. "No. Honest, I haven't."

"Well, what were you doing?"

Marty shook his head. "I was . . . just playing. Honest."

"Humph! If your Uncle Bill finds out, you know what happens."

The boy's eyes grew wide. "Uncle Bill said I could go in the shed. As long as I don't play with his tools. *Honest*."

"Don't you fib to me, Martin Colter." I shook my finger at him. "If you fib to me, you go to that awful state orphanage." I pointed at my chest. "We don't *have* to care for you. We're only letting you stay with us because your mother was Uncle Bill's sister." I grabbed him by both of his shoulders and shook him. "But understand this, Martin Colter: Bill loves your mother's memory; *not* you! It's our *duty* to take care of you, but that only goes *so far*!" Tears dribbled down his cheeks. Such a crybaby. "Do you understand that, Martin Colter?" I shook him harder.

"Yes . . . yes, Aunt Pam. I understand. Please. *Please* don't send me away. I'll be good. I *promise*!"

I stopped shaking him, bent down and gave him a peck on his cheek. "Mind yourself, then. Now stop crying. No one has hurt you." I pulled a crumpled tissue from my pocket and dried his tears. Blubbering all the time, that boy. I pointed him toward the door and patted him on the behind. "Now you go out and play until I call for dinner. And you stay out of mischief, hear?"

The boy nodded and walked slowly through the door, not looking back. I shook my head and went to the stove. "Such an actor. Boo hoo, boo hoo." I lifted the lid on the big pot and stirred the pot pie with a wooden spoon. Bill still wasn't back from town. "If that man is late again, dinner will be ruined. Some people just don't give any thought to what others have to go through."

I replaced the lid and went to the sink. I always try to keep up with the dishes while I'm cooking. If I don't, who will? I looked through the window and saw Marty sneaking into the tool shed. "That *boy*! I never!"

I closed the tool shed door behind me. Motes of dust danced in the thin streams of sunlight that entered the shed through the chinks in the planks. I moved around Uncle Bill's workbench, stepped over the tangle of tools on the floor, then crawled around a large cardboard box and sat in the corner, my back against the wall. I closed my eyes. When I opened them, I was in the prison. The gray, featureless wall, the ceiling that extended to infinity. I lifted my fist and shook it at infinity. "Darn you . . . darn, you! Dish it out! Just watch me . . . I can take anything! Anything . . ."

I *opened my eyes*. Square one. I sat up, ran my fingers through my hair, then placed my elbows on my knees and my face into my open palms. Prisons. There are *all kinds* of prisons. Shackles of guilt, withheld love, threats. I looked at little Marty Colter's prison of choice. Here he was not guilty. Here the issues were clear. Here he was still suffering; but he *knew* he was innocent; he *knew* they were evil; he had a *right* to scream at them, hate them, defy them.

I looked up at that endless ceiling. "They" were up there, somewhere in that malevolent nothingness. They. The forces of pain, oppression, and evil. Those little parts of me. Those unadmitted, unrecognized little parts. I would tell those unhappy, troubled children to take on those parts—become them; admit them; see them for what they were. I looked down again, and I sat before Doctor Sing's desk. That sour taste was in the back of my mouth

before my desk was the next student. A heavy set, muscular lad who looked more as though he should be going out for the football team than into psychotherapy.

I cleared my throat. "Name?"

The boy jumped slightly. "Colter. M-M-Martin Colter."

I smiled. "Very well, Martin. I am Doctor Sing, chairman of the department. I like to have a little chat with each of the students before classes begin." I studied him. Doesn't look very bright. The way he fidgets and looks around one would think he was a hunted animal—or in jail. "Martin, why are you interested in psychotherapy as a career?"

He coughed. "Children. I want to work with troubled children."

"I see." I brought his transcript up on the screen and studied it for a few moments. "You seem to have done very well in school." I looked at him. "Did you have many friends in school?"

Colter's cheek muscles twitched. Very defensive. Almost as though he were under attack. "No. Not many."

"Any?"

Colter's eyes narrowed. "No."

"I see." I pursed my lips and folded my arms. "Martin, a very high percentage of students who enter this work do so because they are, themselves, emotionally disturbed. I hasten to add that this is not necessarily bad. However, it is important that such a student be aware of his motivations."

Colter nodded. "I understand."

"Good. Now, why do you want to work with children?"

The student shrugged, but his eyes held the fright of a trapped animal. "I just do. There are plenty of children that need . . . help. I want to help."

I leaned back and tapped the armrest of my chair with my fingertips. "Is there something about your own childhood that motivates this? Some experience; some trouble?"

It was as though Colter had erected an impenetrable wall between himself and his pain. He laughed, shook his head, and relaxed. "No. No, Doctor Sing. I came here to learn how to cure; not to *be* cured." He shrugged. "Sure I had childhood problems. Who doesn't? But it was nothing out of the ordinary. I'm not carrying any scars."

I looked at Doctor Sing. Silly little man; chalkboard academic. He must be dying to get someone on a couch—anyone. Just for some practical experience. I stood up. "Was there anything else, doctor?"

Sing looked at the top of his desk, pushed a few papers around, then sighed as he looked at me. "There are so many of them. So many."

"So many what?"

"People. People and problems."

I frowned. The old boy seemed a little around the bend. He looked at his office window, then turned back to his desk. "Thank you, Mister Colter. That is all. Please send in the next student."

A lost feeling clutched at my heart. It was . . . a lifeline; extended, being drawn back. My vision thumped in and out of focus with my hard, rapid pulse. Doctor Sing looked up at me. "Is there something else, Mister Colter?"

"No." I turned and walked from the office, closing the door behind me.

Outside, on the grass in front of the building, I vomited . . .

* * *

Return to square one.

A minute is five years.

Prison is whatever my mind calls prison.

To escape, turn off the switch.

I opened my eyes. The grays walls were gone; the floor, gone. Geometric flashes of shape and color whirled about me. I felt for something—anything—resistance. A wall, a limit. I clasped my hands together. They could feel each other. The shapes and patterns constantly swirled, swept this way and that, whirlpooled out of sight, then flooded down upon me. "What prison is this, Krenmyer!"

The shapes and colors flattened, dulled, settled around me forming a softly undulating horizon of rainbows.

Prison is whatever my mind calls prison.

"This is the key, Krenmyer..." Krenmyer. To beat Krenmyer. The wish, the feeling, the desire, the obsession—was different. I walked toward the horizon, a mist at my feet. *Prison is whatever my mind calls prison.* My semantic reaction to the word "prison" had changed. This. This was now my "prison." Above me was blackness sparked by tiny flashes of colored light. Beneath me and around my legs was the mist. Before me was the rainbow horizon. The distances were vast beyond comprehension. I moved more quickly. I did not want to escape from this prison; I wanted to—had to— explore it. This prison was the real one; the one it had always been; the one Krenmyer's machinery was tuned into. This prison was my *mind*!

A *minute, a year*, is of no importance.

My prison is my mind.

Escape is of no consequence.

Square one: I reach out my hand and touch the rainbow. Up comes my hand and a stream of blue crosses the blackness above. Within the blue, spots of green surrounded by bands of red.

Doctor Sing's image spoke to some part of me. "All thought is in symbols. We imagine a tree—see bark, limbs, leaves, rot. But what actually happens in the mind? Discharge thresholds are reached, chemicals react, colloids alter, patterns of connections are repeated, compared, identified by other patterns. Some of us symbolize in colors: red or black is pathologic, perhaps green or blue healthy . . ."

The green surrounded by red. I bring the green to me. It is in there—what it is—

—M . . . *Martin Colter. His hands wrapped around fat Aunt Pam's throat; her face purple; her sausage tongue protruding*—

—reject it! The red fills my vision. The red points me away; points me toward . . . others. Aunt Pam is good, kind, generous. Just ask her. *There are thoughts you must not hold!* She will find out; she will know; she will get *even!*

The red: deception. Sing: "These thoughts. They are horrors, but to deny them is to deny yourself. Admitting that the thoughts are yours—are part of you—does not make the wishes, hates, desires things of reality. But admitting them is what you must do to make yourself whole. You can deny them, but your mind cannot."

I reject the red. I plunge into the green. It is there; her fat sweating neck beneath my fingers. I squeeze. Symbolic execution. "I hate . . . I hate . . . I *hate* you!"

I've said it. Admitted it. Felt it. Expressed it. It is me; a part of me. I release the pig's neck and stand. It, the green, fades. The red is still there, but is weakening. The hidden emotion that gave it its strength has been accepted; made a part of me. The red—hate for the prisons, for the prisoners, for their keepers. It fades.

I stood in the center of that mist, surrounded by the rainbow horizon, beneath that streak of uninterrupted blue. My hand rose and wiped the blue from the sky. I lifted my hand again. With it came another streak of green and red speckled blue. Each green an honest feeling; each red a fiction—a diversion to hide the feeling.

I brought them to me; the greens, the reds. The pains, the lies. The joys, the lies that forbade them to me. My hand rose again and again, crossing the blackness with colors, with pain, with lies, with happiness, with truth—

Square one. I studied the horizon. No longer was it multicolored. Its blueness covered all. Here, there, a speck of green, a flash of red. I touched them, absorbed them, rendered them honest.

Peace.

This is my prison. This is everyone's prison. And it is me.

Square one. All is blackness. It changed. What my mind calls prison changed. Within me were walls within lies within hidden pains, and they are gone. The horizon . . . there is no horizon. My horizon—my limit—is no more. Out stretch my hands, and forth come unnamed colors, shapes without form. I beckon to the shapes, unafraid; their blinding lights engulf me.

These are . . . the powers—the gifts we never see. Never use. Can never find. And my key is there, if I want to use it. To escape I must turn off the switch

No. Frame the rule: to escape the switch must be turned off—by someone, something.

Square one. Prison is what my mind *calls* prison. What my mind calls anything is *my choice*. I can *choose* how I react, how I feel, how I think about anything. This is my special power as a human. Then. My mind can call any part of reality "prison."

I opened my eyes to see the audience frozen in rapt attention. Starks, a frown of cold iron on his face, stared at me. Tabby Glennys's concrete stare aimed at Krenmyer. Krenmyer, his hand still on the switch, smiling at me. I stood and moved next to the silver suitcase. I expanded my prison to admit Krenmyer.

He blinked, looked at Starks, the motionless audience, then at me. He said nothing, but I saw the tears in his eyes. "Krenmyer."

His chin rested upon his chest. "You have won, Colter." He moved his hand to cut the switch.

"Don't! Don't turn it off, Krenmyer."

The old man, eyes confused, studied my face. "But you have won. You have beaten me."

I extended my hand. "Come with me."

He stood, face contorted with fear. "What? *No!*" He held his hands in front of his face.

I reached out a hand and touched his arm. "You will come with me, Krenmyer."

Square one. I stood at the center of my mind; Krenmyer at my side. He stared wide-eyed at the endless black. A black not of color nor color's absence. A black of limitlessness.

Krenmyer grasped at my arm and stared at my freedom in terror. "Colter . . . what *is* this?"

"My prison. Now I will show you yours."

Square one. Twisted, gnarled shapes; browns, grays, blacks. Krenmyer was rigid. I turned him around. In the distance was a small mound of stone slabs. "You are in there, Krenmyer. Even before you can reach here and touch your thoughts directly, you must break out of there."

The whiteness of his eyes stood out from the drabness of his colors. "You're . . . like the rest of them Colter! Against me! Fighting me at every . . ."

I placed my hand on his shoulder. "I am not fighting you." I held out my hand. "Look at what you have accomplished, Krenmyer. You are so obsessed with proving your own worth through locking people up, you never saw what you had created."

"What?"

"This is you, Krenmyer. And I can guide you through this nightmare; helping you to end it." I called forth one of the blacks. It covered us.

"No!"

"Look at it, Krenmyer."

"No, no." He was there; young, intense, brilliant, unrecognized. If he, if he could just do better—better than all of them—if he gathered the honors, medals, he would be . . .

"Say it, Krenmyer! Say it!"

". . . loved." The black faded and was replaced by a tint of yellow. "Loved. Respected." Krenmyer closed his eyes. "By others, damn them. I wanted them, so much—" He held his hands to the sides of his head. "This is too much, Colter. Too much. You've won. *You've won*, damn you. Can't you leave it at that? Turn off the switch. *Let me out of here!*"

"Krenmyer, you still don't see it! With this we can solve

. . . so many problems. We can go directly to pain, our lies, our hidden selves. We can know ourselves, and guide others through their own prisons. We can tap all of the power of the mind. That is what you have accomplished, Krenmyer."

Krenmyer held back his head. He frowned; stood silently looking at his colors. He lifted a hand and a blackness began to come closer. "No!" He forced it back, then looked at me. "You will turn off the switch, Colter. Then I shall be destroyed. I will be a laughingstock—once again."

I brought us back to the limitlessness of my prison. "No, Krenmyer. I will serve my time. You will have won. It is important to you, and it is nothing to me."

"Why? Why do you do this?"

I held out my hands toward the black. "There is much for me to do; to see; to learn." I looked back at the scientist. "You will not be embarrassed, and I will be happy here. But before my sentence is ended, I want you to think about the value of what you have created. I am wealthy, Krenmyer. I can support your work. Between us we can solve many problems."

I waved my hands, fading Krenmyer out of my prison. I turned around, picked a direction, and flew toward it, eager to see what was there—

I opened my eyes, looked at the audience, then turned toward Krenmyer. He withdrew his hand from the switch, looked at me, then closed the silver suitcase. The scientist held his hands to his face, then sat down in his chair. Armand Starks leaned toward Krenmyer. "Are you all right, doctor?" Krenmyer nodded without removing his hands from his face. "Why don't you turn on the switch?"

Krenmyer lowered his hands. He stared at me. "I did. There seems to be something wrong with the equipment."

Snickers came from the audience. Starks held up his hand for quiet. "Isn't that the way? Now, folks, these things do happen."

Tabby Glennys looked crestfallen. She assumed her mask then swung her gaze in my direction. "I suppose, Mister Colter, that you have some little snide comment to make."

I looked from her to Krenmyer. The scientist studied me.

I turned my head and faced the audience. "I only have an announcement. I am retiring—" A big "Awww" of disappointment came from the audience. I looked back at Krenmyer.

Krenmyer studied me. He opened his mouth to speak, then shut it. A struggle fought itself across his face. I had seen part of his prison; I knew a small part about the armies that warred within him. One of them gained an advantage; it hadn't won—Krenmyer had a long trip to take to give that army victory. But it gained an advantage. He faced the audience. "Mister Colter and I..." He looked at me. He was wired tight; he was not allowed to... to trust. His prison walls did not allow it. Yet, there was a crack. He had seen a bit—enough. He was a scientist, after all. "Mister Colter and I will form a partnership. We... we will be working together."

Starks laughed. "Well, this *is* a surprise!" He shook his head then looked at me. "Tell me, Marty. Will this new partnership be in the business of putting people *in* prisons, or busting them *out*!" The audience laughed. Krenmyer studied me, anticipating the answer.

I looked at Starks. "Yes."

The idea for "The Initiation" came from a din of newscasts a few years ago about how New York City was about to go bankrupt; this in combination with the practice of measuring the social success of an organizational structure by the longevity of the organizations that utilize the structure. I had also recently completed reading The Valachi Papers.

The Initiation

Dino Gitaglia wiped the bead of perspiration from his upper lip, then looked nervously at the *soldato*, DiPalermo, standing at his side.

DiPalermo returned the look, then let his swarthy, scarred face break into a broad grin. "Hey, *compagno*, don't worry." He nodded toward the hand-carved double doors. "You'll do fine in there." They stood in silence for a few moments, then DiPalermo sighed, shrugged, and laughed. "What do you think of the Yorkers this season?"

Dino Gitaglia shook his head. "I don't follow the Yorkers." He smiled. "Put me down for the Yankees."

DiPalermo nodded. "Good. The Chief will like that. Respect for tradition."

"Checking up on me?"

DiPalermo shrugged, then patted Gitaglia on the shoulder. "Just asking. How do you think the Yankees will do in twenty-fourteen?"

Gitaglia shrugged. "Who knows? It was a dumb move trading Vitelli."

The double doors opened, and the one called "The Irishman" leaned through and looked at Gitaglia. Then he looked at DiPalermo and cocked his head toward the open door. DiPalermo took his companion by the elbow and steered him toward the door.

"This is it, *compagno*. Just stay cool."

As Gitaglia entered and was ushered to a chair against the wall, he looked at the faces seated behind the grand banquet table. He recognized Johnny "Three Fingers" Provacci, Frank Manterro, and Joey Capuzzi. Seated in the center was Don Salvatore "The Chief" Callace. Don Salvatore nodded in his direction, and Dino nodded back.

The Chief pushed himself to his feet and held out his arms for quiet. Instantly the room hushed. Don Salvatore lowered his arms, pulled the stub of a cigar from his mouth and dropped it into an ashtray. Grasping a coat lapel with each manicured hand, the Chief looked from one end of the banquet table to the other, then turned his eyes toward the antique cut-glass chandelier.

"This is a time of war, so I will make this short." The Chief looked down at Dino seated against the opposite wall, then held out a hand in his direction. "Look at this fine boy . . . and the other side says we are *finished*!"

Don Salvatore smiled as those seated around the table laughed and applauded. They became quiet, and the Chief nodded. "Finished. Well, we almost *were* finished." He pointed around the table. "Ask Johnny there, or Frank. They remember the days when it was worth a good man's life to join." The Chief nodded. "No money, frozen out, everyone's hand turned against us, all the families at each other's throats. I can admit it now, they almost had us back in ninety-eight. Remember, Frank?"

The one called Frank Manterro nodded. "Who could forget, *padrone*?"

Don Salvatore nodded, then made a fist and slammed it down on the table. "We lost many good friends and brothers to the . . . *maiali*!" He pointed around the table. "But, here we still are! And soon we go to the mattresses and hit them," he punched a fist into his own hand, "hard!"

The Chief nodded at Dino and motioned with his hand. Dino Gitaglia stood, walked to the table, and stood across it from Don Salvatore. "Boys, this is Dino Gitaglia. He comes on Vincente DiPalermo's recommendation." The Chief studied Dino, then turned and looked at those seated at the table. "I look at this boy, and I think. We have done many things—

adopted from the other side many ways—just to survive."
Don Salvatore looked at Dino and smiled with a look of fierce
pride.

"Many said that we would *never* survive, no matter *what*
we did." He nodded and held out a hand toward Dino. "But,
look! Look at Dino Gitaglia, and tell me such as this swears
his life and soul to a dying organization!"

The Chief motioned to one side and the "The Irishman"
walked up and placed a gun and a knife on the table between
Dino and Don Salvatore, then withdrew.

"Dino Gitaglia, this represents that you live by the gun
and the knife," he held out his fist, "*and* that you *die* by the
gun and the knife! *Comprende lei?*"

Dino nodded. *"È intesso, padrone."*

"Cup your hands." Dino put his hands together and held
them over the weapons. The Chief crumpled up a sheet of
paper, placed it into Dino's cupped hands, then struck a match
and ignited the paper. "Say this: This is the way I will burn
if I ever betray our secret."

Dino looked up from the burning paper with unblinking
eyes. "This is the way I shall burn if I ever betray our secret."

The flame died and the Chief nodded. "Never forget what
I now tell you. Burn it into your mind. Betraying our secret
means death without trial. Violating any member's wife means
death without trial. Look at them, admire them, and *behave*
with them."

Don Salvatore held up his hands. "Everybody up, and
throw a finger from one to five."

Everyone stood and held out one hand, either as a fist, or
with one or more fingers outstretched. The Chief counted up
the total, then began counting from the left end of the table,
stopping on Johnny "Three Fingers" Provacci. Don Salvatore
turned toward Dino. "Well, Dino, that's your *gombah*—responsible for you as your godfather."

Johnny Provacci laughed, stood up, and walked around
the table, stopping in front of Dino. Provacci held out his
hand. "Give me the finger you shoot with."

Dino held out his right index finger. Provacci pricked it
with a pin and squeezed it until the blood ran. Don Salvatore

spoke. "This blood means that we are now one Family." The others, seated at the table, stood and applauded.

"The Irishman" reached out and handed a small leather case to the Chief. Don Salvatore opened it and pinned the badge on Dino's left shirt pocket. "Welcome to the ranks of the finest, Dino Gitaglia. Welcome to the New York City Police Department."

One morning a large envelope from artist Jack Gaughan arrived in the mail. In it were wads of roughs that were used in illustrating several of my stories that had appeared in Asimov's. Along with the roughs was a letter in which Jack explained that it was either mail them to me or toss them in the garbage. He was running out of room.

Seeing my stories illustrated has always been one of my big thrills. A non-artist reader can say nice things like "I could really relate to such-and-such a character," but it's special to see what I had in my mind go out through my fingertips and return back through my eyes the same way that I sent it. Needless to say, Jack's envelope was like getting gold in the mail rescued by chance from a lazy eccentric who discovered that the post office was closer than the city dump.

That morning I was scheduled to inflict some more of my writing wisdom upon my friend's sixth-grade English class, and I brought the drawings along to show the students. They were flabbergasted. Later that day I wrote Jack to thank him for the roughs and to tell him how excited the students were with his illustrations.

Characteristically he wrote back offering to illustrate ten stories by those same students. I passed the word to their teacher, and she wanted me to select the ten stories. Since I am not about to hand eighty eleven-year-olds their first rejections, I said no. The class formed its own editorial board and then ensued a period of back-stabbing competition sufficient to warm the cockles of any robber baron's heart. Days later I was presented with the ten stories, along with three more that the teacher snuck in while the editorial board wasn't looking.

I mailed the stories to Jack along with my thanks and an offer to crank out a story should he have a spare illustration gathering dust on a windowsill somewhere. The return package arrived a few days later. In it were all thirteen stories and their illustrations. The package also contained something else.

I won't elaborate on the students' reaction to the illustrations beyond mentioning that those kids are all hooked into writing way past any possible reclamation. It sort of gives me a warm glow to have had a small part in turning a bunch of normal carefree kids into bloodthirsty fanatics.

The other thing that was in Jack's package was a book. When I opened it my mind was permanently bent. Since he was eighteen Jack Gaughan has been keeping what amounts to a diary in pictures. Whatever happened to be on his mind, project illustration ideas, roughs, some written observations, cartoon after cartoon, a unique kind of trip through another person's head and life—and the volume I happened to be looking at was number seventy-six!

By return mail I wrote Jack that I knew the story I wanted to do, but to do it I would have to have the other seventy-five volumes. A few days later he telephoned me, and after spending fifteen minutes trying to convince him that I was serious, he gave in. At the same time he informed me that the volumes were now up into the eighties. We agreed to meet at a science fiction convention in New Jersey. There he would drop the first load of books on me.

Since then I have accumulated a mountain of these sketch books. The estimated total contained in those volumes is around seventy thousand items. The bane of my existence right now is trying to boil all of this fantastic material down to a publishable size without losing this sense that I felt of tripping through another person's mind.

What does all of this have to do with where I got the idea

for "The Portrait of Baron Negay"? In the original volume that Jack sent me was a sketch of a defeated old man sitting dejectedly before a huge easel. On the easel was an enormous blank canvas. And I have put in plenty of my own time sitting in front of blankness, trying to fill that horror of white with my own art, and failing. Five minutes after seeing that sketch I began the following story.

It is the first story I ever wrote with illustration in mind. Unfortunately, with the confusion of a rewrite and some subsequent changes in the art department at Davis Publications (publishers of Asimov's), Jack never got to illustrate this piece. Someday I hope he will.

The Portrait of
Baron Negay

*When the fabric of the United Quadrants of the Milky Way
Galaxy tore under the weight of its own corruption, resulting
in the period called Darktime (2661–2940 GS), the inter-
ruption of trade and the devastating consequences of constant
warfare isolated all but a few of the galaxy's human-
populated planets. Among the many planets that suffered
severe damage and loss, and were then left in rubble and
barbarism to fend for themselves, was the agricultural world
of Demeter. When the fighting moved to other quadrants, the
remaining population on Demeter banded together to form
the small self-defense organizations that evolved to become
the oppressive feudal baronies that epitomized the beginning
of Demeter's third century of Darktime.* Andurant, Demeter
and Darktime, *(Republic Press, 3230 GS)*

Tomasi the forger stood in his resplendent maroon satins
and watched as the wealthy young Baron Negay traversed
the polished marble floor of the audience chamber examining
the painting on the easel. Next to the baron's gaudy throne
stood a yellow-robed old man with white whiskers and balding head. The baron placed his gem-encrusted left hand against
his hip, leaned back, and scratched his nose with his right
forefinger. He raised his left eyebrow and looked at Tomasi.
"And you ask forty thousand for a single-layered work?"

Tomasi shrugged. "It is a genuine Sabro, Excellency. A

great find. Forty thousand hardly covers my expenses in bringing it from New London which must come from my commission—"

Negay waved his hand. "Yes, yes." The baron looked back at the semi-abstract crowded with images of human and almost-human hands. "The price is satisfactory—provided that the painting is genuine." The baron looked again at the forger. "We are quite knowledgeable about art in my barony. And quite harsh on forgers."

Tomasi lifted his hand and placed it gently upon the frame of the painting. "I assure you, Excellency. This is a Sabro—"

"We take the fingers off of forgers, Tomasi." He grinned around the horrors he used for words. "Then we burn them, using the ashes to make my fields more fertile."

Tomasi held out his hands. "As well you should, Excellency."

The baron turned to his right and nodded at the old man, then returned his glance to Tomasi. The old man pulled a coder from his pale yellow robe and moved to the painting. "Old Peter will examine the work. He is our resident expert."

Tomasi met the old man's glance, then held out his left hand toward the painting. "The great Sabro and I have nothing to hide."

Old Peter reached out his right hand and touched the paint. Tomasi recognized expert fingers feeling the texture and dryness of the work's surface. The forger's expression was one of genuine unconcern. *I am an expert, too, old man.* The forger smiled as Peter turned and faced Baron Negay. "The composition, style, technique, period, and medium appear to be Sabro's. As do the choices of canvas and frame." He looked back at the painting and lifted his coder. He drew the small red box across the face of the painting, read the numbers that appeared in the coder's tiny screen, then replaced the box in his robe. Tomasi frowned as he saw the same hand withdraw a pocket art register. *These fools have already been burned.*

The old man flipped through the pages of the register, then stopped. He studied the small book, then turned to the Baron. "Excellency, the work may be genuine. The magnetic code number matches that of Sabro's missing work entitled 'Hands.'" He turned toward Tomasi. "However, this work is recorded as having been destroyed in the Yorkton fire. This piece may be a forgery—an excellent forgery—but still a forgery."

Tomasi smiled. "My dear Peter, the great artist himself was killed in that fire. The register only shows works that had been registered as sold prior to Sabro's death, along with the few that have been turned up since in the Western Colonies. Two such paintings I had the honor to represent to Queen Loren's court myself. Both fine Sabros, and both authenticated by Mersiat and Steben of Her Majesty's service." Tomasi again placed his hand on the frame. "I assure you that this painting is as genuine as the others that have been authenticated since the fire." Tomasi nodded. *I know; I forged those, too.*

Baron Negay frowned at the old man. "Peter, how long will it take for you to be certain? I need no forgeries at my sister's birthday festival. At this moment much depends upon Elena's good graces, and I can tolerate nothing that would put me in a bad light with her."

"Your Excellency, I must do an analysis of the paint's composition then research the many photographs that Sabro took in his studio. There are several of the artist's missing works recorded there." Peter frowned and scratched his beard. "That, and I must study all of the artist's work on hands. As I recall, Sabro was never much taken to hands as a subject."

Tomasi issued a polite chuckle. "Then, Peter, why did he paint a work entitled 'Hands'?"

Peter looked at Tomasi. "Many times Sabro used symbolic titles." He looked at Baron Negay. "It will take me three to four days, Excellency."

Negay nodded. "Then be off. Elena's birthday celebration is in four days."

Shortly after the old man picked up the painting and left the room, two armed and helmeted guards entered. Tomasi raised his arm, glanced at his timepiece, then held out his hands. "Excellency, I had not planned on imposing on your hospitality for such a time. I must return to New London and catch my flight if I am to keep my other appointments."

The baron turned his back and motioned toward a hallway. "Come with me, Tomasi."

The forger remained standing. "Please, your Excellency. I must insist." Tomasi heard the two guards approaching. *Negay's argument gathers strength.* He shrugged, stepped off and followed the baron through a stone arch into a gallery lined with the blinking and flashing screens of mind-paintings. Negay held out a hand toward one of the screens.

"What do you think of it, Tomasi?"

The forger fought to keep his lip from curling into a sneer. *Snapshots; electronic garbage.* He studied the screen. The image was formed and altered by the constant repetition of two shapes, each trace of the first shape, an inverted "L," changing the screen from blue to red, while the second shape, a reclining "L," changed the screen from red to blue. *Mindless computer graphics.* Tomasi shook his head, then faced Negay. "Excellency, I fear that I can offer no opinions on works in this medium. Mind-painting is not my area of expertise."

"You are quite a snob, for a commoner, Tomasi." Baron Negay cackled and moved to the next screen. Tomasi followed, half-surprised at the degree of cruelty evident in the young baron's laughter. The baron lifted his hand again. "Here, Tomasi. What do you think of this one?"

The forger glanced at the screen. The image was a summer landscape, serfs toiling in the fields. Particle by particle the image changed to colored trees, browning grass and countless serfs engaged in the baron's harvest. Winter came, and the serfs cut wood for the baron's mansion. "For a mind-painting, Excellency, it seems adequate."

"This was done by Balum, our court artist. Have you heard of him?"

"No, Excellency."

"Balum came to the art from a family of serfs when my father was alive." Negay studied the ever-changing image, half-talking to himself. "Frightening to think that those pieces of meat in the fields might have thoughts of their own." He motioned toward the forger. "Come." Tomasi followed the baron down the hallway, noticing as he glanced to his left that the two guards followed them. The baron stopped before a one-layered painting on canvas. "A bit old-fashioned, but this one may be more to your liking."

The forger stopped at the baron's side, took one look at the knife-painting, then felt faint. It was the most awkward forgery of an Xavier he had ever seen. *Jarouls the forger— his work.* Tomasi brought his face close to the canvas, then turned and faced Negay. "I . . . am terribly sorry, your Excellency. This is an obvious forgery."

Baron Negay nodded. "Yes. A forgery for which I spent much money. Money that my tax collectors worked long hours suffering much abuse to collect."

Tomasi found that a lump blocked his throat. "How did your Excellency discover the forgery? It is . . . very well done."

The baron's eyes narrowed. "Do not patronize me, Tomasi. My hide is not as thin as you might think; nor my mind as dull."

"Your Excellency, I never—"

"After purchasing this, it was put on display in the village for the serfs to help them keep their lazy minds off of their fat bellies. One of the first ones to see it—a woman named Voya—saw that it was a forgery. Quite a surprise, a serf with a knowledge of Xavier. She did me a great service." Negay glanced out of the corner of his eye at Tomasi. "You can imagine what my embarrassment would have been if the display had continued. After that experience, I hired the services of Peter. It is never wise to give the servant reason to laugh behind his master's back."

The forger nodded and pursed his lips. *Serfs never laugh, Negay.* "The woman is dead, of course."

"Of course." Negay motioned for the guards to approach. "Dead as well are the eight or ten other serfs who also saw this painting."

The forger frowned as he felt the strong hands of the guards grip his upper arms. "But, Excellency—"

"Tomasi, if your Sabro is genuine, you will have my sincerest apologies for your detainment; if it is a forgery, I shall find the slowest, most painful punishment that exists for your lesson." Negay looked down and touched a finger to his lips. He then looked up at the guards, pointing the finger at the

forger. "Yes. Put him in the cell with Balum. The old fool
will never finish my portrait unless he receives some assis-
tance." He looked at the forger. "I have Balum preparing my
portrait in the old-fashioned style as a present for my sister.
If he should finish my portrait in time for my sister's party,
I shall set you free—forger or not. It is that important to
me." Negay turned abruptly and continued down the hallway.

"Your Excellency—"

Tomasi felt a jerk on his arm, he was turned around and
aimed at the arch. The deep voice of the guard on his left
rumbled. "Come along."

The forger's feet hardly touched the floorstones as he was
whisked through the audience chamber into the mansion's
flag-decked grand hall and from there to a door behind a cut-
and-polished stone double staircase. As he was dragged
through the doorway, the three entered an elevator car. The
door closed and Tomasi felt his stomach lift as the car began
its descent. The car hissed to a halt and the doors opened
revealing a gray, split-stone hall lined with harsh lights and
solid metal doors. Two leather-clad brutes in the hallway
pushed themselves up from a table and approached the door
of the car. Tomasi heard the screams of someone pained
beyond reason.

The guard holding the forger's left arm laughed and addressed one of the dungeon keepers. "Gunder, your man with
the hot irons is in good form today."

The keeper called Gunder grinned through missing teeth
and examined Tomasi. "My, isn't this a pretty one?" He looked
over at the guard. "And, Kile, what would Negay have me
do with this ornament?"

The guard laughed again. "Don't spoil him until you get
orders from the baron, Gunder. He is to be put in with Balum."

The guards shoved Tomasi into the hallway causing the
forger to fall to the hard floor. Gunder grumped and nudged
Tomasi's ribs with the tip of his boot. "Another addition to
our art department."

Kile snorted out something between a laugh and a sneeze.
"You'll get your tongs on Balum soon enough, Gunder."

The keeper grunted. "The old fool wants the mind-painting

equipment from his apartments brought down. See to it, will you?"

"Right away." The elevator doors closed.

Tomasi's stomach squirmed at the familiar smells of sweat, pain, blood, and fear. Another person's screams joined the first. Tomasi felt strong hands grip his upper arms. The guards pulled the forger to his feet, then began pushing him toward a closed cell door. The barrel-chested one on Tomasi's left looked over the forger's clothing. "Bah! Gunder, why do the well-dressed ones come in such small sizes?"

The other guard chuckled. "I think the baron prefers that those our size be friends rather than enemies." The unknown prisoner continued screaming as the guards roared out their laughter.

They stopped before the cell door and the guard on the right removed a lockbox from his waist and held it against a white plate set into the surface of the door. The door opened and the guards shoved Tomasi through it. Again the forger went to the floor. A voice boomed out over him. "Balum!" The forger turned to his left and looked up from the stone floor to see the back of a huge easel and canvas. "Balum!"

"Eh?" An old, shaggy-headed man peeked around the edge of the canvas with half-closed, red-rimmed eyes. "What do you want, Gunder? I am busy and must not be disturbed."

"We have a helper for you."

The old man snorted, then disappeared behind the canvas. "Remove him. I need no help."

"The baron ordered it, Balum. He has doubts that you will finish his portrait in time for Lady Elena's birthday party." The guard laughed again as he slammed shut the door.

Tomasi pushed himself to his feet and brushed off his satins. He looked with disgust at the small tear in his right slipper. Muttering, the forger looked around the dark cell. Two raised platforms covered with thin mattresses and single sheets served as beds while a sink and toilet against the far wall met sanitary needs. The only light came from behind the canvas. Below the naked light bar Tomasi noticed a light array for reading multi-layered paintings. He walked toward the canvas, moved around it to his left, and stopped at a table littered with tubes, mixers, brushes, scribers, solvents, pallet papers, and other implements of the painter's trade. On the other side of the table, squatting in a paint-spattered longshirt upon a low stool, the one called Balum stared in disgust at the canvas. Tomasi looked at the face of the canvas and frowned. "What is it?"

Balum quickly turned his head to his right, then pointed at Tomasi. "Get away from me! If the baron insists on you being here, I cannot stop you. But keep away from me!"

Tomasi raised his eyebrows and pointed his thumb at the canvas. "What is it?"

Balum leaned his right elbow on his knee and rubbed his eyes. "It is a foot."

The forger laughed. "A *foot*?" He shook his head. "Off of what kind of creature came that foot?"

Balum lowered his hand, then reached to the table and picked up a pallet knife. He paused, then began scraping the paint from the canvas. As he finished, he wiped the knife clean with a piece of paper, then threw the paper to the floor atop a pile of similar papers. The canvas had been scraped many times. Balum looked at the forger. "It is not quite right."

"I noticed," Tomasi sneered. "Mind-painters, bah!" He waved a hand at the canvas. "Why does the baron have a mind-painter attempting art?"

"Art?" Balum stood, his face reddening. "I *am* an artist!" He waved a hand at the forger. "Who are you to judge art?"

The forger bowed. "Tomasi, dealer in fine art; mind-painters, fools, cripples, and children need not apply."

Balum nodded and turned back to face his canvas. "I hope you are as successful as our most recent forger—"

"I am a dealer in art; not a forger!"

"—but with Peter sniffing around, I doubt it." Balum looked at Tomasi. "Have you ever seen a hand without fingers?" He shook his head. "Quite unartistic."

"I am no forger!"

Balum snorted. "Of course." He pointed toward the bed platforms. "Now if you will be so kind, dealer in fine art, I have work to do."

Tomasi folded his arms. "Look, you old fool, I can help. I am supposed to help."

"I need no help."

"If that is the best you can do for a foot, Balum, you need help!" Balum lifted a large brush and began whiting out the canvas. "I deal in art and know quite a lot about it." Tomasi swallowed and looked around the room. "I have also done some brushwork of my own—certainly better work than that foot. You should have remained with your mind-mush; better still, in the fields grubbing potatoes."

Balum turned his head and lowered his brows. "Forger, my art took me *out* of the fields!"

"Potato digger." Tomasi glowered, then looked among the items littered upon the table. He saw the paints and reading lights for multi-layered paintings. *Surely there must be a coder.* He found a roll of magnetic stripping, another larger roll of gel. Between them was the red case of a coder. He reached out, picked it up, turned it on and began walking around the cell. Several times he paused, saying "Da, da, da."

"What are you doing?"

After sweeping the entire cell with the coder, Tomasi returned to Balum's side and dropped the red box on the table. "A coder makes an effective detector of listening devices. The cell appears clean."

Balum finished whiting out the canvas. "I suppose you learned *that* in art school, too, eh forger?"

Tomasi reached over the table, grabbed the cloth of Balum's longshirt beneath the old man's beard, and spoke in a harsh whisper as he pulled the mind-painter off of his stool. "Hear me, you old fraud. I will not let my life depend upon you and your pitiful skills. I will do the portrait. All you must do is to claim it as your own. Then we will both be out of the soup."

Balum's face remained impassive. "No."

Tomasi relaxed his grip, letting Balum sink to the stool. "No? It is the perfect solution—"

"Is this *more* that you learned in your school of art, Tomasi? Taking credit for another's work?" Balum turned back to the canvas. "I am an artist, forger. If this portrait is to be under *my* name, *I* will be the one who will do it." Tomasi began moving around the table. Balum spoke without turning around. "And if you force me to let you do it, I will deny that it is my work."

The forger stopped and stared at the old man's back, then shook his head. "If you fail to produce a portrait in time, what then?"

Balum lifted a brush and made a timid spot of yellow on the expanse of white. "I will be burned." The old man's voice faltered. "I . . . I do not want to end tied to a stake, Tomasi. Leave me to my work."

The forger shook his head, and held out a hand toward the canvas. "How long have you been at this, old fraud?"

Balum was silent for a long moment. "Twenty-eight days." He turned around on the stool and faced the forger. "I am a mind-painter—an artist that paints on screens directly with thoughts." He pointed the brush at the canvas. "It takes time to learn how to force those thoughts through fingers." Balum again faced the canvas. "But I *will* do it, because I *am* an artist."

"Bah!" Tomasi pushed the old man from his stool and stood before the easel. "Watch this, you ancient fake." The forger picked up the pallet knife and scraped the white and yellow paint from the canvas. Balum struggled to his feet.

"Don't! I need the background—"

Tomasi slapped the paint-covered blade of the knife into Balum's hand. "Feel that paint, *artist*. It dries very slowly, and if you attempt to place other colors on top of it before it dries, the colors will smear."

Balum wiped the paint from his hand onto the front of his longshirt. "I knew that."

Tomasi squirted a length of black from a new tube onto a pallet sheet. He selected a brush and tested the paint for thickness. "Then, Balum, you of course know the medium you selected takes at least six days to dry sufficiently to add more paint." The forger glanced at the mind-painter then brought the brush to the top of the canvas. "You don't have six days, Balum." With a single, swift stroke, the forger bisected the canvas vertically with an even, straight line. He again touched the brush to the pallet, then bisected the canvas horizontally dividing it into four equal segments. Tomasi threw the brush to the table, opened four tubes of paint and squirted lengths of red, blue, yellow, and white onto the pallet. Selecting several brushes, he faced the canvas, thought for a moment, then began painting the upper left quadrant with bold strokes.

Balum stared as the quadrant rapidly filled with the face, right shoulder and upraised right arm of a military figure. "Tomasi, what . . . what are you doing?"

Tomasi moved to the lower left quadrant and continued. "You are correct, mind-painter. Putting your thoughts through your fingers takes time to learn." The lower left quadrant filled as rapidly as the first, continuing with the same military figure, but in a radically different style and color arrangement. Tomasi stood, threw his brushes to the table, and picked up the pallet knife. He looked at Balum. "Old fool, it takes *years!*" He mixed and scooped color from the pallet with the knife, and using the knife, the figure was continued in the upper right quadrant—the same form, but done with heavy sweeps, slashes, and moldings of color.

"Fraud, I began my schooling in art when I was six years old—my sole study for twenty years." He completed the knife-painting, threw both knife and pallet to the table, then picked up an array of color-banded, black scribers. He stooped and began filling in a background in the lower right quadrant with the scribers. He completed the background, retrieved the roll of gel, and placed the roll against the canvas, trimming the sheet to fit. Again with the scribers, he continued with the background. Layer upon layer, the quadrant filled with a continuation of the same military figure, but with such depth of color and perspective that it seemed real.

Tomasi stood and faced Balum. "I spent another ten years on my own trying to make a living with my work." He tossed the scribers onto the table, then poked Balum with his right forefinger. "I was not good enough, *artist!*" He lifted his hand and held up his little finger. "And there is more art in *that* than you contain in your entire carcass!" The forger stared down the mind-painter, turned, walked to one of the bed platforms, and dropped onto it. He shouted at the easel, "When you want my help, ask." Tomasi interlaced his fingers, put them behind his head, and stared at the dark ceiling. Sounds of movement came from behind the easel, then silence.

"Tomasi." The forger rolled over on his right side, his back toward the easel. "Tomasi."

"What?"

"Your fingers are very skilled. I envy you that skill. But your fingers contain no art."

"Mind-painting as a court toady, Balum, is swampy ground from which to make such judgments."

"Tomasi, I see the feeling and style of Pordaan here, Cordalayne down here, Xavier and his knife up here, and the layered magic of Mahdina down here. Even the subject—I recognize it—the general Manet on the fields of Preyas as painted by the great Thoam."

Tomasi snorted. "At least you recognize some of your betters."

"Yes, I recognize them." Balum remained silent for a moment. "Where are *you* in this painting, forger? You have borrowed everything—even the subject. You are an excellent copier; forger. But you have no art."

Tomasi bit his lower lip, then turned his head toward the easel. "I do not claim to be an artist, Balum. But if I am not, what are you? What chance have you to save your skin? You don't even know where to start." He turned back to the wall. The forger listened to the silence for a long time until it was broken by the scraping of a pallet knife upon canvas. The scraping stopped.

"As little as you think of mind-paintings, Tomasi, it is art. It is art because *I* am in every piece that I do. At this moment I would give my fortune for your fingers. Perhaps I will not be able to complete the portrait in time; but if I do, it will be *mine*."

The forger stared at the wall. "You are a fool, Balum."

"Perhaps."

Tomasi closed his eyes and drifted off to sleep to the sounds of scraping.

The forger awakened with a start as the cell door slammed open. He sat up, swung his feet to the floor, and rubbed his eyes. Gunder, the keeper, handed two metal trays to Tomasi while the other keeper moved several large wooden crates inside the door. Gunder faced the back of the easel. "Here is your mind-painting gadgetry, Balum."

The old man's voice came from behind the canvas. "Leave it and go, Gunder."

Gunder stared at the easel, then he grinned. "Sooner or later, Balum, I'll have you in my fun room."

"Until then, go away."

Gunder shook his head and the two keepers left, slamming the cell door shut behind them.

"Balum, there is food." Tomasi looked at the two trays and wrinkled his nose at the food's odor. He shrugged. *At least nothing is looking back.* He lifted the trays, stood, and brought them to the sleeping platforms. "Balum." He placed the trays upon his bed, then walked to the easel. "Balum?" As the mind-painter came into view, Tomasi saw the old man bent forward, his arms on his knees, his head cradled in his arms. The forger looked at the canvas, then shook his head. The arms were too short, hands and feet too small, the face as flat as if it had been hit with a skillet, the gaudy clothing without a stress or drape as though it had been borrowed from a paper doll.

Tomasi sighed and put his hands upon Balum's shoulders, pulling the mind-painter to a sitting position. Balum half-opened his eyes and weaved upon the stool. "It is done, Tomasi. See? It is done."

The forger nodded. "Ah, yes." He pulled Balum to his feet and led the old man toward the other sleeping platform. He seated the mind-painter on the bed and reached for one of the trays. When the forger looked back, Balum had lowered his head to the mattress and was fast asleep. Tomasi sighed, replaced the trays, and lifted Balum's legs onto the platform. He then took a few experimental bites of the dungeon's cuisine. After washing down the food with weak tea, the forger moved to the easel and sat down upon the stool.

He lifted the pallet knife, and in a few moments, the canvas was scraped clean. At the end of three hours, a highly complimentary portrait of the young Baron Negay looked down from the canvas. The image was garbed in Arine furs and purple-trimmed shiny black leathers; an increase in rank and status that would stroke the little despot's ego. The baron's face had been configured into one of strength, virtue, and beauty. Perhaps no one but Negay would see himself in the portrait, but that Negay would see himself in it the forger had no doubt. He had done portraits before. Each wart removed increases the artist's reward.

He wiped his hands, tossed the rag onto the table, then went to his sleeping platform. As he turned to sit down, he noticed that Balum had not moved. "With luck, old fool, you will think that you painted it; and I shall declare myself wrong and praise you to the heavens." Tomasi snickered, placed the trays upon the floor, and stretched out.

The forger awakened with strong hands around his throat and Balum's reddened face screaming at him. "Fiend! You *devil*! You—"

Tomasi brought up a knee and thudded it into Balum's ribs. The old man dropped to the floor of the cell, writhing for his breath. "Balum, you . . . damned old—" Tomasi coughed, got up from the platform, then delivered a telling kick to the mind-painter's thigh. "—damned old fool! What were you trying to do?"

Balum, clutching his thigh, breathed deeply and rapidly. "You *corrupter*!" He pushed himself to his feet and stood facing the forger, his face contorted with rage. "Corrupter! Evil filth! Moral slime!"

Tomasi stared at the old mind-painter as Balum's face changed from rage to shame. "Balum, what is wrong?"

Balum's shoulders slumped, then he lowered himself gently to the forger's sleeping platform, his face covered with his hands. "When I awakened I knew . . . I *knew* the portrait I had done was poor. I *knew*!" The old man shook his head, then uncovered his tear-streaked face. "I went to the easel to salvage what I could . . . then—" He pointed a shaking finger at the forger. "—then *I saw what you did*! Your beautiful painting . . . your beautiful, false, phoney portrait! Even stealing technique and style from the masters, you must use their truths to tell *lies*!"

Tomasi rubbed his throat and shrugged. "Negay would not

approve of truth, old fool. As court toady, you should know as much. Should I have shown the twisted, indulgent parasite that feeds off of the backs of a malnourished people? A torturer? Murderer? Thief? Should I—"

"Silence!" Balum wiped the wetness from his face with the backs of his hands. "It is not your lies, forger. It is that I have spent hours on that stool, staring at that painting, trying to convince myself that I should do as you said and take credit for it."

Tomasi sighed and held out his hands. "Do not our skins have value? I am not a corrupter, Balum; I am a survivor. Let this one lie pass and you will remain alive to exercise your toady's integrity upon your mindless mind-paintings—"

Balum stood and walked to the easel. "Stay away from here, forger."

Tomasi sat on the edge of his platform and looked at his timepiece. He looked back at the easel. "You have less than three days remaining, Balum."

"Forger, touch this canvas one more time and I will kill you."

Tomasi sighed as he heard the sound of scraping.

Hours later, after napping, eating, washing his face, and listening to the constant discomforting muffled screams coming through the cell door, the forger had exhausted his environment's entertainment potential. During those hours, he heard the paint being scraped from the canvas six times. He paced for a while, then climbed to his sleeping platform in the dark end of the cell and sat with his back against the cold wall, his feet upon the edge of the bed. As he rested his elbows upon his knees, his fingers interlaced, he wondered about the man examining his most recent effort. Old Peter would find nothing in the composition of the paint to give him away. Better experts had performed the same tests, authenticating his forgeries. In Sabro's photographs were several distant views of a half-completed work that could very well be a beginning to the painting Peter had in his laboratory. Tomasi shrugged. His work had always passed the most exacting tests. The forger frowned. But, this was the first time he had ever been under confinement awaiting a decision.

"Tomasi."

The forger looked at the back of the easel. "What is it, *artist*?"

"The lights. What are they for?"

Tomasi looked above the easel to the light array beneath the light bar, then laughed. "You needn't worry about them, old fraud. They are for use in doing scribed multi-layered paintings. You have more than you can handle with one layer."

"What are they *for*?"

The forger shook his head. "They are used in sequence to enable the neophyte artist to read only one layer at a time."

"You did not use them."

"I am hardly a neophyte, Balum." Tomasi cursed the opening he had given Balum to point out that he was no artist either.

"I have never seen them in galleries where layered paintings were on display."

Tomasi lifted his legs, swung them to his right, and stretched out on his mattress. "They are for painting, Balum. Not viewing. A layered painting is meant to be viewed in normal light. That is how it achieves its effects of depth and perspective. As with any other kind of work, a layered painting is meant to be viewed as a totality. The lights separate the layers to keep fuzzy-headed beginners from getting confused."

"How old is this medium?"

"Not as old as mind-painting. After the popularity of mind-paintings had pushed most real artists out of work, layered gel was developed in hopes of dazzling the host of illiterate clods back to real art. It was not very successful." Tomasi turned his head toward the easel. "Why?"

"Nothing. Curiosity." Balum remained silent for a minute. "Tomasi, I need your help."

The forger barked out a laugh. "*My* help?"

"Yes. Come here and look at this." Tomasi remained on his platform for a moment, shrugged, then got to his feet. He walked around the right side of the easel and looked at the mind-painter's most recent effort. A much improved, but still grotesque, image of Baron Negay looked back at him—

almost. The baron's eyes appeared to be pointing in two different directions. Balum pointed a brush at the image's right hand. "What is wrong with that hand? I have done it over a hundred times. Close up it looks fine . . . but it just isn't right."

Tomasi raised his brows. "It isn't just the hand."

"I know. But let us begin with the hand."

The forger looked down, then looked at Balum. "Lift your right hand."

"Eh?"

"Your right hand. Lift it and place the heel of it against your chin." Frowning, Balum complied.

"Well?"

"Touch your fingertips against your face. Where do they touch?"

Balum tried twice. "The middle of my forehead almost to my hairline."

"Use the end of your brush and measure the good Baron Negay's hand against his face."

Balum held the end of a brush against the image's hand, marked the end of it with his thumb, then brought the exposed end of the brush and placed the part marked with his thumb against the image's chin. The end of the brush rested just above the tip of Negay's nose. Balum's mouth fell open. "Incredible!"

The forger shook his head. "No Balum. Inexperience; quite believable inexperience."

Balum frowned at the forger. "My mind-portraits have no problems such as this!"

Tomasi made two fists and shook them over his head. "Idiot! You old, old, *idiot*!" He pointed at his head. "A mind-painter orders his machine to play a thought. The machine already knows the limits and proportions of the thought, or if it doesn't, it searches your literal subconscious for the information." He slapped his hands together. "Blap! The machine squirts the proper intensity, order, and code of electrons upon a sensitized piece of glass! Less work and less skill than it takes to sharpen a hoe. *That* is what you call *art*!" The forger folded his arms. "When you have to consciously understand limits, proportions, colors, orders and then make your tools comply with them, it is *different*. Is it not, *artist*?"

Balum slowly turned his head back to the painting. "Yes." He lifted his knife and began cleaning the entire canvas. "Tomasi, I shall repair the hand. I also want to know how to put the wrinkles and folds into cloth, as well as the different shades of color according to the angle of the source of light. And shadows. How do I make red darker to show red cloth in a shadow? I add black to it and it turns brown. I must know the colors of skin in different planes at different angles of light. How do I use the shading to make the subject stand out and assume substance rather than remaining as flat as the background? And the proportions of the body. I must know that. All of the facial expressions. Which muscles do I tighten and which do I leave free to make a smile—"

"I cannot compress twenty years of training into a couple of days." He turned and walked from the easel. "If you want me to be of help, let me paint the portrait." He stopped beside his bed platform, placed his hands upon his hips, and turned to look at the crates next to the door. "Why did you have your mind-painting equipment brought here?"

"I thought it might help me to think, relax. I simply don't have the time for it."

Tomasi sat on the edge of his platform, looked around the cell, then let his gaze come to rest upon the crates. He walked over and began opening the first crate.

Balum's head appeared around the edge of the canvas. "What are you doing?"

The forger pulled a black-and-gray metal box from the crate and examined it. "I'm bored waiting for your execution."

"Leave my equipment alone."

"I won't harm it." Tomasi snickered. "And what difference will it make in a few days in any event?" He opened the second crate as Balum disappeared behind the canvas.

Tomasi sat cross-legged upon one end of his sleeping platform looking at the video screen propped upon the other end of the bed. The screen was blank. The forger cursed beneath his breath, adjusted the pick-up band around his head, then turned a knob on the black-and-gray box. "Balum, I cannot get this thing to work."

"I cannot be bothered, forger."

Tomasi snorted, tore the pick-up band from his head, and began rummaging through the small box filled with cables, connectors, and other assorted things. He found another pick-up bank, hooked it up to the machine, and placed the band upon his head. Everything in place, he twisted a couple of knobs at random, then gasped as his eyes went dark and his mind filled with a scramble of horrible images. He felt the band torn from his head, and he sagged and breathed heavily as he rested against the machine. He opened his eyes to see Balum looking down at him. Balum sneered. "It seems that I am not the only fool in this cell." The old man pointed at the machine. "Look at what you have done. You have the equipment arranged for collaboration, at full power, and with one of the bands empty—besides the one that was on your head."

Tomasi swallowed. "My head. It filled with the most terrifying images."

"Of course. You left the second band connected, but empty. Hence, it picked up the available thoughts in the immediate area." Balum looked at the wall next to Tomasi. "You probably picked up whoever it is on the other side of that wall."

The forger frowned. "What do you mean: collaboration?"

Balum turned and walked back to the easel. "Certainly you must know what a collaboration is."

"In mind-painting?"

"Of course. The machine, in effect, makes the two minds one. I never do collaborations, myself. It's unpleasant enough to use the machine for instructing my apprentice."

Tomasi looked again at the knobs and dials on the face of the black-and-gray box. "Could you arrange this thing so that I could teach you—"

"Impossible. It places thoughts—images—in another's head. It cannot control muscles. That I will have to learn for myself."

The forger sprang to his feet and ran to the easel. Balum

was again scraping the canvas. "The other way around, Balum! You can place into *my* mind what you want painted. Then I can put the paint—"

"No!" Balum fumed for a moment, then looked up at Tomasi. "It is to be *my* painting! *My* painting!"

Tomasi wet his lips. "It would be no less yours than one of your mind-pictures. You put your image into the machine, and the machine does the work. You can think of me as the bristles of a brush, the machine my handle."

Balum's shoulders slumped as he turned and stared at the canvas. "But it must be *mine*! You would add things you have stolen from all the great masters..." He sat back, glanced at Tomasi, then looked back at the canvas. "I think I can set the equipment ... yes." He nodded. "Very well. Let's try it. Help me bring the equipment to the easel."

Tomasi grinned. "At last! Progress!"

The forger awakened as though from the dead. He stretched and winced at the aches in his back and legs, then he looked at his timepiece. Balum had kept him at it until well after three in the morning. Or was it the afternoon? He shook his head. He couldn't remember anything after Balum had thrown the switch. Fear tickled him as he glanced at his timepiece. Ten twenty-eight. Morning or night?

He looked toward the easel. The floor around it was covered with papers from the pad. The walls to the side and behind the easel were covered with drawings, as well as color mixing experiments. As he watched, another sheet of paper leaf-dipped to the floor, then the sound of a scriber on gel. Tomasi sighed and rolled over. After the scratching had stopped, there was a long silence. He turned his head back toward the easel. "Balum?"

"Yes?"

"Is this morning or night?"

"I do not know."

Tomasi rubbed the sand from his eyes. "I can still paint the portrait for you."

"No." There was a short pause. "Thank you, but no. Everything will be fine. The experiment worked."

"Oh?" Tomasi began getting up. "I do not remember doing anything. You did not say the machine would do that."

"Stay away. Wait until I am finished."

Tomasi shrugged and stretched out again. "What did I do?"

"What I told you to do."

Tomasi looked again at his timepiece. If it was morning, the guard would bring their trays in an hour and a half. If the trays came, Balum would have twelve hours added to his two days. If the trays did not come, the mind-painter would have less time. More or less, depending upon when the baron roused himself from his silken sheets. He lowered his arm and curled up, his head resting against the coolness of the wall. He paused, then brought his head away from the wall in horror. His ears could not hear it, but the vibration through his bones painted a picture of screaming terror coming from the other side of the wall. Was the voice male or female, or even human? The forger shut his eyes and turned his back to the wall.

"Balum?"

"Yes?" The scratching continued without pause.

"How did you get out of the fields?"

"A curious question." More scratching. "My hands were injured in a threshing machine. I could do no work and my father gave me to old Yate, keeper of the old baron's accounts. Yate punished me the several times I was caught not doing my assigned work, but this brought me to the attention of Norris. He was the first mind-painter here. He took me on, and when he died, I replaced him."

"Your hands look fully recovered."

"They are. But I enjoyed mind-painting, and it gave me extra money to make my family's lot easier ... while they lived."

Tomasi looked into the darkest corner of the cell. "Did your family die in the last population control plague? Mine did."

Balum was silent and the scratching stopped. "All but my father. He died in the stocks ... for speaking against the baronage." The scratching resumed.

Tomasi felt very weary.

... he dreamt of his father—brutish peasant lout poisoned with brew of his own invention. His mother ... "Tomasi, you

*have a great gift from God. You can be more than we are.
More."* He painted signs for the small village merchants;
cups, plates, and platters for the potter; baubles for the village jeweler. Then the great Sabro, heir to a barony in Yorkton, came to the village. Sabro had seen Tomasi's work and
had arranged for the boy's instruction at the great artist's
own studio. There, with five other boys, he studied, glorying
in his freedom from the fields, from hunger, from endless
brutality. The happy years passed.

"Tomasi. I have no more to teach you. You mimic my
work, and the work of my colleagues and your fellow students
with frightening accuracy."

"Thank you, Excellency."

"That was no compliment, boy. We have machines that do
the work of copying. When will I see something of yours?
Something of your own?"

"I . . . I do not understand, Excellency. I have done everything that I was told."

The great Sabro looked down and shook his head. When
he looked up, his eyes were cold, distant. "I apologize, Tomasi. I mistook your gift for mimicry as a calling to the arts.
I envy you your every skill; I weep at your inability to create."
Sabro lifted the young Tomasi's slender hands and looked at
them. "A waste such as this must have a purpose in Heaven's
scheme. Look for it, Tomasi. Look for it, but not here. Here
we are but mere artists."

Ten years of failure, than an opportunity. Sabro burned
along with an unknown number of his completed and half-
completed works. Heaven's plan, at last, had borne fruit.
Tomasi the hungry became Tomasi the dealer in fine art—

Tomasi lost count of the times he was placed before the
easel, then his mind blanked as Balum again turned on the
machine. There were no images, save a feeling of being
drugged. Each time there was nothing on the canvas as he
was placed under, nothing when he awakened. Then Balum
told him to go to sleep, and to stay away from the easel.

Tomasi awakened and the cell was dark. He could hear
Balum's gentle snoring coming from the other sleeping plat-

form. The forger rubbed his eyes and pulled the lace collar from around his throat, begging the Holy for a simple soap and shower. Sitting up and swinging his feet to the floor, he studied the dim outlines of the easel and canvas made visible by the crack of light from under the door. He stood, stretched his aching muscles, walked behind the canvas, and illuminated the light bar. Turning, he saw the image of Baron Negay spring from the canvas. He nodded and smiled. The old man's visions appeared to have worked. Layer by layer Tomasi had worked the gel. Balum himself had assembled the layers.

The forger sat on the stool and examined the multi-layered painting. The depth and perspective were excellent, and the image of the baron showed the little pirate at his best—at better than his best. The drape of the baron's cape was rich and realistic.

Tomasi sighed. It had worked. He looked again at the painting—the baron's eyes. A small thing, but the eyes made Tomasi feel uneasy. He felt an urge torn between laughter and rage. He stood and backed away from the painting. Yes. Laughter and rage . . . and, was it, could it be, hope? The forger frowned. It was a competently done portrait; but no more than that. From where came the humor? What caused the feeling of anger? The painting disturbed him.

Reaching to the wall, Tomasi extinguished the light bar and illuminated the first whitelight. He turned to the painting and sank to the stool in laughter. Baron Negay stood naked, his face attempting to maintain a measure of dignity while his eyes looked down and his hands covered the obvious.

—Second whitelight. The naked baron's features were exaggerated into a comic representation of a human—thickened lower lip, protruding upper teeth, bulging eyes, knobby knees. Again Tomasi laughed. "Balum, this deserves a medal."

—Third whitelight. Still a representation, but no longer comic. The eyes, mouth, and posture spoke of arrogance, cruelty, sadism. The background, skillfully hidden by the first layer's trees and shrubs, became numberless, nameless corpses. Tomasi studied it for a long moment. The figure spoke for his dead mother—for everyone's dead kin. There was the rage. The rage that all put aside in favor of immediate survival. Tomasi reached out his hand.

—First redlight. Negay, fear upon his ugly face, clutched his bleeding belly. Blood spattered his pale skin, while the background was one of fire; the dead rising to take up arms.

—Second redlight. The crouching figure rotted. The eyes were gone, the skin purple and coming free from its bones as though in flight. The dead joined the living, marching under the same banner.

—Fourth whitelight. A skeleton, crouching down further, its gray-white fingers clutching after its fleeing subjects. Tall spires of glass and metal rose behind it, diminishing the bones with their power and grandeur.

—Blacklight. The ragged edges of a ghostly apparition fluoresced and clawed against the blackness that surrounded it. The eyes and heart were hollow; the evil remained to survive the corpse.

—Bluelight. The image was gone, replaced by cloud-tufted blue skies dotted with long-winged white birds. It took a moment, but the forger identified the emotion he felt. Elation; freedom.

Tomasi turned off the light array and returned the cell to illumination from the light bar. He looked around the canvas to see Balum sleeping peacefully upon his platform. Emotions swirled in the forger's head: joy, gratitude, hate, envy, sorrow. He looked back at the normal light figure of the young Baron Negay. What would the creature do when he discovered the truth about his portrait? And Tomasi had no doubt that old Peter would discover it. The truth created by Balum would destroy both painting and . . . and artist. *Yes, artist*.

The cell door slammed open. Heavy footsteps approached the easel, and the guard called Gunder came around the edge of the canvas. He glanced at the painting, then looked at Tomasi. "Did you do this?" The guard's thick fingers motioned toward the canvas.

Tomasi shook his head. "No. It is Balum's."

The guard turned his head toward the painting. "Ha! Didn't think Balum had it in him . . ." He cocked his head to one side, then frowned.

Tomasi half-smiled and turned to face the guard. "What do you think of it?"

Gunder frowned more deeply, then shook his head. "I don't

know." The guard studied the painting for a moment longer, then tore himself away as though by force. "You are free to go. The baron is satisfied that your painting is genuine. Your draft is waiting with the attendant standing by your cab."

Tomasi nodded, stood, then began gathering up the penciled studies scattered upon the floor. "Would there be any objection if I took these with me?"

The guard shrugged. "They belong to Balum." Gunder went back to studying the painting.

Tomasi finished selecting the studies that he wanted, then walked to the mind-painter's side. He sat upon the edge of the sleeping platform and shook the old man's shoulder. He whispered, "Balum. Balum."

The old man opened his eyes. "You have seen it?"

Tomasi nodded. "Yes."

"What do you think?"

The forger smiled as his eyes brimmed with moisture. "Do you care what I think, Balum? You know if it is right."

The mind-painter closed his eyes, then nodded. Opening his eyes, he turned his head and noticed the guard studying the portrait of Baron Negay. "We have touched the brute."

Tomasi shook his head. "You, Balum. I was only the brush in your hand. You have touched him."

Balum looked back at the forger. "What will you do, Tomasi?"

Tomasi held up the sheaf of papers he had collected. "May I take these?"

Balum closed his eyes and nodded. "I suppose I am to become the latest victim to be exploited by the great forger Tomasi."

Tomasi smiled and nodded. His face grew grim. "You know Peter will examine the painting with the light array, and what will happen afterwards."

"Yes."

Tomasi stuffed the papers inside his blouse. "Balum, the sole work of a great artist should bring a good price." He smiled as he buttoned up his blouse, then bent down next to the old man's ear. "It may even bring a bloody empire to its knees."

Tomasi stood and touched Balum's hand. *Farewell, artist.*

Gunder walked up and stood next to the forger. "It is time to go."

Tomasi stood and walked toward the cell door. "Tell me, Gunder. Have you come to any conclusions about the portrait?"

The guard left the door open and steered the forger toward the elevator. He shook his heavy jowls, his gaze fixed to the floor. "No. I must look at it again. It ... disturbs me somehow."

Tomasi stepped into the elevator car and let the door cut off the screams of the dungeon.

... Whoever the unknown artist was that made the over fourteen hundred copies of the portrait of Baron Negay, there can be no doubt that the painting became a symbol of the uprising that soon followed its appearance in every dominion of the former empire. Exhaustive investigation has failed to uncover the name of this artist who encoded all of his copies with the simple inscription: "For Balum." The only Balum appearing in the baronage records of the period was an insignificant mind-painter, coincidentally of the Negay household, who was burned at the stake in 2912 GS....

Stanley, Darktime Artistic Curiosities, *(Oxford, 3106 GS)*

The idea for this story, "SHAWNA, Ltd.," was a gift. I was in New York and I dropped by Davis Publications to say hello to the Asimovians. George Scithers and I talked awhile, then he turned to his assistant editor (now editor of Asimov's) *Shawna McCarthy. "Why don't you ask Barry?"*

Her eyebrows went up. "About what?"

"About that thing." *George pronounced the word "thing" as though it had a bad taste.*

Shawna's face lit up, she slid her chair next to me, and she asked, "Idealist philosophy. You know, it's only there because I see it there. I was wondering if that could be rigged up for a faster-than-light drive. See, you'd power the thing by harnessing some philosophers who would think themselves from one place to another . . ."

On my way home, I pondered the fact that I wouldn't be asked questions like that if I was in the aluminum siding business. Nevertheless, I decided to give Shawna's premise a try. Trying to get practical, honest work from a philosopher is the kind of challenge that tests the limits of credible fantasy. I didn't want her to think I was chicken.

SHAWNA, Ltd.

SHAWNA—(Supraliminal Hegelian Absolutized World Neotranspatial Amplifier), a device that amplifies the component of mind that creates and alters reality. SHAWNA theory, rooted in the work of the early idealistic philosophers, was first made practicable in 2134 by physicist-philosopher Leonid Veggnitz, at which time it was first used in transportation over multiparsec distances (See: SHAWNA, Ltd. under Space Lines, Commercial).

—*Encyclopedia Galactica*

As the huge, swept-wing liner taxied out to the run-up pad at the end of the runway, Enoch Rawls began wishing he had never taken up Leonid Veggnitz's offer. The brain behind SHAWNA, Ltd. had coaxed the semanticist into converting the premises and applications of SHAWNA theory and flight from Aristotelian to non-Aristotelian logic. "Soup it up," as Veggnitz put it. The philosopher pilots he had been introduced to as he took his seat in the cockpit seemed confident enough, but Rawls had never been up before. As the engines grumbled, he turned to his right. Captain Sanford, director of the spaceline's philosophical flight school, looked back. "Is there something the matter, Doctor?"

"Captain, why does this ship have engines? I thought all we had to do was think our way to Betelvane."

Sanford chuckled and nodded his head toward the four pilots in the seats forward of theirs. "They have to get us into the air first. Otherwise, we'd leave a dandy hole in the runway. Because of the extra weight we'd pick up, we probably wouldn't make our destination."

"I see."

"SHAWNA flight is limited right now, but as I understand Doctor Veggnitz, he hopes that your work will make us SHAWNA, Unlimited—bigger payloads with fewer philosophers."

Rawls nodded and looked toward the front. First Philosopher Wheeler reached to a panel, picked up a mike, and keyed it. "Tower, this is SHAWNA one to seven, PFR to Betelvane, over."

Rawls saw the First Philosopher listen into his headphones.

"Roger, tower; one one seven cleared for immediate take-off." Wheeler turned to his right. "Okay, Hansen, throw the coal to it." The one called Hansen, Second Philosopher, grasped the throttles with his left hand and gradually pushed them forward. The ship trembled and began rolling forward.

Hansen called off the markers as they rolled down the runway. "Twenty . . . nineteen . . . eighteen . . ."

Third Philosopher Valdez called off the airspeed. "Ninety . . . one-thirty . . . one-ninety . . . two-eighty, and rotate!"

Rawls felt his stomach sink to his lap as Wheeler pulled back on the wheel, shooting the great craft up into the atmosphere. Wheeler nodded at Hansen. "Gear up."

Rawls' buttocks quivered as he heard the multiple whine-clunks of the landing gear retracting.

"Gear up."

"Flaps."

"Flaps up."

"Heading two one zero."

"Two one zero."

Rawls watched as the philosophers flicked switches, turned knobs, and pulled at controls. Wheeler turned a knob and then keyed his mike. "This is the First Philosopher, Captain Wheeler, speaking. Welcome aboard SHAWNA flight one

one seven en route to Hajii Field, Betelvane. We will be at jump altitude in approximately eight minutes, and we estimate Hajii Field at 2:72, Interstellar Standard Time. Local time will be 8:91. Enjoy your flight, and please pay attention now while the stewardess in your compartment explains the ship's emergency equipment and procedures. Thank you." Wheeler hung up the mike.

Rawls felt a hand shaking his arm. He turned toward Sanford. "Yes?"

"Before the jump, I should explain what you are going to see, since neither of us will be allowed to talk during the jump." He smiled. "Distracting the philosophers during the jump could be very dangerous."

"I see."

Sanford pointed at the four philosophers. "Those seats swivel around, and they will turn at jump time. This is so they will not be looking out the window. You see those helmets suspended from the overhead?"

Rawls looked up and saw four gold helmets, coils of red and orange wires leading from them, dangling from hooks. "Yes. Are they the links to the amplifier?"

Sanford nodded. "They'll put them on after they've turned. You see, they can't chance having their vision contradict their thinking about where they are."

Rawls nodded. "I can see why, but what about simple human doubt? I know these flights have been going on for years, but I have doubts."

"These philosophers are the cream of a very select crop. They are screened and re-screened until the last doubting Thomas is removed, then screened again." Sanford smiled and raised his eyebrows. "I think you can see why we can't afford a rogue skeptic getting into the driver's seat."

Rawls nodded, then the cockpit door opened. A stewardess entered carrying a cup-laden tray. "Coffee, fellas?"

She carried the tray to the four philosophers, who each took a cup, then she turned toward Rawls. "Coffee, Doctor?"

Rawls took a cup. "Thank you." Sanford took a cup, and as the stewardess left, Rawls sipped at the steaming brew. He was half-finished as the philosophers put the ship on autopilot and swung their chairs around. Wheeler smiled at the Doctor, then reached down and placed his coffee on the deck. Then he reached up and pulled down the helmet above his seat and placed it firmly upon his head. The other philosophers did the same.

Sanford leaned over to Rawls. "Doctor, until after the jump, we must do no talking."

Rawls nodded and watched the philosophers. Wheeler loosened his necktie, checked to see that the other philosophers were wearing their helmets, then turned to Hansen. "Right, Dicky, engage the amp."

"Check." Hansen fiddled with a small panel of knobs recessed into the armrest of his chair. "Amp engaged, power reading at 100 percent, all green."

Wheeler turned to the Third Philosopher. "How are we holding up, Pancho?"

Third Philosopher Valdez checked the instruments on the console attached to his chair. "Airspeed four twenty, altitude twelve thousand, bearing one two zero, all green."

Wheeler turned to the Fourth Philosopher. "Anything in the way, Tony?"

The Fourth Philosopher examined the CRT readout next to his chair. "All clear, Captain."

"Very well, engage the sweep." Wheeler turned to Rawls. "The sweep is what we call the field that moves out from the ship to exclude organic materials from the jump area. It wouldn't do if we brought an air pocket full of germs with us to Betelvane." Rawls nodded.

The Fourth Philosopher looked up from his controls and turned toward Wheeler. "Clean as a whistle, Captain."

Wheeler nodded. "Are we ready to throw the old scow into Berkely, then?" The other three philosophers nodded. Wheeler faced to his front, stabbed several buttons set into his chair's armrest. "Into first, then: objects depend on mind for existence; objects have no meaning apart from the knower, and the knower is mind; objects cannot exist apart from mind."

Rawls watched as the four philosophers concentrated on the statements. Wheeler looked at the others. "Are we ready to shift into second?" The other philosophers nodded. Rawls looked out the window and saw no difference. Wheeler cleared his throat. "Terms and relations logically determine one another; ultimate reality is a system of judgments; truth is defined in terms of the relation of these judgments in the formation of a consistent whole."

Rawls noticed that the sky had taken on a curious blue-purple shade, and the clouds a rippling sheen. Wheeler pulled a hanky from his pocket and dabbed at his forehead. The First Philosopher looked at his fellows, then took a deep breath. "Ready for third, lads?" Nods all around. "Here we go, then: subject and object are reciprocally dependent upon each other; there can be no subject without an object and no object can exist without a subject; complete reality is a unity of subject and object."

Outside, the sky began pulsing from red through purple to black, then back to red. The clouds radiated with metallic gold color. Wheeler dabbed again at his forehead, then looked at the Second Philosopher. "Very well, Dicky, run the dissolve tape."

"Check." Hansen jabbed a button, and Rawls watched as the four philosophers went rigid. Outside, the golden clouds blurred, then melded into the purple sky. The sky itself faded until there was nothing—not even the color black. Rawls felt a poke on his arm, turned toward Sanford, and took the note from Sanford's hand.

"Dissolve tape runs at high speed, philosophically showing this reality dissolving. Creation tape will construct the reality of this ship being in Betelvane's atmosphere." Rawls nodded his understanding, then turned his attention back to the philosophers. Wheeler came out of it, shook his head, and looked over the faces of all the others.

"Anyone for a break? Pancho, you look all in."

Valdez shook his head and gasped for air. "Let's get it over with, Captain. I'm up for it."

"Are you certain? I can have the stewardess bring in more coffee."

Valdez shook his head. "I'm okay."

"Very well. Anyone else?" Wheeler saw the heads shaking, then he turned to Hansen. "Run the Betelvane tape, then, Dicky."

Hansen put his hand to the control. "Betelvane tape, check." ·

The philosophers went rigid again as the blankness outside

the cockpit filled in with pale blue sky, high, thready cloud formations, and strange reptilian flying creatures. Wheeler and the other three officers sagged in their chairs, then Wheeler sat up. "There we go, Doctor Rawls. Another successful jump." He turned to Valdez. "Pancho, what shape are we in?"

Valdez, a dazed look in his eyes, squinted at the controls. "On the button, Captain. Airspeed four twenty, altitude twelve thousand, bearing two one zero. Hajii Field in . . . fourteen minutes." Valdez slumped back in his chair.

Wheeler nodded at the Fourth Philosopher. "Tony, take over Pancho's console after you collapse the field, will you? He looks all in."

Valdez smiled at Wheeler, then closed his eyes. "Thanks, Captain."

Wheeler looked at Rawls as Hansen swung his chair around. "We have to keep the helmets on for a while, but it's all right to talk now."

Rawls nodded. "Thank you, Captain Wheeler. That was quite impressive."

Wheeler turned his chair and faced the front as Sanford leaned toward Rawls. "You see, Doctor, the reality of Betelvane has changed since that tape was made. They must keep linked up to the amplifier to program the new tape, and also to establish our own part in this reality. You know, sort of firm things up a bit."

Rawls nodded, then rubbed his chin. "My mind was so occupied with what was happening during the jump, I really didn't have time to consider the application of non-Aristotelian logic to the arguments. I suppose the application should extend to the tapes too?"

Sanford nodded. "This is merely a familiarization flight, Doctor. I suppose your real work will be done in the science research center at SHAWNA back on Earth. But, offhand, what do you think?"

Rawls pursed his lips. "Well, Captain Sanford, the first step in the transformation of any system from Aristotelian to non-Aristotelian logic is the problem of identity. Your flight propositions are rooted in Aristotelian identity: mind is matter; matter is mind; A is A. One of the foundations of non-Aristotelian logic is that A is almost never A."

Wheeler laughed and turned his chair around. "Come now, Doctor. I don't think anything could be more self-evident than A is A."

Rawls pulled a pen from his pocket and scribbled "A is A" on a scrap of paper, then handed it to Wheeler. "Now, Captain, you agree with that statement?"

Wheeler shrugged. "Of course."

Rawls smiled. "The word 'is' in that statement functions the same as the equal sign in mathematics. The statement, as it is used, means that the propositions, objects, realities, or whatever, on either side of the word 'is' are identical; that is, equal in all respects. Look at the paper and you can see that they obviously are not equal in all respects. With my handwriting, I'm certain that the letters are shaped differently, and they are on different sides of the word 'is.' I'm sure I used more ink on one than the other, and so on."

Wheeler studied the paper. "But, Doctor, this is a piece of paper stating or symbolizing a concept, and on the conceptual level, A is A is a tautology."

Rawls nodded. "But, Captain Wheeler, language—that is, symbols—is only a map to reality. Language is not reality; a map isn't the area it describes. I defy you to find one instance of identity in the real world. You might say an apple is an apple, but *is* apple number one equal in all respects to apple number two?"

Wheeler studied the paper, frowned, then shook his head. Sanford lifted his hand and found it covered with black goop. He felt the armrest under his other hand going mushy. "Wheeler, stop thinking about that! We're going into a dissolve phase!"

Wheeler looked up, saw the structural braces of the cabin bending. "Hansen! Hansen! Run the Betelvane tape again, on the double!"

Hansen looked over the back of his chair. "I can't, Captain! I . . . I don't believe it, but we're in Hegelian Overdrive!"

Wheeler swung around and took over Hansen's console. Rawls looked at Sanford. "What's happening?"

Sanford wiped a hand over his face. It came away wet. "Hegelian Overdrive. It's only been theorized so far; this is the first time—" Sanford turned to Rawls. "We've had reality go soft on us before, but another run of the tape usually cures it. But this . . ."

"I don't understand. What's Hegelian Overdrive?"

"The ontological argument first used to . . . prove the existence of a supreme being founds the theory for the Overdrive . . ." Sanford looked around Rawls, his eyes widening. "Wheeler, it's Valdez! He's *praying*! Get the damned helmet off of him!"

The Fourth Philosopher reached out and pulled Valdez's helmet from his head. Valdez wrung his hands. "God, we're dissolving. Heavenly Father, please accept this, Your most unworthy child to your bos—"

"Shut up!" screamed Wheeler. Valdez appeared to come out of it.

"What—what happened?"

Rawls stood and went to the window. As far as he could see, a carpet of soft billowing clouds spread before them. In the distance, tall gleaming spires glinted with an inner light. A being garbed in flowing robes, playing a harp, flew by the window, then into the distance. Rawls turned and faced Valdez. Wheeler was shaking the Third Philosopher by his collar. "You idiot! How did you ever get through screening?"

Valdez blubbered as he held out his hands. "Captain, I haven't thought about religion since I was a boy! It's just . . . I was scared, Captain!"

Rawls saw Sanford turn from the opposite window. "Valdez?"

"Yes, Captain Sanford?"

"Do you believe in Hell?"

Valdez shrugged. "I don't know, Captain. I didn't even know I believed in Heaven. Why?"

Sanford turned back to his window. "There's a guy out there with a long beard and a big book, making a list and checking it twice." He turned back toward the others. "And I don't think he's Santa Claus."

Rawls gulped and turned back to his own window. A group of cherubs were playing king of the mountain on a cloud below. *Dear me*, thought Rawls, *I wonder where semanticists are sent? I hope my bag doesn't get lost in the confusion.*

This story, "A Time for Terror" was an experiment. Just before I wrote it, the recombinant DNA controversy was all over Science News. *Now that we know how to do it, the argument went, anyone can create novel lifeforms. The safe method is to isolate the desired property from the DNA one wishes to introduce into the host lifeform, leaving only whether it will work or not to the unknown. But DNA is very complicated stuff. Identifying a plasmid sequence with a particular property, and then isolating the sequence makes child's play out of finding a particular grain of sand in the Sahara.*

The easiest and least expensive way of introducing a particular property into a host is through what is called the "shotgun" approach. The shotgun is a quick and dirty technique that hits a bunch of the host lifeform (E. coli bacteria is preferred) with the proper enzymes along with a few yards of the foreign DNA containing the property that the experimenter wants to introduce into the E. coli and have it reproduce, the hope being that some of the offspring will exhibit the desired property. Then the experimenter sits back and waits to see what happens. It's sort of like running it up the old flagpole and seeing if anything begins dripping insulin.

The trouble with the shotgun technique, as the argument continues, is not only the desired property, but all of the properties in the foreign DNA, get introduced. Countless novel lifeforms are created, and the shotgunner has no idea what they are or what they can do. Keep in mind that a generation of scientists reared upon 1950 vintage SF films does not lack imagination when it comes to projecting the kinds of horrors that might be created. An additional argument is that E. coli bacteria is commonly found in human intestines. Anything that escapes from the lab, therefore, might set up housekeeping in your gut.

The scientific argument, if the reports are to be believed, was supplemented several times by academic gang rumbles, demonstrations, and (gasp!) fisticuffs.

While all of this abstract flapdoodle was going on, another airliner was hijacked by another group trying to call attention to its cause by sacrificing a number of innocent lives. And this particular hijacking cost a few.

I usually go a little crazy thinking about being caught up in a situation like that, but this time I decided to try something. I wanted to do a first person story and throw my point of view character into the hands of a mean bunch of terrorists. Then I sat back to see what happened.

A curious footnote to this tale. Every time George Scithers has bought a story from me he has telephoned me upon having finished reading the manuscript—except for this one. After I sent this story to George there was a big silence from Philadelphia. I figured on getting a raspberry back in the mail, but instead I received a contract offer. The galleys came and went, the story was published, and never a word.

My wife and I visited him in Philadelphia some months later, and as we were on the front porch concluding the visit, Jean couldn't stand it any longer and she asked him what he had thought of "A Time for Terror."

"It disturbed me," he answered.

That is all he has ever said about the piece. I could understand his feelings. It disturbed me, too. It didn't end quite the way I had planned.

A Time for Terror

The others were dead. As I lay there, my hands bound behind
me, searching the darkness for a speck of light, it kept running
through my mind: They're dead; they're dead, all dead. . . .
The Terranists had hit us as though they were storm-driven.
One second the new commandant of security was putting the
number-two Terranist on display for the press—then, chaos.
The commandant and guards fell a split moment after the
doors blew off their hinges; I saw that hack reporter Dubord
get it an instant later.

All dead.

The dryness of the dark place could be felt, and I turned
my face from the dusty floor, coughing. With effort, I worked
up enough spit to wet my tongue, then my cracked lips.
Lowering the back of my head to the floor, I held my breath
and listened for the mass drivers. They said you could hear
them anywhere on the Lunar surface if you were against
bedrock. So, either I wasn't on the Lunar surface, against
bedrock, or they were full of it. Voices, dim and distant.

Doubling up, I pushed against the dusty floor with my
shoulder and right knee and teetered into a sitting position.
The gravity said Luna. More voices, soft footsteps against
dusty rock, a hand on a door latch. In the dark, flashes of
the Terranist commandos exploded before my eyes. Men,
women, police or civilian—no difference—all dead. Loud,

muffled orders from behind a door. The lump in my throat, my fear, grew to where it became difficult to breathe. A light metal door slammed open against a wall.

Outlined by the dim light from outside was a hand against the door and the muzzle of a weapon. As dim as it was, the light made me close my eyes. When I opened them, the outline of someone in surface gear filled the doorway. Behind the figure, others were moving back and forth, shouting and carrying things.

"On your feet, munie." The figure waved the gun at me. "Let's go; move it! You're not dead. Yet."

I looked behind me and saw a rough-cut wall. Pushing my legs, I backed up against it and used my hands and shoulders to inch up the wall. Still leaning against the wall, I turned toward the armed figure. "Where am I?"

"Come out of there."

"Can I at least have some water?"

The figure stood motionless for a second. "Laddie, your only chance of lasting out the next thirty seconds is to do exactly what I say." The figure backed out of the doorway and waved the muzzle of his gun. "Let's go."

I pushed off from the wall, made it to the door, and stepped out into the corridor. As I worked my jaw around, I could feel the blood caked on the right side of my face. Nameless with the gun gave me a dig in the kidney, and I turned right. I'm usually ready to give a man with a gun any kind of slack he asks for. But that only applies when the gunsel trades me my life for following his orders. When it's a plus or minus thirty seconds in exchange for bruised organs, to hell with it.

I whirled around to plant a knee amongst his family jewels but, instead, met a rifle stock upside the right side of my head. Unfortunately, I didn't black out. When the chimes in my head quieted down, I spit out the dust from the corridor floor, along with a few teeth, and looked back at my keeper. He wore the traditional grayish surface suit, helmet cracked back, except his suit looked in bad repair and had a broad red stripe painted around the chest. He waved his gun up and down.

"Get up, stupid, and head down the walk. Another performance like that will earn you a bolt through your kneecap."

On my knees, I looked up at him. "You're not going to kill me, are you?"

His face was round, dark, and cruel. He smiled, and a laugh started somewhere around his feet and rumbled out of his mouth. "Laddie, that depends on how much trouble you are alive."

Another red-banded figure pulled up to us carrying a crate and nodded toward my keeper. "Need a hand, Ahmis?"

He shook his head. "No." He cocked his head toward me. "On your feet, harmless." Again, he waved his gun up and down. I put one leg forward and stood, spitting blood on the floor. I looked at the four gleaming white teeth among the blood and dust of the corridor floor, remembering out of a childhood long forgotten that the most terrible thing in the world was getting a tooth knocked out. I looked at the face of my keeper. There was no remorse, nor even a hint of pity. "Turn around and stop at the next door on your left."

I turned, my cheek and jaw throbbing with indescribable aches. Three more red-banded figures, two women and a man, raced past headed in the opposite direction. One slow foot at a time, I walked the remaining few meters to the door. As I reached it, I stopped and turned toward my keeper. "I'd open it with my teeth, but I left them back in the walk."

My keeper nodded. "Very brave, little boy. Perhaps one of us will live to tell the Earth how brave you are."

He reached out and unlatched the door, pushing me in after. The room was much like the one I had just left, except for the light and the company. Behind a rude metal table sat a bearded fellow with a crown of brown hair circling his otherwise hairless dome. His facial features were identical to every representation of Jesus Christ I'd ever seen, except for the dark, haunted eyes. He pointed at a stool before the table. "Sit. My name is Rudy Vegler." He nodded toward a figure seated in the shadows. "You have already met Raymond."

I lowered myself onto the stool, trying to make out the face of the number-two Terranist. I had seen him at the news conference, but for some reason couldn't remember his face. My keeper stood behind me, his gun at the ready. Both Vegler and the one called Raymond wore surface gear.

"Why am I here?"

Vegler nodded slightly. "Yes, Mark Lambert, why are you here? You are alive because we cannot answer that question. Tell us."

I laughed. I suppose I resigned myself to being a dead man, and that helped ease my tension. After I was dead, I couldn't be hurt. Go out with style, or something stupid like that. "I didn't kill twenty men and women and drag me here. You tell me."

Vegler shook his head. "It was only eighteen." He leaned forward, the red band of his surface suit against the edge of the table. "Lambert, do you know what being surfaced is?"

"No."

"We kick you outside with no suit." He rubbed the side of his nose. "I understand that boiling blood is a very, very painful way to go." He smilied, exposing a gap in two rows of yellowing teeth. "Of course, those in a position to know are in no position to tell. Why are you here?"

I shrugged. "Honesty won't get me any points. Why should I tell you?"

Vegler dropped his smile. "Lambert, we don't have time to waste—you don't have time to waste. Why are you on Luna?"

There it was: the question. I dropped my glance to the red band around Vegler's chest. "I'm a sound tech with the *Los Angeles Telejournal*. I was sent up with Harvey Dubord to cover..."

Vegler held up his hand. "I said we don't have time." He lowered it to the table. "Feed your cover story to the lock-watchers, but to us, nothing but the truth."

With puffy lips, missing teeth, and blood dribbling from my mouth, I managed the best sneer I could. "Why should I tell you anything? You're going to kill me, aren't you?"

"No decision has been made."

I snorted, dribbling more blood down my chin and cov-eralls. "I saw you bastards slaughter innocent men and women with less compassion than I throw out my garbage."

In the shadows, the one called Raymond uttered a brief, bitter laugh. "Lambert, we have more compassion for your garbage than we do for the munies." He leaned forward, bringing his face into the light. His fine blond hair was matted and caked with blood, his skin pale and greenish around his almost delicate jaw. The narrow-set, pale blue eyes were almost hypnotic in their attraction. "Lambert, we are evacuating this site. When we leave, we will make it useless. What we need to know is whether or not it is worth our while to spend surface gear, water, and air on your survival."

I turned to Vegler. "I find it hard to believe that anything I can say will improve my chances one bit."

Vegler rubbed his nose. "The information we have from Earthside says you are a reporter working undercover for the *L.A. Telejournal*. Your exact assignment is somewhat vague, but it concerns an investigation into the possible manipulation of news from Luna."

I felt as though Ahmis, the happy jailer, had tapped me again with his gun butt. Only five persons knew: me, my editor, the publisher, the lawyer called in to hand out a heap of ignored advice and the New York Bureau chief, Margate. But Margate had said that to feed a fake ID to the MAC VI would involve developing mob contacts. You tell the mob and you tell anyone who has the price of a whisper. It had been assumed that no one on Luna, particularly the Terranists, could raise the ante. "If you know that, why the question? Why not just kill me and be done with it?"

Vegler unlatched the collar ring on his suit, pulled the seal to the middle of his chest, reached inside and scratched. "Tell me, Lambert: Is this information we've discovered, or crap that we've been fed?"

"What difference does it make?"

"If it's true, you live; if not . . ." Vegler pointed up toward the surface.

"What else would I be?"

"A police spy."

I smiled and immediately regretted it as the throb in my cheek grew. "What about you? What if this is some production number by the police to get me to admit to something?"

Vegler resealed his suit. "You overestimate your importance. It will be a long time before the lockwatchers have a commandant killed just to ferret out a reporter." He raised his eyebrows. "That would be even too extreme for us."

I shrugged. "What if I am what you say I am?"

Vegler looked at Raymond. Number-two nodded a permission, then leaned back into the shadows. Vegler turned back to me. "Then you may be of some use to us. We have been trying to get the truth to Earth for a long time."

"Terranist truth."

"Explain."

"I'm not here to do propaganda pieces for the Terranist League. Remember, I've seen you killers in action, and all it does is confirm everything I've seen or heard about the Terranists."

"Be that as it may, Lambert, there is still the small matter of convincing us that you are a reporter. If you can't, it's the last time you'll see anyone or anything in action."

I think that, for the first time since entering that room, I began believing I might somehow get out of my predicament in one piece. "What do you want to know?"

"Begin with why none of the registers, the official ones, list you as a reporter."

"I never have been listed as a reporter. It's a new position for me, but because of its nature, I couldn't be listed." Vegler was frowning. "Look, up until a few weeks ago, I was a sound tech. But I've been trying to get in reporting for years. I'd pestered the station editor about it so many times, he told me to come up with an idea and, if it was any good, he'd see. He liked my idea."

"What was the idea?"

"To come up here as a sound tech, poke around and see if the governor's office has anything to hide. I got the idea from a camera jock who was with our team covering the capture of Tralcor. The story he told me about the press conference didn't seem to have anything to do with what the reporters on Luna put on the tape loops."

Vegler nodded. "And?"

"Then I overheard one of our reporters a few days later. He had been assigned the story, but Immigration rejected his blood test. The *Telejournal* sent Morton Dubord instead, and the reporter I overheard was complaining. Dubord is what we call a 'safe' voice—a reporter the government can count on not to embarrass it." I felt as though my fingers were about to fall off, and nodded back over my right shoulder. "Is there something you can do about my hands?"

"We're doing it. Go on."

"Well, I thought of another reporter that had been turned down, then did some checking. From the *Telejournal*, at least, nothing but safe voices have ever been sent to Luna since the Plague. That includes writers as well as..."

Vegler held up his hand. "And you suspected that the government was using the blood tests as a way of screening reporters?"

"Yes."

"For what purpose?"

I shrugged, sending darts of pain from my wrists up my arms. "I don't know. That's what I'm here to find out."

Vegler looked at Raymond, then turned back toward me. "One more question: How did you plan on getting your tapes back to Earth?"

"The mass drivers. The *Telejournal* has arranged for a small ship to pick the tapes out of the dirt track before they reach the catcher station." My throat felt raw from the dryness. "From there, the tapes would be taken to the New Eden industrial station at El Five and then broadcast."

"I see." Vegler nodded. "Wouldn't those pulses in the driver wipe the tapes?"

I started to shake my head, but thought better of it. "I had a specially shielded case. It was with me at the news conference...."

Vegler nodded at my keeper. I felt the muzzle of his gun dig in between my shoulder blades. "Get up, laddie."

I stood and heard the door open behind me. I kept my eyes on Vegler. "Well?"

"Well, what?"

"Do I live or die?"

Vegler shook his head. "As I said, no decision has been made." He nodded at the guard and I felt a hand fall on my shoulder. The guard turned me around and shoved me out into the walk. He followed and closed the door, pulling a long knife from the belt of his surface suit.

"Turn around." I felt the knife slip between my hands,

and the bonds part. Immediately, blood, feeling, and pain began flowing from my arms into my hands. I turned and faced my keeper.

"I thought no decision had been made about letting me live."

The guard smiled, then rumbled forth another laugh. "Rudy hasn't made that decision about me, yet." He pointed down the walk toward my old room. "Let's go."

Before the guard closed the door, plunging the room into darkness again, a quick look around showed me a small rectangular alcove carved out of solid rock. In the darkness, I felt along the walls finding nothing but moon dust. The stuff was everywhere. Gray, fine and adhesive, the powder seemed to be in everything. Stock joke earthside: Moon miners get gray-lung.

The joke had come back with the original miners that operated the first experimental mines on Luna. But that was before the Plague and before the miners had been replaced by thousands of carriers sentenced to Luna to separate them from the rest of the population. At first, the press had called Luna the new Molokai, then simply the leper colony: one hundred and forty thousand carriers of a novel lifeform product of late 1980's recombinant DNA research known as "Megabug." They were guarded and managed by five thousand immunes, or "munies." For three generations, the leper colony had mined the mountains between Imbrium and Serenitatis, feeding the seven mass drivers that provided raw materials for the New Eden industrial station, which, in turn, fed products to Earth. But, the carriers wanted to come back, and Terranism was born.

I put my back against the wall and slid down to a sitting position. Rubbing my wrists, I thought back to my meeting with Vegler and Raymond. Why was I still alive? The Terranists had claimed responsibility for bombing the shuttle to El Five from Luna, a disaster that claimed the lives of fifteen young children among many others. Why would they spare my life simply because I'm innocent?

Voices again, outside the door. What use did they plan to

make of me? I was no safe voice, but I certainly had no sympathy for the Terranists. The door unlatched, then opened, exposing Ahmis the guard. "Let's go, laddie."

"Where?" I pushed myself to my feet.

"It's time to fit you with some walking gear. Looks as though you'll be with us for a while."

Endless hours later, clad in scavenged surface gear, a wide red band sprayed around my chest, I followed the doctor who patched up my head through a wide, low gallery lit by a single string of dim green light bars. Even without being bound, I found movement difficult. To move forward in the clumsy gear, I had to lean forward as though I were trying to walk through a gale-force storm. To stop, I had to lean backwards and dig in. It took a few drifts to the floor of the gallery to polish my technique. The effort of getting back to my feet, as well as the strain of the bouncy pace we kept, soon mixed the acrid smell of the moon dust in the suit with my sweat, and the leftover smells of the previous occupant. Since my suit's radio had been removed, the only sounds I could hear were the circulation motor and my own breathing.

Ahead of the doctor, a string of Terranists made their way to the open end of the gallery. It opened on the dark side of the mountain, but sunlight from the slope opposite the entrance hurt my eyes. Behind, my faithful keeper Ahmis kept a close watch on me. He had chuckled as he showed me how to patch the holes in the suit's plastic lining with crosses of plastic tape. I had asked the cause of his humor, and he pointed out, in detail, how the suit was obtained from its previous occupant.

While she cleaned my wound and covered it with plasti-skin, the doctor had remained silent. She bounced along in front of me, and came to a halt at the gallery entrance. Leaning backward and digging in, I managed not to run into her. Ahmis pulled up beside me and we could see a figure in front, outside the entrance, giving hand signals. In a few moments, the doctor started off and Ahmis and I followed. Behind us were, perhaps, ten others.

Outside the gallery, I saw that we were on one of the old access roads. The old mounting braces for the ore-belt support could be seen every few meters, which meant that we were still in the Caucasus. Far in front, a six-wheeled ore extractor turned right off the road and headed down a large gully. Those in front turned and followed after. As we walked out of the mountain's shadow, I saw the rim of Calippus. It had to be. Calippus was the largest crater near the ore belt system, which meant we were far north of Bee Town. An hour or more later, we reached the end of the gully and gathered again. As I looked around, I could see thirty-two in surface suits. One of them mounted the ore extractor and entered the airlock. Soon after, the figure emerged and the extractor turned right again and headed off across the low rolling hills toward the darkness of the higher Caucasus west of Calippus. Those of us on foot turned left and headed south.

As my suit struggled to keep out the blistering heat, I began feeling dizzy. I kept up, but before I realized what was happening, the doctor had fallen back beside me and had plugged a black cord from her helmet into mine.

"How do you feel, Lambert?"

I laughed. "After getting my head beat in with rifle stocks, how do you expect me to feel?"

"Are you dizzy; a little sick to your stomach?"

"Yes."

She held up her hand and Ahmis stopped next to us. She pulled the air coupling from my pack and inserted it into a cup she pulled from a pouch at her belt. I could feel that no air was entering my system, and began to panic, but she soon plugged the coupling back in and my nostrils were assaulted with a new odor: something like rotted leaves mixed with some kind of commercial hand cream. "The feeling should be gone in an hour or so." She pulled the cord from my helmet and wound it up and attached it to her own. As she turned and followed the others, Ahmis tapped my shoulder and pointed after her. I leaned forward and followed.

I looked from the black sky to the Earth hanging huge over the horizon and wondered what purpose I was serving. One bouncing foot in front of the other, each one lifting that gray dust that settled quickly to the surface again. As I reached a slight rise I could see wheel prints in the dust extending off toward the golden tan horizon. We followed the tracks for another hour or two until we reached the end of another abandoned access road. At that point, my dizziness had cleared up, but the effort of walking with mostly unfamiliar muscles had my legs aching. Hand signals went up for a halt, and I turned to see how our passage had marked the Lunar surface, but no tracks could be seen. At the end of the column two figures with what looked like hockey sticks were erasing the evidence. The column moved again, then walked into the shadow of a cliff and stopped.

The doctor turned and connected the cord from her helmet to mine. "Is the dizziness gone?"

"Yes." She reached up her hand to pull the plug.

"Wait. As long as we're stopped, could we talk for a while?"

"Why?"

"I'd like to ask a few questions." She reached up again to pull the cord. "Look, if you people want your side reported, you're going to have to talk to me."

She hesitated, then dropped her hand. "What do you want to know?"

I sighed, grateful to have someone to talk to. "Well, to begin, what's your name, Doctor?"

"Kit."

"Kit what?"

"You'll find most of us use single names, usually adopted. We still have families in the pits." Her voice came through the speaker cold and brittle.

"What about Rudy Vegler?"

"The lockwatchers killed his family when he was just a boy, right after he joined the Terranist League."

"Why are you a Terranist?"

She gave a sharp laugh. "The same as everyone else, Lambert: to go back to Earth." She reached up, pulled the plug and turned away. More hand signals from up front, and the column moved out.

As we bounced down the road past dark, abandoned mine entrances, I thought of the Terranist goals and could almost understand. The novelty of being on Earth's moon wore off tense hours ago, and seeing that blue-white globe hanging above the bleak, gray, airless mountains made me long for fresh air, trees, and water. To be able to stretch my naked arms in the sunlight, to splash into a clear pool, even to scratch when I felt like it, had become luxuries beyond price. It would seem even dearer to those who had never been to Earth, and the band of cutthroats I'd seen were at least third, possibly fourth-generation carriers. But, they were carriers, and could never come home to Earth. The Terranists had no sympathy on Earth; to let them back on the planet meant certain death for at least four-fifths of the human race. I looked at the Great Lakes and took a sip of warm, tasteless water through the tube in my helmet.

As the column reached a sharp turn in the old access road, hand signals went up and we fled off the road back into the shadows. I looked up and saw a formation of four police fighters streak toward Calippus. We waited for a few moments, then were motioned back on the road. Ahead, five-wheeled vehicles turned right off the main road onto a track that led straight into the mountain. As I came abreast of the feeder road and turned, I saw it enter the opening of one of the countless abandoned mine shafts that dotted the base of the mountain.

Inside the shaft, we came to a gallery-wide airlock and stepped in, leaving the vehicles outside. After a few moments, I could feel the pressure of the chamber equalizing the pressure of my suit. Vegler, Ahmis, and the others removed their helmets, and I fooled with the lock on mine until it opened, allowing me to push my helmet back. Ahmis reached out a beefy hand and shut down my suit's systems.

Vegler turned to me. "All the gear we picked up at the news conference will be brought in. Identify yours and bring it with you. Ahmis will show you the way."

"Would it be a breach of security to ask why?"

"You're about to do your first story from the leper colony; that's what you're here for, isn't it?"

I ground my teeth a little—the ones that remained. "I said I'm not here to do puff pieces for the Terranist League. What makes you think I will?"

"Two things: First, it doesn't matter whether you approve or not, the Terranists exist and they are news. Or are you one of those safe voices you mentioned?"

"No." What could I do but agree; he was right. "What was the second thing?"

Vegler grinned. "With your mouth shut, you're no use to your station, the munies, or to us. You may as well be skinny-dipping in the moon dust."

I nodded. Both points were well taken.

Loaded with my equipemnt, Ahmis and I followed Vegler and three other Terranists through the dark shafts until we came to a section illuminated with light bars. The greenish light, dim and flickering, mixed with mournful, wailing voices. It took a moment to realize it was singing. We moved around a slight turn in the shaft and were waved on by a red-banded figure in the distance. Where the sentry stood, the shaft seemed to narrow to a single passageway almost two meters wide, but as we came closer, I saw that the gallery walls had been filled in with rough-cut blocks.

I entered the passage behind Vegler and saw that the gallery had been divided into rooms, and in the rooms were people. Only a few steps into the mine shaft town, the smell of the ever present moon dust was overpowered by the smells of unwashed bodies, urine, and burnt grease. A very old woman, her legs missing from the knees down, sat in the passageway and reached out a hand toward Vegler as he passed. The Terranist stopped, squatted, and touched the old woman's cheek with the palm of his hand. She took his hand in hers, kissed it, then released it. Vegler watched as she nodded, smiled, and pulled herself into a dark doorway. He looked down at the dusty floor for a second, then stood and looked at me.

I pointed toward the dark doorway. "What was that, a Terranist groupie?" Vegler backhanded me across my face with the armored glove of his surface suit, sending me sprawling into Ahmis, then onto the floor. He turned and stormed off. Ahmis grabbed my shoulder and pulled me to my feet. "What is she, his mother?"

Ahmis reached down and picked up my equipment, dumping it into my arms. "No. She's just an old woman."

"What happened to her legs?"

"Mine accident, like a lot of old people here."

A bit weavy on my feet, I stumbled off after Vegler. There were many dark doorways, and many old faces. The deeper we got into the area, the stronger became the smells. Ahead, Vegler turned into one of the doorways. Before entering, I stopped and faced Ahmis. "What is this place?"

"This is where you go when you're too old to work the mines. We call it the boneyard."

Ahmis pointed at the doorway, and I turned and entered. The dark room looked and smelled like all the others. Its single difference was a false wall where the hard rock of the gallery should have been. Ahmis nodded toward it, and I stepped through into a black, narrow hall. Feeling along the rough walls with my fingertips, I made a turn and saw white light ahead. A few steps further and I entered a smooth-walled white chamber with a low ceiling set with yellowish-white light panels. Along the far wall stood racks of weapons. On either side of the racks were closed doors and immediately in front of me were several metal chairs and a table. Vegler stood with his back toward me talking to Kit and a frail old fellow dressed in coveralls. It took a moment, but I finally made the face. It was Charles Towne, the molecular biologist stationed with the Luna Immune contingent, kidnapped by the Terranists four years earlier and presumed dead.

Vegler cocked his head in my direction. "Towne, this is Lambert, the reporter I told you about."

Towne's watery blue eyes darted at me, then back to Vegler. "If I cooperate, then you'll release me?"

"We'll see." Vegler looked at me. "This is your show; how do you want to work it?"

I shrugged, then looked down around the room. "I'll set my stuff up, then we'll just sit down and talk.... Will we be going someplace other than this room?"

"Perhaps."

"Then I may need someone to work the camera in transit."

Vegler scratched his chin and looked at Ahmis standing next to me. The Terranist guard had his arms loaded with gear. "You feel like a camera jock, Ahmis?"

The guard grinned. "Sure, Rudy." Ahmis lowered the gear to the floor, removed the gloves to his surface suit and rubbed his hands together. "Where do we start, laddie?"

I raised an eyebrow at Vegler. He smiled and sat in one of the metal chairs. "Whenever you're ready, Lambert."

Hours later, I sat in the room staring at the five centimeter screen of my editor, trying to shake off the feeling that more had gone on at the interview than I had gotten on tape. I skipped over some experimenting Ahmis had done with the camera's zoom lens, checked the index and stopped, backed, then stopped again. I pushed the playback and watched a miniature representation of Charles Towne rub his nose, then fold his arms.

"The Lunar Genetic Center was established in '91, immediately after the contained carrier population had been removed to the moon. The original purpose of the center was, in effect, to find a cure for the carriers."

Lambert: "You said 'original purpose.' The purpose changed then?"

Towne squirmed, looked off screen, then looked back at Lambert and nodded. "It was when the New Eden station at El Five was just beginning construction—before my time."

Lambert: "About 2005."

Towne: "Yes. Well, you see the Center had been examining both carriers and immunes on Luna on a regular basis. The nucleotide sequence that gave immunity to the so-called megabug had been identified. But, another thing was beginning to make itself evident: The particular strain of *E. coli* that carried the recombined plasmids that were found to be pathogenic—"

Lambert: "The megabug."

Towne: "Yes. Well, the frequency of occurrence appeared to diminish as time passed. Samples on record show—"

Lambert: "You mean the bug was dying out?"

Towne: "It did die out. No traces have been found since 2008."

Lambert: "You mean that the carrier population has been free of the diease since '08? They could be returned to Earth with no harmful effects?"

Towne nodded. "That's when the Center's purpose changed. By then, Luna had four mass drivers and the New Eden station was beginning to supply products to Earth. The mass drivers had to be fed, and it was decided to keep the news secret until they could be sure. All information concerning the so-called plague was collected and filed at the Center."

Lambert: "And?"

Towne: "And that's where the situation stands today, sixty years later."

Vegler: "Except that now there are seven mass drivers to feed." The picture moved until Vegler's head filled the tiny screen.

Lambert: "What you're saying, then, is that the carrier population—actually, its descendants—are being used as . . . as . . ."

Vegler: "'Slaves' is the word you're looking for."

Lambert: "For what possible reason?"

Vegler: "The original miners on Luna were well paid and their quarters and facilities were extravagant. You've seen Bee Town?"

Lambert: "Yes."

Vegler: "That was the original settlement, but now the immunes live there. The immunes pay us in food and minimal living conditions. They literally control the air we breathe. You've seen how we live; it's cheaper."

I pushed the stop and looked at Vegler's frozen face. If true, that would explain what the United States of Earth had to hide on Luna. But how much of Towne's statement could be trusted? Towne and Kit had taken me into another room, crammed with equipment and wire files. They showed me slides, documents, records, and other things the Terranists had snatched at the Center when they kidnapped Towne.

But I couldn't judge what I'd seen. All of us had guns stuck in our ears. Even so, just finding Charles Towne alive would make the story, not to mention the follow-up potential in a story on carrier living conditions. If it was true that the bug had died, so much the better. It would be the cover-up of the century. Just thinking of the number of high officials and different administrations that must have been involved to pull it off made my mouth water. It was true; no one on Earth would lift a finger to help the carriers, even if the bug had died out sixty years before.

I went fast forward until I saw Vegler stabbing his finger

at the air, then hit the play. ". . . like the Indians on the old reservations. They don't ask why they wound up on the reservations; all they can think of is that the government has been paying their upkeep. Why, then, should anyone give them back their land? That's what they think of us now. A planetoid full of welfare bums; why should we let them back on Earth? We do that, and the next thing you know, they'll want their properties back."

Lambert: "Will terrorism turn that indifference into sympathy?"

Vegler shook his head. "No. But we're not looking for sympathy."

Lambert: "What, then?"

Vegler: "Action."

Lambert: "You are, of course, aware that the few Terranist apologists on Earth have made the claim that the present containment of carriers is based on a hoax. It's regarded as nothing but Terranist propaganda."

Vegler: "Those pictures in your school books, the streets choked with black, rotting corpses, won't be countered by words alone. Before, you asked what we hoped to accomplish by bombing the shuttle to El Five. It's simple. We're giving them new pictures of horror to counter the old. If we make them horrible enough, we'll get the action we seek—"

I hit the stop. But then, if words won't do it, why go to all the trouble of keeping me alive to conduct an interview? That's what was bothering me. The edited tape loop had been packed in the shielded case, and the case given to a party to put in one of the mass drivers. They could just ditch the case, but what would be the point? They could have accomplished the same thing just by killing me at the news conference. I feather-touched the back button and hit the play.

". . . new pictures of horror to counter the old. If we make them horrible enough . . ." I hit the stop, ejected the tape and picked the first tape off the table, feeling sick to my stomach. I hit the fast forward and watched the miniature figures jerk about until the one named Kit sat still for a moment, looking at the one called Mark Lambert. Stop. Back. Play.

Lambert: ". . . seems to me, that with the training and equipment you and Towne needed to do the checks on the carriers, and to understand all this, you ought to be able to do your own recombinant DNA work."

Kit: "Such as?"

Lambert: "Well, on Earth the research has many applications in food production, medicines—things that could improve conditions up here."

Kit looked at Towne, then leveled her eyes at Lambert, a hint of a smile on her lips. "We've done a little of that, yes. . . . " I hit the stop and turned off the editor.

I just bet they'd done a little of that. ". . . new pictures of horror . . . " The tape container would be picked up from the dirt track, taken to the New Eden station and opened, releasing . . . what? Two and a half million men, women, and children were at New Eden. I felt my skin prickle as I realized that cargo and passenger shuttles to Earth left New Eden in a steady stream. The Earth . . .

Kit entered the room from the door to the right of the rifle racks, looked at my face and smiled. "It looks like you figured it out." She raised a rifle and pointed it at me. All I could do was sit there with my mouth hanging open. I looked at the floor and examined the equipment there. The signal coder by which I would know when the pickup had been accomplished was gone. If I had it, I could signal the pickup ship to abort. I looked at Kit. "Rudy has it."

"Where is he? You don't understand; I've got to stop him!"

She laughed. "If I wouldn't understand, who would?"

"You don't know what you're doing!"

She waved the muzzle of her rifle at me. "Stay seated and stay alive, Lambert—"

Before she could finish, I reached under the table and turned it over on her. The edge of the table deflected her rifle toward the ceiling. She fired, the rifle's blinding white beam blowing rocks and rock powder down on both of us. Without stopping, I ran across the overturned table, then kicked her in the side of the head. I picked up the rifle and a helmet sitting on one of the chairs. I seated the helmet in place as I headed toward the door, wondering why the helmet locks were so easy to work. I had taken my gloves off to work the editor.

I went back for them, clipped them into the suit's cuffs

and bounced down the dark passage, turned and came to the false wall. It was a sliding slab of rock, perhaps as thick as ten centimeters. I could see a crack of light along one edge, but couldn't find a lock. I pushed on the slab, trying to move it, but it didn't even shake.

Unslinging the rifle, I aimed it at the crack and fired. The slab shattered diagonally, opening the upper part of the entrance. Ahmis' surprised face stared back at me. Jumping through the opening, I slammed the stock of my rifle into his face and ran over him into the passage. Faces up and down the passage were sticking out of dark doorways.

I turned left and bounced back the way I had been led in. Where the shaft opened, I looked for the guard, but he was gone. I stepped out into the open part and a rifle bolt flashed over my head from behind me. I turned and saw Ahmis, blood running from his nose, bounding down the passage. I lifted my rifle, but there were too many others in the passage behind him. I turned and ran, stopping when I reached the slight turn in the shaft. As Ahmis came through the opening, I fired several times, filling the shaft at his end with moon dust.

I knew I had missed him as I turned and bounded off into the unlit shaft ahead. In moments, I was at the large airlock. I checked my suit's systems, closed the face plate, opened the door and stepped in. At the other end of the lock, I felt for the valve set in the door, found it and turned it wide open. In a few moments my suit was tight and I undogged the outside door and opened it. It was weighted to close automatically behind me to make the cell operational for the next person wanting out. Since the next person was going to be Ahmis, I picked up a fist-sized stone and jammed it in the closing door. It held.

One of the wheeled vehicles along the side of the gallery was missing. I climbed up on the next and lowered myself into the tubular frame driver's seat and studied the few controls. It was a simple cargo rover with little more than a charge indicator, throttle, brake, and steering wheel. I moved the throttle to the reverse position and the rover jerked to life and swayed out of the shaft entrance. The road was wide at the entrance and I backed around, turned the wire mesh wheels downhill, and gave it forward throttle.

In moments I reached the main access road, then stopped, wondering where to go next. To the left I knew the road just ended, but Vegler and company might have gone that way to avoid the security police. But, however they went, they'd have to wind up at the mass drivers, and that's where the old ore belt access roads went. I turned right and gave the rover full throttle forward.

The road went straight, until it ran into a tee where two old ore belt routes joined. The mass drivers were south of Calippus. I turned right, held on for dear life around a curve and stopped just in time to miss an ore extractor making its way across the road. Behind it, raised on metal frame supports every few meters, was the beginning of the ore belt system in use. From the mountain rising to my right, smaller belts led from gallery entrances to dump their loads onto the main belt.

I swung around the ore extractor and followed the access road in and out of the forest of ore belt supports. To my left, the emptiness of Serenitatis made me stop and think. As the rover came to a halt, I tried to visualize the layout of the mass drivers and ore belt system. The drivers were at the edge of the *mare*, directly south of the eastern Caucasus, which is where I had to be if I could see Serenitatis. When the road turned to the right to follow the line of the mountains, I turned off the road and continued south.

In minutes I was lost. All landmarks had dropped below the short horizon and my only directional aids were the rover tracks stretching out behind me. Although not much help to me, they would be invaluable to Ahmis as he rolled down the access road and saw the tracks running off across Serenitatis pointing a big red arrow at my back. I leaned forward to put full throttle to the rover, but found it already at maximum. The charge indicator showed negative, and in bright sunlight. I pulled up, stood and stepped on the seat to check the solar cell panel. There must have been a centimeter of moon dust on it. I brushed off what I could with my arm and turned to step down off the seat. In the distance a flash of silver followed by another announced the mass driver complex.

I quickly checked back the way I had come, but Ahmis was nowhere in sight. My stunt at the airlock must have worked. I dropped into the seat, hit the throttle, and headed toward where I remembered the glint of silver. The charge indicator was still negative, but less so. In a moment, it didn't matter.

As I reached a slight rise, the kilometers of gleaming bars and whizzing buckets of the mass driver complex stretched out right to left, from horizon to horizon. The buckets scooped up a load at the slow end dump, then were propelled by synchronized magnetic pulses along the length of the tracks until they reached escape velocity. At the fast end, the buckets opened, shooting the compacted ore into the dirt track orbit where the catcher station gathered it up. The buckets were decelerated and returned to the slow end for another pickup. The buckets I could see were slowing them from left to right, and I turned right toward the slow end.

The rover lurched and bounced around a small, house-sized crater, then up a steep hill. From the crest I could see the cargo rover Vegler and his group had taken next to three rovers mounted with environmental support vans bearing the insignia of the security police. Behind them rose the long, tapered bin of the dump being fed by two huge ore trunk belts. A flash from one of the police rovers kicked up the dust in front of me and I turned left and headed for the dark safety of the spaces underneath the mass driver tracks. More flashes and it seemed as though I was caught in a dust storm. The dust cleared, and I realized the rover wasn't moving. The two wire mesh tires on the right side looked like aluminum spaghetti. I jumped off the left side and bounded for the driver tracks.

As I approached the tracks, bringing my attention with me in the form of police fire, answering fire aimed at the police vans began coming from under the tracks. A red-banded figure stood out from behind a support and waved me on. When I was within five meters of the shadows, I was lifted from behind, slammed into one of the inside track supports, then buried in moon dust.

My head swam and I drifted in and out of consciousness as I felt hands digging me out. My body felt like a sack of broken glass. Gloved fingers wiping the dust off my face plate; Vegler's face looking back at me. He pulled a black cord from his helmet and plugged it into mine.

"Lambert?"

"You monster," I hissed. "Where is the case?"

A beam flashed behind Vegler's helmet, but he didn't seem to notice. "It's gone. Who told you, or did you figure it out?"

"Does it make a difference?"

"Lambert, the lockwatchers will be on us in a few seconds. You answer me now, or I'll fry a hole through your head."

"That seems to be the Terranist answer to everything; can't get an answer, fry a hole in somebody's head. Can't go back to Earth, wipe out the damned human race—"

"Shut up and listen. What's in that case is something that will make megabug look like a case of diaper rash by comparison—"

"That should get some attention, Vegler—"

"You're damned right it will! But there's something else. The bug Kit and Doc Towne cooked up takes from two to four months to kill, and no one on Earth knows a cure for it. Even if they did, it would take them two or three months to begin production—"

"My god, Vegler . . ."

"Listen. We have a cure; another organism that can compete successfully with the first. We have enough of it stashed away in abandoned mine shafts right now to immunize everyone on Earth. When we go back to Earth, we'll bring it with us."

"Blackmail."

"Yes. You have a better solution?"

"Why are you telling me this?"

"Lambert, we need time—eight or ten days for the organism to spread. If they know what's going on, they'll be able to contain it at the New Eden station . . ."

I laughed, then stopped as I felt the loose ends of a couple of ribs grind together. "What is it, Vegler? You want me to keep my mouth shut, is that it?"

"Yes."

"Why don't you just shut it?"

Vegler seemed to have the same look on his face that he had when he touched the old woman's cheek back in the boneyard. "I don't want to kill you, Lambert. Someday, when it's a time for law again, we'll need people with your naïve abhorrence of violence."

"How do you expect me to keep quiet? My god, even if they do finally agree, you know how long that would take? You know how slow governments work."

"Why should we be the only ones who have to pay for the government's inertia?"

Breathing came very hard. Someone ran by Vegler and tapped him on the helmet as he passed. "Vegler, how do I know you have a cure . . . ?" Pieces of rock showered down on us. The lockwatchers were closing in. "Kit—" Vegler teetered, then fell over on top of me. "On the road—" A loud ringing in my helmet, we were both lifted up, then slammed hard.

I opened my eyes, the memory of rotted leaves and hand cream still in my nostrils. I felt ill and Kit had taken my air hose . . . But, was that proof? The white haze in front of my eyes swam, then shaped itself into a face. "Lambert?"

"Who are you?" I whispered.

The face turned. "Captain, I think he can talk now."

The first face left and another took its place. "I'm Captain Manion, Lambert. It's a real stroke you made it alive. The Terranists usually aren't that careless."

"Manion? Are you with the police?"

"Yes. I hate to question you now, but I have no other choice. What were they doing at the mass drivers? They know that if they mess with the drivers, we'll cut off the air to one of the residential galleries."

"Cut the air off?"

"Yes. It sounds harsh, but we have to protect the drivers. Both Earth and the New Eden station depend on them." Manion must have seen the look on my face. "We wouldn't do it to production workers or anything vital; just one of the boneyards. You know, they're only carriers." He turned away and came back holding a small red plastic box. It was the signal coder and the pick-up light was still off. The case was still in the dirt track. "You know what this is?"

I looked at the ten numbered keys. All I had to do was punch in four-four-three and the pick-up would be aborted. That's all. "I don't know, Captain. It looks like a pocket calculator."

Manion raised his eyebrows and shrugged, then turned to the other one. "All right, Doctor, you can have him back." He left the compartment. It lurched; we were in a police van.

The doctor's face swam into view. "Sorry we can't get you back to Earth right away, Lambert, but you're pretty banged up. We'll probably keep you for two weeks or so."

I closed my eyes. "That should be time enough."

"Enough for what?"

I opened my eyes and looked at the doctor. "The Terranists are planning an announcement about then."

"Oh?" The doctor peered at a plastic sack filled with clear liquid that drained from a tube into my arm. "More demands?"

I bit my lip and closed my eyes to force back the tears. "It's a surprise." Vegler at the interview: *"There are no innocents, Lambert. If because you do nothing, nothing is done, you are guilty. There is a time for terror. Perhaps you will come to understand this...."* I laughed.

"Where's Rudy Vegler?"

The doctor nodded toward the back of the compartment. Stacked like cordwood, the five Terranists, still in their torn, filthy, blood-caked surface suits, jiggled with the motion of the police rover across the Lunar landscape. On the bottom, nearest me, Rudy Vegler stared at me through a shattered faceplate with empty sockets. His skin was purple—almost black. "We got all of them."

I looked back at the doctor. "Not all. There's still a few left."

The doctor shrugged. "Ten or fifteen?" Might as well be all. How can a dozen fanatics fight the entire world?" The doctor patted my arm, turned and left the compartment.

"As I said, Doctor, it's a surprise." My voice sounded tinny in the empty compartment. The tears began to flow freely and I turned my head toward the pile of dead Terranists.

"Damn you. Damn you, damn you, damn you!"

The telephone rang. I put aside important work to answer.

"What about intelligent dinosaurs from Earth's past that show up in the present to reclaim their planet?"

"Hi George." It was Scithers. Again I pondered that I could go for twenty years without being asked a question like that if I was in aluminum siding.

There were some new findings related to dinosaurs, and new theories to accompany them. The newly discovered Dromeosauris had a much larger brain in relation to body weight than any dinosaur previously discovered. And, so the theory went, it was possible that the dinosaurs weren't reptiles at all but were warm-blooded. Also much evidence that either a supernova or a planetoid impact with Earth coincided with the disappearance of the dinosaurs. What if they saw it coming and made tracks for safer parts? He'd send me what he had on the critters.

George was on a roll.

He seemed to be leaning in favor of time travel as the vehicle in which said critters show up in the present. "Collector's Item" notwithstanding, I am not a fan of time travel stories. I have found very few of them that have been convincing. Well, I told George that I'd see what I could come up with. Then it was time to hit the books and learn about dinosaurs and what things were like back in the good old days. By the time I was finished with this piece, I knew a lot more about that time period and dinosaurs than I wanted to know. Something must have clicked somewhere, however. After it was published in Asimov's *"The Homecoming" was nominated for a Hugo.*

The Homecoming

Lothas draped his heavy green tail between the seat cushion and the backrest. Extending a claw on a scaled, five-fingered hand, he inserted it in a slotswitch and pulled down. The armored shield on the forward view bubble slowly lifted as the control center went to redlight. Lothas felt the strange pain grow in his chest as he looked through the filter at the target star, now no longer a point of light but a tiny, brilliant disc. He leaned against the backrest, his large dark eyes glittering as they drank in the sight of the star.

It has been so long. Even though I have been out of suspension for only a total of six star cycles, yet I still know it has been . . . seventy million star cycles. A third of a galactic cycle.

Lothas noticed his own reflection in the filter, turned his long neck left, then right, and marveled at the absence of change. The large eyes, occupying a fifth of the image, were clear and glinted with points of red, blue, and yellow light reflected from service and indicator lights. The skin, gray-green and smooth, pressed against and outlined the large veins leading from his eyes down the elongated muzzle, with its rows of thick, white, needle-sharp teeth. His focus returned to the star as he reached and pressed a panel with one of the five clawed fingers of his right hand.

"This is Lothas Dim Ir, on regular watch." He paused and

examined the navigation readout, then switched to a display of the rest of the cluster formation of ships. "The formation is normal; no course corrections necessary; the homestar Amasaat now at—" he examined an instrument "—four degrees of arc."

He pressed another panel, signaling to all the watches on the rest of the ships. The display showed all but three of the two hundred ships answering. Lothas studied the display, slightly confused that he felt nothing about the missing ships. Automatic recording systems had shown the three ships wrecked by the same meteor.

But that was . . . millions of cycles ago. Difficult to feel pain for deaths that old.

He pressed another panel, and the display began filling with life unit survival-percentage figures transmitted by the watches on the other ships. Automatically an average was made and a total rate of survival and unit count was made. 77.031 percent; 308,124 life units surviving. Lothas nodded. There had been no change in the figure for . . . over thirty million star cycles. The three wrecked ships, and the others who could not survive the suspension process.

But, the rest of us shall see Nitola.

Lothas looked around at the empty control center. Moments after he gave the initiate-desuspension command, the center would be a hive of activity. . . . *a hive of activity; I wonder if the little stinging sweetsects have survived?* He looked at the banks of receiving equipment, sensor and analysis piles, and the rest of the tools that the knowing ones would use to see how Nitola had changed.

But, this moment there is still quiet—this wondrous, jeweled loneliness of space. I ache for my home planet, but this, too, has become my home.

He reached out a claw and closed the shield, cutting off his view of the homestar. As the center returned to yellow light, Lothas pressed the initiate-desuspension command. As the ships answered, he listened to the sounds of life stirring in his own vessel—motors whined, draining the clear suspension from countless lengths of veins and replacing it with warm blood. Lothas looked at the drain set into the skin of his own arm. He pulled it free and watched as the blood pooled slightly, then began clotting. He tossed the drain into a recycler.

We will need them no longer. We are almost home.

Carl Baxter, garbed in regulation briefs and tee shirt, looked up from under the bed. "Where are my socks?"

The lump on the bed, sheets pulled up over her head, mumbled. "I don't wear 'em."

"It's my last pair of clean socks. Now, where are they?"

The lump pulled the sheets down, exposing a sleep-mussed tousle of black curls framing a pretty, if angry, face. "You'd have clean socks if you'd do the laundry more often. We both work. There's no reason why I have to be the—"

"Yeah, yeah, yeah." Baxter pulled out the dresser and looked behind it.

"Yeah, yeah, is it?"

"Yeah." He pushed the dresser back against the wall. "Look, it's not like we had the same kind of job, Deb. I have to be at the base at oh-six-thirty six days a week, and sometimes seven. I'm lucky if I can drag it home in time for Johnny Carson. And, you want me to pitch in with the laundry, grocery shopping, housecleaning—"

"Look, supersoldier!" Deb pushed her hair from her eyes. "You think keeping the agency going by myself is easy? Just last week that idiot layout man you hired before you were called up totally feebed the Boxman Spring campaign. I've been putting in sixteen hour days to try and have it ready in time! You want laundry on top of that?"

Baxter concluded his third survey of the dresser drawers by slamming the upper right. "Why don't you hire some help? We can afford it."

Deb's eyes widened. "Yawl means dat Massa Baxter gonna let dis nappy ol' head actually hire someone? Me, a *woman!*"

"Oh, knock it off!" Baxter frowned and sat on the bed. He put a hand on Deb's shoulder. "Look, I'm sorry, Deb. I know I said no hiring until I got back, and I know it's been tough on you. Go ahead and hire whatever you need in the way of help. I'll give Boxman a call and try and straighten things out."

Deb put her hand on Baxter's and looked up into his eyes.

"Carl, when is the Air Force going to be finished with you? This whole thing is so silly. One day we are running a successful advertising agency and living in a nice condo, and the next we're stuck here in the middle of nowhere in a shack that hasn't been repaired since Billy Mitchell was a P.F.C. Tell me there's a light at the end of the tunnel."

Baxter shrugged. "I don't know." He raised his head and looked at her. "That trip to Santa Barbara every day is getting you down, isn't it? Maybe you'd be happier if you stayed at home?"

"Look, Baxter, I'll stick it out as long as you do, and how much longer can that be? Your six months is almost up, isn't it?"

Baxter stood up and resumed his search for the missing pair of socks. "You think I might have left them in the living room?"

Deb's face developed an instant frown. "Isn't it?"

"Isn't what?"

She shook her head and pounded on the mattress with her fists. "Oh, no! You didn't! Tell me you didn't get extended, Baxter! Tell me you didn't, or I'll brain you with the alarm clock."

He sighed, shrugged, scratched his head, then held out his hands. "I didn't have any choice, Deb—"

"Oooooooooo! You . . . you . . . monster!" She threw off the covers, swung her legs to the floor, then stormed off to the bathroom. The door slammed, then clicked.

"Deb?" Baxter walked to the door. "Deb, honey? Don't lock yourself in, honey. I still have to shave."

"Go away."

"Deb, I'm all they have in public relations right now to promote the Air Force's argument for the combined shuttle, not to mention the new bomber, and the—"

The door opened, a pair of socks flew out, and the door slammed shut.

Wearing one regulation blue and one not-so-regulation yellow and red Argyle sock in addition to his uniform, Captain Carl F. Baxter pulled away in the blue staff car assigned to him. He came to the cross-street stop sign, screeched to a halt, and rummaged through the glove compartment for his electric shaver. A honk came from behind, and Baxter looked over the top of the headrest to check the honker's rank. Seeing only single golden bars, he returned to his search. *Damned thing has got to be in here.*

His hand closed on the ancient Remington, a gift from his mother-in-law, and he sat up and removed the cap. The driver behind honked again, and Baxter extended a finger in the Hawaiian good luck tradition, then returned to the shaver. With an angry squeal of tires, the lieutenant pulled around Baxter's car, ignored the stop sign, and pulled out onto the base's main drag. With his shaver humming, Baxter pulled out and turned right.

Baxter caught a flash of a sign, "ODQ-D7," recalling Deb's comment when she first saw it. "This is our new home? Oh, I like the name; it's so much nicer than Hollywood Hills or Sutton Place." He snorted and leaned on the accelerator as he came abreast of the parking ramp for the experimental aircraft. Deb was ready with a comment for that, too. "Oh, what a nice view—Baxter, I want a divorce!" She didn't really, but she was not happy, and neither was Baxter. An experienced test pilot, he had left the Air Force during the testing cutbacks of the late sixties to begin his own advertising agency. As a reserve officer, he had assumed that, if he ever was called up, it would be as a pilot. But, the Air Force had found his advertising skills much more desirable, and dropped him in public relations. Baxter glanced out of the side window at the black, needle-pointed craft on the ramp being readied for a test. *Dammit, it is a beautiful view!*

He turned back to his driving and concentrated on missing the larger pieces of traffic. The Congressional delegation would show up in two days, and the presentation on the combined shuttle was still in search of a theme—or at least a theme less obvious than "Gimmie bucks!"

Then, there was still the planning board in town to deal with. The proposed recruiting facility violated the town's zoning ordinances, and it was feather-smoothing time. Even though Federal departments aren't obligated to be governed by local zoning regulations, bad press is still bad press. The theme: cram the new facility down their throats, but in a manner that makes it look like the Air Force is doing the town a big favor.

The Concerned Women from town still had to have a number done on them. In the office, the group was known as the Anti-Slop Chute and Whorehouse League. The dear ladies objected to men from the base supplying a market in town for the growing number of bars and ladies of negotiable virtue. Theme?

Perhaps we could have all the men castrated, ladies. How would that be? Baxter chuckled, then resumed his sober expression as he remembered the school board *had* to be dealt with. The screams over supporting the educations of the base's dependent children were getting loud, and the charge that a group of Air Force brats had introduced pot to their playmates was no help . . . "Ah, nuts!"

Baxter drove it all from his mind as he pulled up to the guard shack at the security gate. An AP, three times larger than life, with a jaw the size, shape, and color of a cinder block, saluted and bent down to the car's window. "Captain Baxter?"

Baxter nodded. "Yes, I'm Baxter."

"Carl F.?"

"That's right."

The AP opened the door and motioned with his hand. "Please slide over, sir."

"What?"

"I'm supposed to drive you to a security area, Captain. Please, slide over."

Baxter reached for the door and tried to pull it shut. The AP's grip on the door might as well have been a ton of reinforced concrete. Baxter looked into the guard shack and saw Wilson, one of the regular AP's on the gate. "Wilson, will you call off this trained gorilla? I have a lot of work to do today, and no time to fool around."

Wilson stood in the doorway and shrugged. "I'm sorry, Captain, but Inovsky has his orders."

Baxter looked at the gorilla. "Inovsky, huh?"

"Yes, sir."

"You sure you got the right Air Force, Inovsky?"

The AP unsnapped the cover on his holster. "Please, Captain Baxter. Slide over."

Baxter shrugged and put the car in park. "Sure. Why not?" He slid over and watched as the huge AP slid in, slammed the door, then squealed off, heading the car in the direction of the experimental parking ramp. "What's this all about?"

The AP shook his head. "I don't know, Captain. I was detailed to get you to the experimental station." The man cracked his first smile. "But, with all the brass that's been landed out on the field during the past hour, it looks like you're going to see some important people."

"How important?"

"The Secretary of Defense, the base commander, and just about everything in between, from what I hear."

Baxter looked out of the window on his side, and tried to inch his right trouser leg down over his Argyle sock.

"A question rests without answer in my mind, Lothas."

Lothas turned away from the side port where he had been drinking in the sights of the blue-white planet Nitola—now called Earth. Medp stood next to him. "Medp, have the knowing ones among you time now for idle thoughts?" Both of them looked at Nitola.

"What is the question, Medp?"

Medp nodded in the direction of the planet. "How does a race such as that select a representative to treat with us?"

"The hue-muns?" Lothas paused, wondering how his own race would have reacted at the news of seventy-million-cycle-old visitors from the past. "I cannot even speculate, Medp." Lothas held out a clawed hand. "All those separate tribes, such confusion—I know not." He turned toward Medp. "How are the surveys progressing?"

Medp looked at a readout strapped to his wrist. "We have over twenty distinct languages, with as yet uncounted dialects, entered in the lingpile, and this from only their radio and television. Many more languages are yet to be entered. However, the tribe who is sending the representative speaks the English, and that we have entered in quantity."

Lothas turned back to the view port. "And, the other surveys?"

"Everything is much as predicted. Residual radiation is negligible; vegetable and animal life is reestablished, although the forms are highly mutated. As I said, it is all much as predicted."

Lothas nodded toward Nitola. "All except this hue-muns creature. That we did not predict." He reached up and touched a panel that dropped armor over the view port, then turned to Medp. "I have a question of my own, knowing one."

"Speak."

Lothas lowered himself into a couch and closed his eyes. "How would we choose a representative, Medp, if the positions were reversed?"

"That is easily answered; we would send the wisest of our race. Nothing less could serve such a moment."

Lothas nodded. "Perhaps the hue-muns will do the same."

Baxter looked around the room at the circle of seated high-ranking officers and officials. "What in the ever-loving, four-color-processed Hell are you people *talking* about?"

The Secretary of Defense looked at the Chairman of the Joint Chiefs of Staff, and the Chairman and the Secretary of the Air Force both looked at Baxter's base commander, General Stayer. Stayer's glance seemed to lower the room's temperature by twenty degrees. "You don't understand, Captain. You aren't being asked; you're being ordered. You're it."

Baxter found a chair and lowered himself into it. He realized that he was coming across as being a little wild-eyed, and he took several deep breaths before he continued. "Gentlemen, what I do not understand is how I drew the black marble on this one. It's been seven, no, eight years since I flew anything even resembling the Python."

An unnamed colonel seated next to the Secretary of the Air Force leaned forward. "Captain, you are familiar with the XK-17 Python, are you not?"

Baxter shrugged and shook his head. "Only for publicity purposes. I never flew it, or even checked out in it. The things I know are things people want to know, like cost figures, performance—"

"And, all your tickets are up to date?"

Baxter held out his hands, then dropped them. "Yes."

"And you are in top physical shape?"

Baxter nodded again. "But, Colonel—"

The colonel held up a hand. "Captain, you will be surprised how fast we can check you out in the XK-17—"

"Colonel!" Baxter was startled by the loudness of his own voice. "Colonel, there must be at least five pilots I can name who are checked out on the Python, and who are on the base right now."

General Stayer gave a curt wave of his hand at the Colonel. "Let's cut through the crap. Baxter, you're it. None of those pilots are trained in public relations. You are."

"What about whatsisface? The astronaut in the Senate?"

Stayer shook his head. "Too old, his tickets aren't up to date, and we can't locate him. He's somewhere in Canada right now, fishing." The general leaned forward and pointed a finger at Baxter's throat. "You are the closest thing to a flying diplomat that we can get off the ground within the next twenty-four hours, because the Python is the only vehicle ready to go right now."

The Secretary of Defense moved his head a fraction of an inch, signaling his desire to speak. "If I may, General?"

"Of course, Mr. Secretary."

The secretary, a blown-dry glory in four-hundred-dollar pin stripes, let his gaze wander around the room as he talked. "Captain Baxter, I realize you are being asked to perform a difficult task, but we have little choice. The..." he waved a hand up in the air "... aliens, or whatever they are, made a broadband contact. In other words, their invitation was extended to whomsoever can make it up there. The Russians, of course, will get there, but—" he held up a finger, "it will take them at least three days to get off the ground. Am I making myself clear?"

Baxter folded his hands over his belly and nodded. "Yes, Mr. Secretary."

The secretary nodded. "Good. While you are there, you will be in constant touch with the Department of State, and with the White House. There will always be someone with whom you can consult on any matter."

Baxter nodded and smiled. "This is what I mean, Mr. Secretary. If all I'm supposed to do is carry a radio for the State Department, why not use another—qualified—pilot? I don't see what particular use my training in public relations will be."

The secretary nodded. "You must know the value in eyeball-to-eyeball negotiations, Captain. When you deal with groups and committees on behalf of the Air Force, do you telephone or appear in person?"

Baxter nodded, noting the chains being locked in place. "And what am I supposed to attempt to accomplish?"

"Your meaning?"

"Mr. Secretary, the only purpose of public relations, or diplomacy for that matter, is to get people to do things that they would normally not do. If everyone did what we wanted, there would be no need for PR types or diplomats. Now, just what is it that I am supposed to get them to do?"

The secretary frowned. "I don't know."

"You don't *know*?"

"Captain, if these beings are what they say they are— inhabitants of Earth from over seventy million years ago— it is possible that they are thinking of reclaiming the planet for themselves. In such a case, discourage them." The secretary raised his eyebrows and held out his hands. "However, they may be from another solar system and bent on conquering Earth. Then, perhaps, in either case, it may prove beneficial to have them on our side. They are obviously more advanced . . . but, then again, it might be better to sic them on the Russians." The secretary dropped his hands into his lap. "All I can say, Baxter, is look out for the interests of your country, and the interests of your planet and the human race, while you're at it."

An hour later, as two technicians stood waiting to help him into his pressure suit, Baxter remembered that he had forgotten to telephone Boxman about the Boxman Spring account. He sat down on a cold metal bench and untied his shoes. Security on the base was locked up tighter than a million uninflated dollars, and no calls allowed. *Deb! I can't call her! She'll kill me!* He removed his red and yellow Argyle sock and held it in his hand. It had a hole in it. *I guess it's just going to be one of those days*.

Lothas studied the circle of eight faces seated around the polished black table in the half-light of the governor's conference compartment, aft of the control center. Deayl brushed a clawed hand over his muzzle, then let the hand drop to the surface of the table. "Lothas, it is still my mind that we wait no longer. The hue-muns are divided, and they have nothing that can protect them against the Power. We can brush them aside."

Lothas examined the other faces. "How many of you have this mind?" Four clawed hands went forward toward the center of the table. "The mind that counsels us to wait, then, still prevails."

Deayl put two fists on the table and turned to the ones who had not voted with him. "After seventy million cycles traveling from and to our home, we are to sit here polishing our claws? We are so close!"

Lothas noted that two who had voted with him were wavering. The desire to go home was strong, and Deayl's argument appealed to that desire. The desire twisted with no less strength in Lothas, but he held out his hands. "Our knowledge of the hue-muns is but pieces—what they are, and what they can do. The hue-muns' knowledge of us is even less—what we are, and what we can do." He lowered his hands to the table. "We must also grant that the sense of right we feel in our cause is shared by the hue-muns in their cause. They grew to dominate and control Nitola, much as we did. By what we acknowledge to be the right—"

"No!" Deayl crossed his wrists. All could hear the angry swishing of his tail across the deck. "We do not know that. What if the hue-muns are from another planet? What if they invaded our home planet, and now simply stand to defend their conquest?"

Lothas nodded. "The hue-muns must have like suspicions about us, Deayl. After all, they are on the planet; we are the ones in space ships." He brought his hands together. "We

have much to learn about each other, if we are to avoid error."
Lothas looked around the table and stopped on Deayl. "Do
you wish another vote?"

Deayl leaned against his back rest. "No. Not at the present."

Medp entered the compartment, bowed toward those seated
at the table, then turned toward Lothas. "We have just been
told that the hue-muns' representative has been launched.
Other hue-muns, speaking the Russian, have said that the
true representative will be launched in three days, and that
we should refuse to see the other."

Lothas looked at the table top, then raised his glance and
looked at Deayl. "We do have much to learn. Deayl, I will
leave to you the task of instructing our visitor in what we
can do. If hue-muns understand *the* Power, they will understand *our* power."

"Yes, Lothas."

Lothas stood and bowed toward the ones seated at the
table. The others stood and bowed in return. Lothas turned
toward the control center and entered, Medp at his side.
"Medp, do you have contact with the representative?"

"Yes. He is called Captaincarlbaxter."

Lothas nodded. "Is everything in readiness?"

"Yes. It will take him approximately a tenth of a cycle to
come into safe power range."

Lothas tucked his tail between the seat and backrest of a
chair before a monitor and sat down. He lifted his head and
looked at Medp. "Deayl will sway some minds before the
council sits again."

Medp nodded and pointed at the monitor. Nitola hung blue-
white in the blackness of space. "The feeling is very strong,
Lothas. All of us can see, and . . . we have been away for a
very long time."

Lothas turned toward the monitor, studied once more the
beautiful planet, then nodded. "Have you assembled enough
information to comprehend this squabble and division among
the hue-muns?"

Medp shifted his weight from one foot to the other. "We
can see a little. We have determined from their transmissions,

and our sensor surveys support this, that there are over four billion hue-muns belonging to the various tribes."

"Four billion?"

"And, they grow in numbers every day. This does not explain all, but it lets us see a little."

Lothas changed the positions on several slotswitches, then energized a panel, causing a tiny dot to appear on the monitor. He pressed another panel, and the dot expanded until the monitor was filled with an image of a sleek, black ship, just separating from a cluster of acceleration tubes. "Such a tiny craft. Have you come to a determination about the hue-muns' rite called humor?"

"It is exasperating. The loud reaction—the laughing, chuckling and so on—appears to be pleasurable. But, the causes of the reaction—pain, misfortune, shame, misunderstanding—all are causes of grief as well." Medp looked at the monitor. "It needs more information for sense to be made of it. Still, they are fascinating creatures. I could devote my remaining cycles to studying them."

Lothas extended a claw toward the monitor. "Part of your wish approaches now, Medp: Your first specimen, Captaincarlbaxter."

Baxter was surprised at how familiar everything was. The wing drop from the mother plane, the slam of the initial and secondary burns, even the attitude correction rockets. He looked out of the tiny canopy windows, little more than a hand's breadth from his faceplate, to see himself floating on the outer limits of Earth's atmosphere. Above, the sky was star-studded black. He searched the space above for a visual sighting, but could see nothing. He looked down, and the cluster of ships was indicated clearly on his screen. As he studied the screen, he finally realized what he was about to do. The frustrations of the morning and the skull-popping briefing by the Python's pilot, plus frantic phone conversations with several Undersecretaries of State, along with a brief inspirational call from the President, faded as the thought of meeting . . . whoever they are, filled his mind.

This is a bigger event than walking on the moon. This is

what generations of movie makers and novelists have speculated about.

"Messenger, this is Mission Control."

Baxter opened his channel. "This is Messenger. Go ahead."

"Messenger, we're patching you into a line connected with the State Department. Stand by."

Baxter listened to a series of clicks, howls, and crackles. "Captain Baxter, this is Undersecretary Wyman. Can you hear me?"

"Loud and clear, Mr. Wyman."

"Baxter, our most recent information on the Soviet mission indicates that they will have a man up in less than three days. They are sending Lavr Razin. Razin is a former cosmonaut, now attached to the Soviet mission to the U.N. Understand?"

"Affirmative. Can you tell me anything about him?"

The channel went dead for long moments, then came to life. "Baxter, since we don't know, we are assuming that none of our transmissions are secure from the . . . visitors." Another pause. "We can tell you to watch out. Razin is no Fozzie Bear, savvy?"

"Affirmative."

"Goodbye, and good luck, Baxter."

Baxter signed off with Mission Control, wishing that Undersecretary Wyman's goodbye hadn't sounded so final. He gave his instruments a casual sweep, then looked out of the left side canopy window. Green fire danced upon the Python's skin. "Captaincarlbaxter?"

"This is Messenger. Go ahead, Mission Control."

A long pause. "I am called Deayl. Are you Captaincarlbaxter?"

A strange feeling began tugging at Baxter's stomach. The voice sounded . . . ultranormal—the ideal of every midwestern radio announcer. "Yes, this is Baxter."

"Greetings. Our instruments inform us that, unless you remove the force of your engines, you will be destroyed." Baxter turned back to his own instruments. Every dial was either pegged or dead. "We have you in the grip of our power. With it, we shall bring you into our control ship. It will not harm you, unless you fail to turn off your engines."

Baxter raised a gloved hand, hesitated, then began punching and flicking switches according to the Python's shutdown SOP. "The craft is shut down . . . Deayl."

"Sensible. I am curious, Captaincarlbaxter. What were you hue-muns seventy million years ago?"

Baxter swallowed and tried to recall his ten minute high-speed briefing on the lineage of Man. *"After all, Baxter, they may want to establish the authenticity of our claim to this planet."* "At that stage, we were prosimians—the apes hadn't evolved yet. You know what I mean when I say 'apes'?"

"Yes. We have seen them on your transmissions."

Baxter frowned. *What if those guys can pick up every radio and T.V. transmission on Earth? They could assemble quite a body of information.* "Interesting."

"What did the prosimians look like?"

"Well, I understand that they were small, long-tailed creatures that resembled present-day squirrels. Probably, they were adept at securing food by leaping about in the trees, eating fruit, seeds, eggs—"

"Ah, the tree jontyl. I recognize them. That is very curious, Captaincarlbaxter. Tree jontyls were very well-known to my race when we occupied this planet. My mouth has been watering for one for over seventy million years. I am looking forward to seeing you."

They called themselves Nitolans—Earthlings in another tongue. As his craft approached the ship in the lead center of the armada of Nitolan vessels, Baxter felt the awe he experienced when, as a boy of ten, he had been taken into St. Patrick's Cathedral in New York. One hundred and ninety-seven ships, and any one of them large enough to dwarf a supertanker. The ships were long, cylindrical, and with ridges along the sides that could be retractable wings. As he observed the smooth skin and flowing configuration of the ships, Baxter realized that the vessels were designed for atmospheric flight.

"Captaincarlbaxter?"

"This is Baxter. Deayl?"

A pause. "This is Deayl. This shortening of the name; is this a friendly gesture of you hue-muns?"

"Yes . . . everybody just calls me 'Baxter'—even my wife."

"Your mate?"

Baxter nodded to himself. "Yes."

Another pause. "Very well, Baxter. I will accept this gesture in kind. I am known as Illya..." Baxter listened while the Nitolan supervising his approach seemed to be wrestling with a thought. "This gesture, Baxter. Understand that it does not obligate me to anything."

Baxter smiled. *This guy could have come straight from a Middle East peace conference.* "I understand, Illya. Is there anything I should know about being taken into your ship's landing bay?"

"If your craft has surface landing apparatus that is now retracted, you should prepare it. Otherwise, we can suspend your craft in a neutral field. Air will be normal to you."

Baxter noted the existence of artificial gravity. None of the ships were spinning. The Python landed on two fixed rear skids and a nose wheel. He threw the switch and felt the wheel lower and lock as his eyes confirmed the event by observing the safe/go light for the landing gear. "Landing gear down and locked, Illya."

"Noted."

Baxter watched as the underside (toward Earth) of the ship opened, much like the iris of a camera. Dull red light came from the bay, and as the Python closed on the iris, Baxter felt a slight panic at the size of the opening, then at the size of the bay. *I feel like a pea rattling around in a fifty-five gallon drum!*

The Python rose just above the opening, and Baxter watched open-mouthed as the enormous iris blinked shut. His craft was gently lowered to the deck, and he let out his breath. He checked his instruments, shut down the works, and waited. In the distance he could see four jumbo-jet-sized ships parked off to the side. The bay switched from red to yellow light, and Baxter's mouth remained open as a hatch opened and a delegation of gray-green, long-necked, heavy-tailed creatures entered.

They walked toward him on powerful legs with clawed feet. Although bipedal, they stooped forward, carrying their long, thin arms in front. Baxter's gaze went from the clawed toes to the clawed fingers, then to the gleaming rows of teeth. As he unstrapped, removed his helmet and cracked the Python's canopy, Baxter ran a dry tongue over equally dry lips. He stood, stepped over the side of the cockpit, pushing his toes into the step holes, and climbed down from his craft. He turned as the delegation of creatures came to a halt. Stooped over, the creatures were only a little taller than himself. One of them rotated its body, bringing its neck and head well above the others. Baxter cleared his throat and croaked. "I bring you greetings from the President of the United States."

Deayl watched the scene of the docking bay reception a moment longer, then closed his eyes. *If so long ago we had not abandoned our gods. If I could only lay my burden at the feet of old Sisal, or old Fane*. He extended a claw and shut off the monitor. Energizing another monitor, he watched Nitola, and his pain eased.

I do not do it for myself, but for all of us. He kept his eyes on the image as he pressed the signal to Lothas' quarters.

"Lothas."

"Deayl, Lothas. Baxter has landed safely, and Medp brings him now to the quarters prepared for him."

"Deayl, is 'Baxter' the representative's name of friendship?"

Deayl lowered his muzzle to his chest. "Yes. And I extended mine to him."

"This is good. He shall rest for the remainder of the cycle, then you shall demonstrate to him the Power. I shall meet with him after."

"All will be as you wish, Lothas."

"Deayl, with your mind concerning the return to Nitola, exchanging names with the hue-muns was a fine gesture." A pause, as though Lothas expected some sort of comment. "Deayl, I know you disapprove of my direction as governor, but I know you to be a strong and determined champion of our race. I would exchange names with you. I am called 'Dimmis.'"

Deayl wiped a shaking hand over his muzzle, then nodded. "I am called 'Illya.'"

"A home for you, Illya."

Deayl pressed the panel, extended his fingers, and placed his palms over his eyes. *Ah! Ah, it comes! The pain returns*.

How many disgraces must I bring upon myself before my task is done? How many?

In his quarters, Baxter sagged as he tried to get comfortable in the strange chair. As near as he could figure it, he had just completed a three kilometer dead run from the docking bay, trying to keep up with the delegation. He opened his eyes and looked around the room. The white bulkheads were bare, except for the three iris-like doors. One door led to a closet, another to the corridor, and the third to a bathroom straight from one of Baxter's more imaginative nightmares. He had been literally relieved to find that he could use the equipment, although with some difficulty. On the deck, several thick cushions were arranged for sleeping. His chair had a black metal frame and was upholstered with a soft green fabric. Baxter sat on one side of the seat, since the center-rear was open to comfortably seat the Nitolan tail. The backrest, tilted forward to accommodate the creatures' stooping backs, dug into Baxter's shoulderblades. His ankles reached to the edge of the seat.

He reached to his belt and pressed the switch to his radio that, through the relay set in the Python, would keep him in touch with Earth. "Mission Control, this is Messenger."

"Messenger, report on your situation."

"I'm established in quarters. At the moment, I'm supposed to be resting . . . although that's going to be a little difficult. At about oh-four-hundred GMT tomorrow, I'll be taken on some kind of demonstration, then meet Lothas. The best their language mechanics can make out of his title is 'governor.' Then, whatever negotiations there will be will begin."

"Acknowledged, Messenger. From now on, until you begin preparations for reentry, your communications will be handled by the State Department mission control. Stand by."

Baxter looked down from the chair at the knee-high thick pallet on the deck that would serve him as a bed during his stay. "Baxter, this is Wyman. Do you read?"

"Five by five, Mr. Wyman."

"Good. Wnat have you found out?"

"The Nitolans, first. They look like a cross between a kangaroo, an ostrich and an alligator; general shape for the first, eyes for the second, claws and teeth for the third—lots of teeth. The head is pretty large."

"I understand, Baxter. The ships?"

"Incredible."

"Could you be more specific?"

"The ships are enormous. I can't even tell you how wide they are. Everything seemed to extend out of sight. But, I'm pretty sure they are monitoring our commercial radio and television broadcasts. The lingpile—the thing they use to convert their language into and out of English—talks like Merv Griffin. They have some sort of force field or tractor beam that pulled me into their lead ship, and I think the same thing allows them to simulate gravity on board. Gravity appears to be Earth normal, and there appears to be no inducement of this by centrifugal force or other physical means. That's it, except that they seem friendly—and curious."

"Baxter, do they appear secretive or evasive about themselves?"

Baxter shook his head. "Not that I can tell. In fact, they provided me with a reader of some kind in case I wanted some diversion when I wasn't sleeping. They prepared something for me that contains a nutshell history of them, their mission, and so on."

"You will begin on it at once, Baxter."

"Mr. Wyman, I'm a little bushed right now—"

"At once, Baxter! Until we know more, all of us are groping in the dark—including you. Now, do your homework."

"Yessir."

"One more thing, Baxter."

"Go ahead."

"We must establish to a certainty from where they came. If they, in fact, have come from Earth's past, we must be sure. Do you have any indications other than their appearance? Things they've said? Answers to your questions?"

"Mr. Wyman, I haven't asked them Babe Ruth's all-time batting average, or the words to 'Yankee Doodle,' if that's what you're talking about."

"I understand. I'll see about preparing a suitable list of

questions—things based on our knowledge of the period they claim to be from. Is there anything you need?"

Baxter thought a moment. "How is all this striking the public?"

"Officially, we are denying everything, and so are the Soviets, but rumors are spreading fast. Too many people picked up that initial broadband contact, although it hasn't grown serious yet."

"What about the Russian?"

"Launch is still go for the day after tomorrow. We still don't have a line on what they plan to pull. That it?"

"Yes. Baxter out." He released the switch, sighed and slid to the front edge of the seat, then dropped to the floor. The edge of the seat came to his waist. Baxter walked to the door panel, reached up and pressed the platter-sized button with both hands. Part of the wall dilated iris fashion, exposing a wide corridor and a Nitolan standing guard. The creature walked to the opening, its heavy tail scraping harshly against the deck, and stooped in Baxter's direction.

"May I help you, Captaincarlbaxter? I am Simdna."

Baxter nodded and pointed at the swept-screened contraption attached to a chair by a swinging metal brace. "Yes. Medp said that I could use the reader if I wanted, but I am ignorant of its operation." Baxter walked to the reader chair, climbed up and settled in as the Nitolan followed, then pushed the reader more closely to the chair. "Now, what do I do?"

Simdna picked up two pancake-sized tabs and held them out to Baxter. "Put one on each side of your head. They will attach themselves."

Baxter held one tab in each hand, then held them to the sides of his head. "What now?"

Simdna pointed toward a panel. "This will begin the record." He pointed at a slotswitch. "The more you pull this toward you, the faster will run the record."

Baxter nodded. "Thank you. I don't think I'll need anything else."

Simdna turned, left the room and the door closed after him. Baxter studied the screen then looked at the panel for starting. He leaned forward and pushed it with the palm of

his hand. At once, a feeling of mild intoxication swept him.
It stayed as he pulled the switch, and images and narratives
attacked his senses at high input levels. He realized this, but
realized also that he understood it all, as fast as it was. He
pulled again at the slotswitch...

    *...The Nitolans were a highly-evolved race, with self-
made imperatives of right and wrong, a structured social
system, great cities, long before man thought these even to
exist. In the midst of the great reptiles, the Nitolans had
science, law, and the creation of wealth, for the Power was
theirs. They studied truth...*
    *...And the knowing ones read their instruments and saw
the death of every creature that could not hide within the mud
or beneath the waters. The night brightstar would grow in
brilliance, until it washed all other stars from the sky, and
even paled Amasaat from the day sky. To survive, the Nitolans
must leave the planet for as long as the planet took to again
become green and alive with creatures.*
    *While the wisest of the knowing ones searched the future
for a time that would serve the race, others of the knowing
ones spread across Nitola to tell the things that they had
learned. "We must leave Nitola, else the race shall die." ...
Many believed and helped to construct the great ships that
would protect precious cargo through the vacuum of space
and the emptiness of time. Others did not believe and the
Power was turned against itself as the factions decided the
issue through blood.*
    *As the ships were completed, the war concluded, and the
victors gathered among the ships to depart Nitola. The knowing ones looked at their planet and saw the ravaged cities,
the gaping wounds of mines and quarries, their own structures for building the ships. They wondered if this evidence,
if left behind, would lead an alien visitor or a newly evolved
race to find them and destroy them as they crossed the void.
The Power was turned against the cities, and the other marks
they had made, removing all trace of their existence. Then,
they swept the planet and removed all traces of the substance of the Power, should they return to find a newly evolved*

race using the Power and turning it against the homecomers.
    When all was done, the ships were filled, the travelers'
life processes were slowed, and the journey begun . . .

"There are many of us who share your mind, Deayl."

Deayl looked from Nozn to his companion Suleth, then
back to Nozn. "My mind has been voted down by the council.
What brings you to my quarters?"

Nozn studied Deayl. "We read the piles and can see what
the hue-muns do. Many of us would not wait until the creatures render Nitola unfit for habitation."

Deayl turned away and studied a blank wall. "If there are
such as you talk about, they would disgrace themselves by
acting against the common mind."

Suleth looked from Nozn to Deayl. "We have had enough
of these word games, Deayl. Do you plan to take an action?"

"Action?"

Suleth nodded. "Will you lead us?"

Deayl lowered himself to his sleeping pallet, placed his
head on his cushion, and looked up at the overhead. "I will
speak with you two later."

Nozn placed a clawed hand on Suleth's arm to quiet him,
then nodded at Deayl. "It is my mind that this task would be
bonded by our exchanging of names. Is this your mind as
well, Deayl?"

Deayl rolled over and propped himself up with an elbow.
His black eyes fixed Nozn to the deck. "No! Treason to our
race is no excuse for friendship!" He lowered himself back
to his cushion. "Leave me now. I will call you if I wish to
converse further."

Nozn and Suleth bowed and left Deayl's quarters. Deayl
rolled to his left side, his eyes tightly shut. *I belittle myself
enough by the enterprise I have undertaken. I shall not suck
others into the same mire.* He opened his eyes and spoke to
a dark corner of the compartment. "You are my governor,
Lothas, and you speak for the common mind." Deayl sighed.
"But, you stand between us and our home. Isn't yours the
greater crime?" Deayl closed his eyes and tossed. The question was yet to be answered in his own mind.

* * *

Midway through the next planetary cycle, Baxter bid farewell to his Nitolan friend Illya, then entered his quarters and flopped onto his sleeping pallet. He detached the insulated gloves from his suit, threw them aside and placed his hands against his cheeks. His face felt drained of color. Without rising, Baxter keyed his transceiver. "State, this is Messenger." He opened his eyes and looked at the overhead. "State, this is Messenger. Do you read?"

"Go ahead, Baxter. This is Wyman."

Baxter licked his lips, took a deep breath, then sat up. "Wyman, are there any manned missions on the Moon—secret things that I don't know about?"

"I'm sure there aren't, but I can check it for you. Is it important?"

"It's important. I also want to know if the Soviets have anything on the Lunar surface, and if so, where."

"Understood. What's going on, Baxter?"

Baxter shook his head. *I'm rattled, that's what's going on. Calm down.*

"I was taken on a demonstration today. It's a thing they call 'the power.' I saw a quarter of the Lunar surface turned into glass in less time than it's taking me to tell you about it." Baxter licked his lips again. "My guide took me down about two hours later and I walked the surface. The dark side now has a *mare* that makes Imbrium, Serenity, and Tranquillity together look like a wading pool." The radio remained silent. "Did you copy that, Wyman?"

"Baxter, what is your feeling about it?"

Baxter's eyes widened. "My *feeling*? How in the Hell do you think I feel about it? If these lizards want to, they can fry my entire planet in about twenty minutes!"

"What I meant, Baxter, is your feeling about the purpose of the demonstration."

Baxter thought a moment, then flushed. "I suppose its purpose was to produce exactly the kind of hysterical gibbering I've been doing; correct?"

"Correct. Look, Baxter; you are not dealing with an overweight Congressional committee or the local school board. You can't make a mistake, then go back and patch it up later with an apology or some syrup from the White House. You have to keep your head clear and your feelings out of it, while you look for angles, feel out the edges, find out where to push, and where to back off. You understand?"

Baxter shook his head. "You diplomatic types have all the sensitivity of an oyster."

State paused for a long moment. "It's not lack of feelings, Baxter; it's called guts. Grow some. Wyman out."

Baxter released the key on his transceiver, stood, and began shucking his pressure suit. *At least I wasn't as rattled as Deayl.* The Nitolan had walked the Lunar surface with him, and had been strangely quiet. Deayl's answers to direct questions were brief, shaken, and almost incoherent. *I wonder what my old buddy Illya was nervous about?*

The iris to Baxter's compartment opened and the Nitolan called Simdna entered. "I extend an invitation from Lothas, our governor, to meet with him in private before you meet with the full council."

Baxter nodded. "I am most happy to accept his invitation." *I'm already beginning to talk like a diplomat.* "When does Lothas wish to see me?"

"Is it convenient for you to come now?"

"Yes."

Simdna backed away from the door and held out a clawed hand. "Then Lothas would see you now."

On the way to his quarters, Deayl sagged against the corridor wall. He turned his head up, then closed his eyes and let his muzzle drop to his chest. The claws on his fingers dug into his palms, the pain almost blotting out the waves of self-condemnation that threatened to drive his mind empty. He heard the sound of someone approaching, and he pushed himself away from the wall and opened his eyes. It was Nozn.

"There you are, Deayl."

"Here I am."

Nozn turned back, and seeing the corridor empty, returned his gaze to Deayl. "The hue-mun still lives, Deayl. If you cannot perform the task, leave it to someone who can."

Deayl hissed, his eyes sparking. "You forget your place Nozn!"

Nozn closed his eyes and performed a shallow bow. "I meant no disrespect, Deayl."

"I shall do what needs to be done, and with no one's help. That I can keep all others but myself clean from this act is my only claim to honor. Do not take this from me by becoming involved."

Nozn bowed again. "It will be as you wish, Deayl." He stood and half-turned to go. "But, if you should fail, there are others who will not." Nozn nodded once, then moved off down the corridor.

Deayl placed a hand against the corridor wall, turned his gaze toward the deck plates, and saw the glassy surface of Naal, the child-moon of Nitola. Baxter had stood on the thin crust of the molten pool, and it would have taken only a slight shove to have removed the creature from existence. The Council would have accepted the event as an accident, while the humans on the planet would have ... *Are the hue-muns that sensitive that they would attempt retaliation on the basis of one suspicious death? Will they adopt an attitude that will make their removal the only option left to the Council, for just one death?* Deayl wiped his hand over his muzzle, then let it drop to his side. *Or, will the hue-muns' tribes be more reflective, making the murder I will commit a futile gesture?*

Deayl, still supporting himself by moving his hand along the corridor wall, walked the few remaining steps to his quarters. He pressed the panel and the iris opened. Inside, the compartment was black, making the door appear as the dark, slathering maw of some nightmare-begotten creature. *If the hue-muns know it is a murder, the Council will as well. But, perhaps this is the only way—exchange my future for the future of my race.* Deayl stepped into the iris, and it closed behind him.

Baxter stared at the upholstered, wing-backed chair in disbelief. From its wooden claw-on-ball legs to the garish oranges and yellows of the fabric, the chair appeared to have been cloned from a discount department store's loss leader. He looked over to Lothas. The Nitolan governor reclined on several of the familiar thick cushions. "Where did you get this?" Baxter held out a hand toward the chair.

"Do you like it? I hope it is comfortable."

Baxter lowered himself into it, did one or two experimental bounces, then leaned back and crossed his legs. "It's fine."

"That pleases me, Captaincarlbaxter. It was constructed according to information gleaned from your television transmissions. It was felt that you might find our furniture out of size."

Baxter smiled. "Thank you very much . . . do I call you 'governor'?"

"I am Lothas. If you would exchange names, I am called Dimmis."

Baxter nodded. "Very well, Dimmis. I am called Baxter. I appreciate the chair very much."

"Another like it will be placed in your quarters, and one more in the conference compartment where you will meet with my council."

"Excellent." Baxter wondered if he should mention something about the horrible pattern, but decided against it.

"We can prepare you one of your beds, if you wish."

Baxter held up his hands. "Thank you, but that would be quite unnecessary. I find the cushions in my quarters very comfortable."

Lothas nodded. "Baxter, you know of us and our mission, do you not?"

"Yes. I watched the record you prepared before I slept."

The governor nodded again. "Still, you know too little of us, and we, too little of you." The Nitolan sat up and pulled a table console to where he could reach it. "The knowing ones have amassed a great deal of information from your radio and television, and from the visual and sensor surveys they have done. Still, we know too little to judge properly what we should do."

Baxter nodded. *These lizards don't know what to do any more than I do.* "I understand. If you will tell me the information you want, perhaps I can arrange to get it for you."

"We understand that your information storage piles can talk to each other, is this not true?"

Baxter nodded. "Yes. Computers."

"The information we need appears to be contained in a number of your . . . computers. I would like to send three of our knowing ones down to a place that can talk to your computers."

"I'll see if I can arrange it."

Lothas sat quietly for a moment, then lifted his head. "There is much, Baxter, that we must learn about each other, as well."

Baxter followed the direction of the governor's gaze and saw nothing but an inverted green dome set into the overhead. He looked back at Lothas and shrugged. "I agree, we must..."

Baxter's vision blurred as Lothas removed a hand from the console beside his cushion bed.

"It is good you agreed, Baxter. Trust is important." Lothas's hand rose to the console, and Baxter felt himself expanding, whirling up and out, as the compartment went black.

He felt his gorge rise as he realized he was standing off to one side observing while another thumbed and sorted through his memories. From memories to automatized interactions and responses as memories were let to play, mesh, divide, and redivide according to their own dictates.

... *the job; the goddamned job* ... *still haven't called Boxman. Deb. That damned Argyle sock* ... He felt his thoughts pulled from one area, then forced into another ... *a documentary; stacking them up like cordwood in Auschwitz* ... *Eichmann in a little glass booth* ... *Korea, Lebanon, Vietnam, Gaza, Suez, South Afr* ...

His thoughts plunged down a dimly lit hole ... *a little red balsa wood plane with a wind up* ... *Christmas, and Grandma's there, so we'll say grace this time* ... *high school, college* ... *planes at the grass strip near Evanston* ... *testing at Lockheed* ... *Air Force* ...

A cesspool of repressed fear yawned before him ... *The Python, panic* ... *what to do, God, what to do?* ... *the size of them* ... *why me?* ...

Baxter opened his eyes and saw Lothas removing his hand from the console. The Nitolan stared at him for a long time, then held its hands over its eyes for a moment. Lothas let his hands fall to his knees. "Baxter ... you, your race ... you are everything..." He waved a hand toward his compartment's iris. "Please leave. Take no offense, but please leave. I must think."

Baxter stood, a feeling of panic rising in his chest. He watched as Lothas put his head down on the cushions and appeared to sleep.

Back in his quarters, seated in a duplicate of the wing-backed chair, Baxter shook his head at his transceiver. "I don't know, Wyman. After I woke up, Lothas seemed very upset. Then, he asked me to leave."

"I don't know what to make of it, Baxter. You think it's some kind of mind-reading machine?"

"I'm sure of it. Should I make a break for it? I know the way to the docking bay, and—"

"No. Baxter, get control of yourself. Since we don't have any plans, Lothas couldn't have uncovered any hostile intentions. We just don't know, so sit tight until we do."

"Sit tight."

"You read me correctly."

Baxter listened to the static as he reviewed language forms he had not used since high school. He let out his breath. "Wyman, has anyone gotten in touch with Deb yet?"

"Deb?"

"My wife."

"I'm sure someone has. Is it important?"

Baxter could feel himself becoming wild-eyed again, and he took several deep breaths. "You're damn right it's important, Wyman, I want you—you personally—to make sure that my wife is notified."

"Very well. I'll let you know as soon as I can about that visit from your friends. There shouldn't be any problems with letting them down—the slip-stick jockeys down here are as curious about them as they are about us. As far as access to computers, it depends on what they want. We aren't about to hand over classified information to a potential enemy. Do you know what they're interested in?"

"No." Baxter wiped a hand over his face. The hand came away wet. "What about the Russian?"

"No change. Lift-off is tomorrow. We still don't have a reading on the approach he's going to use."

Baxter laughed. "I think I do. He'll probably use the same one I'm using: sort of a combination of Alice in Wonderland with Blind Man's Bluff."

"Baxter?"

"Yeah?"

"Hang in there, Baxter. Okay?"

Baxter closed his eyes and nodded. "No sweat. And thanks. Baxter out." He released the key on his transceiver and studied the overhead. It was eggshell white, smooth and seamless. Images from his stay under Lothas's machine flashed through his mind, and he gripped the armrests of the chair to keep his hands from shaking.

I don't believe it! I'm scared. I am finger-shaking, head-sweating, pants-wetting scared.

The iris to his compartment opened, and he jumped and began backing away from the door. It was Simdna. "Captaincarlbaxter?"

Baxter held his head back as the muscles at the back of his neck knotted. "What is it, Simdna?"

"Lothas wishes to inform you that the council meeting has been postponed."

Baxter studied the guard, then nodded. "Thank you."

Simdna left, the door closing behind him. Baxter lowered himself to the knee-high pallet on the deck and exhaled.

"Now what?"

Baxter tossed on his pallet, his fingers clawing at the throats of his mind's monsters. *He saw himself, a fraud in man's clothing. A creature of petty evasion, weak, frightened—above all, frightened. Thin hands reached out to work levers and turn knobs; watery eyes, reflective and darting, sought out lights and dials. Shaking and pain-whipped, the creature operated a machine. Baxter's view faded back, through the wall of the machine, into the light. He stumbled back as his view of the machine reached a point of recognition. With thick painted lips, gleaming cardboard teeth, and dime store flashlight bulbs for eyes, Carl Baxter raised a hand in his direction . . . the machine-Baxter buzzed as the creature inside screamed . . .*

* * *

Baxter bolted upright, looked around the compartment, then wrapped his arms around his body to still the shaking. A low buzzing sound drew his attention to the transceiver on the wing-backed chair. Baxter stood, walked over to the chair, and keyed the instrument. "This is Baxter."

"Wyman here."

"What is it, Wyman?"

"Hold on for a moment while we patch you back through Mission Control. Remember, you won't have long."

"Wyman..." Baxter could hear the static shifts as Wyman went out and unseen hands fed unseen signals over new routes.

"Baxter?" The voice was clear, husky, yet soft.

Baxter stared at the transceiver. "Deb? Is that you?"

Baxter heard a familiar sniff, and knew she would be nodding her head and crying. "What have you gotten yourself into now?"

He swallowed, picked up the transceiver, and sat in the chair. "This is a fine mess I've gotten us in, Ollie." Baxter felt the tears welling in his eyes. "Has anyone explained... you know."

"Yes. I see from your new friends down here that you've become a real social climber." She laughed. "You want to know who sat up and held my hand last night?"

"Who?"

"Her husband lives in a white house." She sniffed again. "And you voted for the other one."

Baxter smiled and shook his head. "This'll teach you to mismatch my socks. Hey, you'd never believe the bathroom in my quarters. There's a machine in there that can clean and dry my uniform and underwear in twenty seconds flat—and you should see my laundress. His name's Simdna... cooks too—"

"Baxter, I love you."

He bit his lower lip. "Deb, is there anyone else listening in?"

"Only three or four hundred people that I know of."

Baxter shut his eyes. "Deb... there's something I... something I want to tell you."

"I know."

"How do you know?"

"I've been holding down my side of your bed for a bunch of years, Baxter. I know. You can handle it. Do you understand that?"

"Sure."

"I know you don't believe it, Baxter, but it's true. You've got what it takes."

"Deb . . ."

"I have to go now, Baxter. Don't forget where you live."

"The house with the view, right?"

"Right." The audio filled with static as the frequency was returned to State. *I love you, Deb. God, do I need you.*

"Baxter, this is Wyman."

"Go ahead."

"It's go on the trip. Mission Control will get in touch with the Nitolan mission directly regarding the landing field and time. Still go on the Russian."

Baxter nodded. "I copy. And Wyman?"

"Yes, Baxter?"

"Thanks."

"You're welcome, but for what?"

"You know. The call to my wife."

Wyman chuckled. "Don't thank me, Baxter. That call was made at the orders of the President because of an urgent request by your friend Lothas. I thought you knew."

"Lothas requested that you put me in touch with my wife?"

"Affirmative. What do you make of it?"

What I make of it is I needed, very badly, to hear from Deb—to have her tell me I can handle it—to prop up my crumbling self-esteem. That, and that Lothas knew that. "I haven't a clue. I'll keep in touch."

"Wyman out."

Baxter released the key, leaned his head back against the chair, and fell into a troubled sleep.

In the control center, Lothas leaned against his chair's backrest while Medp shut down the receiver. "Medp, why would Baxter forget where he lives?"

Medp swung his chair in the governor's direction. "It is a joke, Lothas. It is said as a substitute for 'I want you to come home.'"

Lothas held up a hand toward the receiver. "Baxter did not laugh at the joke."

Medp shook his head. "There are jokes not to be laughed at. It is but another facet to this humor that still eludes me."

Lothas let his hand drop to his knee. "Why did his mate, Deb, not simply say 'I want you to come home'? There would be less confusion."

"Lothas, I am sure Baxter understood. This is what he meant by saying 'the house with the view,' when, from what you said, Baxter believes his mate to detest the view from their house. Another joke."

Lothas hissed, then let his muzzle drop to his chest as he passed a hand over one eye. "The melding showed me Baxter's mind, but it did not give me an understanding of it. On the outside, he functions as you or I; inside he is a warren of screaming agonies." Lothas turned to Medp. "I have never witnessed such confusion . . . such pain." He leaned forward. "Do the creatures use the humor to hide the things they feel from others?"

Medp nodded. "And from themselves as well."

"How can they hide what they are from themselves? It is impossible."

"You saw it for yourself, Lothas. All I have seen shows them to be complex, contradictory, self-deceptive, and even self-destructive."

Lothas leaned back in his chair. "Medp, the melding process not only makes clear to me the workings of Baxter's mind, you know that it will do the same for him. If what you say is true—as improbable as it sounds—then Baxter will have seen himself for the first time."

Medp nodded. "Possible."

"We cannot hide our motives from our own minds; to do so would cause us much pain and confusion. But, if a creature cannot see himself, do we damage it by allowing it to discover its motives?"

Medp leaned back and looked at the overhead. He then lowered his head and turned toward Lothas. "It is outside of my experience to imagine that knowledge of oneself could be damaging. But the hue-muns are also outside of my experience. Perhaps it could be damaging." Medp turned to a monitor displaying but a crescent of night-shrouded Nitola. "A more important question, Lothas, is can we live together with such creatures in peace?" Medp looked at Lothas.

"My mind thinks not."

Lothas looked at the monitor and nodded. "Perhaps Deayl is in the right." He turned to Medp. "In any event, we shall know once you obtain the information from their computers. Prepare your mission well, Medp. The future of this curious race may depend upon what you find. Our own futures, as well."

In his private quarters, Lothas reclined on his cushions and studied the hue-mun sitting nervously in the wing-backed chair. Baxter would cross his legs, uncross them, then cross them again. His eyes would dart about, then look in one direction for long, unblinking minutes. "Are you well, Baxter?"

The human raised his glance and looked at the Nitolan. "Well?" He nodded, then smiled. "Yes, and you?"

Lothas nodded. "I am well." He watched as the human's appearance altered to become calm, his motions unhurried. *Perhaps this denial of the self is a means of hue-mun survival.*

"What did you wish to see me about, Dimmis? Has the new meeting with the council been arranged?"

"No. Baxter, we are very different creatures from each other."

Baxter laughed. "This much even I could see."

Lothas waited for the hue-mun to quiet himself, then sat up. "I do not talk of skin, bones, shape, and size, Baxter." Lothas held up a five-fingered hand. "Our bone structures are similar, we are both carbon-based lifeforms—two eyes, two nostrils, two arms, two legs. I believe your race originated on my planet, as you must believe that my race did as well."

Baxter shrugged. "That judgment is for others to make, Dimmis. But, for myself, I believe you are what you say you are."

Lothas nodded. "There is a difference. Your thinking, Baxter; it is *alien*. But I can see it is alien by your own choosing.

What I do not see is why. I know of no form of life that acts against its interests by choice, except yours."

Baxter frowned, then wiped a hand over his face. "I'm not sure I know what you mean." His hand came away wet. "Do you mean wars?"

Lothas shook his head. "No. We have had our own wars, Baxter. Wars can be an expression of self-interest." The Nitolan pointed a clawed finger at the human. "I talk about your thinking, and how your thinking makes you act. During the meld, among your many pains, I saw the need for your mate. Yet, when you talked with her, you made jokes; you hide the things you mean to say."

Baxter flushed. "That's my business. I would like to thank you for making the request."

"Is this what you mean, Baxter, or is this a joke? I do not understand. Understand that, to my mind, there are only a few ways that this situation can be resolved: First, we end hue-mun life on Nitola and resume control of our planet. We can do this."

Baxter blanched, then leaned forward, his elbows on the chair's armrests. "That would gain you nothing but a dead planet, Dimmis. To kill us from orbit, you will have to kill everything. If you land to kill us, then we can fight back, and we will."

Lothas nodded. "This is why my mind has not been in favor of this choice, although the minds of many Nitolans do favor it." Lothas waved a hand, dismissing the option. "Of course, I think it impossible that your race could attack and destroy mine. We have the Power. This leaves us with both races living together on Nitola, in some manner."

Baxter nodded as he exhaled a nervous breath. "I would prefer that."

"But the more we examine that course, Baxter, the more impossible it appears. We see you destroying the home planet, and this we could not tolerate. But your tribes are so divided, how could they agree to stop? I find that you do not represent all hue-muns, but only a small number. The Russian also represents only a small number. Yet, even so, you could not agree. I see that your tribes would try to use us each to gain an advantage over the other." Lothas shook his head.

"Another way is for the hue-muns to leave Nitola."

"Leave?"

"Yes. Find another planet."

Baxter leaned back in his chair and stared at Lothas. He placed a hand over his chest as he felt his heart beating, threatening to come loose of its supports. "How can we?"

"We have these ships, and we can build you more. Enough to vacate the planet."

Impossible! Baxter shook his head as he remembered that it was not his decision to make. "I don't know, Dimmis. It seems unlikely, but I will talk with my people."

"Such of them as you represent."

Baxter nodded. "Yes." He stood.

"Before you go, Baxter, you should understand that these talks with me and with the council are different in substance to us than they are to you."

"How do you mean?"

"In you I read an attitude . . . a desire to use this experience to gain an advantage for your race. To us, we are learning. When we know enough, the proper choice will become obvious. Such a choice is not something subject to concession or negotiation. We will see where the right is, then we shall pursue it. This right we seek is independent of either my desires—or yours."

Baxter gently rubbed his temples as he reviewed his meeting with Lothas and waited for Wyman to get back to him. State had not been pleased. *The whole damned thing is falling apart.* Baxter leaned back in the chair, thinking. *This whole thing—it's like trying to stop the fall of mountains by stringing spools of rotting thread across the Grand Canyon.*

Lothas had pointed at the dying oceans, the poison air, the sheer number of human mouths. *"Still, Dimmis, we have a right to our future—and, on Earth. It is the future you committed us to. We didn't bail out and take the power with us—you did. If you had left us the power, perhaps things would have been different."*

Lothas had swept the argument away with a wave of his clawed hand. *"As lifeforms, you are freaks—self-destructive, murdering freaks. And what is your answer? 'We are only hue-mun.' You use this phrase to excuse it all. But, Baxter, this defines you as a lifeform; it defines you as flawed, unworthy. And this is how you define yourselves."* The Nitolan had leaned forward. *"If we had left you the Power, there would be none of you left."*

Baxter leaned forward, placed his elbows on his knees, then lowered his face into his hands. He had reported the talk to Wyman. *"Baxter, are you insane?"*

"Wyman, dammit, we both know I didn't ask for this! I knew I didn't know what I was doing, and so did you people! Now Lothas knows it, too. Wyman, you have got to get some-one else up here. When Medp takes down the ship to get at the computers, what about putting a State Department mission—or something from the U.N.—on board?"

There had been a long silence, then Wyman came back on the air. *"I have to talk to some people about all of this, Baxter, then I'll get back to you. One thing I can tell you now: if and when you have any more meetings with Lothas or with his council, keep your transceiver keyed and your mouth shut. We shall inform Lothas that State will attempt to deal directly with him. Understood?"*

Baxter let his head fall between his hands, then began kneading the knot of muscles at the back of his neck. Wyman had taken the responsibility off of him, except for working the transceiver—something Baxter felt confident enough to handle. But, still, he felt no relief. He leaned back in the chair and bit his lower lip. He was coming across as a complaining, whining, incompetent loser. "Dammit, Wyman," he said to the overhead, "don't you understand that they're messing with my mind? How would you weather a good look at yourself, you brass-plated diplomat?"

His transceiver buzzed, and he pressed the key. "This is Baxter."

"Wyman. Well, boy, it looks as though you have royally screwed up the works. To tell you the truth, I wouldn't give two cents for the chances your tailfeathers have if you ever set foot in this country again."

"It's nice hearing from you too, Wyman."

"Okay, here is the drill. We have put together a mission, and we're waiting now for Lothas or his council to decide whether or not to take them on board. The communications we've had were not encouraging. Just in case, we're going on full alert, and a spit-and-baling-wire arrangement is being put together to coordinate the military defenses of every nation on Earth. By the way, we've had at least one break. The Russian isn't going to make it. He bought it during the launch—"

"Wyman, you twit! A *break*? You call that a *break*? What brand of bumwad are you using for brains? I need *help* up here, and fast—"

"Grow up, Baxter! Help, from the Soviets?"

Baxter shook his head. "No, Wyman. Help from another human." Baxter felt himself giggling. "You haven't gotten the message yet—you people down there. We're all in this together . . . all of us." He shook his head as his giggles turned into quiet tears. The transceiver clicked, then clicked again. Wyman had keyed in, then keyed out—nothing to say.

The transceiver clicked again. "Remember, Baxter. Do nothing without authorization, and make sure they understand that, from now on, they will be dealing with us directly. Wyman out."

Baxter released the key on the transceiver. He shrugged, released the catch on his belt, and stood, leaving the belt and transceiver in the chair. The iris to his compartment opened and Simdna entered. "Captaincarlbaxter, Deayl would speak with you if it is your desire."

Baxter looked at the transceiver on the chair, then back at Simdna. "Yes. I will see him." Simdna left through the iris and Deayl entered. "It is good to see you again, Illya. Are you feeling better?"

Deayl stared down at the hue-mun; the creature's image wavered before his eyes. *Better? Do I feel better?* The iris closed and Deayl took a step forward. "Baxter, we have exchanged names."

"Yes, Illya."

Deayl wiped a clawed hand over his muzzle. "Do you remember I said this obligates me to nothing?"

"I remember." Baxter frowned, then looked once again at the transceiver. He turned back and faced the Nitolan. Deayl had come another step closer; his frightful clawed hands were outstretched.

"Still, I must tell you why I do this, Baxter."

Baxter began edging away from the Nitolan. "Do what?"

"Baxter, the knowing ones have left for Nitola to talk with your computers. The hue-muns below struggle with the same problem: how are we to live together in peace—a thing that can never be."

"How do you know? You're upset—"

"The longer we wait to take back our planet, the harder it will be. Even now the hue-muns prepare. But, I must make this clear to the council, and to do this I must provoke the hue-muns. You see, I must murder you."

"Murder..." Baxter watched as Deayl came closer, his black, dagger-sized claws glowing softly in the light of the compartment. The hands struck out, and Baxter ducked. He turned, grabbed the wing-backed chair and threw it at the Nitolan. Deayl swatted it away, splintering it, and smashing the transceiver. Before the pieces hit the deck, Baxter reached the panel controlling the iris and slapped it with both hands. "Simdna! For God's sake, Simdna!" As the iris opened, Baxter felt Deayl's hands encircling his chest, the long claws ripping into his lungs...

A week passed, and many of those on Earth marveled at how easily arms and territorial agreements between nations could be reached, now that they—in the face of the power—had become meaningless. The strange Nitolan vessel squatted silently next to the hangar where human technicians maintained the links between the ship and a vast array of computers located in almost every nation of Earth. No one saw the Nitolans, and for a week, there had been no communications from either Lothas or Baxter.

In a motel, near the airbase, a diplomatic mission headed by the Secretary of State waited impatiently to board the Nitolan ship. On the other side of the field, a task force of commandos practiced their assault plan on the vessel. In Washington, Moscow, Paris, London, Peking, Cairo ... haggard faces circled cup- and butt-littered tables, waiting by

brand new communication facilities for some kind—any kind—
of news.

The base commander, General Stayer, heard it first. A
shaken voice—one of the technicians in the hangar. No warn-
ing. The Nitolans had disconnected the links to the hangar
and rose into the night.

The waiting began in earnest.

Deb Baxter listened to the rain spatter against the window
and let her arm fall on the empty side of the bed. She opened
her hand, palm down, and caressed the overstuffed quilt. She
made a fist, then rolled over and pulled a cigarette from a
half-empty pack on her night stand. She had been three years
off cigarettes, and she realized as she struck a match that she
was already back to two packs a day. In the light of the match,
her eyes were puffy, with dark circles. She touched the match
to the end of the cigarette, then shook it out. Taking a pillow
and propping it up against the headboard, she propped herself
up against it and studied the dark surrounding the warm coal
that brightened with each drag she took.

She had faced that Baxter wasn't coming back, learned
she could survive the fact, then accepted it—almost. Nights
without sleeping pills still became vigils. She threw off the
covers, swung her legs to the cold floor and walked barefooted
to the bedroom window. Holding the dark curtain aside, she
stared at the security lights surrounding the experimental parking ramp. Somewhere out there, some poor jerk who had
been conned off the farm with promises of becoming an
"Aerospace Technician" was walking guard, rifle muzzle
down, head and shoulders hunched under a poncho against
the rain. She shook her head. "Stupid. It's not even supposed
to rain in the desert."

She heard sirens in the distance, and then red lights streaked
down the base's main drag, between her and the lights around
the experimental ramp. There were always sirens. Baxter used
to roll over and mumble something about the AP's playing
cops and robbers, then sink back into sleep. She listened as
the sirens grew dim, then gradually increased in volume. *Must*
be turning into the area. She smiled and shook her head. *An*
area. I don't call it a neighborhood, or even a development,

anymore. An area. She felt an ash brush her knuckles as it fell from the cigarette to the carpet. "Damn!" She stooped down to make certain that she had not ignited the cheap pile, then held up her head as she heard the sirens grow very loud, then die amidst a squeal of brakes. Immediately a loud pounding came from her door.

She looked around the dark bedroom, found her robe thrown over a chair, and began putting it on. "Mrs. Baxter! Mrs. Baxter, are you in there?"

She tied the sash with trembling fingers. "Just a minute!" She ran into the living room and to the front door. Unlocking the door, she pulled it open. In the street before her house was a blue staff car flanked fore and aft by AP jeeps, red lights still flashing. She turned on the outside light and a graying Air Force officer, accompanied by an AP, removed his hat.

"Mrs. Baxter. I am the base commander, General Stayer. I must ask you to come with me."

"I . . . General, is this about my husband? Is it?"

The officer looked down. "I'm sorry. I don't know. Please hurry. We haven't much time."

Deb turned from the door, opened the hall closet and pulled out a raincoat. As she put it on, she found the first thing handy, and slipped Baxter's rubber galoshes over her bare feet. Moments later, she sat by the general in the back of the blue staff car as the procession screamed its way toward the field.

The car stood silently on the edge of the field, the dim blue taxiing lights diffused by the droplets on the windows, illuminating Deb's face with a cold glow. She looked across the back seat through the windshield, but could see nothing but the rain. Pulling the raincoat around her, she shivered.

"I'm sorry, Mrs. Baxter." The general turned to the driver. "Bill?"

"Yessir?"

"Turn on the car and let's have some heat."

"Yessir!" The driver hit the ignition, the motor caught, and in moments warm air blew against Deb's legs. She turned toward Stayer.

"Thank you. I didn't realize how cold I was."

Stayer nodded, then reached for a microphone attached to the back seat. He keyed the mike. "Tower, this is Stayer. Has GCA got 'em yet?"

"Affirmative, General. Ground con—"

Stayer switched the frequency indicator next to the mike hanger, then keyed the mike. "GCA, this is Stayer. You have an ETA yet?"

"This is GCA. Yes, General. They should be over the field in about a minute, although with this visibility you probably won't be able to see them until they land. The other ship didn't use lights."

"Stayer out." The general hung up the mike, looked at Deb, then turned back to the driver. "Bill, hit the wipers."

"Yessir." The car's electric wipers whined and thumped back and forth, but the field before them, as well as the sky above, remained empty.

Stayer leaned back, keeping his eyes on the deserted runway. "This is the first contact of any kind that we've had with them for three weeks, Mrs. Baxter. I know how difficult this is, but they specifically asked to meet with you. We tried to ask, but they ended the transmission before we could ask about your husband."

Deb nodded and turned to face Stayer. "I'll do whatever I can—"

The entire field grew bright with a blinding, yellow-white glare. Deb put her hands over her eyes, then peered through her fingers. The driver was leaning forward, over the steering wheel, looking up through the windshield.

"Jesus!" The driver craned his neck further, trying to get a vertical look. "Jesus, General, the size of it."

Stayer, his head pressed against the rear window, simply nodded. Deb held her breath as a glittering shape filled the landing field before her. She was startled to realize that the only sound she heard was the car's motor and the patter of the rain on the roof. Without thinking, she reached out a hand and grasped Stayer's forearm.

The area beneath the ship grew bright as it came within a few meters of the ground. Red light joined the white as the belly opened, and a small, black craft was gently lowered to the runway. "It's the Python, General. And there's something else. Looks like two boxes."

Somewhere on the ship, a blue panel illuminated. The general took a breath, leaned forward and tapped the driver on the shoulder. "That's the signal, Bill. Get going."

Deb saw the driver looking at the controls on the staff car as though it was the first time he had ever seen them.

"Damn!" He put the car in gear, the car jumped forward, then died. "I'm sorry, sir . . . I . . ."

"Take it easy, Bill. Just start it up, and take it easy."

"Yessir." The car started, then began approaching the ship. Deb's hand dropped from her eyes as she stared at the vessel, growing larger just at the moment she would have sworn it could grow no larger. The car stopped. Deb watched as an illuminated ramp extended from under the blue panel on the ship and touched the ground. A moment later a creature with massive legs for walking, smaller clawed legs held in front, and a thick tail behind, walked down the ramp and took up a position next to it.

"Mrs. Baxter?"

Deb turned toward Stayer, realizing she still held his arm. "What . . . what do I do?"

Stayer nodded at the creature. "Go over to . . . that. It'll tell you what to do. Good luck."

Deb opened the door, stepped out, and stood facing the ship. She could tell it was still raining, but none fell around the vessel. Leaving the door open, she walked toward the ramp, keeping her eyes on the creature. When she was ten feet from it, she stopped. "Well?"

The creature looked down at her. "You are the mate of Captaincarlbaxter?"

"Yes." She looked up the ramp into the ship, and at the top she saw a familiar face. "Baxter!" She ran past the creature, onto the ramp, and then reached the top. Tears streamed down her face as she looked at him, then ran to him and held him tightly.

"Easy, Deb." He kissed her and held his cheek tightly against hers.

She pushed back and held him at arm's length. "Baxter." She sniffed, then laughed. "That's some dynamite entrance you've got there, Baxter!"

Baxter smiled. "Wait until you see the rest of my act." He looked from Deb's wet hair, to his old raincoat, then to his old rubber galoshes. He looked back at her face and shook his head. "That's my Deb. All class. Why didn't you dress up? You're going to meet some important people."

"Oh, you jerk!" She embraced him again, then withdrew her arms as she heard a rasping sound behind her.

Baxter nodded in the direction of the open ramp door, where the creature Deb had seen was now standing. "Deb, I would like you to meet my friend, Deayl. If you would be friends with him, he would be called Illya."

Deb nodded at Deayl. "My name is Deb."

The creature nodded back. "You must call me Illya, then."

Baxter bent down, picked a helmet up from the deck, and turned to Deayl. "Illya, there's something I have to do. Would you keep Deb company for a few minutes?"

Deb frowned. "Baxter!"

He kissed her, turned and walked down the ramp. Both she and Illya stood at the head of the ramp as Baxter went down, walked to the edge of the concrete runway, and knelt down. She turned to Deayl, "What is he doing?"

"Something that he wishes to do." He turned his head down toward Deb. "I asked Baxter if I could explain to you what has happened, and he consented." Deayl looked back at the hue-mun kneeling on the edge of the runway. "I tried to kill Baxter." Deb looked at the creature's clawed hands, then to the coal black eyes. "I hurt him very badly. This was to make you humans angry, and make impossible a settlement between us."

Deayl nodded toward Baxter. "Our medicine saved him, then he saved me. I was to be tried by the council for my act, and Baxter interceded. What was said is not important, but he showed us something we had never seen before." Deayl looked back at Deb. "When we see the right, that is what we accept and follow. But the right says Baxter should have demanded my death. Instead, he pleaded for me. He understood why I had acted the way I did. He . . . showed mercy.

You hue-muns are everything evil that we had feared becoming, but you are also greater than we could hope to be. Because of this, and because of the things the knowing ones found, our ships will leave. Earth is yours for as long as you can keep it."

Deb looked down the ramp and saw Baxter at the bottom. In his arms he carried his helmet, and as he came close to the door, she saw that the helmet was filled to the brim with mud. He stopped, held it out toward Deayl, and smiled as the Nitolan took it and bowed. "A home for you, Baxter."

"A home for you, Illya."

Deayl stood up, turned and went through an open iris. It blinked shut behind him. Baxter took Deb's arm and steered her down the ramp. When they reached the runway, the ramp retracted, the ship became dark, then it lifted quietly away from the field. Deb felt the rain on her cheek as she followed Baxter to where the Python stood on the runway next to the two cubical containers. General Stayer got out of his car and stopped next to them.

Baxter patted the nose of the Python and turned toward the general. "There you are, General. I'm returning your property, and I even saved you some fuel."

Stayer placed a hand on Baxter's shoulder. "I'm glad to see you, Baxter. You'll never know how glad."

"The feeling is mutual, General." Baxter looked up as he saw a stampede of siren-screaming, light-flashing vehicles moving toward their location from the tower area. "I guess that'll be all the brass." He turned toward Stayer. "General, I have two favors to ask."

"Shoot."

Baxter went to one of the containers. "General, this is the information the Nitolans pulled out of our computers. It's been put together with their information and processed in ways I don't pretend to understand. It shows, day by day, the human race lasting another hundred and twenty years at the outside. Their predictions are accurate, which is why they left. What they saw told them that they could come back in a few hundred years and pick up where they left off—that humanity will have eliminated itself by then." Baxter nodded, then held Deb around the shoulders. "But, Medp told me that this particular prediction of theirs has one very large, unpredictable variable. That's us: humanity. If I were you, I'd have the container moved to wherever it was the Nitolans linked into those computers and get to work."

Stayer nodded. "And the other favor?"

"Before all the brass shows up, I'd like to borrow your car and driver. I want to go home."

"Baxter, there are briefings, the Secretary—"

"General, I want to go home."

Stayer motioned at his car, it started up, and began rolling in their direction. The car's headlights illuminated the Python and the two containers. "One more thing, Baxter."

"Yessir?"

"What's in the other container?"

Baxter pulled on Deb's arm, stopped next to the car-sized cube, and pressed a panel set into the side of the container. It parted into two sections and swung open, exposing two wing-backed chairs, claw-on-ball feet, yellow and orange floral pattern. "I'd like these sent to my house."

Deb looked at them, then began laughing. "Oh . . . oh, Baxter . . . they're *horrible*!"

Stayer shook Baxter's arm. "Get going, Captain. And expect an early call. You have quite a selling job to do."

"Yessir. Thank you, sir."

The two entered the rear door held by the driver, and after shutting it, the driver ran around the front of the car and entered. In moments, the car moved off. Stayer felt the rain, hunched his shoulders and walked to the container with the chairs. As waves of vehicles pulled up, lighting the area with their headlights, the General took a last look, then pressed the container's panel. The cube closed with a snap. He nodded. "She's right. They are horrible." Shaking his head, General Stayer turned to greet the brass.

Lothas closed his fingers over the handful of dirt and looked up at the image of receding Nitola in the monitor. He held the closed hand toward the monitor and turned toward Medp. "In suspension it will be nothing to us. Perhaps a few planetary cycles, then we shall go home."

Medp studied the monitor. "Perhaps not."

Lothas nodded. "I hope you are right, Medp. They are special creatures, aren't they?"

"Indeed. It will take me many star cycles to absorb the information on them that I have acquired."

Lothas turned back toward the monitor. "Have you found an answer to the humor ritual?"

Medp gave an involuntary snort, then shook his head. "Perhaps there is no answer." He giggled.

"You seem to have discovered the cause of the reaction. Please explain."

Medp nodded, then looked up at the overhead. "Very well. Do you know of mice?"

Lothas nodded. "The small rodent."

"Yes." Medp giggled again. "And the mythical being of Santa Claus?"

Lothas leaned against his backrest, half-closed his large, dark eyes, and studied the knowing one. "Yes. You explained that in your report on hue-mun beliefs. Explain this behavior."

Medp held out his hands. "Lothas, why are a little gray mouse and Santa Claus similar?" Medp closed his eyes, shook, and gasped for breath.

"Are you well?"

Medp waved a hand. "Yes, yes. Answer the question."

Lothas thought a moment, then shook his head. "It escapes me, knowing one. Why are a little gray mouse and Santa Claus similar?"

Medp reached out a hand and grasped the back of Lothas's chair, apparently to keep from falling to the deck. "You see, Lothas . . . they both have long white beards—" tears began streaming from the knowing one's eyes "—*except for the mouse!*"

The control center rocked with the sounds of Medp's laughter as the knowing one slapped Lothas's back, then staggered through an open iris, leaving Lothas alone with only a puzzled expression for company. Lothas shook his head. "Truly, there is much to learn." He reached out a claw finger to press the panel for the voice log. His finger stopped short of the panel, he closed his eyes and nodded.

Then the dinosaur laughed.

The dinosaurs finally behind me, I thought, I got on with other things. However, before the contract offer for "The Homecoming" arrived in the mail, George telephoned me again. He wanted another story about intelligent dinosaurs, and this time make it time travel.

After George hung up, I telephoned my brother-in-law to see if I could still get in on the ground floor of his aluminum siding company. No luck.

I didn't want anything more to do with big lizards and I couldn't think of anything to write. About then I was reading the letters column in Asimov's and in it there was a reader complaining at length because he hated twist endings.

I suppose it was then that Herman, an imaginary creature I dress up in various costumes to do time as one of my story characters, began speaking to me. I think I must have gone a bit crazy prior to writing the following piece, "Twist Ending." So did George. He bought it.

Twist Ending

GerG clasped his three-fingered, clawed hands, rotated his stooping torso on his massive hind legs, and closed his eyes in respect to the Great Ones.

> *"All right! Hold everything!"*
> *"What's the matter?"*
> *"Look at me! What silly getup have you stuffed me into this time?"*
> *"Why ... you're an offshoot of the Dromaeosaurus—the last of the warm-blooded dinosaurs. Probably the most intelligent—"*
> *"I look like a bald ostrich with claws!"*
> *"Come on! You're holding up the show."*
> *"Well ... this better not have one of those twist endings—can't stand them."*
> *"Trust me."*
> *"Okay, okay! Get on with it!"*

"You are prepared, GerG, to enter the time frame and scout the future site for our dying race?" Of the Great Ones, the Presence towered above the others, then held out a clawed hand. "There exists but one node of time-future open within the range of our frames. You must go there and prepare the way for our exodus. Else, the supernova shall extinguish us all."

> "That's it! I'll buy one outrageous assumption per story, but not three in one paragraph!"
>
> "What are you talking about?"
>
> "Intelligent dinosaurs, time travel, and now a supernova thrown in—ridiculous!"
>
> "Look, there's evidence supporting the existence of a supernova in Earth's past, and no one has a better explanation for the end of the dinosaurs."
>
> "What about intelligence from a brain the size of a walnut?"
>
> "The evidence shows the Dromaeosaurus had a very favorable brain-to-body-weight ratio. It's not outrageous to assume that a race of dinosaurs existed along with them much the way we now exist in relation to chimps and apes."
>
> "What about time travel?"
>
> "Well . . . you said I could have one."
>
> *sigh* "Okay, but how about giving me something to counterbalance this body? My back is killing me."
>
> "Sorry, I forgot."

GerG swished his heavy tail and opened his large dark eyes. "I am prepared, O Mighty Presence."

The Great Ones nodded, and GerG turned from the chamber and stepped into the corridor. He felt filled with the importance of his mission. *To be the savior of my race, and more. To be the messenger of the past to seventy million years in the future. If there are intelligent beings in that future, how they will venerate me! I will be their key to the wisdom of the ages!* At the end of the corridor, he came to the massive stone doors behind which stood an army of anxious scientists—and the door to the future. He placed his clawed fingers on the massive brass handles, then paused.

> "You're sure, now, that this doesn't have one of those twist endings? I won't put up with it, if it does."
>
> "I said to trust me, didn't I?"
>
> "Yeah. Okay."

GerG pulled open the doors. Before him spread the huge laboratory, its far wall occupied by the shimmering blue-green of the time frame. Standing in front of it, a group of seven scientists twitched their tails as they checked computations, adjustments, and a mass of other detail. One of them looked in GerG's direction, then turned back to the others. "It is the Chosen One."

"The Chosen One!" repeated the others in hushed voices.

GerG approached them and extended his clawed hands. Each of the scientists in turn bowed, touching his forehead to an outstretched hand. "I am ready. You may rise."

One scientist remained bowing. "Please step this way, Chosen One." The scientist pointed with his head.

GerG saw a small table littered with instruments, then walked over. He pointed a claw at a black box attached to a wide belt. "Is this the language translator that will allow me to communicate with any intelligent race I should find?"

> *"Language translator?"*
> *"Knock it off! I'm on a roll."*

The scientist bowed. "Yes, Chosen One." The scientist pointed at another instrument. "And this is your weapon, should you meet anything hostile." The scientist placed the instrument into a holster and held the belt out. GerG lifted his arms as another scientist pulled the ends of the belt around GerG's waist and buckled it. Another scientist placed the strap holding the translator around GerG's neck.

GerG stood tall and faced the time frame. "Is all in readiness?"

All the scientists bowed. "Yes, Chosen One, and may the Great Phlabod be with you."

GerG walked until he stood before the frame, then stopped. The shimmer of the surface filled his vision as his skin prickled with the aura of energy surrounding the doorway. He took a deep breath, placed a clawed hand upon his weapon, and stepped through.

"Hey! Why don't you watch where you're going?"

GerG looked down to see a furry amphibian nursing its bruised tail. "I beg your—"

"Watch out!"

GerG stopped his descending foot just in time to avoid crushing a fan-shaped mollusk. "I'm terribly sorry—"

A five-foot-long dragonfly buzzed angrily about GerG's head. "Get in line, you overgrown toad!"

A pink, hairless biped walked over and poked GerG in the arm. "Here, take a number."

GerG looked at the square plastic chip the human held. He looked up and held out his hands. "What is this?"

The human raised its brows and continued in a bored voice. "Look, all you extinct creatures are piling in here through the same time node. You'll just have to wait your turn."

End

> *"Oh, no! Not a twist ending! I told you I won't put up with it!"*
>
> *"Aw, c'mon."*
>
> *"C'mon, nothing! Move aside! I'm taking over!"*
>
> *"You can't take over; I'm in control."*
>
> *"I can't, huh? Just watch me!"*

GerG pulled the weapon from his belt, aimed it at the human, and blew off its head. Turning quickly, he shot the dragonfly in the air, then cut the amphibian in two. He saw the mollusk cowering in a corner. "We'll just see who has to wait in line, my crunchy friend." GerG lifted a foot and stepped on the shelled creature. Lifting his foot, GerG expected to find a mess, but, instead, found a squashed bundle of wires, integrated circuits, and broken bulbs. "Eh? What is this?"

He looked at the human, the amphibian and the dragonfly—nothing but wires, integrated circuits, tiny motors. Frowning, he looked at the surrounding landscape, aimed his weapon at it, and fired. A great hole tore in the scenery, he walked toward it, stepped through, and found himself back in the laboratory.

A scientist bowed. "Congratulations, Chosen One. You have passed the test. We are now certain of your ability to pave the way for our race's survival—that is, once we invent time travel."

End

"*There!*"
"*That's a twist ending, too.*"
"*What?*"
"*Look at it.*"
"*Hmmm. I see. Those endings do kind of grow on you, don't they?*"
"*How true. But, you know what the real twist ending on this piece is?*"
"*No, what?*"
"*You don't even exist!*"
"*. . . . !*"

As my years begin to add up it becomes clearer and clearer to me that the only thing that stands between us and Utopia is this word "Utopia." Any social construct one wishes to put forward as Utopia can be shot down by saying "but it's not perfect." One's mind is hard put, however, to come up with an example of "perfection" that exists in either mind or reality. Of course when this proposition is offered, the devoted student of philosophy leaps bodily into the fray armed with a satchel full of definitions, a mouth full of logic, and a head full of semantic nonsense. "Perfection" to one is not necessarily "perfection" to another. It's a value judgement. Language and human judgement, you see, are far from "perfect."

So what are we all trying to do? Where do we want to go? Where should we want to go? How do we force the rest of humanity to want it too? All fun questions. The kind of questions that keep psychologists, philosophers, clerics, sociologists, economists, politicians, and political consultants in constant demand. It's a puzzle with no solution. A game. In terms of human doubt, pain and death, a very expensive game.

The phrase "If it ain't broke don't fix it" has come into wider circulation recently in an effort to cut through this semantic game—this fog of meaningless words and non-issues—to come up with some sort of practical approach for dealing with the current social mess. The first time I became

216

acquainted with that phrase was in 1962 as HAWK missile technician in the Army. The phraseology then seemed to have deeper—earthier—roots, and I would commend the original form to our age's social thinkers. As my missile chief phrased it: "If it works, don't fuck with it."

Since I couldn't even begin to improve upon that poetry, I wrote "Catch the Sun."

Catch the Sun

Synya squatted in the snow, her thorny back toward Kadnu's dying light, as the last of the far vine-masters joined the circle. She glanced at the two vine-masters to her right, then looked up above the ring of gray-maned heads for the light among Kadnu's Sparks that would grow bright, bringing the future of the vine people.

She tossed her mane and swiped at the snow with a clawed hand, sending a spray of crystals into the air. She looked at the soft whiteness in front of her, then dug the claws of her hands into her haunches. *Better that the ice should claim us than the future.*

"Synya." Nothing but a click and a hiss, but to the vine people it was a name. "Synya, we are all present."

Synya looked up and stared with unblinking eyes at the speaker. "I see this, Morah. Kadnu has not blinded me despite my many growths."

The one called Morah squatted silently for a long moment, then held out his long muscular arms. "Why are we here, Synya?"

Gray manes nodded. Another vine master, a long leap to Synya's left, turned his head. "It has taken me three growths of fast travel to meet here at your call. The people of my vine will not see me for more than another three growths if I should leave at this moment." He clawed at the snow. "Look at this, Synya. I must move with Kadnu for a growth before turning toward my vine if I am to avoid the ice. Why are we here?"

Synya looked again at the two vine-masters to her right. Shadig, the closest to her, shook his mane and cast down his glance. The next vine-master, Neest, folded her arms across her breast and studied the snow. "You are the oldest, Synya. It is your place."

Synya looked around the circle of squatting bodies, then looked up again for the spark that would grow bright.

How to tell them that God is but a ball of burning air, that Kadnu's Sparks are but more such balls—many much larger? How to tell them that the Endless Trail is not endless, but is nothing but a futile trek around a great ball? That we will never find the Lost Ones? That there is no God?

She brought her glance down to the ring of faces. "We must wait here. There will be a visitor." Visitor. Synya shook her head. *I use the word for Kadnu's Sparks that streak the sky because we have no word else to name them.* She again dug her claws into her haunches. *But the streaks are but stones that burn in our air. And they ... they are not stones.*

Morah snorted and shook his head. "Synya, no one reveres Kadnu's visitors more than I, but is this why we are called? Can we not watch the visitor from the snowfields at the backs of our own vines?"

Synya took a deep breath and snorted steam from her nostrils. She closed her eyes. "The visitor, Morah, is not from Kadnu. The visitor will only be seen here."

Morah opened his fanged mouth in surprise. "Have you— has your sign-reader seen a vision? Do the Lost Ones—"

"Silence!" Synya turned toward Shadig and held out her left arm toward Morah. "You speak now, Shadig! Tell them of the visitor not from Kadnu!"

Shadig glanced at Synya, then returned his gaze toward the snow. "Morah, the sign-readers did not see this ... this visitor, nor its purpose. I, Synya, and Neest met here long ago to plot the rooting of our respective vines. It was then that we saw the ... visitor." Shadig covered his eyes and mouth; still all heard him whimper.

Morah stood erect. "Say this, Shadig! What do you struggle to keep from us?"

Shadig only shook his head. Synya looked at Neest, but the vine-master's gaze was frozen to the snow. Synya turned toward Morah. "The visitor told us to gather all of the vine-masters here to meet twenty-seven growths from the visitor's departure. This is the end of the twenty-seventh growth."

Morah expelled the air from his mouth and wrinkled his upper lip into a sneer. "Pah! And how would this visitor know where the vines would be within twenty-seven growths? We do not even know this for five growths. To plot that far toward Kadnu would anger God and death-burn those foolish enough to approach so close. Tell us, Synya, how would this visitor know?"

Synya nodded slowly. "The visitor knows."

Those lights, those slivers of metal, those pale traces on shiny sheets of warm ice . . . the thing that took the three of us away from the ground to show us the Endless Trail to be a ball floating in nothing . . . "Morah, the visitor knows. I cannot explain how because I do not know the method. I do know we must wait."

Morah looked around the circle of vine-masters. "I have come a long way. For that reason I shall wait." He looked at Synya. "For a while." He held out his hands. "But I shall not wait squatting in the snow. I go to my hut!" He turned and left the circle. One by one the others stood and moved toward their vine-bark huts until only Synya, Shadig, and Neest remained.

Shadig turned toward Synya. "Why did you not tell them?"

Synya tensed her arm muscles, restraining them from bringing her clawed hand across Shadig's mouth. "You were there too, Shadig! You could have told them!"

Shadig hissed, moving into a half-crouch. "It is you who should have told them! You are the oldest!"

Neest stood erect. "We all saw the same things and none of us told of the things we saw and for the same reason." She turned and looked toward Kadnu's fading light. "They would have done what we would have done in their places. They would have taken us for mad." She looked down at Shadig and Synya. "Or blasphemers."

Neest turned and walked toward her hut. Shadig stood, turned, then left Synya alone in the snow.

Synya looked at Kadnu's Sparks. *If you were but sparks . . .* Two visitors in rapid succession left brief streaks across the sky. Synya looked down at the snow. *Stones burning in air.*

She stood, turned, and moved toward her hut.

The ice wind carried the roar of the visitor to Synya's ears. She could hear the shouts of the other vine-masters and the soft padding of their running feet through the snow. She did not move, but instead kept her gaze fixed on the deep pink of Kadnu's glow as the pale light entered the open end of her hut. The roar of the visitor was a familiar one. The light at the open end of her hut was blocked by a dark, hulking figure. It was Morah.

"The visitor has come, Synya!"

She lowered her head. "It is as we told you."

"Then, come! It is you who called us. Do you not wish to hear the visitor's message?"

Synya looked up at the darkness of the figure blocking her doorway. "I have heard the visitor's message, Morah. Now it is your turn."

Morah paused for a moment, then turned and ran toward the sounds of the other vine-masters. Synya picked at her clawed toes for a few moments, then crawled from her hut. She stood and turned in the direction of the chattering to see the vine-masters standing a respectful distance away from the visitor. It was a blue-and-white-colored container supported by five telescoped legs. It was at least a growth long—much longer than the earlier visitor—and its top and sides bristled with points, lumps, and whirling things in clear bubbles. From beneath it came bright white lightning and great billows of steam.

Synya felt a clawed hand on her left arm, and she turned to see Shadig looking into her eyes. "These growths, Synya. All these growths! I prayed that the thing we saw was a dream; that the visitor would not return. I . . . prayed! To Kadnu, I begged!"

Synya pulled her arm free and snorted. "You would pray

to a ball of burning air?" She cocked her head toward the circle of vine-masters gathered around the strange craft. "Come, Shadig. Let us meet our future."

When they joined the circle, Synya saw that Neest was already there, squatting in the snow while the others stood. Neest glanced at her and Shadig, then she returned her gaze to the craft.

Out of the steam walked four beings talking the strange yodel of the things called "humans." Their skins were green, with black fur around their faces; but they were different from the other ones. The tall muscular one beat his hands against his arms. "By the beard of the Prophet, Miklynn, your big mouth's gotten us stuck in some pits before—"

"How would you like to pick your teeth out of those pits, Assir?" The speaker was not as tall as the other, but he was fat and talked with authority. Following them were two others, both slender, one a head taller than the other. The fat one motioned behind and the short, slender one moved up to his side.

"What is it, Red?"

The fat one pointed at the circle of vine-masters. "Tell these creepy-looking things we're ready." The fat one looked around, pulled a smoking stick from his mouth, then frowned at the short, slender one. "Dean, where in the hell are the others? We're supposed to pull the whole damned population off this rock. There can't be but thirty or so here."

The slender one looked at the circle of vine-masters, then he spoke in the sounds and words of the vine people. *"Are the ones named Synya, Shadig, and Neest among you?"*

Synya stepped through the circle and stopped a short leap before the speaker. Shadig and Neest joined her. *"I am Synya."* She moved her clawed hand from her breast, then indicated her two companions. *"Shadig, Neest."*

"I am called Dean." Dean pointed at the fat one. *"This one is our master and he is called Red Miklynn."*

A growl of anger erupted from the circle. The fat one slapped Dean on the arm and shouted at him. "What in the hell did you say?" He pulled the smoking stick from his mouth and threw it down to the snow. "Dammit! I know I should've pulled Jerzi out of that funny farm. Helluva communications man you make, Dean—"

The one called Dean wrinkled his face and bared his small teeth. "Look, fatty, I told you to—"

Synya stepped forward. *"Dean."*

Dean looked at her. *"I am Dean."*

"Dean, you called this other 'Red.' " Synya pointed at the dying glow of Kadnu. *"This is one of the names of our God. It is one of his many colors."*

Dean nodded, then pointed at the fat one. *"This one needs only to be called 'Miklynn.' I meant no disrespect."*

The vine-masters nodded, then the fat one poked Dean in the arm. "Well? Where's the rest of them?"

Dean turned back to Synya. *"We were told by the others who came before us that all of the vine people would be ready by the twenty-seventh growth. Where are they?"*

Synya held out both of her arms indicating the others of her kind surrounding the four humans. *"We are all that can come. These are the masters of their respective vines."*

Dean frowned. *"The vine people do not know?"*

"We could not tell them. They would not believe."

Dean looked around the circle of vine-masters, then brought his gaze to a halt on Synya. *"What about the other vine-masters?"*

Synya shook her gray mane. *"None of them have been told. You must show them."*

Dean turned toward the fat one called Miklynn. "Red, we got troubles."

Miklynn grimaced and nodded. "It figures. It's not bad enough to get stuck with a farming job. We have to do one on Gaum's troubleshooting and followups."

The one called Assir snorted. "Miklynn, if you'd keep your big mouth shut, Gaum would be farming and we'd be troubleshooting."

Miklynn held up his hand. "All right! You've worked your jaw enough for one day, Assir. Unless you want it wired shut, button it up!" He turned toward Dean. "What's the trouble?"

"Red, these are just the vine-masters. The people haven't been told. In fact, neither have the vine-masters. This one," he pointed toward Synya, "says that you'll have to take the other vine-masters up and show them. Otherwise they won't believe."

Miklynn raised an eyebrow, then looked around the circle. "A joy ride." He looked back at Dean. "I count around thirty. Where are the rest of the vine-masters?"

Dean looked around the circle, then faced Synya. *"I see only half of the vine-masters. We know there to be over sixty vines—"*

Snorts and hisses greeted Dean's remarks until Synya held up her hands for quiet. When all was silent, except the wind, Synya looked at Dean. *"These are all the vine-masters."*

Dean looked at the fat one. "Red, she says this is it; there ain't no more."

Miklynn rubbed his chin, then kicked snow from his right boot. "Do these characters follow the sun or the ice?"

Dean looked around the circle. *"How many of you follow Kadnu?"*

Shadig snorted. *"All of us follow Kadnu. If we did not the ice would destroy us."* Shadig scooped up a handful of snow and flung it into the air to punctuate his observation.

Dean turned toward Miklynn. "Red, these guys are only the vine-masters from this side of the habitable belt. There's no one from the opposite side of the ring."

Miklynn nodded. "Gaum must've spent all of ten minutes troubleshooting this rock."

Dean shrugged. "Should I ask them why the other vine-masters aren't here?"

The fat one looked around the circle, then turned toward the tall slender one standing behind him. "Parks, do you think that these people even know about the population of the other side of this planet?"

The one called Parks moved up and stood between Dean and the fat one. He looked at Dean. "Ask them . . . ask them if they have a legend about . . . about a missing population."

Dean turned toward Synya. *"Does your belief in Kadnu suggest . . . does it include a missing people?"*

Synya's head snapped back as though it had been slapped. *"The Lost Ones. Dean, do you speak of the Lost Ones?"* Dean turned and nodded at Parks, then turned back to Synya.

"Synya, where are the Lost Ones?"

Synya held a clawed hand toward Kadnu's light. *"We know not, Dean. Kadnu will lead us to them."*

Dean turned toward Miklynn and raised his eyebrows. "Red, they don't even know about the others. A search for the 'Lost Ones' is part of their belief."

Miklynn stomped around in a small circle for a few seconds, then stopped and poked Assir's chest with a gloved forefinger. "You take this mob up for the joy ride and put enough distance between you and that sun so they can tell it's just like any other star."

Assir heaved a sigh. "Red, that will take days—"

"But before you take off for the long ride, you hop on up to the base ship, grab another communications man, then pick up a few of those Lost Ones. Got me?"

Assir nodded. "Yeah—"

"And while you're at the base ship, send down enough rock-hound teams in landers to recheck Gaum's data—iceside and hot-side both."

"What?"

The fat one placed his fists on his hips. "If that idiot Gaum can miss half a planet's population, would you trust his seismic data? Before I plant eight hundred thrusters on this rock, I want to make certain we won't tear it apart." The fat one glowered at the one called Assir. "Move it!"

Assir shrugged, then turned toward the craft. Lifting his right hand, he waved the vine-masters to follow him. Dean looked around at the circle. *"You are to follow him into the craft. You will not be harmed."*

Synya noticed that all of the vine-masters were looking at her. *"The visitor has something to show you . . . something you must know. Shadig, Neest, and I have already seen it."*

Morah looked at the snow for a second, then turned and faced Synya. *"If this is a good thing we shall see, are you not coming with us?"*

Synya shook her mane. *"The goodness of the thing is not for me to judge. I have seen it once, and that is enough."* The vine-masters continued to look at Synya. *"I am your senior, and I tell you to go! This is what you have traveled so far to see. You must see this!"*

Shadig looked toward the craft, then looked at Synya. *"We will go. For me ... I must see it again. I ..."* He turned and began moving toward the craft. Neest watched Shadig, then looked at Synya and nodded. Neest turned toward the craft and one by one the remaining vine-masters followed.

The one called Dean looked at Synya standing alone in the snow. *"Will you go with them?"*

"Pah!" Synya's long arms swiped at the icy air. *"My eyes have spoken once to me. I listened then!"*

Miklynn walked up to Synya and studied her, as she studied him. She had height and strength, but the fat one brought the terrible future. He turned to the one called Dean. "What's the chatter about?"

Dean shrugged. "She's seen the Terraform Corps' act before. She doesn't want a rerun."

The fat one looked back at Synya. "Ask her where she will go now."

"Synya, where do you go?"

Synya turned toward Kadnu's light and held out a clawed hand. *"I go to tend my vine."* She lowered her hand and looked from Miklynn to Dean, then to the remaining human. *"What is this one called?"*

Dean looked at the tall slender one, then turned back to Synya. *"He is called Parks. He is our ..."* The one called Dean seemed to search for his words, *"Parks advises us ... on matters ..."* Dean looked at Parks. "Parks, I don't have any way to describe a social structural engineer with the vocabulary Gaum's communications man stuffed into the computer."

The one called Parks looked at Dean, then shook his head. "I don't speak the language."

"Give me some other description—some other words."

Parks scratched his chin with a gloved finger, then shrugged. "Beliefs, customs, historical trends, organization?"

Dean held up a hand toward Parks, then turned toward Synya. *"The one called Parks advises us on matters of faith, tradition ... ritual—"*

Synya's gray mane came up sharply. *"Parks, then, is your sign-reader?"*

Dean shook his head and turned to Parks. "She doesn't

understand. She thinks you're a 'sign-reader.' That's their name for witch doctor, seer, priest, or whatever."

The one called Parks appeared to laugh within himself. But his eyes held none of this laugher. "That's close enough, Dean." He returned his glance to the one called Dean. "I used to be a chaplain. Go ahead. Tell her that I am a sign-reader."

Dean frowned and looked at the fat one. Miklynn waved an impatient hand. "I don't give a damn."

Dean pursed his lips, then addressed Synya. *"The one called Parks is our sign-reader."*

Synya moved toward Parks and studied his face. *"He has the eyes of a sign-reader. Strange eyes. But those of a sign-reader."*

Dean turned toward Parks. "You've passed inspection—"

Synya leaped backwards as a beeping noise came from the fat one's belly. The fat one pulled a dark object from his belly and spoke to it. "What?"

"Miklynn, we're ready. Are you clowns coming?" Synya recognized the distorted voice of the one called Assir.

The fat one thumbed the object. "Keep your turban on." He turned toward Dean. "Is your little chit-chat over?"

Parks shook his head. "Wait, Red."

"Wait for what?"

Parks rubbed his chin, looked at Synya, then back at the fat one. "Look, Gaum has screwed up everything else. We ought to check his data on social structures."

The fat one appeared angry. "Parks, I don't give a damn if they know which fork to use—or even if they know what a damned fork is. All I want to do is get this job over and done with as fast as possible."

Parks walked over and poked the fat one in the chest. "Well, Red, what if they don't want to leave? What if, instead of calmly boarding the landers, they decide to stay? For all we know from the job that Gaum did, these people could be planning to wage war on us."

The fat one looked down at the finger stabbing at his chest. "You want to keep that finger?" The stabbing stopped and Parks folded his arms across his chest. Miklynn turned toward Synya, glanced at Dean, then spoke at the object in his hand.

"Assir, dump out three K-packs and let us get clear before you take off. We'll be here on the skin for a while." The object clicked and the fat one replaced it on the strap around his belly. As the one called Parks ran toward the craft to pick up the packs, the fat one looked at Dean and pointed a finger at Synya. "Tell her we're coming along."

Dean faced Synya. *"The fat one asks if we may go with you to see your people."*

Synya looked from Dean to Miklynn. *"Will the sign-reader called Parks come with you?"*

"Yes. It was his request."

Synya looked back at Dean. *"Then you may come. I would have your sign-reader observe what is, then consider what is to be."*

Dean looked at Miklynn. "She says it's okay." Dean pointed a thumb toward the craft. "Why the K-packs? Why not use a cart?"

The fat one pointed at Dean's feet. "See those?"

"What about them?"

"That's locomotion on this planet, dirtbrain. All we need is to come roaring up to her tribe in a cart to scare the living daylights out of them."

Dean fluttered his eyelashes and held his head to one side. "Why, you old softie."

"Dean, how would you like me to rip off your lips?"

Parks ran up, distributed the packs, and while the humans put them on, Synya looked toward Kadnu's light. *Does being a ball of fire, does knowing what you are, make you not a god?* She looked down at the snow, knowing but refusing to recognize the answer.

"Let's move out." It was the voice of the fat one.

Synya looked at Dean. *"We are ready, Synya."*

She walked a few paces to a mound of snow, reached under it and lifted her hut. She shook the snow from it, rolled the vine bark and tied it with woven strands of softened fiber, then slung the roll across her back. She faced the three humans, then turned toward Kadnu and began walking.

Synya set a strong pace toward Kadnu, the three humans half-walking, half-running to keep up with her. Each time she looked over her shoulder, however, the fat one was only a short leap behind while Dean and Parks fell further back. Synya increased her pace to a comfortable run, then looked back again. Dean and Parks were left far behind, but the fat one remained but a short leap back, his face reddening, his stubby legs pumping against the thinning snow.

Synya frowned, then turned her face toward the light and ran as though the ice scavengers had picked up her scent. She maintained her speed until she felt the sting of the cold air in her lung. She slowed to a walk, then stopped and looked back. The fat one, streams of wetness on his face, stood a short leap behind her, sucking and blowing at the air. The others were lost over the horizon. "Wha..." The fat one gulped more air. "What's the ... matter, you ... creep? Can't run any ... faster'n that?"

Synya frowned, then hissed and clicked at the human. *Your legs ... not made for running. Mine are. Why ... do you try and prove differently?"*

The fat one pointed at the right side of his head. "I don't ... speak the lingo." He pointed toward Kadnu. "If you are all ... rested up, then let's get going."

Synya pointed at her own head and pointed away from the light. *"Wait for Parks and Dean. Our tracks ... covered soon by the wind."*

The fat one nodded. "Parks ... Dean." He pointed at the snow. "Wait for them?"

Synya nodded, then looked with surprise as the fat one fell as a stiff branch to the snow, apparently asleep. Synya, still breathing hard squatted next to the human. *I envy your ability to sleep, fat one. My sleeps have been too troubled.* Synya looked away from the light to see two dark specks against the white of the snow. She studied them until she was certain they were not scavengers but the remaining two humans. She looked back at the fat one and jabbed his arm with her clawed fingers. He did not open his eyes. *"You must not sleep so soundly on the snow, fat one. You must be on guard against the cold and the ice scavengers."*

The human did not stir except for the heaving of his chest. Synya unslung her hut roll and busied herself putting up her shelter. When she was finished, she squatted in it and watched the human until his two companions arrived. Parks slung down his pack and rushed to the fat one's side while Dean squatted in front of the opening to Synya's hut. *"Synya, what happened?"*

"The fat one and I moved too fast for you and Parks. We decided to wait here for you." Synya looked down at the snow, then back at Dean. *"Why could the fat one run with me when you and your sign-reader could not?"*

Dean looked over his shoulder. "Parks, how's Red doing?"

Parks stood, picked up his pack and began opening it. "He's out cold. And I do mean o-u-t out. We better get him into a shelter."

Dean looked back at Synya. *"The fat one has things to prove to himself that the sign-reader and I do not."* Dean chuckled. *"It's a good thing that you did not challenge the fat one to a fang-growing contest."*

Synya's forehead wrinkled in confusion as she observed Dean's short flat teeth, then licked her tongue over her set of tearing teeth. *"Surely the fat one would lose such a contest."*

Dean stood and unslung his pack. *"No, Synya. Miklynn would probably win, but it would be..."* Dean frowned as he searched for an expression, then he shrugged. *"It would not be good for his gums."*

Synya watched as Dean and Parks erected a shelter of fabric, then pulled the fat one inside. She curled herself into a ball, her sensitive ears searching for threatening sounds, and began to doze. She licked again at her fangs, then tried to imagine the fat one with a similar set.

I must have not understood the one called Dean. She sighed. *Words can be so mysterious.*

Synya awakened with a start as her ears picked up noises her instincts said should not be there. Her ears altered direction until she identified the curious yodel of humans speaking. To be certain of their safety, she moved from her hut, walked around the two shelters, sniffed at the air, then returned to her hut. She again curled into a ball, letting the soothing human voices calm her.

"Red, you are about the stupidest sonofabitch I ever met."

"Parks, you and me don't go back *that* far. How about I feed you a few knuckles?"

"You tell him, Dean."

"Yeah, Dean. You tell me."

"I'm not an authority, Red."

"What's that supposed to mean?"

"I don't know how many stupid sons of bitches Parks has met. I bet you're way up there, though."

"You little schoolboy snot, I ought—Parks, are you getting your jollies or something? You want to quit feeling up my leg?"

"Red, unless we get your circulation going, you can kiss these lovely little stems of yours good-bye."

"The joy juice'll do that."

"I'm just helping it along. Why don't you try and get some sleep?"

"Hah! Wouldn't you just like that? Get me while I'm asleep—"

"Dean. Hit him with another shot. I'm tired of listening to him."

"Dean, you squirt me with any more of that . . . stuff. You crummy . . . little . . . sonof . . . abitch . . ." The voice of the fat one died away.

"What's his temperature?" The voice of the one called Parks had concern in it.

"It's up. Stick the heat sheet over him and I think he'll be okay." Synya heard fabric being spread, then the voice of the one called Dean. "I'll stand first watch over him."

"Okay. Dean, lend me your language chip."

"Why?"

"If I'm going to be a sign-reader, I think it would help if I knew the language. It's all right; I'm adapted."

"Even so, you can't learn it in just a few hours. It took me four straight days."

"I'll learn what I can, when I can . . ."

Synya dozed, her ears standing her own watch.

. . . The one called Gaum had pointed at the view of the great ball, half-shrouded in darkness. Synya looked with horror at the thin band between the light and the dark—a narrow

*thread of life in the midst of so much death by ice, death by
fire. As the craft swung around the great ball, Synya saw the
lopsided mound of ice. It extended toward Kadnu farther than
any of the vines; but farther than that, extended a great body
of water. At the edge of the water, where once again the soil
could be seen, the water steamed. The one called Gaum had
said that the ice, water and hot desert were the things that
had kept the vines and the vine people from crossing over to
the world where one must flee Kadnu, instead of follow him.
But the one called Gaum had never spoken about the Lost
Ones . . .*

She brought her eyes open as her ears heard feet in the
snow. Through the open end of her hut she saw the fat one
standing, looking at Kadnu's light. He reached to his neck
with his right hand, unsealed his green skin, then took something from within it and brought his hands around the stick.
Smoke erupted from his hands; and when he brought his hands
away, the end of the stick glowed. The fat one sucked on the
stick, letting the wind from the ice carry the smoke toward
Kadnu.

Synya crawled from her hut, walked over to Miklynn, then
squatted beside him. She pointed a clawed finger at the thing
in Miklynn's mouth. *"Fat one, what is this for?"*

Miklynn pulled the object from his mouth and looked at
Synya. "So, you're finally up. Thought you'd sleep forever."
She jabbed her finger at the smoking stick. The fat one looked
at it. "This?" He held it out toward her. "Cigar. This is a
cigar."

Synya frowned. "Che . . . che-gah. Che-gah?"

The fat one shrugged. "Close enough." He unsealed his
skin, withdrew another stick, and held it out to her. "Want
one?"

Synya frowned, then took the stick in her hands. It was
soft—a roll of leaves. She held it to her nostrils and the
bittersweet smell intrigued her. She placed one end into her
mouth and pointed at the other. The fat one exposed his teeth
in a smile, then brought a flame from his hand to the end of
the stick. Synya sucked on the cigar as she had seen the fat

one do, and delicious smoke filled her mouth. She opened her lips, letting the ice-wind carry away the smoke. She nodded her mane at the fat one.

"The burning leaves taste good."

The fat one nodded as if he understood, and resealed his skin. He puffed on his own stick of leaves; and Synya joined him puffing the delicious smoke and looking at Kadnu's light.

"For crissake!" It was the voice of the one called Dean. "Parks, Red's teaching her how to smoke."

Synya looked over her shoulder to see Dean standing by the fabric shelter and the one called Parks emerging from it. Synya raised her clawed hand and delicately removed the cigar from her mouth. *"Dean, there is concern in your words."*

Parks stood, looked at the fat one's back, then shook his head. "Come on, Dean. Let's tear down the tent."

"But what about her health? What's one of Red's weeds going to do to her?"

Synya replaced the cigar between her thick lips and took another puff. Parks turned to the tent. "She seems to be handling it better than we do. Let's go with the tent." As Dean and Parks began repacking the shelter, Synya looked back toward Kadnu. She puffed again and watched the wind speed away the smoke. She turned her head toward the fat one and held out her cigar. "Che-gah."

The fat one puffed and nodded. "Put hair on your chest." He looked at Synya, observed the thick mat of hair on her chest, then shrugged and looked back toward Kadnu's light.

After a few moments, Dean and Parks walked up to them. They both wore their packs, and Dean carried the third. He held the pack toward the fat one. "Red, are you strong enough to carry this? Parks and I can switch off."

Synya saw the fat one's face grow angry as he turned and pulled the pack from Dean's hand. "After this job I'm going to throw you two smartmouths so deep in the stockade neither of you'll remember what sunlight is!"

As the fat one strapped on his pack, Synya turned toward Dean and removed the cigar from her mouth. *"Is the fat one angry with you?"*

Dean shook his head. *"It is only his manner."* Dean looked

toward Kadnu's light, then looked at Synya, again puffing on her cigar. *"Synya, this time could you walk a slower pace?"*

"Did the fat one ask this?"

Dean glowered at the fat one for a moment, then returned his gaze to Synya. *"No, it is for the sign-reader and I. We cannot keep up."*

Synya nodded. *"If it is for you and the sign-reader, I will walk more slowly."*

Dean turned toward Miklynn. "Red, we're going to keep the pace down."

The fat one's eyebrows rose. "Oh? Did Synya find our last little run too fast?"

Dean sighed and shook his head. "No. I asked her to slow it down."

The fat one nodded, smiled around his cigar, then turned and faced Kadnu's light. He patted Synya on the back, then pointed with his thumb toward Dean and Parks. "I guess we better hold it down. Those two are a little out of shape." Synya nodded and the pair began walking toward the light.

Dean turned toward Parks as the two began following. "Dammit, but Red makes me mad! Another run like that would kill him."

Parks hunched up his pack and kept putting one foot in front of the other. "Dean, just be grateful that the wind is at our backs."

"Why?"

"The cigars."

Dean nodded, hunched up his own pack, and followed in silence.

By the end of the walking, the bright edge of Kadnu peered over the horizon, casting long shadows from the regular mounds of soil covering the severed root-ends of Ashah, Synya's vine. During the walk, she had noted the larger mounds, and had told the human sign-reader their significance: with the root-ends were also buried the dead of her vine. She taught the sign-reader, through Dean, how to read the shapes of the mounds to identify the dead. They passed Nogda, the old sign-reader who had foretold the poor rooting of the fourth growth; and Synya's father, Garif, who had been slain by the ice scavengers; and others.

As Synya curled to sleep inside her shelter, she again listened to the humans talk. Dean and Parks were practicing to speak the language of the vine people. The human sign-reader had difficulty forming the words correctly, but he knew them. The fat one spoke the yodel of the humans.

"You two've been hissing and clicking at each other for hours. You want to knock it off so I can get some sleep?" The practicing stopped. Only silence came from the humans' shelter until, again, the fat one spoke. "Dean, you got that language chip on you?"

"What?" The one called Dean sounded astonished.

"Language chip, dirtbrain. You know what a language chip is—"

"Yeah, Red. I thought you said your skull was already too full of grunts and groans. Why the chip?"

"If I want you to know, I'll tell you. Maybe the next time I offer the lady a cigar, I'll want to do so as a gentleman."

"I don't think the chip has a word for cigar, except weed that croaks—"

"Just hand me the chip, Dean. And if I want any wise-ass remarks out of you, I'll stomp on your head'n squirt 'em out your ears."

Synya heard movement inside the shelter, then silence again. It was broken by Dean's voice. "Parks, what do you suppose he wants to talk to Synya for?"

"Maybe he's in love. Red's a haunch and claw man, you know."

Dean laughed. "Think you'll be best man?"

"No." Parks chuckled. "This love is destined to fail. She's too good for him."

Synya listened to the yodeling sounds, then drifted off to sleep, her ears standing guard.

The next three walks brought Kadnu into full view, the only remaining snow, mere patches hiding in the mound shadows. As they stopped to rest at the end of the walk, Dean and Parks set to the job of erecting their shelter while clouds crossed Kadnu's face, bringing with them a light rain. Synya completed her shelter, then walked to where the fat one was squatting on the bare soil. She could see where he had scooped up a handful of the soil. The fat one was letting the soil trickle through his bare fingers as he studied the horizon. Synya squatted next to Miklynn.

"Upon what are you thinking, fat one?"

Miklynn frowned at Synya. *"I am called Miklynn."* He spoke the language of the vine people well. *"Do not call me fat one."*

Synya sat back on her haunches and studied him. The description bothered him. Why that was concerned only him. *"Miklynn."*

"Yes."

"Why do you feel the soil?"

The fat one pointed from left to right at the horizon. *"Look, Synya. How flat it is. There are no . . . mountains . . . large mounds as there are on many other worlds. The soil is rich and fine-grained."* He held out a small, flat object. *"This is the largest stone I have found. The visitor Gaum explained farming to you?"*

Synya nodded her mane. *"The planting, the harvesting, and much more."* She looked down at the soil and clawed at it.

"Synya, after we have done our work, this world will farm. This soil can grow things almost from pole to pole. Do you understand?"

Synya sighed. *"Gaum explained these things. He showed us with his magic ice pictures."*

Miklynn studied the horizon, then scooped up another handful of soil. *"Synya, just think of the farm this world would be."*

Synya looked at the handful of soil she had clawed from the surface. *"I have thought upon it, Miklynn. For many growths, I have thought of little else."*

Miklynn stood, his glance still surveying the horizon. *"Synya, do not misunderstand me. This is not my kind of work. But, still, there is something to be accomplished here. This world will produce food—many kinds of food—for many kinds of worlds."*

With a claw extended from her left hand, she pushed about

the small mound of soil she held. *"This is why you come to do this to us?"*

The fat one looked down upon her, the space above and between his eyes wrinkled. *"Do to you?"*

"Your people will arrive at some gain by changing my world?"

The fat one moved his shoulders. *"Yes. But so will the vine people. That is why the ... big shots, the Quadrant ... why others have committed great ..."* The fat one shook his head. *"You don't have the word for wealth, the big credit."* He rubbed his chin. *"That is why others have committed a lot to this work. Both your people and mine will arrive at gains."* The fat one nodded his head. *"As I said, it is not my kind of work, but just think of what this world can be."*

Synya knocked the soil from her claws, then stood. *"I have thought on it, Miklynn."* She looked at Kadnu, hanging low above the horizon. Kadnu would not be followed, for he would travel too fast—no, the ... ball would spin too fast. It would melt the ice, warm the cold, and cool the hot. There would be no need to follow Kadnu. The vine people could stop their endless walk.

Synya shook her mane. *"I ... I have thought on it, Miklynn. I am grateful that my death will come first."* She turned and went to her shelter. Miklynn studied her back until she disappeared inside.

Synya listened to the soothing yodel of the humans as she curled and tried to sleep. Thoughts of Kadnu flying across the sky too fast for her to chase were thoughts she drove from her mind by concentrating on the human talk coming from their shelter.

"Dean?"

"Yeah, Red?"

"Who was the commo man with Gaum?"

"Keffer. Sheena Keffer. I don't know her. Why?"

The fat one was silent for a while. "I talked to Synya about increasing the rotation on this planet, about how it could be farmed ... she didn't exactly jump for joy. You think this Keffer screwed up?"

"Screwed up how?"

The fat one paused. "She as much as told me she'd rather be dead than see it."

"Keffer's job was to get the words, meanings, grammar, and contexts down. She's done that all right as far as I can see."

"Why didn't the original three vine-masters tell their people? Gaum's group must have scared the hell out of them."

Parks laughed. "No, Red. Look at it from Synya's point of view. The universe is a long road extending to infinity. The road is lighted by Kadnu, their god. Kadnu leads them along the road and draws their life-sustaining vines along with them. He gives them water, warms them, and is always there. Synya's god has never failed her or her people."

Dean snorted. "Which is more than you can say for most of the gods we've come across."

"So what, Parks? The Corps has shown Synya the truth about her road, but it showed her how we will turn this rock into a garden."

"A garden." The one called Parks was silent a long time. When he again talked there was a strangeness in his voice.

"Red, when Gaum took Synya and her two buddies on the grand tour, they weren't just shown that Santa Calus and the Easter Bunny are myths. They didn't only have their concept of Kadnu the god blown up in their faces—they had everything that they *know to be true* turned over, shook up, and flung out into space. Their universe has been destroyed, Red, and you wonder why a couple of plows and a manure spreader don't seem to compensate them for it."

The fat one laughed. "Careful, Parks. Keep it up and the Corps will have you back in your chaplain's collar."

"Why don't you just shut the hell up?"

The fat one was silent for a moment. "Dean, what put a wild hair up Parks's—"

"Shut up, Red. We can all use some sleep."

Silence came from the humans' shelter. After a long while, the fat one emerged from the entrance shouldering his pack. He stood looking at Kadnu for a moment, then began walking toward the light. Synya watched Miklynn march toward the light until she dozed. There would be no danger from the scavengers this close to Kadnu. The fat one would be safe.

At the end of the resting period the one called Miklynn had not returned. Synya and the two humans packed their shelters and continued toward the light without him. They walked in silence, reaching the short brown grasses, Kadnu growing ever higher above the horizon. The one called Dean yodeled the human speech at Parks, then Synya spoke. *"We all speak the language of the vine people. Do you hide things from me?"*

Parks shook his head. *"Dean was asking me about Miklynn; if we should be concerned."*

Synya looked at the one called Dean and saw no lie in his manner. *"Parks, then should you be concerned?"*

"No. Miklynn does as he wants when he wants."

Synya nodded. *"Then he has no fear."*

Parks studied the ground as he walked. He glanced up at Kadnu, then returned his gaze to the ground. *"We all have fears, Synya. Even Miklynn. Even you. Is this not true?"*

Synya and the others walked in silence. As they approached the place where green blades appeared among the brown grass, she turned toward Parks.

"You asked about my fears, sign-reader. All my fears have been brought by the humans. Before the one called Gaum came, one only needed to follow Kadnu and serve Ashah, our vine, as it followed Kadnu."

Parks frowned. *"You do not fear your god?"*

"Pah!" Synya swiped at the grass with her claws. *"The one called Gaum showed us the 'god' to be nothing but fire! We cook with fire! Fire serves us; we do not serve fire! What is there to fear, sign-reader?"*

Parks nodded, then faced Synya. *"Before Gaum came—did you fear Kadnu then?"*

Synya thought back. *"No . . . no, sign-reader. Before Gaum came we did not fear Kadnu. The light showed us the way to life. It fed and watered Ashah, it warmed our briths, and watched as we danced. You do not fear such a thing; you love it."* Synya choked as she suppressed a cry. *"But that was before Gaum came."*

Parks nodded, glanced at Kadnu, then studied the mounds of still fresh soil. *"Synya, what is death to the vine people—what was it before Gaum came?"*

"In death we served Ashah and were reborn with the Lost Ones." She waved her clawed hand at the nearest mound. *"Now what is it? Burial next to a root? The end of life?"*

The one called Dean slapped Parks's arm and pointed toward the horizon. "Look." Dean faced Synya. *"What is that?"*

Synya narrowed her eyes and studied the horizon. Directly beneath Kadnu there was a distinct bump marring the otherwise featureless surface. *"It is Ashah. The vine my people tend."*

Synya stopped and looked from the light, back toward the snow they had left behind. Regular mounds of soil reached to the horizon. Above, the sky was dark blue. Kadnu's light had drowned even the brightest of his sparks.

"To my eyes, sign-reader, it is as it always has been." She dug her claws into her breast. *"But to this—here inside of me—to this nothing is the same! What is this pain inside of me, sign-reader? Name it!"*

Parks studied Synya, then turned away as she looked at him. Before he turned, Synya had seen wetness in his eyes. *"I have no name, Synya. But I know the pain. I know it . . . very well."*

Parks resumed walking toward Kadnu. Synya saw Dean standing, watching Parks. Dean's brow was furrowed. *"Dean, what is this I see on your face? Anger?"*

Dean turned toward Synya, then shook his head. *"No, Synya. Doubt—confusion."* The one called Dean looked at the back of the other human. *"There is much we humans do not know . . . about each other."*

Dean began following Parks while Synya looked from one to the other. She held out her arms, extended her claws, and roared at Parks's retreating back. *"You know this pain, sign-reader! Is what you bring us worth this pain? Tell me!"*

Parks continued walking, not turning back, and not answering.

At the end of the walking period, they erected their shelters a few long leaps from the end of Ashah, the vine of Synya's people. Dean erected the fabric tent for the humans while the one called Parks sat cross-legged, studying the activity at the end of the vine. With their sharp claws, the vine people were stripping finger-thick sections of bark from the plant, while others cut free sections of the huge stem's meaty interior.

The strips of bark were handed down to others who would arrange them into close-fitting rows, which would then be spread with the thick sap of Ashah gathered by others. Synya talked among the workers for a long while, then returned to the two humans and squatted next to Parks. With her she held in her hands a piece of the vine's interior. She tore off a small portion and handed it to Parks. He took it, smelled it, then bit into it, and chewed.

"It is good, Synya—sweet. But does it spoil? How are the others tending the length of the vine fed?"

Synya waved a clawed hand at the air as she talked around a mouthful of food. *"It is still cold at this end of Ashah. The sections that are being cut free will soon be crust-covered. That protects the food as it is carried forward."*

Parks nodded. *"The vine-water dries in the air."* He felt the stickiness on his fingers, then pointed at the workers laying the strips of bark and spreading them with the sap. *"I see how your shelters are made. But is that one so large for a reason?"*

Synya shook her mane. *"It was the fat one who told them to build it."*

The one called Dean walked up and joined them, squatting on the short, green grass. "Did she say Miklynn's been by here?"

Parks nodded, then pointed at the workers. *"Miklynn told them to build something."* He turned to Synya. *"Did they say the purpose?"*

Synya shook her mane and handed Dean a piece of vine meat. Dean bit into it and raised his eyebrows. *"This is good."*

"It is the body of Ashah. It could be nothing else."

Dean nodded and looked at Parks. "What is Miklynn up to?"

"I do not know. Synya, did they say where the fat one went?"

"Only that they saw him continue toward Kadnu. They had many questions about the fat one. Many questions."

Parks smiled. *"And what did you tell them?"*

"That you are the sign-reader of the humans, and that you will answer their questions in due time."

Parks snorted, then looked at Dean. Dean only shook his head. Parks returned his glance to Ashah and the workers. *"The one thing I can never do is try to explain Miklynn."* He looked at Synya. *"Is your sign-reader near?"*

Synya pointed at one of the workers high atop the body of the great vine. *"Volyan. My grandson. He is one of our seven sign-readers."*

Dean began shaking as his face turned red. Synya frowned at him. *"Are you not well, Dean?"*

Dean nodded, laughed, then gasped for air. *"I cannot wait to tell Miklynn that his foot race was with a grandmother."*

Synya tossed back her mane. *"But I am not merely a grandmother."* Dean frowned, and Synya continued. *"Volyan's children are all mated, and each of the unions have been blessed by Kadnu with babes. All of them are now grown, have mated—"* Dean fell backwards, laughing uncontrollably. Synya turned toward Parks to ask the reason; but the sign-reader, too, was fighting for air to feed his laughter.

Later, inside the humans' shelter, Volyan joined Synya and the two humans. Volyan's mane was gray but streaked with brown. He pointed at Parks. *"What is the purpose of the large shelter with the strange design the fat one told us to build?"*

Parks shook his head. *"I do not know."*

Volyan pointed at Parks's belt. *"I know you can talk to the fat one if you choose. I saw him use such a thing to talk to creatures in a great craft, high in Kadnu's light."*

Parks pulled the communicator from his belt, studied it, then replaced it. *"If Miklynn wishes to talk with me, he will call."*

Dean pulled out his own communicator. "Well, I'll ask him if you won't. Damned if I know what it is." Dean pressed the object. He pressed it again.

"What?" Synya recognized Miklynn's voice.

"Red, we're at the end of the vine. What do you have these people doing?"

"I guess I was wrong, Dean. You are as stupid as you look." Dean's face flushed. The object spoke again. "Is Volyan there?" Dean held out the object toward Volyan and pointed at a small silver plate set in its surface. *"Speak in there."*

"Miklynn? This is Volyan."

"Do you still have that thing I left with you?"

Volyan nodded. *"I do."*

"Give it to Synya." The box remained silent for a moment, then spoke again. "Dean?"

Dean took the box from Volyan's hand. "Yeah, Red?"

"Don't call me any more unless it's important, got me? That call signal liked to scared the crap outta the people I was talking with. Miklynn out."

Dean looked at Parks, shrugged, then looked at Volyan in time to see him hand Synya a cigar. "Oh, for crying out loud!"

Synya inserted the proper end into her mouth then pointed a clawed finger at the other end and spoke to Volyan. *"Fire."* As Volyan left the tent, Synya nodded at Parks and talked around her cigar. *"The fat one remembers. He thinks of me."*

Parks grimaced. *"Yes, Synya, the fat one is a regular . . . sweetheart."*

"This last word, sign-reader. What does it mean?"

Parks sighed. *"It means that such a person is . . . a polite and . . . loving—"* Parks turned toward Dean. "You're the communications expert. You tell her."

Dean rubbed his chin and smiled. "It is not for me to divine the cryptic meanings of your visions, sign-reader."

As the human sign-reader pointed at the portion of his body upon which he was sitting and yodeled in the human speech at Dean, Volyan entered the tent carrying a leaf from the vine. He squatted before Synya and opened the leaf. In its center was a bright, glowing coal. Synya touched the end of her cigar to it and puffed until the cigar was lit, filling the tent with the bittersweet smoke. At the suggestion of the human sign-reader, they all moved outside of the tent to continue their discussion.

They sat on the grass outside of the tent facing each other.

Volyan laid the coal and leaf on the ground between them, and Dean leaned forward and picked it up. *"Parks, I can hardly feel the heat of the coal through the leaf."*

Parks took the leaf from Dean, held it for a moment, then nodded. Synya pointed at the leaf. *"We must wear wraps made from Ashah's leaves to protect us against Kadnu's heat at the growth-end of the vine."*

Volyan looked at the two humans, then at Synya. He studied her for an instant, then looked at the burning coal. While the humans watched the end of Ashah, and as Synya puffed on her cigar, the look on Volyan's face grew more concerned. He turned to Synya.

"Synya, first this fat one, then these two others. Boxes that speak, huge crafts in the sky, you making smoke from a stick. My sign-reader's eyes do not see the meanings. I see change, but what will that change be?"

Synya pulled the cigar from her mouth and hung her head as she closed her eyes. *"I almost forget, then I am reminded."*

She threw the cigar away and it hit the ground in a shower of sparks. *"There will be change, Volyan—many changes."* She nodded her head at Parks. *"Their sign-reader should tell you instead of me."* She shook her mane. *"I cannot."*

Parks pulled a blade of grass from the ground, pulled it apart, then dropped the pieces back to the soil. *"How can I tell him, Synya, when neither you, Shadig, nor Neest could tell the people of your vines? You all said that you would not be believed."*

Volyan studied the human sign-reader, then studied Synya. *"I see the same pain in you both. Synya, after what I have seen, I am prepared for the unbelievable."* He reached out a clawed hand and placed it on Synya's arm. *"You are my grandmother and the master of my vine. I can see truth from lies in you; and if you say the one called Parks tells the truth, I will believe."*

Synya remained still for a long moment, then nodded at Parks. *"Tell Volyan what the other vine-masters are being shown."*

Parks licked his lips then turned toward Dean. "Get one of those weather balloons from the tent." Dean left and Parks looked at Volyan. *"The masters of all of the vines are being shown that Kadnu is a great ball of burning air. Then they will be taken far, far away from Kadnu to show them that . . . Kadnu is nothing more than one of many thousands of such burning balls. Those are the lights you call Kadnu's Sparks."*

Dean returned and handed a small container to Parks. Volyan looked at Synya, then back to Parks. *"There is more, sign-reader. I see there is more."*

Parks nodded. *"Yes, Volyan. There is more."* Parks triggered the container and from its top emerged a white fabric that soon grew into a perfectly round ball. Half of the ball was lit by Kadnu; the other half was dark. Parks pointed at the ball.

"What you call the Endless Trail looks like this. It floats in space around Kadnu."

Volyan sat back for a moment, turned and looked at Synya, then returned his gaze to the ball. *"And . . . and there is yet . . . more."*

Parks pointed at the line between the light and dark sides of the balloon. *"This is where the vine people live—where we are right now. The ball—it is called a* planet—*moves very slowly. Like this."* He held his finger on the ball and rotated it until his fingertip was in the dark. *"This is why Ashah and the vine people must move every growth, like this."* He moved his finger from the dark back to the line without moving the ball.

Volyan stood, looked at Kadnu, then turned completely around, peering at the horizon. when he stopped, he was looking down at Synya. *"Grandmother . . ."*

Synya nodded, her eyes shut tightly. *"It is . . . it is true! It is true, but . . . there is still more!"*

Volyan remained standing, looking with astonishment from his grandmother to the human holding the ball. He squatted, and dug his claws into his haunches. *"Parks."*

Parks did not meet Volyan's glance. *"Yes, Volyan."*

"If . . . if what you say is true . . . and Synya says it is true. Synya says it is, and I see no lie in her, but if the Trail is a . . . ball, what of the Lost Ones? We will never catch the god and meet . . . the Lost Ones?"

"Look at the other side of the ball, Volyan."

Volyan stood and walked until he stopped beside Dean. Parks continued rotating the ball in the same direction. *"Just as your people must follow Kadnu, on the other side there are more people that must move from Kadnu. They follow the ice. I believe them to be the Lost Ones."*

Volyan swiped at the ball with his claws, exploding it. *"This . . . this, this thing you say . . ."* He looked at Synya. *"This cannot be true! Grandmother, this cannot be true!"*

Synya stood, pain and anger contorting her voice. *"You see no lie in me! It is true! My own eyes have seen this thing, and there is still more, Volyan! Still more! The humans have great machines that they will plant on this ball of ours! The machines will make the ball spin faster! So fast that our strongest runner could not keep up with Kadnu's pace! The ball will spin so fast that the ice will melt and the death-burn will cool!"* She held out her arms. *"The entire ball will be much like it is here, right now."*

Volyan squatted and clawed at the green grass. *"But Grandmother, why do they do this to us?"*

Synya squatted. *"We will grow things—food. More food than we can ever use. Then great crafts will come to take away the food and they will give us leaves for the food. With the leaves we can have others come to us and make us shelters of stone, teach us things . . . we will be . . . prosperous."*

Volyan rocked back and forth on his feet, digging at his haunches until he broke the thorny skin that covered them. *"I see, Grandmother. I see. And what shall the vine people do when the ball spins too fast to follow Kadnu, yet not fast enough to melt the ice?"*

Synya looked at Parks, then squatted. *"Tell him, sign-reader."*

Parks had his elbows resting on his knees, his face resting in the open palms of his hands. He shook his head. Dean looked at Synya, but talked to Volyan. *"The population will be removed from the planet until the proper rotation speed is achieved and the air masses have adjusted to the new surface temperatures. Right now the wind always comes from the cold side of the ball to the warm side, where it rises and returns to the cold side. In the centers of both the cold and hot sides, the air does not move. At the new speed, the coldest parts of the ball will be...at the top and bottom. The air will change. The wind will come from the top and bottom, meet in the middle where it will be warmest, then it will rise and return. the change will cause terrible storms—"*

"Aaahh!" Volyan held his hands over his ears. When he let his hands fall, he looked at Synya. *"How long have you known?"*

"Twenty-seven growths."

Volyan looked at the grass before him. *"How could you keep this awful knowledge within yourself for so long..."* He turned to Dean. *"How long will we be away from... here?"*

Dean thought a moment. *"Between seventy and eighty growths."* He shrugged. *"Maybe more. It depends on many things."*

Volyan looked at Synya. *"You will be dead before you see this."*

Synya nodded, then looked at Dean. *"Ashah. What will happen to Ashah and all of the other vines?"*

Dean shrugged and shook his head. Parks lifted his face away from his hands and looked at Synya.

"They will die. They will all die."

Synya looked at the human sign-reader's face. It was streaked with wetness. *"Parks, is there a chance that this will not happen?"*

Parks barked out a laugh. *"Not with the fat one in charge, Synya. Miklynn will see that the job is done. He has to."*

In her hut, Synya curled to sleep, rearranged her position, and curled again. The yodel of the nearby human voices, this time, was not soothing.

"Dean, I've been with Miklynn for too long. He doesn't like this job, but it's the job he's been given to do, and he will do it."

"Parks, if he doesn't like it..."

"The only reason he doesn't like it is because it's a post-followup operation—a milk run. He could care less about vines, vine people, or anything else."

"Parks, what if the people won't go? What can Red do about it?"

The one called Parks was silent for a moment. "Dean, you are stark-flapping out of your marbles if you're thinking of working against Red." He was silent for another moment. "What did you have in mind?"

"What about denouncing Red as a heretic?"

Parks laughed. "What about the vine-masters? Synya?"

"We can say . . . tricks were played on them. That what they saw was all lies. From Volyan's reaction, which do you think the vine people would *want* to believe?"

There was a long silence. "Two problems, Dean. The first one is that we would be part of this conspiracy. Second, have you seen the claws on those suckers? Besides, we'd be putting Red in danger." Parks sighed. "Anyway, if it wanted to, the Terraform Corps could probably get this population removed by force under the Savage Planet Regulations."

"Parks . . . we just can't go along with this."

"Of course we can. And we will. Read your enlistment papers sometime." Synya heard movement inside the humans' shelter. "That's it for me, Dean. I'm hitting the sack."

The humans were quiet for a long time, then the one called Dean emerged from the shelter and walked away from Kadnu for a long time. Still Synya's keen ears heard the beep of his talking box, then she heard Dean speak the humans' yodel. "This is Dean. Put Arango on the horn."

Silence, then a strange voice. "Arango. What's up, Dean, and why are you on this frequency?"

"Because that's the frequency I picked, okay?"

The talking box was quiet for a moment. "What're you up to, Dean?"

"I want the data the orbiting station has on the other side of this planet."

The box was silent again. Then the strange voice spoke. "I shot down all that stuff to Red forty hours ago."

The one called Dean paused a moment. "So shoot it down to me. Parks and I haven't seen Miklynn for longer than that."

"Okay. You on record?"

"Yeah."

"Here it comes." Synya heard a series of squeaks and bips that lasted but a short breath. "That's it. Now, you want to tell me why you're on this frequency? Your team is supposed to be on channel eight."

"I just didn't want to wake up the others."

"Uh huh. You mean you don't want Red to find out."

"Maybe, Arango. Maybe."

"It better be, if you know what's good for you, Dean. Arango out."

Synya heard the talking box make a clicking sound, then it began to speak in a voice similar to the human yodel, but devoid of emotion or degrees of expression. She dozed and when she awoke, the flat yodeling still came from the box.

Synya noted the shadows Ashah made by Kadnu's light. The shadows had moved a few grains. The human Parks would awaken soon, yet the one called Dean had listened to his talking box the entire time. She listened to the flat yodel a moment longer, then heard a click followed by a series of bips and squeaks. For a long while she heard nothing but the steady wind from the ice, then she heard Dean's boots grinding against the soil. He was walking even further from Kadnu's light. She heard him stop, then talk to himself.

"Dammit. Aw, Goddammit all to hell." He was unmoving and quiet for a moment, then he shouted, "Parks!" He waited for a moment, then shouted again, "Parks!"

Synya saw the other human emerge from the fabric shelter, sealing the top of his green skin. "Dean?" Parks looked toward the vine, shielding his eyes from Kadnu's light. "Dean, where are you?"

"Back here."

Parks turned around and faced the darkness. "What is it?"

"Come here." Parks began walking away from the light. "It's Volyan. He's dead."

Synya stood between Dean and Parks as the three looked into the pit that had been dug, exposing one of Ashah's severed root ends. At the bottom of the pit, curled among the root branches, was the sign-reader, Volyan, his throat slashed with his own claws. The one called Parks turned toward Synya.

"I am pained at this, Synya. Believe me."

Synya stared at the body of her grandson, then she squatted

and began pushing the soil back into the pit with her hands.
The two humans stood still for a moment, then began kicking
the soil into the hole with their boots. Synya stopped and
looked first at Dean, then at Parks.

*"Do not use your feet. The soil must be replaced with the
hands."* The humans paused, then knelt next to her and pushed
in the soil with their hands. Synya returned to scooping the
soil into the pit, wondering about the wetness on the faces
of the humans.

When they were finished, the soil over the root end was
mounded and smoothed. Synya gathered several pieces of
vine bark and began pressing them into the mound as she
talked.

*"Volyan, sign-reader and son of my son, may you in death
serve the Lost Ones as in life you served Ashah and its people."*
Synya finished the vine-bark design on the mound: three
horizontal pieces. She looked at the design. *"Will you serve
them Volyan? Will Kadnu ever shine upon you again?"* She
shook her mane. *"How to feel?"*

She stood, the humans at her sides, then the one called
Dean pointed at the design. *"Synya, what is the meaning of
that mark?"*

Synya looked at the design. *"It represents the name of my
grandson, Volyan."*

Dean nodded. *"Synya, I wish that we had not told him. I
feel as though Parks and I killed him."*

Synya turned from the grave and began walking toward
Kadnu. *"He would not have believed you except for me. We
are equal in Volyan's death. With each other and with . . .
truth."*

The two humans glanced at each other, then followed her.

The ice wind flew at their backs, bringing the rain as they
walked past the vine people cutting the meat from Ashah, and
the others still occupied with the fat one's project. The
humans studied the thing Miklynn had instructed the vine
people to build, but could not divine its purpose. Neither did
those who worked on the project know its purpose.

Synya had asked them why they worked so hard for an
unknown objective at the instruction of a strange creature.

They had answered that the fat one had a certain manner about him that left little room for objections, and he had said that Synya would tell them to continue the construction when she again returned to Ashah.

The ones called Parks and Dean had watched Synya's face as she thought for long moments. Then she had instructed her people to complete the fat one's assignment. Afterwards the three continued their journey toward Kadnu.

The three walked in silence, ignoring the food-burdened vine people passing them to bring the vine meat to others who would, in turn, pass the food forward to nourish those who tended the great vine. The one called Parks studied the twists and bends of the vine, the thick, curled roots leading from Ashah's massive body across the ground. The path they followed twisted with the vine as it kept near the body, allowing the heavy food traffic to pass beneath great loops under the vine or its gnarled roots.

Ashah was leafed only along its root branches, and Parks could see where many of the leaves had been harvested. As they reached the great scar that encircled the body of Ashah, the thickness of the vine diminished, marking the beginning of the next growth. Beneath the scar, Synya led them from the path to a smaller path following one of the great root branches. Smaller roots led from the branch to the ground, and Parks could see where clawed hands had dug channels from small pools of water to feed the roots. Huts, both large and small, were located near the branch, but none were occupied. Parks spoke to Synya, raising his voice against the sounds of the wind and rain.

"Synya, why have you taken us on this path?"

Synya shook the water from her mane, then stopped and faced Parks. *"I must tell my son, Royah, of Volyan's death."* She held out a hand toward a cluster of huts near the end of the branch. *"It is not far."*

The one called Dean hunched his shoulders against the rain and began walking in the direction of the huts. Parks and Synya followed. Synya glanced at Parks's face, then looked toward the huts. *"There is a question on your face, sign-reader."*

Parks nodded. *"You read my face well."*

"You would ask why I told them to complete the fat one's assignment."

Parks nodded again. *"Yes. Miklynn and the rest of us are here to change everything that you and your people hold dear, yet you would do Miklynn's work for him. Why?"*

Synya walked in silence for long moments. *"Sign-reader, who is to say that the future you bring us is not better than the present we now occupy? This future is beyond my experience; beyond my wisdom. But the fat one knows."*

She again shook the water from her mane. *"I must trust the fat one, whatever the purpose of the thing he told my people to build. I trust the fat one to do what is best for my people."*

Parks bit his lip, then faced Synya. *"How can you be certain?"*

"I can be certain of nothing, sign-reader. Your people have shown me. All my certainties have been proven false. All that remains is trust." She looked at Parks. *"And I read a dislike of this task in the fat one's face."*

Parks laughed and wiped the water from his face with a gloved hand. *"You read his face with accuracy. Synya."* His face again grew somber. *"But you have read wrongly his motives."*

"Tell me, sign-reader. Tell me of the fat one."

Parks walked in silence searching for words. *"Synya, all of the people like me that you have seen belong to a ... group—a people whose purpose it is to change ..."*

"Planets."

Parks smiled and nodded. *"Yes, planets."*

Synya looked at the muddy path, the boot-prints of the one called Dean filling with water. *"As the Endless Trail is a planet. And to make them better places."*

Parks nodded. *"There are different parts in the process of changing a planet. The first part is called troubleshooting. Each planet is a puzzle that must be solved before it can be changed."*

Synya looked up at the gray sky. *"As the one called Gaum did here?"*

"Yes." Parks looked toward Synya. *"It is a special task,*

different from the actual process of what we call terraforming, *changing the* planet."

"*As we have special ones to read the signs, find the water, dig the channels?*"

Parks nodded. "*The ones who change the* planet *take the solutions of the* troubleshooters *and perform the task of change.*"

Synya again shook the water from her mane. "*But what of the fat one?*"

"*He, Dean, and I are trained to be* troubleshooters. *The fat one commands a group of* troubleshooters."

Synya stopped and placed a clawed hand upon Parks's arm. "*Then why . . . why are you here, if the one called Gaum has already done this—solved our puzzle?*"

Parks grimaced. "*It is a punishment. The fat one is in disfavor with his superiors—*"

Synya's eyes widened. "*The fat one has superiors?*"

Parks shrugged. "*Yes, but not that he acknowledges. That is why they do not smile upon the fat one and have given him—and us—this punishment.*"

Synya studied Parks's face. "*You find the first task exciting, but the second without interest?*"

"*Synya, the job we do has challenge, danger. We are scraps of flesh with nothing but our minds and instruments. Take this and throw it against a strange* planet—*skies that rain fire, great pools of water that can reach out and destroy a mind, flying and crawling creatures that can kill with only a touch—*"

Synya turned and resumed following Dean. "*And the fat one is nourished by this danger, but is starved—*" She pointed at her breast. "*—in here at finishing the task when the danger is past.*"

Parks nodded. "*He will finish the task here, Synya, as fast as he possibly can. Just to be done with it. That is the dislike of this task you read in his face.*" Parks shook his head. "*He could not stop what is happening here if he wanted.*"

Synya looked down at the muddy trail. The brown flash of a tiny creature fled into the grass. "*That is why you believe I should not trust the fat one?*"

Parks shut his eyes and nodded. *"Yes."*

They walked in silence for a long moment. *"Sign-reader, I think you to be wrong. My mind is not settled on this, but I think you to be wrong. But there is something I do not understand."*

Parks shrugged. *"What is that, Synya?"*

"You speak this way about the fat one, that I should not trust him. And when you were together speaking in the humans' yodel, I read anger and disrespect in your words towards him." Synya faced the one called Parks. *"Yet you hold a great love for the one called Miklynn."*

Parks studied Synya's face, then turned his head and again faced the direction of the trail. *"Yes."*

"Why is this, sign-reader?"

Parks shook his head and continued walking. Synya read the signs of a struggle within the human sign-reader. The one called Parks slowed to a stop, his gaze still fixed on the trail ahead. Synya stopped beside him.

"Synya, I once faced a moment such as that which killed Volyan. The details are unimportant. But my god was dead—it had never lived. All that I knew of the universe and my place in it was smashed...I think I would have done the same as Volyan, but then Miklynn came along. He gave me planets to test myself against. He forced me to find a new place in the universe, a new meaning. Yes, I love him."

"Then, sign-reader, in what do you believe?"

Parks looked down. *"In myself, to a small degree. For the rest, I believe in Miklynn."*

Synya stood erect. *"You think the fat one to be a god?"*

Parks laughed, shaking his head at the same time. The laughter brought the wetness to the sign-reader's eyes. *"No, Synya, no. Miklynn is no god."*

"But you trust him?" Synya watched as Parks turned and continued down the trail. She remained standing, and shouted against the sound of the rain. *"You trust him, yet you tell me not to trust him?"*

Parks stopped and turned back toward Synya. *"I do not trust him to be always right. He can have my life anytime he asks for it. I owe it to him. But he is not always right."*

Synya watched the sign-reader move down the trail. She turned and followed, her mind troubled.

After the tenders had returned to their huts, Synya and the two humans sat on beds of dried grass in the large shelter of her son, Royah. Synya's son had brought coals and dried vine bark to build a fire of celebration. The visit of his mother and her strange companions would be cause enough for the fire, but it had been planned for a long time. Royah's grand-daughter and her mate and the babe were to leave and move toward Kadnu. The babe, Vidnya, would begin with Ashah's new growth and gather its size, strength, and gray hairs tend-ing the growth, until it and the growth were touched by the ice wind and charged with feeding the people of Ashah.

As the hut warmed, the humans pushed back from their heads their fur-ringed skins, then unsealed and removed them altogether, exposing the fabric of their thinner, interior skins. As the fur of the two vine people dried, Synya noticed a strange smell. She looked at the one called Dean. His face held a strange expression as he turned toward Parks. "Parks, old buddy, you are getting just a little bit ripe."

Parks pulled out the neck of his green skin and sniffed. "Hmmm." He leaned toward Dean and sniffed again. "I wouldn't put money on who stinks the most."

Synya nodded her head toward Parks. *"Sign-reader, what is this smell? And why do you two talk the yodel?"*

Parks faced Synya and smiled. *"We meant to keep nothing from you."* He held out his hand toward Dean. *"It is past due for Dean and I to ... perform our ... water ritual."*

Synya's eyes widened. *"What ritual is this?"*

Parks rubbed his chin, then held out his hands. *"We must cover our bodies with water—"*

"Are you crazy, Parks?" Dean pointed toward the open end of the hut. "You know how cold that water will be?"

Parks frowned at Dean, then returned his gaze to Synya. *"The one called Dean objects to discussing our ritual with strangers. I will attempt to show him that you are both friends and understanding."* He turned toward Dean. "Dean, you and I stink already, and this hut is just warming up. What do you think it's going to be like when the rest of the party shows up?"

The one called Dean grimaced at the human sign-reader, then faced Royah and Synya. *"Synya, Royah . . . I see my error. Is there a pool of water in which we may perform our ritual without offending Ashah or its people?"*

Royah's face grew angry. *"You would dip your bodies in waters that feed Ashah, that people drink?"*

Dean licked his lips, then continued. *"There must be pools that do not feed Ashah, from which the vine people do not drink."*

Royah held out a clawed hand. *"I cannot see poisoning any of our waters to serve some . . . ritual not of Kadnu, not of Ashah."* He leaned forward toward Dean to make a further point, but returned to his place, his nose wrinkled in disgust. *"Whew."* He shook his head. *"What is the purpose of this ritual?"*

Dean grinned. *"It will remove our odor."*

Synya placed her right hand on Royah's left shoulder. *"My son, it seems that the ritual is a necessary one."*

Royah nodded. *"It is Kadnu's own truth."* He pointed toward the back of the hut. *"Beyond the end of the root— way beyond the end of the root—there are pools. Use one of these pools and mark it well."*

Parks and Dean stood and lifted their packs. Parks turned toward Royah. *"How shall we mark the pool?"*

Royah thought for a moment, then turned toward Synya. *"How shall they mark the pool?"*

Synya made an 'x' in the soil of the hut's dirt floor, then looked at Parks. *"Take two lengths of bark with you and stick them into the soil so that they stand upright, but crossed in this manner."*

Dean studied the mark, then pointed at it. *"What is the mark's meaning?"*

Royah covered his mouth and snuffled into the hair on his broad chest. Synya held out her hands. *"It is not important. But should the vine people see this, they will avoid the pool."*

Dean frowned and his voice took on many of the qualities of the fat one's voice. *"What is the mark's meaning?"*

Synya lowered her hands. *"It is a sign-reader's mark. There are tiny boring worms, other creatures that appear as only a slight brown tint to the water—they are not good for Ashah. They make Ashah's roots die. If the vine people drink from such waters, their waste is painful and thin."*

Dean turned toward Parks. "Diseased. I've got half a mind to sit in here and stink up the place."

Parks pushed Dean from the hut. "I can't stand it any more than they can. Let's go." Parks waved at Synya, then followed Dean.

Synya listened to their boots sucking at the mud for a long while, then she faced Royah. *"You have heard about Volyan?"*

Royah nodded. *"This is why you have come?"*

"Yes."

Royah looked at Synya. *"Volyan now serves Ashah and the Lost Ones. It is my own wish when my time comes."* He looked at the fire and took a deep breath. *"The smell improves."* He looked back at his mother. *"Did he fall from the vine; or did he wander too far looking for signs, falling to the ice scavengers?"*

Synya turned her eyes from Royah and looked at the fire. *"My son, Volyan dug his own root-end and caused his own death. The ones called Dean and Parks, and I your mother, replaced the soil and built and marked the mound."*

Royah's eyes widened. *"Volyan . . . was mad?"*

"No."

Royah looked at the fire. *"The creatures with you. Do they . . . have something to do with this?"*

Synya wiped a clawed hand across her face. *"Something, but they did not kill Volyan. They bring with them an awful knowledge. Volyan chose death rather than life with what he knew."*

Royah looked out of the open end of the hut. The rain was thinning. Soon the clouds would leave Kadnu's face, letting his light warm the ground. *"Synya?"*

"Yes, my son."

"Do you have this same knowledge—that which brought Volyan to end his own life?"

Synya nodded. *"Yes. I have held this knowledge for many growths."*

Royah looked at Synya. *"Yet you choose to live."*

Synya shook her mane. *"Royah, I have not chosen to die."*

"There is no difference."

Synya closed her eyes. *"There is a difference, Royah. I cannot explain it to you, but there is a difference."*

Royah was silent for long moments. *"Then I must accept what you say. You are my vine-master."*

"Royah, do you trust me?"

Royah stared at Synya. *"You are my vine-master. You ask strange questions."*

Synya held out her hands, claws extended, then she pointed the claws at her own breast. *"Do you trust me? Do you trust me to be always right?"*

Royah stared at the fire, then added a stick of bark to the flames. He looked down at the ground between his legs. *"I do not know how you would have me answer your question."*

"With the truth."

"Vine-masters make mistakes. They are not gods, Synya. You are not a god." He lifted his gaze to the fire. *"You made a mistake four growths toward Kadnu when you argued with the sign-reader about where to root Ashah to keep the vine moving toward the light. It took another three growths for you to correct the mistake."* Royah looked back at the ground. *"And other vine-masters have made mistakes."* He looked at Synya. *"This is a hard question, Synya."*

Synya nodded. *"I still need an answer."*

Royah held his hands to his head, then clasped them beneath his chin. *"I do. You make mistakes, but I trust you to be always right."* He held out his hands. *"If I did not hold this trust, I should have to challenge you for the position of vine-master. I would have to because not to trust you I would have to think myself superior to you in my knowledge of Ashah, Kadnu, and the good of our people."* He shook his mane. *"I do not think of myself in this manner. I trust you to be always right because you are the superior in knowledge."*

Synya covered her eyes with her hands. *"Even though I can make mistakes."*

Royah nodded. *"What choice have I? I must trust you to be always right."* He shook his mane. *"These are strange questions, Synya. The answers hurt my head. Why do you ask them?"*

"I must place my trust in the same manner, and for the same reason."

Royah pointed a claw toward the back of the hut. *"In one of those two creatures?"*

"No. The other that went before us."

"The fat one who has the cutters and carriers building the strange shelter?"

Synya nodded. *"You have seen him?"*

"No. News of his instructions reached me, but I did not see him." He wiped a clawed hand across his face. *"Synya, this knowledge that Volyan could not bear; am I to share it?"*

"No."

Royah nodded, then looked at Synya. *"Have you fear that this trust you have in the fat one may be a mistake? Synya, do you trust yourself; do you trust yourself to be always right?"*

Synya stared at the fire. *"In asking hard questions, Royah, you are easily my superior."*

They both sat in silence while the fire crackled and the strange beings splashed and cursed in the cold water far beyond the end of the root.

Synya—oldest and master of the vine—stood closest to the fire holding the babe, Vidnya, in her arms. Royah, flanked by the babe's parents, Ahrmin and Dathroh, squatted in the first ring around the fire, while their friends and relatives completed the ring. In the third ring, against the wall of the hut, the ones called Parks and Dean listened and observed the ritual of the newborn and the new growth.

The babe, although thickly coated with hair, had no claws or fangs. Synya held Vidnya out, the babe's face and body toward the fire. *"Vidnya, observe the heat, the flame. Love them and mind them, for they are the nature of Kadnu. Ob-*

serve the light, for Kadnu will direct you as you grow to tend Ashah's new beginning."

One of those squatting in the first ring pulled forward a sack made of vine leaves glued together with sap. The sack was opened, exposing a mound of snow. The snow was made level with clawed hands, then Synya turned her back on the fire and placed the back of the babe upon the cold, soft bed of ice crystals. The babe whimpered at the feeling of cold on its back.

"Vidnya, observe the cold and whiteness. Fear them, but mind them, for they bring the ice and death." Synya held her clawed hand over the babe's eyes. *"Observe the darkness, for it brings with it the end of the growth you shall tend. And when your growth of Ashah has fattened, then fed and sheltered its people, your duty and your life shall end, your body to become a part of Ashah, to bring the life of Ashah to those who wander in the darkness. In death you shall serve the Lost Ones as in life you shall serve Ashah."*

Synya lifted the babe from the snow, held it aloft, then handed the child to its mother. A roar of approval filled the large hut, then those near the hut's entrance brought in great pieces of vine meat. Synya removed herself from the center circle as others began the task of cooking the feast. She stepped through the first and second rings and squatted next to the one called Parks. She read a curious look in his eyes, a calmness in his face. When she spoke, she kept her voice low, that only the humans could hear.

"Sign-reader, do you find our ritual savage—childish?"

The one called Parks slowly shook his head. *"No, Synya, I found it beautiful; its form, its meaning, its purpose."* The human sign-reader kept his gaze on the activities in the center of the hut—the preparations for the feast, the touching of the babe, the rough well-wishing to Vidnya's parents. The one called Parks observed this as he leaned back against the wall of the hut, his mind closed to all but his eyes.

Synya looked past the sign-reader to see the one called Dean sitting cross-legged, his elbows on his knees, black anger upon his face. He too studied the activities in the center of the hut. Synya licked her tongue over her fangs, then spoke. *"And you, Dean. How do you find our meaningless ritual?"*

Dean abruptly turned his head toward her. *"It is not meaningless!"* He spat out the words in a hoarse whisper, then pushed himself to his feet. *"It is true!"* He stepped around Parks and Synya, then went through the entrance of the hut.

Synya watched the one called Dean until he left, then stared open-mouthed at the empty doorway. She turned to Parks to see the human sign-reader's mouth also hanging open. *"The one called Dean, sign-reader; what did he mean?"*

Parks closed his mouth, frowned at the doorway, then slowly shook his head. *"I do not know, Synya."* Parks stood and faced the doorway.

Synya held out a hand and placed it on the sign-reader's arm. *"Parks, does the one called Dean have gods, or a god?"*

Parks shook his head. *"No."*

"What can he mean then—that our ritual is true? What can he mean?"

The one called Parks held out his hand toward the entrance. *"Synya, let us find out what he means."* The sign-reader stooped, picked up the packs of the two humans, then stepped around Synya and left the hut. Synya took her shelter roll and followed, after bidding her son farewell.

A third of the way toward the main path, Synya and Parks caught up with the one called Dean. He was sitting on the low curl of a root branch, tossing his talking box from one hand to the other. Synya read anger in his face. Dean looked up at them, then back at the box he tossed from hand to hand. After long moments, the one called Dean looked up again at Parks, then spoke the yodel of the humans. "Red won't answer his communicator. Neither will the orbiting station or the command ship."

The one called Parks pulled his own talking box from his belt and spoke to it. "Red?" He waited. "Red, where in hell are you?" He waited, shook his head, then turned a small knob on the box. "Arango? This is Parks. Answer up." The human sign-reader studied the box for a moment, then he smiled. "Arango, I'm willing to believe that one communicator is not functioning, but not two at the same time, and if you don't answer I just might tell Red about you and a certain somebody named Julia."

A long silence, then the box spoke. "This is Arango, you sonofabitch. Red ordered communications shut down, and you better hope like hell that he isn't listening in on this channel."

Parks thought for a moment, then held the box to his mouth. "Where is Red, and what's going on?"

"Red's at the hot end of the same vine you're at. I don't know what's going on." The box crackled for a moment. "The bunch Assir took up is on its way back. Red ordered Assir to put down near where he is now."

The one called Parks frowned, thought for a moment, then spoke into the box. "Thanks, Arango. And I didn't really mean that—telling Red about Julia."

"Fry in hell, Parks. Arango out." The box went dead.

Synya watched as the one called Dean raised his eyebrows at the sign-reader. "You mean Arango got Julia—"

"Zip it up, Dean." Parks looked at Synya, then back at Dean. *"Synya and I want to know what you meant about the ritual."*

Dean hung his talking box on his belt and stared at the still-moist ground in front of his feet. *"It is true. All of what Synya said in the ritual is true."*

Synya squatted in front of the one called Dean. *"How can this be?"* She held a clawed hand against the soil. *"This is but a great ball floating in nothingness. Kadnu is a ball of burning air . . . and the Lost Ones. They walk the other side of this ball. How do we serve the Lost Ones? How will Vidnya bathe in Kadnu's light—"*

"Look." Dean bent over and drew a great circle in the moist soil. To the right of it, he drew another, smaller circle with lines coming from it. He pointed at the smaller ball. *"This represents Kadnu."* He moved his finger back to the original circle. He marked off a small segment at the top and an equal segment at the bottom. Above the top segment, he drew in an arrow pointing away from Kadnu.

"This is the direction in which the planet rotates." Underneath the arrow, Dean drew a smaller arrow pointing toward Kadnu. *"This is the direction in which Ashah grows."* He pointed at the dark end of the segment. *"This is the end of Ashah that feeds the vine people, and where the root ends*

and branches are severed." He looked at Synya. *"And this is where Volyan is buried next to one of the severed roots."*

Synya studied the picture in the soil, then nodded. *"But, Dean, then comes the ice."*

The one called Dean nodded and pointed around the half of the circle away from Kadnu's light. *"Volyan is buried deep, and as the planet rotates, both he and the root end will go under the ice. But . . . while this happens, Volyan will . . ."* Dean looked at the sign-reader, then back at Synya. *"He will become part of that root end—nourishing it and keeping it alive."* Dean's finger followed the curve of the ice side until he reached the bottom segment. *"This is where your Lost Ones are."*

He drew a small arrow beneath the segment pointing away from Kadnu. *"This is the direction they must travel to avoid the death-burn."* He moved his finger to where dark turned to light for the Lost Ones. *"And this is where Volyan, as part of Ashah's root end, breaks through the soil. The vine-masters there train the sprouts to root and grow together, forming a single vine body."* Dean pointed along the Lost Ones' segment toward Kadnu.

"At the hot end, the vine is fat, and it is cut to feed the vine people there. They tend their portions of their Ashah in much the same manner as your people." Dean sat up, folded his arms, and rested his elbows on his knees. *"And when the Lost Ones die, they too are buried along with severed root ends of their Ashah."* He unfolded his arms and pointed at the side of the circle facing Kadnu. *"In the heat that reaches deep into the soil, the bodies of the Lost Ones and the vine roots . . . change. They both . . . come apart, then become one with the soil."*

Synya shook her mane. *"That makes no sense to me."*

The one called Dean moved his finger around the hot side until he came to the growth-end of Ashah. *"What do your sign-readers look for here, Synya? What do they do?"*

Synya studied the diagram. *"At the growth end of the vine, the sign-readers study the soil with their eyes, claws, and tongues. Then they mark the places where Ashah's roots must be . . . led. Where the water must be brought . . ."*

Dean nodded. *"The sign-readers are looking for the old*

*graves of the Lost Ones—fertile soil in which to root Ashah.
The Lost Ones, and Volyan, then become parts of the new
Ashah."*

Synya stood, looked at the great body of Ashah stretched
across the horizon, looked at Kadnu, then back at the diagram
at her feet. *"And they will serve Ashah and the Lost Ones as
Ashah has served them . . . And Kadnu's light will shine upon
them forever."*

The one called Dean looked up at Synya. *"Do you know
what the Lost Ones call your people?"*

"They know of us?"

Dean nodded. *"First by legend, then by their vine-masters
being taken up and shown what your vine-masters are being
shown."*

"What do they call us?"

Dean looked down, but not at the diagram. *"In their language, they call your people the 'Lost Ones.'"* Dean looked
up at the human sign-reader. *"I had Arango shoot me down
the stuff on the other side before Volyan killed himself."*

Parks looked at Synya. Her eyes were raised toward the
vine. *"It is true. Despite everything we have seen, it is true.
The light of Kadnu shall shine on Volyan—and all our dead—
forever."*

Parks looked down at the diagram, then erased it with his
boot. *"As long as Ashah and the other vines live, it is true."*
He threw Dean a pack, then began shouldering his own. *"But
you forget, Synya; we are here to kill your vines. We will
make you fat and rich and we shall have brought to you the
many wonders of many worlds to teach you, to do your work,
to amuse you. All you must do in exchange is . . . deny that
which you know is true. All you must do is kill your god."*

Dean stood and shouldered his pack, then faced Parks.
"What're you going to do?"

Parks shook his head as he looked at the vine. "I don't
know. Why did Red order a communications blackout?" The
sign-reader looked down for an instant then pulled the talking
box from his belt. He pressed his finger against it several
times, then spoke at it. "Red, this is Parks. Answer." The
box was silent. Parks pressed his finger against the box several
more times, then spoke again at the box.

"Red, I'm going to keep beeping your box until you answer." Still the box remained silent. Parks pursed his lips, then held the box to his mouth. "Red, what if I told Arango about you and a certain person named Julia?"

The box crackled for an instant, then Synya recognized the fat one's voice. "Parks, you sonofabitch, you are going to look damned silly with your leg shoved down your throat—hip first! Now, I ordered a blackout; what'n the hell're you doing on the damned horn?"

"Why the blackout, Red?"

"Parks, have you gone stupid on me all of a sudden? Now, it wouldn't make much sense to order a blackout, then to tell you over the horn—with everyone listening in—just why I don't want them to hear what you want me to say." The box was silent for a moment, then spoke again. "Where are you and Dean?"

Parks spoke into the box again. "We're on a path just beyond the first growth."

"I want you two to move up to the hot end as fast as you can. Is Synya still with you?"

"Yes." Parks paused for a moment. "Volyan is dead."

The box crackled again. "One of you had to shoot off his big mouth, right? Put Synya on the horn."

Parks held out the talking box to Synya and pointed at the small silver plate in the box's surface. *"The fat one would speak with you. Talk in there."*

Synya held the box. *"Miklynn?"*

"Synya, I am pained to hear about Volyan. Believe this."

She looked away from the box, glanced at Kadnu for a moment, then turned back to the box. *"I believe you."* She was silent for a moment, then spoke again to the box. *"Miklynn, we have learned much since you left us, and I must tell you of these things."*

"Not on the talking box, Synya. I know the things that you know, and I will take care of everything. But no one must speak of these things on the box. Do you understand?"

Synya nodded her mane. *"I understand."*

"Do you trust me, Synya?"

She looked at Parks and read both the pain and the doubt there. She read the same in the face of the one called Dean.

The tiny box in her hand seemed very heavy. *"Miklynn..."*

"Yes, Synya."

"Miklynn...I trust you," She handed the box back to the human sign-reader.

Parks lifted the box to his mouth. "Is there anything else, Red?"

"Yeah. Do you two meatballs figure you can keep your traps shut and follow orders for another thirty or forty hours?"

Parks smiled. "Are you asking me if I trust you, fat one?"

"I'll give you a fat one... What about it? You two going to follow orders or not?"

Parks looked at Dean. The one called Dean kept his eyes down, shrugged, then faced the sign-reader and gave a single nod. Parks spoke into the box. "Okay, Red. We'll see you at the hot end." He hung the talking box on his belt.

Synya studied the sign-reader's face. *"Sign-reader, did the fat one ask for your trust?"*

"Yes." Parks nodded. *"In his own way."*

"And will you trust him? I remember what you told me before about your trust."

Parks studied Synya, then looked toward the vine. *"I trust him just this time."* He shook his head. *"I do not think I have a choice."*

The ice wind blew, but the sky remained clear as Synya and the ones called Parks and Dean came to the main path and turned in the direction of the food carriers. They offered little in the way of greetings to those vine people that saw them; they offered nothing in the way of explanations. As they passed each growth scar encircling Ashah's body, the vine grew thinner, the grass taller, until at the twenty-seventh scar the vine was no thicker than Synya's height. Kadnu was higher, and the three erected their shelters in a shadow made by a high curl and twist in the vine. The people serving the twenty-seventh growth were in their middle years, and Synya watched them at their work and play as she listened to the yodel of the humans coming from their shelter.

"Parks, how do you think Red will get them off this rock?"

A long silence. "I don't know. Maybe he has some other answer."

"What answer?" The one called Dean snorted. "With the figures we have now, it'll take maybe six or seven years to bring this planet up to speed, then another I don't know how long for the air masses to adjust. Then there's reestablishing the population, getting them set up as farmers, establishing a social framework, seeding the damned place . . ."

The one called Parks laughed. "Red's not going to like that, but he has a reputation to protect. No planet's ever licked Red, and he certainly won't throw a farming job—"

Synya heard the beep of a talking box, then she recognized the voice of the one called Assir—the one who had taken the vine-masters away. "Red?"

She heard the fat one reply through the same box. "What is it?"

"Do you want me to shoot down the data the rockhounds dug up? I have—"

"Assir, I ordered a commo blackout. Didn't you get that from the orbiter?"

"Yeah, but I thought—"

"Quit bragging, Assir. If I want the data before you land, I'll ask for it. Just put that crate down near the hot end of this vine as soon as you can. But not too close. Put it down around a thousand meters north of the vine. Understand?"

"I understand. Assir out."

Synya listened, but the fat one made no reply. Instead, she heard the movements that spoke of the humans making ready for their sleep period. They were quiet and still for long moments, then the one called Dean spoke in a quiet voice. "On a compassion scale of one to ten, where would you place Red?"

"Off the scale." The one called Parks paused for a short moment. "But which way, I don't know."

"Red isn't exactly a bleeding heart, Parks."

A long silence. "We don't always bleed for the entertainment of others, Dean."

"What's that supposed to mean?"

"How much do you know about Red, or me, or yourself for all that goes? I've been with Red longer than anyone in the group, and I know that I don't know him. On the outside, he blusters and blows a lot, but you know the scrapes he's gotten us through. He's smart, he's got guts, and he's loyal to us—the people in his group. He . . . he's also got this thing about the job. I suppose it's a kind of loyalty to himself. But what he feels inside, about anyone or anything, I don't know. I don't even know if Red knows that."

One of the vine tenders came into view not far from Synya's shelter. The vine tender shielded its eyes from Kadnu's light and looked toward Synya. Synya motioned with her hand that she was not sleeping and the vine tender ran to stand in the grass in front of the shelter's opening. *"Synya, vine-master."*

Synya studied the vine tender's face. *"Your name?"*

"My name is Tuneh, vine-master." Tuneh glanced from Synya to the humans' shelter then back to the vine-master. *"Vine-master, these strange creatures following on the heels of the fat one that went before. There is much talk."*

Synya turned from the female and curled into her sleeping position. *"There is always talk."*

"But what is the meaning, vine-master? What will they mean to the vine people?"

Synya moved her position slightly, then settled herself more comfortably. *"Of these things I must not speak."* She listened as the vine tender moved away with slow steps. The fat one had said to speak of nothing on the box. Synya nodded as she began to doze. Even without the box, silence appeared to be sound advice.

The sky was clear despite the wind at their backs as Synya and the two humans left the scar of the twenty-seventh growth behind and followed Kadnu. The humans had removed their thick outer skins and wore only their thin inner skins. As they approached the thirty-fourth growth, the seed pods on the tall grass stalks were fat and covered with insects waiting for the pods to open that both they and the seeds could move toward Kadnu. Tiny brown-furred creatures moved through the grass to meet the insects when they landed.

The light green of the humans' inner skins were stained dark with wide patches of moisture as they moved ever closer to the newest growth. Past open seed pods being emptied by the wind, the vine tenders became younger and wore caps made from Ashah's leaves. At the scar of the thirty-ninth growth, the tenders wore both caps and capes of leaves. Synya and the two humans left the scar in similar attire.

At the forty-fourth growth, the vine—now no thicker than the leg of the one called Dean—lay across the bare, seeded ground. The heat of Kadnu shimmered from the soil making each breath for the humans something thin and ungratifying. They paused there to watch leaf-covered vine tenders and their young gathered away from the vine, performing some ritual. The one called Parks, his breath short, turned toward Synya.

"Synya, what are they doing . . . and in this heat?"

Synya narrowed her eyes against Kadnu's light and examined the tenders and their activities. She stopped, turned toward the one called Parks, then shook her leafed head. *"This ritual has no meaning for me, sign-reader."* She looked at the one called Dean. *"Do you know what this is?"*

Dean frowned and studied the vine tenders. *"Synya, it looks . . ."* Dean shook his head, then nodded as he saw a puff of smoke erupt from one of the leaf-covered beings. *"They are playing a game we call* baseball."

Parks frowned, then closed his eyes as his body began shaking. Synya shook her head and looked back at the vine tenders. She too saw smoke erupting from one of the leaf-covered beings. The creature was bent over, peering across the head of a squatting tender. In front of them both, another tender stood holding a heavy stick made of bark. All three of them were facing another tender who was whirling about with his arms. From the gyrating tender flew an object toward the three facing him. The one with the heavy stick swung at the object, but missed. The one squatting behind the one with the stick caught the object, while the one who smoked stood erect and made a gesture with a human hand. "Yer out!"

As the one with the stick threw the piece of bark to the ground, another came to take his place. Synya walked toward the group, followed by Dean and Parks. The smoking one turned at the sound of their footsteps, then he motioned for one of the vine tenders to take his place behind the squatting one. He turned toward Synya and the humans and met them a short distance from the play. *"It is good to see you, Synya."*

He turned toward the humans. "It's about time you idiots showed up. What'd you do? Take the scenic route?"

Synya ran her tongue over her fangs. *"Miklynn, we are here."* She held a clawed hand out toward the tenders. *"What do you call this?"*

The fat one looked back at the players, then smiled around his cigar and turned back. *"They are good, are they not? With those claws, Melyeh can put a spin and dip on that gob of dried sap I do not believe myself."* He looked at the two other humans and pointed at the players with his thumb. "I had to do something to kill time waiting for you two."

The one called Parks studied the players, then looked back at the fat one. "The team have a name?"

The fat one nodded. "The Miklynn Fireballs. First team of the Endless Trail League." He then faced Synya. *"We all speak the language of the vine people."* He turned back to Parks. *"The tenders of the other vines will learn of this game, for the Fireballs will teach it to them. Is this hard to understand?"*

Parks sighed and turned toward Synya. *"The fat one will make things clear to us in his own manner, and at the time he chooses."*

The fat one grinned, then looked up at the sky. *"Synya, I am waiting for the one called Assir to bring back the others."* He looked back at the vine-master. *"The vine people will not have to leave the Endless Trail."*

Synya and the two humans stared at the fat one, but he again returned his glance to the sky. "Ah hah!" He began running away from the vine, motioning with his arm. *"Come, Synya. Run, Parks and Dean. Here they come."* They ran toward the speck in the sky which rapidly grew to become the huge craft that had taken away the vine-masters. The craft landed on its five legs before Synya and the others reached it. The fat one slowed to a walk as the underside of the craft opened and the vine-masters began disembarking. The fat one looked at the one called Parks. "Just follow my lead. Got me?"

Parks noticed that neither the Fireballs nor their fans were following them. "What lead? Miklynn . . ."

Synya saw the fat one wave his hand impatiently at Parks. She looked back at the craft, and then she saw them: taller, thinner versions of the vine people, but with no fangs and short, stubby growths where their claws should have been. Their pelts were deep gray, thick and shiny. Synya reached out her hand and placed it on the fat one's shoulder.

"Miklynn, are they . . . the Lost Ones?"

Miklynn nodded as they came into the shade given by the craft. The vine-masters of Synya's kind were chattering with the Lost Ones. Neither of the races were speaking words of comfort or pleasure. A huge, dark human—the one called Assir—separated from the group and approached the fat one. "Red, here they are, and there's no problem with the seismics. This rock has a crust as thick as your head." He swung the pack he was carrying to the ground. "The stuff you wanted is in there."

Miklynn squatted before the pack, opened its flap, and peered inside. Closing the flap, he stood and shouted. *"Still your mouths!"* The fat one turned to the one called Assir. "They all talk the vine-people lingo? This side's?"

Assir nodded. "We adapted all of them. Each speaks the language of the other."

The fat one nodded once, then turned back to the group. *"Silence!"* When all was quiet, the fat one looked over their faces, then he spoke. *"The one called Gaum made a terrible mistake."* A few of the vine-masters spoke in hushed whispers, then fell silent again. *"This place you all call the Endless Trail needs no changes. It shall be as it has always been. We will leave—"*

Parks grabbed Miklynn's arm and swung the fat one around. "What in the hell do you think you're doing?"

The fat one pulled himself free. "Try that again, Parks, and I'll tie you into a big knot."

"Haven't we screwed around with these people's minds enough, Red? Why did you tell them—"

The fat one held out a hand, palm toward the one called Parks. "Now, you shut your mouth. I'm going to need you in a minute, but you won't be much use to me with your teeth knocked down your throat." The fat one looked from

Parks to the ones called Dean and Assir. "Look, do yor dirtbrains want to spend the next six to eight years farming this rock, or do you want to get on with our own thing?"

Assir pursed his lips, then cocked his head to one side "Do these ears of mine hear correctly that Red Miklynn i going to throw a farming job? They'll toss you out of the Corps so fast that—"

"No one is throwing anything, Assir." The fat one looker back at the restless vine-masters. *"I must consult with my companions. Please understand and accept my apologies."*

He turned toward Assir. "Okay, craphead, you're the science officer. You ever see a planet in more perfect ecologica balance than this one?"

"No, but—"

The fat one turned toward Parks. "Is the population healthy happy?"

"As far as I know, but—"

The fat one looked at the one called Dean. "Tell me the vine people's word for crime, or their words for war, rape theft, or government screwups."

Dean shrugged. "They don't have equivalent—"

"They don't have them, dirtbrain, because they don't nee them." The fat one looked down at the ground, then glancer at the faces surrounding him. "This rock doesn't need ter raforming; Earth should be in such good shape. Any damner fool can see that."

The one called Parks laughed, then nodded his head at the fat one. "Go ahead, Red. Do it." He laughed again. Assi and Dean both looked at Parks and began talking at the sam time.

The fat one held up his hands for quiet. "Go ahead, Parks Tell them."

Parks laughed to himself for a moment, then turned to face Assir and Dean. "Red's getting us out of the job. We'r done. Finished." Parks nodded as Assir opened his mouth to speak. "Oh, there will be a fuss, but I imagine that Red can put up a good argument that this rock doesn't come unde the regulations. The population is sapient, with both a spoke and written language. Remember those signs on the mounds And it is a governed society, which places it way outside the

Savage Planet Regs. The government may be a sun and a bunch of vines, but it works better than most."

Assir looked at the fat one. "Red, the Quadrant has big credits tied up in this project. Big enough credits that your argument won't hold enough water to make a teardrop. Nothing's going to stop those eight-hundred thrusters that are on their way here."

The fat one rubbed his chin. "Maybe. But, Assir, I have a hunch that once you examine that seismic data again, you'll find that the crust on this rock is a little less stable than those thrusters will need to bring this planet up to speed in only six or seven years. It'll probably take, say, fifteen or twenty years."

Assir grimaced at the fat one. "So I'll fake it. There are a few ancient faults I can doctor up." He nodded. "And that will make the project a net a loss, so . . ."

The fat one folded his arms. "So, once we get back upstairs, we might as well reassign those thrusters to other farming operations." He looked around at the faces once more. "Are we all straight?" The ones called Dean, Assir, and Parks nodded. The fat one turned and faced the group of vine-masters. *"It is as I have said. Gaum made a mistake. We will leave, and things will be as they have been."*

One of the vine-masters stepped toward the fat one. It was Morah, and his eyes were wild, his claws extended. *"You come here . . . show us our god is false! You show us the Trail to be a circle? You destroy Kadnu, and now you will leave and things will be as they have been?"* A low roar erupted from the vine-masters, and they started moving toward the humans.

The fat one looked over his shoulder. "Parks. It's time."

Parks walked forward, stopped, and held up his hands. *"Silence!"* The roar lowered to a grumble. *"I want silence!"* And there was silence. Parks lowered his hands, then continued in a soft voice.

"We have not destroyed your god. His light shines all around you. Ashah and the other vines of the clawed vine people still follow Kadnu, and the vines still feed you, shelter you, and protect you against the heat and the ice. Still the vines of the gray vine people spring from the soil, and the

god remains at your backs, melting the ice, serving you as it has always done. Still you die and join your vines, becoming parts of them, each vine people serving their Lost Ones, who in turn serve them. We have not destroyed your god."

Parks looked down for a moment, then he turned and looked at the fat one. He frowned for an instant, then smiled and shook his head as he looked back at the vine-masters.

"Think of the Endless Trail. We have not shown you the Trail to be false, for what is more endless than a circle?" Parks pointed toward Ashah. *"At the feeding end of this vine is a structure that we have brought to you. It looks as if it were a huge shelter with no doorways. All of you will travel the length of Ashah to see this thing. Turn it over and it will become what is called a* boat. *It will float on water. First learn to build* boats, *then move along the ice, always keeping Kadnu to your left, past the land of the last vine, and there you will find the waters that will bring you to the world of the gray vine people.*

"You will travel that world, always keeping Kadnu to your left, until you again reach waters. These waters will bring you again to this world. We have not shown the Trail to be false; we have proven it to be true. And you shall prove this to yourselves. We have not destroyed your god; we have shown him to be real by carrying you to a place where you could see it and watch its face."

Morah lowered his arms and shook his mane. *"These things that we have been shown . . . that god is a ball . . . of burning air—"*

A strange look came into the face of the one called Parks. It was a look of pain, yet of anger. *"Your god gives you everything you have. It has served you and will never fail you. Do you demand that your god also be not real?"* Parks looked at the faces of all of the vine-masters from both sides of the Endless Trail. His voice became very quiet. *"Your god will serve you, if you do not demand too much from it. To be real, yet not real, is too much."*

Synya sat in the shade of her shelter, puffing on one of the smoke sticks. The fat one had left her a box of them. She savored the bittersweet taste of the smoke, then looked away from the practice session of the Miklynn Fireballs. The vine-masters had been gone a long time—long enough for them to have seen the boat, long enough for them to have put Kadnu to their left and begun the long journey. They had lingered long enough to study and learn the game the Fireballs played, but the fat one and his craft had left long before the vine-masters had learned the game.

Synya looked down at the second box the fat one had given her. It was of green metal with rounded corners. When he gave her the second box, the fat one explained its use. *"Synya, we and the vine-masters have made a decision for an entire world. None of us knows if this will be the right decision for all time."* The fat one had opened the box as the ones called Parks and Dean looked on. Inside the box was filled with a silver plate. From out of the plate extended a sliver of black. *"If ever the vine-masters change their minds, Synya, all you need to do is to move the sliver of black. It will send out a call, and someone will answer it. If you want the things that we can bring you, all you must do is to move the black sliver."*

Synya opened the box and looked at the black sliver. The fat one had said that the box would last for endless growths. Some vine-master thousands of growths in the future would still be able to send out the call, bring back the humans, and turn the Endless Trail into a farm world. She lifted the object the one called Dean had given her after the fat one had returned to the craft. The object was also of metal, but it was ribbed at its thick end and formed a flat blade at the tip of the narrow shaft that extended from the ribbed end. Dean had spoken as the one called Parks looked on.

"Synya, the box the fat one gave you is very rugged, and it will last forever." Then he had given her the object. *"But you must be careful not to take this—it is called a* screw-driver—*and insert it into those two slots and twist the slots like this."* He had demonstrated. *"If you do that, Synya, the insides of the box will be exposed and can be damaged. If that should happen, the box will no longer be able to send out the call."*

Synya inserted the blade into one of the two slots and thought of the one called Parks as she turned the screwdriver.

What had he said in the yodel to Dean as Dean went back to the craft? The yodel had sounded like this: "I can't be certain, Dean, but I think you have started the first screwdriver fetish in human history."

Parks had turned to her. *"Synya, I am still pained at the death of Volyan."*

She had answered. *"He is one with Ashah. Do not grieve. Have you not yourself proven this to us?"*

As Synya removed the second screw from the box, she remembered the look on the sign-reader's face. *"We have proven that."* He had paused for a short moment, then looked back at the craft. *"I must go now."*

Synya had heard the pain. *"Sign-reader. Your god is dead, but mine is indestructible. Share Kadnu with us."*

The one called Parks had smiled. Synya thought of his answer as she lifted the face-plate from the box. *"I wish that I could, Synya."* He had looked at Kadnu, the light of the god washing his face. *"But I have seen too much, experienced too much."* He had looked at her as he stood to leave. *"Besides, who would take care of the fat one?"* Then he had left.

Synya moved the box out into Kadnu's light, better to see the things behind the silver plate. The things were coated with happy colors and were made of fine threads and dots of gold.

"Vine-master?"

Synya looked up to see one of the middle children who had wandered away from the baseball practice. *"Yes? Your name?"*

"I am called Chiveh, vine-master." The child held out a clawed hand toward the box. *"Could you tell me what is in there? It is so pretty."*

Synya thought for a moment, then held the box out toward the child.

"Reach in and pull out a handful, Chiveh, and we shall see."

With our frame of time perception we treat coral as though they were rocks. Intellectually, of course, we know coral is alive. Diving off Okinawa once I slithered by one of those little red suckers and received a nasty cut that didn't heal for weeks. A cut from a piece of dead coral heals normally. The live coral, on the other hand, is trying to say something. Since I was leaking mass quantities of blood into shark-infested waters, I didn't spend the present moment pondering this particular attempt of a lifeform to reach out and communicate. As a matter of fact I probably broke several swimming records making it back to the beach. Sharks are inspiring. They should use them in the Olympics.

Eventually the cut healed and I was discharged from the service. I can't say that I spent many of my civilian waking moments thinking about coral. At mineral shows I would admire some of the beautiful things that had been made out of coral, but now I was back to looking at the little critters as minerals—rocks.

Did you know that different species of coral war among themselves? I didn't until I watched a National Geographic special on television. I thought coral just sat there, cloning slowing, going "glub, glug" or whatever. However, when they grow, sometimes they grow into each other. The National Geographic special showed one of the fights with time lapse photography. It was a nasty fight, too.

It's true; I get some of my best ideas from watching television. Hence, as I lie there on the couch all day with my eyeballs screwed into the tube and some significant other wants to know how I've spent my day, I can honestly answer: "working." Although I know I'm not lying, I feel as though I am. I'm working on it. As Emerson said, "To be great is to be misunderstood." I don't know how Ralph was fooling around when he came up with that one.

In any event, I was watching The Coral Wars on the tube. That a fight of this sort could take place right beneath a human nose with the human being totally unaware of the contest got me to pondering nights about how we perceive events, and the qualities we attribute to observed events according to the rate at which the event takes place. To us Pet Rocks are a joke. The characters in the following story, however, aren't laughing.

Adagio

> *what this*
> *stand there*
> *why*
> *sign to right*
> *obey or die*
> *why*

Tobias sat on the red stone grave marker and watched as Forrest tortured the rocks with the portable current generator he had taken from the cargo bay. Torture is what Lady Name called Forrest's game. Lady Name was convinced that Forrest was insane.

Tobias raised a grimy hand and rubbed his eyes. Hell, Lady Name was wig-picker bait herself. That's why she was called Lady Name. It was a temporary label designed to provide the others with an identity tag until such time as the woman could figure out just who in the hell she was. All of them were rejects. The passengers. He nodded. So was the crew.

He lowered his hand and let his gaze wander until it came to rest upon the remains of the ship. He could see Lady Name's rag of matted black hair high in the wreckage. As was her habit, she was silently observing Forrest at play. It was entirely possible that Lady Name would kill Forrest. A matter of indifference to Tobias. Somewhere below her in the twisted metal, Cage would be nervously working on the computer. Death still seemed to matter to Cage. His nerves were the direct result of Lady Name frequently sitting just out of his field of vision, staring at him, sharpening her knife upon one of the dead red stones.

The dried and cracked crust that had formed over the surface of the red dust when it had last rained was almost all gone. The little bit of wind, the motion of the rocks, the feet of the humans had eroded it. And it had been such a long time since it had rained.

There were the sounds of footsteps in the dust. Tillson. The footsteps stopped.

"Is it possible, Tobias, that God has done this to us to provide us with a challenge against which to test our virtue?"

Tobias turned to his left and glared up at the chaplain. Tillson was naked again. "Stick it up your ass, Howard."

Chaplain Howard Tillson nodded gravely at the learned response. "You are right, of course. You are very wise, Tobias. Very wise." The chaplain turned and stumbled his way down the back of Graveyard Hill, his droopy buns jiggling with each step.

Tobias pondered again the fact that Tillson had a woman's ass. Another fact to ponder was that rescue had best happen before Tillson's ass got to look much better. He hollered down the hill at the jiggling ass, "Tillson, put some clothes on!"

The chaplain stopped, turned, looked up at Tobias and nodded. "You are right, of course. You are always right, Tobias."

Placing his hands upon his knees, Tobias pushed himself to his feet and dusted off the seat of his flight suit. The fine red dust of the planet's dead agitated by his activity hung in the still air like a bad smell. He turned and looked down at the grave marker. It was a smooth red stone just like Mikizu's and Sheen's. For grave markers they had to use only the red stones. They don't walk off.

The gray stone Tobias had originally used to mark Osborn's grave was now several meters downslope, running like hell, Forrest claimed. It had taken the gray stone five of the planet's month-long days to race the short distance. Gray stones, white stones, green stones, black stones. They littered the red landscape. They were alive. The red ones didn't move. They were dead.

He stumbled down the hill, entered his individual shelter and flopped down on his cot. He closed his eyes thinking of dead red grave markers.

Sheen was dead. A passenger. Never did find out what she did to justify the space she took up in the universe. Osborn was dead. Mikizu was dead. Mikizu was no loss. If it hadn't been for him they wouldn't be stranded. But Osborn. Tobias wished Osborn was still alive. He'd know what to do. But Osborn had to be a hero. . . .

He had sat in the sputtering flashes of the emergency lights watching Osborn's eyeballs leak. The chief engineer was in the wreckage of the engineering deck inhaling vacuum, the seat of his trousers puddling with piss and blood, the fluid from his eyeballs dribbling down his cheeks.

There had been plenty of time for Osborn to get on his suit. The hull damage in aft engineering had only dumped the pressure from that compartment. The rest of the ship only lost pressure because of the warped bulkhead seals. It took minutes for the ship to lose cabin pressure. But Osborn wanted to flick switches, punch buttons and twirl knobs. The rest of them probably owed him their lives. The asshole.

"Tobias?" The headset in his suit spoke. The pilot, Mikizu. His voice. "Engineering? Osborn? Tobias?"

Tobias answered. "What?"

"Osborn?"

"Osborn's dead."

A pause. "Tobias, I need to know the power situation."

Through his suit's faceplate he glanced at the remains of the engineering board. "I can't help but believe, Mikizu, that you know just about as much as I do about that."

"The bridge panel is dead."

"No shit." He leaned back against the bulkhead, glanced at Osborn, and closed his eyes. "We're all dead back here, too."

"I need power if we're going to go down."

"Is there any point?"

"Forrest thinks so."

Forrest. Second pilot. A little bastard, but smart. Tobias shook his head to clear it. Time to knock off the smartmouth. "Main and auxiliary plants are down. Whatever it was that came flying through the hull took out the engines. I couldn't sell what's left for scrap."

Another pause. "What about the fuel cells?"

"They're okay. Osborn got the lines shut down before too much escaped. What's Forrest got in mind?"

Forrest's voice entered his helmet. "We can try for a dead-stick landing. If you can rig the steering jets, Tobias, the computer says we have a chance of making it through the atmosphere."

"How much of a chance?"

Forrest laughed. "Don't ask." He became quiet. "We have a better chance at making a landing than we have trying to stay alive up here. Can you rig something?"

Tobias looked around the engineering deck, the challenges of practical necessity crowding out, for the moment, projections of disaster and demise. With the board shot there would be some wiring to do. He'd have to work off the batteries. And some plumbing, not to mention readjusting the steering jets to use main plant fuel. He didn't really know if that could be done. But there was something else. The entry heat would turn aft engineering into a furnace.

"Forrest, I can make a try at the steering jets, but something has to be done about those holes in the hull."

"Get to work on the jets. When you're ready I'll help you with the holes. We can snatch some plate from somewhere."

Tobias pushed up and began working his way toward aft engineering. He loved doing wiring in atmospheric longjohns. It's like doing watch repair while wearing a pair of boxing gloves. The failing gravity would just make it interesting. He punched the switch and the hatch swung slightly open and jammed. With his foot he kicked it the rest of the way open. He stood in the hatch and looked into the darkness of the engine room.

The only light came from the holes in the hull. Some of those flickers were stars. Most of them were too bright for that. The bright ones were the remains of the crumbled planets that formed the Oids Belt in orbit around a sun called Mantchee.

Merchant crews don't like the Oids Belt and never go there. The union even got it in the contract. Asteroids, planetoids and paranoids. Tobias still had one of the buttons that said "I avoids the Oids."

But there were some passengers and parts to pick up and deliver in strange and wonderful places, and a pilot who believed in shortcuts more than he did in either minimum safety or union contracts. Tobias swore that if he and the pilot managed to live through the landing Tobias's first planetside act would be to murder Mikizu.

First things first.

He returned, grabbed Osborn and dislodged the engineering chief's body from the rapidly freezing fluids that were pinning his ass to the deck. Pulling the body to the hatch, Tobias pushed it toward the large hole at his feet.

The still form somersaulted slowly toward the hole and jerked to a halt. Tobias pulled the light from his belt and aimed the beam at the opening. The back of Osborn's head had been speared and snagged by the hole's ragged edge. One of the thick splinters of metal protruded from Osborn's left eye.

Someday the geniuses will figure out how to puke in a space suit. Someday. He turned away . . .

> this thing
> will serve us
> if we obey it.
>> how will it serve
>> obey
> this thing
> it will stop
> pain and death
>> this thing
> brought us
> pain and death
>> still
> pain and death
> obey

> *this thing*
> *now wants us*
> *to kill.*
> *obey*

"Forrest is still torturing the rocks."

It was Lady Name's voice. Tobias buried his head more deeply into his pillow. "If you don't get out of here, I'll rip out your spine and strangle you with it."

No footsteps moving away. He could feel the woman's hurt gaze on his back. The flimsy shelter almost radiated with terminal sulk. Tobias chased away his nightmares and rolled over on his cot. "Go away, Lady. Take up a hobby, go play with your bunny, anything. Anything but tattling on Forrest. I don't find forty-year-old children amusing."

"I am not tattling, Tobias. I am reporting. One of your men is torturing the rocks. Those rocks are alive."

"Lady, first, they are not my men. If anyone is in charge, it's Forrest. Second, I don't care about the rocks. I really don't. My only problem is keeping sane until someone picks up our signal. Rescue, Lady. Think rescue."

"No one will pick up the signal, Tobias. Forrest told you that. It can't get through the radiation—"

"You don't know that. Forrest doesn't know that for certain. There's a chance."

She stared for a moment, almost looking sane, then nodded toward the shack's doorway. "What are you going to do about Forrest?"

He turned his back and burrowed into his pillow. "Nothing."

Footsteps, finally.

The beacon signal would get through. It had to. Then a curious thought entered his mind. He felt he *should* be rooting for the beacon signal's success. A moral thing. What generations of humans would say was the thing he should be doing right then. The curious thought was that he didn't really care if the signal got through or not.

> *soon*
> *the dark*

> soon
> we kill
> it is
> the wish of
> this thing

The sun called Mantchee rode half-hidden by the horizon.
Tobias entered the main shelter, the red glare of the week-
long sunset casting the interior of the dome in blood. They
were all seated around the low table. Lady Name, as usual,
was watching Forrest. Forrest was entertaining himself with
his own thoughts while Tillson struggled, probably uncomfortable with the unfamiliar feeling of wearing clothes. Nelson
Cage was heavily into a wiring diagram, the symbols and the
problems their relationships represented providing as much
entertainment for him as the rocks did for Forrest.

As he pulled a ration pack from the dispenser, Tobias heard
Cage announce to the others, "I have the computer working."

Tillson: "God doesn't like computers."

Lady Name: "What are you going to kill time with now,
Cage?"

Forrest: "Break it, Cage. Break the computer and fix it
again."

Cage's face flushed red. "I don't know what's wrong with
you people. After five months of hard work I've managed
to—"

Forrest leaned forward holding a finger before his lips.
"Shhhh." He brought his finger down and smiled. "No one
cares. No one cares."

Tobias lowered himself into the chair to Forrest's right,
sipped at the acid-tasting hot beverage, and gnawed at the
nutribar as Cage leaned back, his voice becoming brittle. "We
can use the computer—"

"For what?" Tobias shook his head as he bit again at the
nutribar. "Except for getting rescued, all our solvable problems are solved. We have oxygen, water, rations, and a livable
temperature spread. The only things in short supply are pa-
tience and sanity. Do you have any games you can play on
that thing? We could use some entertainment."

Cage snorted and sat back in his chair. "Games," he repeated in disgust. He looked at Lady Name. "At least I know who you are now."

She looked away from Forrest for a split second. As she resumed her watch on the pebble persecutor she replied, "Cage, you haven't a clue who I am."

Cage smirked. "Barbara Striker. *Doctor* Barbara Striker. I managed to retrieve the passenger manifest. It says you are Doctor Barbara Striker, a biologist formerly with the Dison System colonization effort, currently relieved of your post because you are a fucking crazy."

"Words." She slowly turned her head toward Cage. "I'll be using the computer."

"You will not! I just finished repairing it."

Lady Name grinned as she stood and walked from the dome, obviously headed for the wreck and the computer. Cage leaned forward. "Tobias, you must do something!"

Forrest chuckled and shook his head. "Calm down. Let her play with the machine. It's got to be better than having her perched like a vulture on my shoulder all of the time."

"What if she breaks it?"

"Then you can fix it again. It really isn't very important."

Cage stood abruptly and walked rapidly from the dome. Again Forrest chuckled. "Cage is on his way to the ship to lay down the law to Lady Name."

"Yeah, and when she flashes that blade of hers he'll be back with a wet crotch." Tobias pointed with his thumb toward the door. "How come you aren't out playing with your rocks?"

He closed his eyes. "Things are arranged."

"What's that mean?"

"I have initiated certain things out there. I'm teaching them to serve. When it becomes light again you should be able to see how my subjects have responded."

Subjects.

Tobias finished off the remaining portion of his nutribar and tossed the wrapper on the plastic floor. If Forrest wants to play god, at least he doesn't make a lot of noise. But they are all crazy, though. Every single last one of them. Am I?

There was a scream from the wreckage and a moment later Cage could be seen, holding his arm, running toward his individual shelter. Forrest nodded, his eyes still closed. "It looks as though they've decided that Lady Name gets to use the computer." He opened one eye and aimed it at Tobias. "Is it true that you pissed on Mikizu's grave?"

Tobias finished his beverage and placed the cup on the table. He sat back, clasped his hands over his belly and watched Mantchee slip a little lower behind the horizon.

"Every chance I get."

> *now*
> *we kill*
> *the not green*
> *should know*
> *why we kill*
> *tell them*
> *to ask*
> *this thing*

The dark came.

Tobias tossed beneath his thermal blanket, trying to sleep, flying in the face of the fact that he was all slept out. Had been slept out for hours. Probably days—those twenty-four hour spans of time they call days on a planet whose memory had grown very dim. Back on a planet in a time when there was youth. Ideals, dreams, vast plans. The excitement of school and training.

—the very ordinariness of space. The monotony. All of it reduced to keeping the power plants in second-rate ships coughing along in exchange for a paycheck and a pension that he didn't think he could stand living long enough to collect—

"To hell with this." Long ago Tobias had lost the ability to entertain himself with his own company.

He sat up, still wearing his filthy flight suit, and slipped his feet into his icy boots. The smell of his own body hung around him like a curse. There would be enough light from the Oids to make it to the place where the stream was above ground if he wanted to take a bath. He shivered at the thought. What the hell. Everyone was being tracked by his own shadow of funk.

Keeping the thermal blanket wrapped around his shoulders, Tobias stepped outside. The Oids were bright in the night sky. Maybe they should use the computer to plot the Oids. There was a lot of crap out there, all in the same orbit. Some fine day maybe one of those three hundred kilometer long chunks of rock might slam into the middle of their camp. He spat on the ground. "And if we knew, what could we do about it?"

There was a light on in the wreckage of the ship. Tobias began moving his feet in that direction. Now that it was fixed, the computer might have something to read; something besides his own thoughts with which to occupy his neurons. The other individual shelters were dark. The main shelter had a light on but no one was inside the dome. The open cargo hatch in the belly of the ship glowed with a dim red. Whoever was in the ship, it wouldn't be Cage. The computer man had a moral thing about conserving the ship's batteries. Cage would never leave on a light that wasn't needed. As though it made any difference. The batteries would outlive them all.

Tobias entered the cargo bay and began working his way around and through the jumble of opened containers and scattered contents. Most of it had been destined for a low-budget evaluation mission on some steamy planet out there somewhere. Everything anyone would need to learn the learnable about a planet and then screw it up. They had found the shelters and rations there.

Forward of the cargo hatch another light burned above a stack of strange equipment that Tobias had never seen before. Must have come from the cargo. Cables ran from the stack through the crew's quarters toward the cockpit. He entered the corridor to the crew's quarters, his mind thumbing through the bleeding obvious as he trudged up the slight incline to the cockpit. If a full crew had been on board, maybe. If Mikizu hadn't over-estimated his and his ship's abilities, maybe. If they'd followed company policy and stayed the hell out of the Oids, maybe. If they hadn't been ordered out of their way to pick up the passengers, maybe. Maybe. If. If ending it on this dreary rock wasn't such a fitting end to a dreary life.

If.

He could hear no sound forward except for the almost inaudible whine of the power converter. He stopped at the hatch to the cockpit and peered in. Lady Name's back was toward him. She was sitting back watching, almost hypnotized by the patterns appearing upon the display. Every few moments the image would switch to columns of figures, and then back to the patterns.

He stepped into the cockpit. "Hey, Lady, what're you up to—"

She whirled around, the needle-pointed blade in her right hand. As he froze a slow grin appeared on her face. "You shouldn't sneak up on me that way, Tobias. You almost got to do your pension as a eunuch." She lowered the blade. "Why are you here?"

His gaze still fixed on the knife, Tobias worked his way to the commo station couch and sat down. "I couldn't sleep anymore. Thought Cage's machine might have something to read."

She turned back to the display over the keyboard. "This terminal is busy."

"Are any of the other stations hooked up?"

She didn't answer. He watched her for a moment and then turned his attention to the display. "Does that have anything to do with that gear you have hooked up in the cargo bay?"

She nodded toward the display. "Those are the thought patterns of one of the green rocks. I have one of the small ones in a sensory chamber. When I can get the main sensors hooked up I'll be able to receive from any rock in sight." Turning her head away from the screen, she fixed Tobias with a hate-filled glare. "You refused to do anything about Forrest. Now I'm taking matters into my own hands."

Tobias leaned back in the commo couch and shook his head. "You be real careful, Lady Name. You keep this up and you just might buy a real case of the crazies." He nodded once toward the screen. "Once you have all of that data, what are you going to be able to do with it?"

"Communicate, Tobias. Communicate."

"Talk with the rocks? Hell, if they communicate at the same rate that they move, you'll be an old woman before you can get a 'hello' back. And if you can communicate with them, so what?"

"It looks as though they conceptualize and communicate faster than they move." She faced the display. "Forrest is doing terrible things to the rocks. I've been watching him. On a primitive pain-pleasure level he has divided some of the rocks into armies. And he is forcing them into situations where they must fight each other—"

"Fight?' Tobias burst out in laughter. "That has to be the action event of the century. Hell, Lady, I've been here just as long as you and I don't see any war going on outside."

"It's there all the same. Once I can communicate with the rocks, I'm going to teach them how to fight Forrest."

Tobias glanced at the other terminal in the cockpit and decided that trying to read in the same compartment with Lady and her shiv would not exactly be the ultimate in relaxation. There was another terminal in engineering. However the ghosts in engineering had been sufficient to keep Tobias out of there since he and Forrest had dragged Osborn's remains from the compartment. Suddenly he felt very tired. Perhaps even tired enough to sleep. He got to his feet and slowly made his way out of the ship.

As he stood in the dim red light outside the cargo hatch he noticed one of the white rocks. It was rounded and about the size of a pillow. It had been there ever since...

No, he thought. It's closer to the hatch now. When we landed it was farther away. He shook his head. Another recruit for Lady Name's liberation army. He muttered as he walked toward his shelter. "Enlist now. Avoid the rush later."

As he passed the main shelter he glanced in and froze as he saw Tillson's naked body hanging by its neck from a piece of cargo line tied to the dome's center brace.

He entered the shelter and lowered himself into a chair as a feeling of absolute desolation invaded his soul. What's the point? What is the point of any of it?

"Isn't that just a tad ghoulish for entertainment, Tobias?" It was Forrest's voice. He was standing in the doorway. Forrest nodded toward the body. "Just look at that. The man was totally incompetent. Look at the way he placed that noose, straight up the back."

Tobias closed his eyes and leaned his head against the back of his chair. "It seems to have done what it was intended to do."

"True. But old Tillson must have done quite a mambo before he died. His neck isn't broken. Tobias. He danced. He danced for a long time."

"I guess Tillson wasn't much of a hangman."

Forrest snorted out a laugh. "He wasn't much of a chaplain, either. He just wasn't much of anything."

There were sounds coming from behind Forrest. He turned and Cage pushed past him and came to a halt as the body came into his view. "For god's sake..." Cage looked first at Forrest and then at Tobias seated in the chair. "For god's sake, cut him down!" He moved toward the body.

Forrest studied Tillson's still form. "Wouldn't it be amusing to leave him there for Lady Name? We'd all be eating our rations as though nothing were out of the ordinary, and in she'd come. What would she do?"

Cage finished righting the overturned chair next to the hanging corpse. "Give me a hand, someone."

Tobias pushed himself to his feet and headed toward the door. He paused next to Forrest. "Help him. Help him you sonofabitch or I'll kill you."

A breath of amusement passed over Forrest's face as the man walked over to Cage and began helping him to bring down the body.

Outside, walking rapidly away from the camp, Tobias felt the angry sickness forcing its way through his wall of control. He began running into the dark.

> why
> must i die
> ask
> this thing
> i asked
> this thing
> no answer
> the ways of
> this thing

> *are mysterious*
> *die*

The second Earth-day into the new sunrise.

Tobias stood on Graveyard Hill next to Tillson's grave marker staring at the long shadows cast by the rocks below. One of the shadows moved. His gaze traced along the shadow to its source. It was Forrest moving among the rocks.

Tobias squatted, leaned his forearms upon his knees and clasped his hands together. Curious that no one had questioned that Tillson's suicide was in fact a suicide. The body had been taken down, planted, and never mentioned again.

Tillson's mind had gone, there was no question about that. His shelter had been littered with incoherent scribblings. Mostly theological squirrel droppings; a rambling eternal justification of the author's existence. There were occasional moments of apparent lucidity. Relative lucidity. All things being relative.

Most of Tillson's lucid moments at his papers were crowded with the pain and anguish of a man who knows he is losing his mind. Fragments of the writings still teased Tobias's mind.

. . . Forrest explained that each rock is a small community of the creatures. A community of individuals bound by their physical nature and shared nervous systems to act for the community's welfare, much like the cells of a human body. Each rock, then, can be treated as an individual. The rock color is a genetic thing and has no other significance. The rocks cannot perceive anything that doesn't stay still for at least the equivalent of nine Earth-days . . .

. . . He dispenses pain and death to the rocks according to whether the rocks have acted in accordance with the signs he has made. It must be terrifying to the creatures. Signs suddenly appearing out of nowhere. Signs that if they are disobeyed instantly reap horrible consequences. The creatures must believe themselves to be in the grip of spirits— terrible gods.

. . . Forrest is teaching them good and evil. Doing what Forrest signs is the Good; disobeying Forrest is the Evil.

Before Forrest these creatures had no conception of good and evil. The horrors of moral commandments whose reasons for existence must be taken on blind faith. I wonder if the rocks will survive morality as long as humans have.

...A few moments ago Forrest showed me something. It was a green pebble the size of a blueberry. It seems that several of the rocks, acting in concert, prepared a platform and placed this pebble upon it. Then they left the platform. It must have taken them weeks. But there it is. The faithful tithing to their god. They prepared an altar and placed one of their members upon it. A gift. A virgin thrown into the volcano. A lamb pumping out its blood in the temple. The rocks have learned how to sacrifice.

I am an obscenity.

There was no way of knowing how long after writing those words that the chaplain had hung himself. Or had been murdered, Tobias reminded himself.

I am an obscenity.

Tobias looked down at Tillson's grave marker. "This is a hell of a place to try and judge an entire life, Howard."

A whoop of joy came from below. Tobias turned his head to see Forrest running among the rocks. And the rocks he was running among were of only two colors: green and red. Everywhere else there was a fairly even mix of white, green, gray and black, as well as the red and dead. But in Forrest's little community the only creatures left living were green. The green rocks, in accordance with their god's wish, had killed all those who were not green. There had indeed been a war.

Tobias reached down and picked up a small white rock. The terror, the passion that must exist in those very slow creatures. The pain of those who sacrificed one of their own number to Forrest. It wouldn't be a sacrifice without the pain of loss. And the pain couldn't exist without some form of love.

What about that little green pebble? The article of sacrifice? If the others had time enough to move away from the platform, so did the pebble. It had been green. Alive. And

suddenly disappearing into the horrors of the unknowable
was what had faced it. And it had stood there, waiting for
Forrest.

Courage?

He suddenly felt guilty about holding the white rock and
tried to replace it exactly from where it had come. But he
couldn't remember which side had been up. He stood, wondering how he would feel if the next instant he found himself
standing on his head.

He headed for the ship, being careful where he placed his
feet.

> the green
> kills ours
> why
> the gray
> must kill
> the green
> how
> this thing
> serves the green
> why
> this thing
> will serve
> the gray
> how
> if the gray
> obeys
> this thing

Tobias sat in the commo couch and watched Lady Name
alternately punch buttons and refer to the notes that she kept
on slips of paper in her right breast pocket. The sensors he
had installed above the cockpit seemed to be working, whatever it was that they did.

"There." She pointed at the incomprehensible scramble of
numbers on the display. "That's the key. We'll be able to talk
to them in a bit."

"Forrest can already do that."

"Our way will be much faster. We won't have to fuck over them and wait for them to deduce the message. Direct communication." She faced Tobias. "Did you find the portable units?"

He nodded toward the rear of the cockpit where two heavy-looking brown metal cases stood. "What do we need those for?"

She turned back to the display. "As soon as Forrest figures out what we're doing in here he'll turn this computer into rubble. Once I have the data milked and processed through this thing we won't need it anymore. I'll enter the translation codes into the portable units and we can use them. I hope they're still working."

"They don't look damaged." Tobias looked back at the units as he felt himself squirm in his chair. Lady Name's use of the pronoun "we" made Tobias more than a bit uncomfortable. After all, she was crazy.

"Why don't we just kill Forrest and be done with it?"

"We aren't murderers, Tobias. We are the good guys." Tobias glanced at the knife resting on her lap and raised an eyebrow. She nodded and reached for the keyboard. "Hide the soft suits and portable units while I try it out and see what happens."

>   *the gray*
>   *also seeks*
>   *the signs of*
>   *this thing*
>   *this thing*
>   *serves the green*
>   *we obeyed*
>   *still*
>   *the gray*
>   *seeks the signs*
>   *this thing*
>   *will not*
>   *betray the green*
> This thing will betray you.
>   *who signs*

Truth.
>   *we obey*
>   *this thing*
>   *this thing*
>   *not betray us*

This thing will betray you.
>   *who signs*

Truth.
>   *truth is what*

I am.
>   *does truth*
>   *serve the green*

Truth serves Truth. Will the green serve Truth?
>   *the green*
>   *serves*
>   *this thing*

The gray serves this thing. Truth is stronger. Serve me.
>   *. . . truth*
>   *what have we done*
>   *what have we done*

Lady had been right about Forrest going after the computer. While they had been pulling down rations in the dome, the thing had been trashed. Shortly after, Cage wandered off in the distance beyond the ship. Tobias had followed the man's footsteps in the red ash, between and around the endless rocks, until he came to a bottomless chasm. It was an opening that looked as though real gods had scarred the floor of the plain with a huge razor. The footsteps went to the edge, and that was that.

So long Cage.

From the entrance to the dome Tobias watched Forrest study his subjects in the dying light at the end of another week-long sunset. He was seated on top of one of the large red stones. Surrounding him were nothing but red rocks. All quite alive.

Tobias chuckled as he gnawed at his rations. Forrest's new army, as well as his original force, were immobilized. They wouldn't fight. Lady Name had given the green the command to tell the gray about Truth. The word had even spread to the white and the black. If you don't fight, you don't have to kill. If you don't fight, you don't have to die.

> *this thing*
> *kills us if we*
> *not obey*

Then you must fight this thing, not each other.

> *how to fight*
> *this thing*

Play dead.

Tobias laughed out loud. Play dead; turn red. A simple task for the rocks requiring only the sacrifice of each rock's surface members. The surface dies, but inside they live. And growth takes place against the ground.

He saw Forrest's head turn slowly in his direction. The small man studied him, his face as expressionless as one of the rocks. He called out, "Tobias!" He held up the current generator. "Tobias, what if I kill them all? What if I just go from stone to stone and give each a little shot?"

"Then you'd have nothing left to play with except your radish, Forrest. Your game would be over."

He lowered his shock stick and grinned. "You joined the wrong side, Tobias."

Tobias laughed and turned into the dome. He finished off his nutribar, tossed the wrapper on the floor, and flopped down in a chair facing the doorway. He had taken to sitting and sleeping facing doorways. When someone's out to get you, paranoia is just practical thinking.

He glanced at the position of Mantchee and frowned. Lady Name was going to meet him to explain the new sequence they were going to initiate. She had determined that the rocks had the ability to excrete their waste products in the form of a highly corrosive vapor. It wouldn't kill the rocks. Their ability to obtain what they needed from the atmosphere wouldn't be affected. Creatures with lungs, however, would die. The soft suits and respirators would leave only Forrest inhaling acid. The only real problem was trying to convince the rocks to do it. Lady Name suspected that, for some reason, the rocks might object to wandering around in a cloud of their own shit.

The doorway darkened. It was Forrest and he was holding something in his hands. He squatted in the doorway.

"You know, Tobias, there were many times in my life when I thought I had all my ducks in a row. When I thought I was on top of everything. It wasn't always true."

Tobias hooked another chair with the toe of his boot and pulled it closer, crossing his legs at the ankles upon it. "Welcome to the club."

Forrest looked down at what was in his hands. "It might not be true for you."

"Just stop fucking with the rocks, Forrest, and it'll be all over."

He glanced up and grinned. "You think so?" He placed what was in his hands upon the floor, stepped upon it with one foot, and lifted as the sound of a sharp crack reverberated around the dome. He stood and tossed the object across the space that separated them. Tobias caught it with his left hand as Forrest turned and left the doorway empty.

It took a moment, but Tobias recognized the object. It was the hilt of Lady Name's knife.

> *it signs as truth signs*
> *agreed*
> *still it signs strange*
> *truth do you sign*

Truth is dead.

> *truth cannot die*

Call Truth.

> *we call truth*
> *truth see our sign*
> *truth*

Truth does not see your sign. Truth is dead.

> *who do we serve now*

You know me.

> *this thing*
> *this thing*
> *must we again kill and die to serve*

You know me.
>   *we know you*

By the light of the Oids he had found her among the
mountain of red rocks beyond the ship, on the way to Cage's
Chasm. That's where she had stashed her half of the equipment. Her soft suit had been slashed, her respirator broken.
Her portable communication unit was missing. She was dead.
Tobias extinguished his light and turned away. Forrest must
have taken some time to mutilate Lady Name's body.

Had Forrest found the other suit and communication unit?
Tobias looked back toward the gentle silver gleam of the ship.
To hell with it. Let Forrest play with the damned rocks if
that's what he wants. What did Tobias care? Keep going with
the rations, stay out of Forrest's way, wait for rescue. Simple.

He turned back, knelt on both knees next to her body and
began pushing the red ash over her. "You dumb bitch. You
dumb crazy bitch."

>   *what must we do to atone*
There is another. Kill it.
>   *to kill what we cannot see*
>   *how*
Find a way.

The edge of another new sunrise. Tobias looked through
the dome window at the pink of the slow dawn. How long
had it been since he had seen Forrest? Back when the man
had broken Lady Name's knife. He frowned. Has only one
night passed, or was it two? Or three?

He sipped at his steaming beverage, lowered his cup and
looked at it. Somewhere back on Earth there was a person
with a degree in nutrition who had never stepped outside of
his or her environmentally controlled city. That person had
invented N-669 Beverage, Survival, Hot. More than likely
that person had never tasted N-669 Beverage, Survival, Hot.
At odd moments Tobias had a fantasy about finding that
person, cramming a funnel down his or her throat, and pour-
ing in ten or twelve liters of N-669 Beverage, Survival, Hot.

A sound.

He slowly looked up and turned.

The sound had been something between a groan and creak. He looked up at the inside of the dome. No problem there that he could see. His head turned toward the doorway. As he took a step toward it, half of the dome crashed to the floor next to him, knocking him clear to the wall of the undamaged half.

Another crash. Another.

He cleared his head, opened his eyes and watched the open sky in horror as a ten meter column of rocks teetered, then came falling toward him. He scrambled to his feet and leaped into the rubble to escape, a deafening roar and a choking cloud of dust overtaking him.

The sounds stopped and the dust settled. He opened his eyes and chanced a glance at his surroundings. The dome was nothing but rubble criss-crossed by collapsed columns of rocks. He pulled himself to his feet, climbed up the rocks and rubble until he stood on top. Except for where he was standing, the landscape was unchanged, the long shadows of the morning pointing away from the bit of Mantchee that showed over the horizon.

"Forrest!" Forrest was nowhere to be seen. "Forrest!"

Tobias took several deep breaths and looked down at the destruction of the dome. Without the dispenser what rations he could rescue from the wreckage would last only a few days—Earth days at that. Without the dispenser . . . he looked at the empty cup still gripped by his hand. So long N-669 Beverage, Survival, Hot. There were no more dispensers or rations in the ship's cargo hold. The equipment used to tap into the ground water supply had been crushed along with the dispenser.

Tobias began gathering up the few nutribars he could find and reach. Already his mind was planning what he would do once he broke out his own portable communication unit and set up his command post. There still remained Lady Name's stunt with the corrosive vapor. Tobias didn't wonder about being able to figure out how to get the rocks to do it. He *had* to. But first there was food, water, shelter to arrange. Time. It would take time. But he had nothing but time. He spoke in mutters as he worked.

"I'll get you Forrest. You miserable little son of a bitch.
'll get you."

> we have found truth
> is truth dead
> truth is dead
> it is a strange creature truth
> soft and made of food
> what of the other this thing had
> us try to kill
> we do not know
> some toward the beginning of the new light
> sign about an other there far below the surface
> dead
> in the mound are the two who appeared when
> this thing first appeared
> they are dead
> four of them
> still there is this thing
> this thing is changing
> now it is different
> what will this change mean
> it is unknown—
> there is a sign

Forrest. Forrest. Answer if you're reading Forrest.

> who signs

I look for the one called this thing.

> truth is dead
> you are not this thing
> who
> are you the other

I am God. Where is this thing?

> who is god

I am. God rules all.

> are you like truth or like this thing

No. I have more power.

> even we can see this thing
> if you can not see this thing
> we have more power than god

Serve God or you will suffer.
> *this thing already provides us with what*
> *you offer us god*
> *we serve this thing*

You must serve me.

Communicate. I am stronger than this thing. Answer. An swer. Answer.

From the top of Graveyard Hill Tobias surveyed the result of his efforts. He was standing in the center of a circula enclosure of red rocks, a triangular piece of the dome servin as a roof. Inside were some cushions from the dome and panel he had grabbed from the ship. The panel controlled th array of debris-impregnated seismic charges surrounding hi position on the hill. If Forrest or any of his followers wantee to get at him, they'd need the proper combination.

Next to the cushions was a stack of the seismic charge rigged with adjustable time-delay triggers. They were in cas Forrest told his rocks to do the falling column bit again. Th soft suit and respirator were still in their container, in cas Tobias ever got some of the rocks to see things his way. Nex to the soft suit were his containers of water lugged from th surface stream and his supply of ration bars. In addition t the ration bars, he had managed to salvage intact four con tainers of the powder that the dispenser used to make up goo old N-669 Beverage, Survival, Hot. Vitamins, minerals an old underwear. He wondered what N-669 would taste lik cold.

Next to the rations, on the other side of the cushions, stoo the portable communication unit. Tobias bit the skin on th inside of his lower lip. What did the rocks mean when the said they could see Forrest?

He leaned his forearms upon the edge of the red wall an let his gaze scan the area behind Graveyard Hill. Forrest wa nowhere around. Not even a footprint. And to see Forrest The Thing had to stay substantially in one place for the bette part of nine Earth days. He looked farther to the right, movin his position, until he was overlooking the camp. The shelter had been in place long enough to be seen. And the graves The ship.

He studied the wreckage of the ship. To the rocks it had
suddenly appeared out of nowhere. Huge, gleaming. Silver.
A color the rocks had never seen before. And then they began
getting signs. Certain actions in relation to the signs brought
death. Other actions did not. They learned the penalty of
disobedience. Good and evil came to stay. And it all began
after the ship appeared.

Tobias nodded and sat on his cushions, energizing the
portable communication unit. "Oh, Forest, old buddy. Do
have a num-num for you."

> *who signs*

God.

> *we serve this thing*

I have found this thing. If I kill this thing, will you serve
me?

> *we see this thing*
> *this thing now sees what we think*

I see what you think. Will you serve me?

> *we see this thing*

I will kill this thing and appear to you. Then you will
serve me.

> *we wait*

The directional indicator on the portable unit and a quick
move enabled him to triangulate the positions of two of the
rocks with which he had been communicating. After marking
them, it took only minutes to rig the ship. Remote controlled
seismic charges next to the half-full fuel cells. Tobias quickly
searched the crew's quarters and scanned the cargo hold for
anything additional that he might be able to use. There was
a three-wheeled motorized "mule." He energized it and drove
it over and around the mess in the hold until he was outside,
next to the marked rocks. He worked the forks of the mule
beneath first one rock and then the next. With the rocks
secured, he drove them to the top of Graveyard Hill and
parked them where they could see both the ship and inside
his bunker. Moving the rocks would add some time to the
demonstration, but he would be too vulnerable in the open.

His preparations completed, he sat down and waited. If

he stayed in the same place, in the same position, with onl
brief absences to piss on Mikizu's grave, the rocks would se
him shortly after they were able to perceive the ship. Th
only problem was boredom. But there were entertainment:
Keeping alert for an attack of some kind by Forrest. That an
the voices he was beginning to hear.

All a part of going crazy, he reminded himself. Still h
wished the voices were loud enough to understand. Wh
knows? His insanity might have something interesting to say

He sat back and stared at the two green rocks he was tryin
to convince. A thought passed his attention and he bega
laughing. "Talk about your hard sells!"

When he calmed down, he began the wait.

> *who signs*

God. I have moved you.

> *your power is great*

Do you see this thing?

> *we see this thing*

Do you see me?

> *we see you god*
> *you are very small*
> *this thing is much larger.*

My power is greater.

> *this thing has moved us without us seeing th*
> *move*
> *what you have done is no more*

Will you serve me on faith, or must I kill this thing?

> *you must kill this thing*

Mantchee was slowly moving toward sunset, but enoug
time remained. Tobias pressed the remote trigger and watche
as the ship disappeared in a sheet of light and sound. To
bad, he thought as he watched the heat carry the flames an
black smoke high into the shimmering red of the sky. It's to
bad that it happens so quickly. If they could see it, the flamin
death of this thing would impress the rocks.

He sat back to wait. It would take another nine days fo
the rocks to see that this thing was destroyed.

The portable communication unit began making strang

buzzing sounds. He looked at the operation panel inside the case. The only image on the screen above the tiny keyboard was an instructional line: switch function to normal receive.

He did as instructed and sat back in shock, withdrawing his hand as though it had been burned, as an angry, deep snarl came from the unit's speaker.

"Tobias! Tobias, I'm coming for you! Do you hear me?"

After his being startled passed, Tobias grinned. "Is something wrong, Forrest?"

"The ship! Why did you blow the ship?"

"I think you know, old thing. Shall I put on a nice hot cup of N-669 when you come calling? By the way, old thing, what are you using for food these days?"

The unit was silent. Tobias laughed as he switched the function selector back to the rock channel.

It didn't seem so long a time.

The nine days.

The voices provided some entertainment.

Still they were muddy, too distant.

But at times they even seemed to sing.

Especially toward the end. Strange songs.

Forrest never did show.

It is time to decide.
> *this thing brings us pain and death*
> *god what do you bring us*

The good.
> *god we will serve you*

And now will you have faith in me?
> *god we will have faith in you*

Tell the others. All must serve god.
> *god we will tell the others*

Does perception of time adjust to the local framework of time? Tobias let the thought sit just behind his eyes as he made his weary way to the stream. There didn't seem to be enough time in the day to do everything. Lug water, eat, talk to the rocks and try to get them to understand about the acid vapor.

He had gone back and dug up Lady Name's body, hoping

there would be some clue in her notes. She must have had
some idea about how to get the rocks to expel the vapor. But
her breast pocket was empty. If anyone had those notes, it
was Forrest.

But it was the feel of the dead breast behind that pocket
that had captured his attention. Hard. Unyielding. He uncovered it and found it to be made of gray stone. Her entire
body had been replaced by the gray. Back at Graveyard Hill
he uncovered part of Sheen's body. She had been replaced
by gray and green. He didn't bother to check out Mikizu and
Osborn. Whatever the rocks were doing, they were only doing
it to the dead. That was none of his concern. Not yet.

He came to the bank of the stream and lowered his containers to the ground. The stream was dry. He climbed down
the bank and dug at the cracked surface of the bed with his
hands. Dry.

He sat back on his heels, his gaze resting on the distant
hills. That's where the water comes from, he thought. And
that's where Forrest is. That's where he cut it off.

"And that's where I'm going to kill you."

The light and the dark. Days. It seemed that so much time
had passed that he ought to have forgotten what he was trying
to do. At moments he would forget.

He finished securing the portable communication unit to
the mule next to the driver's seat. In the vehicle's tiny cargo
bay were the remainder of his rations, the water containers,
his soft suit and respirator, and his supply of bombs. He
looked back at the two green rocks that had been keeping
him company for...

He looked at the communication unit. There was a date
and time indicator function. He didn't know his when. Hence
he didn't know how long. For some reason it seemed important to know.

He opened the unit, energized it, and switched the function
selector to date/time. The figures were unreadable; a smear
of flashes. As though the indications had been recorded in
time lapse and replayed at normal speed.

The reflection of his image in the screen showed the face
of an old man.

> *god*

"What?" Tobias looked up and around. He looked back at the communication unit. The function selector was still on date/time. The voices again?

> *god*

He looked again at the two green rocks. "What?"

> *take me with you*

"Why?"

> *there is a new one*
> *more powerful than this thing*

The rock on the right. He didn't know how, but he knew that was the one that was talking to him. Have I slowed down that much, he wondered, or have the rocks finally gotten it into high gear? Or have I finally lost it? My mind?

> *god bring me*

"Why?"

> *i can help you*

"Help me to do what?"

> *i can help you to fight lucifer*

So Forrest is calling himself Lucifer. Tobias leaned against the mule and looked toward the hills. He nodded. "Sure. You can come along."

And he saw the rock move.

It seemed to flow across the red dust. A balloon filled with water. Light and dark. Rapidly shifting shadows. Time. Again light, then dark, light. The rock was next to the mule.

He watched Mantchee streak across the sky, leaving him not in day or night, but in half-light. That fast, he wondered, or have I become that slow?

"Am I seeing this as you see it?"

> *i do not know how god sees*

Tobias reached to pull himself onto the driver's seat. The brace he had grabbed came away in his hand. The metal of the mule was pitted, corroded, like lace. The supplies, the soft suit, the water containers—all dust.

He stood naked, a film of gray over his skin. He sank down next to the green rock. "I can't make it. Too tired. Too old."

> *we will carry you*

Tobias watched the landscape move. Green, gray, black

and white globes flowing around the red. Rapid rivers of shapes. He felt himself lifted and carried. In the sky Mantchee was an even bar of yellow light against the dim pink.

As he was moved along, floating upon that softly undulating river of life, the edge of a thought—what would he do when he met Forrest—came and left many times. My mind, he said to himself, really is going. But Forrest will be just as old, if he's still alive.

He was at the hills. He could not push himself up to look. The rocks rose beneath his head and shoulders.

"Forrest."

There was no answer except for the stinging pain all over his body. He watched his skin peel and blacken, curling away to expose the bones beneath. The acid. Forrest taught them to shit acid.

"I can't fight him. I am dying."

   god you must live
 become as lucifer

"I am God. Good cannot become as Lucifer. I am good."

   lucifer says he is the evil
   is good less powerful than lucifer?

"I cannot change my purpose."

   change not purpose
 change form
 become as Lucifer.

The thread of a thought spoke. Lucifer had no protection against the acid. Then what has Lucifer become? What must I become to live?

"I am afraid."

   god
 you want us to have faith in you
 have faith in us
 become as lucifer

There was not enough tissue left to force air through vocal cords that no longer existed. His thought was his response. *Very well. I will become as Lucifer.*

He stood, his height above the crest of the hills, his reach wider than the plain beneath his feet. Beyond the hills a massive head leered back at him. The face was rot, corruption, evil.

"You are God," it hissed.

"Lucifer."

A glow invaded the engineer's heart. No more pointless wandering, desperate existence. Happiness born of purpose. To be a giant fighting giants. He reached out his great arms and wrapped his fingers around the hideous monster's throat.

When they came to investigate the weak, garbled signal from the Oids Belt, they quickly located the beacon. It was from a type of commercial cargo ship that hadn't been in use for over a century. Of the ship, passengers and crew the only trace remaining was a curious statue of two naked human men in mortal combat standing upon the bodies of four other humans, the sculpture surrounded by a wall of red masonry. The local lifeform informed them that the statue was titled "Equilibrium."

*And, finally the idea for "Where Do You Get Your Ideas?"
came from an interviewer asking me that question. After
writing the piece I let it sit around on my desk for about a
month. I couldn't think of anywhere to send it. So I sent it
to George, figuring he could use a laugh. He bought it.*

*I suppose the moral of this story, as well as the moral of
this entire collection, is that ideas come from everywhere and
anywhere. The secret in writing is not getting ideas. Every
human on this planet is sitting in an ocean of ideas. The trick
is in learning to recognize this fact.*

Where Do You
Get Your Ideas?

Fred sighed at the pile of dirty dishes Margie had left, shrugged his shoulders, and tied the pink ruffles of the apron around his waist. *Fordan cursed the host of slime-dripping creatures as he swung his mighty arms and donned his shield. "Mysor, the evil seawitch, shall rue this day," he swore.*

He pushed the dishes from the counter into the sink, gave them a squirt of soap, and turned on the hot water. *With a sweep of his mighty blade, Fordan drove the slime creatures into the foam—the blood of Ajax, his stalwart friend who had disappeared beneath the waves. The battle-blood pounded in his veins as he turned the waters of the scalding waterfall upon the foe.*

Fred reached into the sudsy water, took a dish, swished the dishcloth over it, and placed it in the drain rack. *"Har!" Fordan joined battle and grappled with his bare hands as one of the slime creatures struggled to climb back on board. A smile on the warrior's lips, Fordan broke the creature's back, then flung it upon the shore.*

Wiping his forehead on his left sleeve, Fred noticed the tiny cleaver still on the cutting board. He shook his head and picked it up. Thick congealed grease coated the blade. He ripped off a paper towel, wiped the blade, and tossed the cleaver into the sink. *The creatures fought well. Driven to the deckhouse, Fordan unleashed his ax and drove them back into the water. He spoke a fond farewell to his trusty blade, wiped the gore from it upon his heaving chest, then flung the ax into the foam. The screams of a dying creature tore at the fabric of that evil night.*

Billy came in, feeling guilty about watching TV while his father cleaned the kitchen. "Need some help, Pop?" *Vor drove the demons from his heart, struggled to the deck to face the horror, standing next to his brave father.*

"It is I, your son Vor. I shall stand with you, Father!"

Fred cocked his head toward the rack. "Sure, kid. Grab a towel." *Fordan turned to see his son standing firmly upon the blood-washed deck. "Aye. Aye, my son. Man the sheets, and we shall bring the foe down together!"*